PATRICK DOCHERTY

Oxford Truths

For Loveday

Patrick

First published by Oscar Corgi Press 2021

Copyright © 2021 by Patrick Docherty

All rights reserved. No part of this publication may be reproduced, stored or transmitted in any form or by any means, electronic, mechanical, photocopying, recording, scanning, or otherwise without written permission from the publisher. It is illegal to copy this book, post it to a website, or distribute it by any other means without permission.

This novel is entirely a work of fiction. The names, characters and incidents portrayed in it are the work of the author's imagination. Any resemblance to actual persons, living or dead, events or localities is entirely coincidental.

Patrick Docherty asserts the moral right to be identified as the author of this work.

First edition

ISBN: 9798739007285

This book was professionally typeset on Reedsy. Find out more at reedsy.com

For Monica

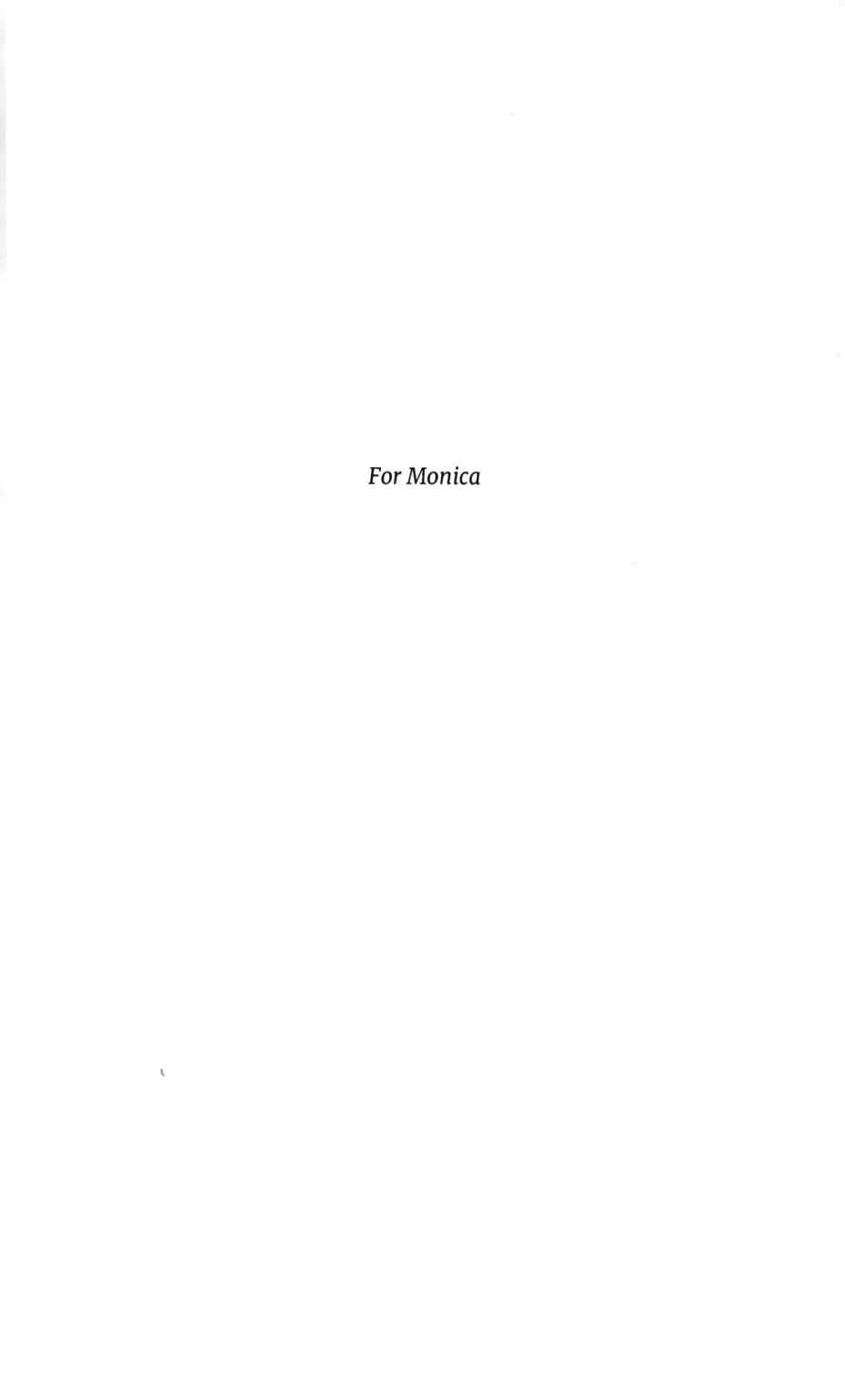

Contents

Acknowledgement		iv
1	Declarations of Intent	1
2	What's in a Name?	8
3	Gap Year	11
4	Signing Off	16
5	Double First	21
6	Cabbages and Queens	25
7	Double Life	27
8	Family Affair	36
9	Kidnap	41
10	King Lear	49
11	Contact	54
12	Fire Sale	61
13	Preparing to Pay	71
14	The Theory of Fairness	75
15	The Practice of Fairness	81
16	Pencil and Paper	87
17	How Hard Can It Be?	93
18	Whose Idea Was It Anyway?	102
19	Extraction	110
20	The Boundaries of Philosophy	113
21	Two Hawks Circling a Full Moon	123
22	Full Disclosure	129
23	An Offer Not to Be Refused	138

24	Philosophical Advice	144
25	Release	150
26	Cold Comfort Farm	157
27	The Younger Son's Tale	166
28	She	176
29	Television News	180
30	Situation Management (1)	185
31	Situation Management (2)	191
32	Closer to Home	198
33	Chief's Powwow	208
34	High Policy, Low Morals	214
35	A Cold Time	223
36	Spooked	235
37	Another Mind	242
38	The Hounds of Spring	252
39	Two Into One Doesn't Go	262
40	Annie and the Detectives	275
41	St. James's Park	287
42	Shades of the Prison House	299
43	The Heart of Things	309
44	Turnaround	315
45	Whatever It Takes	327
46	Show Time	336
47	Unforeseen	351
48	A Very Gentle Knight	359
49	Supporters' Club	364
50	Making Things Right	370
51	Grown Up Conversation	377
52	Storm in a Chafing Dish	381
53	Good Fellowship	386
54	Counted Out	395

55	Vice	402
56	Conditional Surrender	409
57	Scuppering the Master	417
58	Wise Counsel	421
59	Darkness at Noon	430
60	To Russia with Love	440
61	Back in the USSR	449
62	Climax	463
63	Anti-climax	473
About the Author		480

Acknowledgement

This book would not have seen the light of day but for Alan Agnew to whom I owe enormous thanks.

I am also very grateful to Sandra Chua for undertaking the thankless task of proof reading.

Special thanks also to Janis Chow for the cover and back cover sketch, and to Jenny Tan for digital design layout for both covers.

As always to Benson Goh – great thanks apply for crucial computer support.

OXFORD TRUTHS:

Moral truth and terrifying action: how far can fairness stretch?

PATRICK DOCHERTY

1

Declarations of Intent

'I was thinking of writing a novel.'

'Oh why? Isn't one of us enough?'

'Novelists? I thought you'd relish the competition.'

He bit his tongue along with his toast. Did she have any idea what was involved? Why not aerobics? She had been, as he was totally not allowed to say, putting on weight recently. Archaeology? There were any number of stone circles and prehistoric barrows within an 600easy drive of their ample house. Painting, pottery, sculpture? Well perhaps not, as the products of any of those would tend to multiply and soon be challenging them for house room, ample or not.

He realised that she was still looking at him, expecting a serious response.

'What brought this on?'

'Well, the children are grown up. Or at least they behave as if they think they're grown up. I have no particular talents, only a mediocre degree in English Literature. And after all, isn't that what people try who can't do anything and aren't qualified to teach anything? They write. They make up stories. I was quite good at it when I was five or six.'

An unpleasant thought struck him.

'Under what name were you thinking of publishing this work of fiction?'

He had no doubt that if she set her mind to it, she could produce the requisite eighty thousand or so words, and that once written she would find an agent and a publisher on the basis of his own considerable reputation.

'My own. What else?'

What did she mean, her own name? Her married name, aka his name. No, no and no. This had to be stopped and quickly.

'But darling, wouldn't that be...confusing?'

She laughed at that.

'Oh, you are afraid people would buy my books, mistaking them for yours? Then after they'd read mine, they might actually prefer them to yours?'

Wait a minute. Weren't we taking our fences three at a time here?

"Books" plural? She'd yet to put pen to paper.

"Prefer mine to yours"? Who'd ever heard of a husband and wife who were both hugely successful authors of fiction?

But yes, he was concerned about the possibility of a careless keystroke in on-line ordering, of a changeling slipped in amongst the piles of copies of his latest blockbuster in better bookshops. Well surviving bookshops. Or even on library shelves, the shelves of surviving libraries that is.

'There might be the chance of an initial confusion. Of course, once someone started reading your book, they'd realise within a page that they'd made a mistake...'

'Mistake, David?'

''Well, you know picking up the wrong kind of book. After all my books are mostly thrillers, literary thrillers I like to think. And presumably you're going to be writing girlie stuff...romantic fictions.'

'I understand now, David, why your novels are so successful. I've always wondered. Like you, they are so bloody predictable.'

At any moment this was going to get ugly. Urgent containment required.

'Of course, Vina, you can write what you like. I merely meant that...'

'My working title is THE DARWIN FACTOR. Does that sound girlie?'

'It sounds like a thriller.'

'That's good because it is a thriller. I've written forty thousand words already.'

A sense of outrage, of betrayal. He imagined that this was how he would have felt if she had calmly announced that she were having an affair. How in earlier days he had felt when he suspected she was having an affair. How, could she?

And yet, what was actually wrong with writing forty thousand words and failing to mention it to your husband of thirty years? Something certainly, but he could not articulate it. He to whom articulation was bread and butter. What would Manny Kant, principal character of a number of his books, do in a situation like this? Suavely dissemble of course.

'Well darling that is a surprise. Congratulations. How did you manage to do all that without my knowing? It's not as if I have been travelling recently.'

'No, but you have been running regularly. And you have been sleeping early.'

It was his practice, in the late afternoon when energy levels were at their highest, so he had read and believed, to take one of the trails on the Downs which could be easily accessed from the bottom of their garden. He would then run for a good hour or more. Then warm down exercises, a bit of weights and a hot shower. Certainly, he'd not been aware of what his wife was doing during that time. It was also true that he tended to sleep early, leaving Vina to watch television or whatever else she might be doing.

Normally he breakfasted early. Then he would spend the morning writing. He wrote fast when he could write, but when he encountered a block, as happened with increasing frequency, he would abandon his attic study and roam the house and garden in search of inspiration. So, it was unlikely that his wife's secret authorship occurred in the mornings or he would have surprised her at it. As she said she must have been extruding those forty thousand words while he was out running in the late afternoons or at night.

'And then I do quite often write longhand. So, while I'm at the dining room table scribbling away you probably think I'm writing shopping lists or to-do instructions for Felix...'

'But that is so cumbersome. You then have to type up all that stuff, I assume. You must have been at it for months, years.'

'You forget, David, that I am from that generation of well brought up girls who found on graduation that taking a typing course was their only way to a job. That, of course, was in the days when there were still jobs for secretaries. So, it takes me no time at all to type up my longhand stuff.'

'So how long has this...?' He wanted to say 'subterfuge' but did not think it would be well received. '...This...this unknown, unknown to me, writing been going on, darling.'

'Oh, a month perhaps.'

Forty thousand words in a month? Whatever way you looked at it, that was fast, very fast. Of course, one couldn't compare it to his own schedule for writing a book.

Typically, broad structuring for a couple of months. Three months of research in the subject area of the planned novel. A month of restructuring in light of the research. Four months of writing a first draft. Of course, the various activities overlapped. He would need to go back and garner extra background as his restructuring turned the direction of the novel. Early on he might write key chapters on which the rest of the story would hang. On this basis he could just squeeze out a book a year, as demanded by his agent and his publisher.

But no, you could not compare the organized approach of a professional like himself to the fumbling of a neophyte like his wife.

Rather more serious than the forty thousand words, which were probably bilge anyway, was the assertion that her book was a thriller. Serious risk of reputational, not to speak of net worth, damage arising from people picking up her book in mistake for his latest. After all there wasn't much difference between D.H. Cameron and D.L. Cameron.

The door of the kitchen opened with a bang, ricocheting off the wall.

'Is there tea?'

'Could you be a little less exuberant opening the door, dear?'

'Don't call me that. I'm fucking fifteen years old for Christ's sake.'

'Well Felix, what did you do at school today?' his father asked, seeking to lighten the tone, as fathers tend ineptly to do with their youngest.

'Nothing, since the holidays started two weeks ago. But what I did out of school was to write the first chapter of my novel. Perhaps it'll sell more than yours, dad.'

2

What's in a Name?

'David Cameron!'

He had stood, a little dazed, genuinely surprised. That had really been his breakthrough.

'Ladies and Gentlemen, please welcome the winner of this year's Nanki Poo Prize for Creative Writing.'

The Nanki Poo was not quite the Mann Booker, though the money was not to be sneezed at. He'd been in two minds whether to let his publisher submit UP AGAINST IT in competition. But Sam had assured him that this was the year the Nanki Pooh would come of age as a serious award rather than an oddity. Not to speak of the doubling of the prize money.

Sure enough, the cultural media were out in force. Superstitious as he was, he'd not prepared a prize acceptance speech.

But thinking as quickly as his hero Manny Kant in a tight spot, he thanked everybody whose name presented itself to his mind, connected or not to his writing, gave a modest pitch for UP AGAINST IT, and uttered the words Nanki Poo as often as he decently could.

He also mentioned what as a journalist had become a cause for him. That of the unfairness of the growing disparities of income and wealth between rich and poor, globally but also in Britain. As his corpus of novels grew and his public profile with it, he increasingly used his position to campaign for those with any degree of serious wealth and good conscience to give away substantial parts of that wealth to sound charities. And increasingly he used his novels to the same end.

The applause was sufficient, even if it was mainly for the fact that the speech ran for little more than four minutes and did not, as for a moment it had threatened to, set off on any hobby horse of long duration.

David Cameron had won the Nanki Poo a few years before the other David Cameron had risen, from nowhere as far as most people were concerned, to become the Leader of Her Majesty's Opposition and the Conservative Party. In later years, bold and ill-informed interviewers sometimes suggested that his success depended on his sharing a name with the, by then, Prime Minister.

He was always pleased to counter this by recalling an interview in which the Prime Minister was asked how he managed to run the country while turning out a bestselling novel a year. Now both he and the Prime Minister were well enough known that one was not often confused with the other, in Britain at least.

In America, Novelist Cameron privately acknowledged, perhaps as much as half of his considerable sales were down to buyers believing that his book, whichever one it was, had been written by the British Prime Minister and America's firmest ally. But this he would admit to no one, not even to his wife. He just hoped the British Government would keep its foreign policy closely attuned to that of the United States. And that the other David Cameron would keep tight hold of his job.

But whatever his hopes and fears, on the strength of the Nanki Poo he had felt secure enough in his talent to give up the day job completely.

3

Gap Year

'Well, I don't see why not.'

'He's fifteen years old...

'He's sixteen tomorrow. Have you got him a present?'

'No. Have you?'

'I thought we'd agreed he's in your court now. Now he's practically grown up.'

'That's just it. He isn't grown up, practically or in any other way. And he has 'A' Levels this summer.'

Enter Felix reading a book.

'Got a conditional offer from an Oxbridge Coll. Two of them actually. One Oxford, one Cambridge. Faked the school's recommendation letter. Conditions? 'A 'Level maths, further maths, furthermost maths and history, only A*s required. Doddle. So, I'll get the grades, then postpone going up for a year, till I'm emotionally mature enough to get the best out of the Oxbridge experience. In the meantime, I'll take off for the war zone of choice, my choice, in September.'

'Why in heaven's name?'

'To do a bit of good in the world. At least for a year. And, of course, gather first-hand experience for my novel. You don't think I'm going to rely on the tawdry leavings of foreign correspondents' dispatches, other men's scribblings, like you Dad?'

Swallow that...for now.

'And what will you use for money? We are certainly not giving you any.'

This is what the smarter counter-terrorist forces did these days, at least in his novels. Interdict the finance and watch the Jihad or whatever it was wither on the vine.

'No sweat.' Felix had struggled to pull something out of the pocket of his jeans. It turned out to be a wad of fifties, secured with an elastic band. 'I fix people's software for them when it's gone AWOL. That and a bit of hacking for certain friends.'

'What friends? You could go to prison.'

'I'm not old enough. And anyway, I'm far too clever ever to be caught. But just in case I get my friends to sign a release stating that the nature of my work is entirely within the law and that in any event I am not aware of the final nature of the project to which I am contributing.'

'That won't get you very far in a Court of Law.'

'Oh, but it will. I got my friend Tommy in Lincoln's Inn to check it out for me. She ran it past a couple of her QCs. They made a few changes in the text, just to show they weren't brain dead, and said it was fine. Actually, the second QC just crossed out what the first one had put in. Tommy says it happens all the time. It's just one long hoot in Chambers.'

'Do I take it that Tommy is a girl?'

'That's it, Dad. Female the species. You may have come across it.'

'And she is?'

'Barrister, junior one of course, in a good set of chambers in Lincoln's Inn, like I said. She'll do anything for me.'

'Oh?'

'Yeh. She has the hots for me. Don't worry Dad. It's just a phase she's going through. She'll probably have got over me by the time I take off for the Middle East in the autumn.'

'The Middle East!!!!'

'Keep your hair on Dad. We are not talking Iraq or Syria here. Maybe Dubai or Abu Dhabi.'

'And what good works precisely are you thinking of doing there?'

'I don't know yet. Hang out with some opposition groups. Bit of cultural subversion into Iran or Saudi. See what turns up. Hack into the Saudi Defence Ministry's computer. I don't know. By the way, have you got me a present for my birthday tomorrow? When I asked Mum, she said at sixteen I move into your sector of responsibility. Do you think it's this thriller she's writing that makes her talk like that? She didn't used to.'

'We should discuss what...'

'Well sixteen's the key one really. I can legally fuck my own age group and upwards. And now it doesn't matter whether I turn out to be queer or not, which is somewhat of a relief. What's left? Driving? Well, I do that anyway in Tommy's Porsche. Voting? Yawn-a-rama. Owning property. Tommy says I can get effective control of my assets from tomorrow. Actually, I have already. They are mostly in big denominations under the floorboards. That is the part that isn't with various friends. So, thank you for asking. Cash would be great. Or a cheque if you prefer. Good timing as it happens since I'm just off to the bank with this lot now.'

Felix is stuffing his bank roll back into his jeans.

'Tommy's account?'

'Well done Dad. You're catching on. Not Tommy actually but Christie May.'

'My personal assistant?'

'Yeh, that Christie May. Now don't go embarrassing her, Dad, by mentioning it or anything. If you are in something of a quandary as to the amount, might I suggest that a couple of thou would bring a song to a young man's heart. Or three if you're feeling...'

'I have calls to make.'

'Haven't we all, Dad? Calls to make. Places to go.'

Father and son part on the best of terms and the worst of terms, depending on from whose point of view you are looking at it.

4

Signing Off

Three simple desks, each piled high with newly printed hardbacks. A space for each of the three authors to peer between the volumes and execute a constrained signature on a fly leaf held down by a suitably pretty, but credibly bookish, assistant.

It was a breakthrough in global publishing.

New technology. The signature of each of the three authors, as it emerged from the nib of a specially commissioned fountain pen, was replicated in real time on the corresponding fly leaves in New York, Los Angeles, Sydney, Tokyo, Singapore and Dubai.

Old technology. A huge banner stretched over the heads of the three authors. THE CAMERONS ARE COMING.

David Cameron had had his doubts. Davina Cameron had

been delighted. Felix Cameron? Well they had been his ideas. The banner and the globally simultaneous signing screens.

The negotiations between family members had been fraught.

'My publisher? Absolutely and terminally not.'

But that was before he had talked to Sam. His agent was a sufficiently old friend and fixture that she could say what she thought, almost. Not entirely without fear of emotional explosion but with a fair expectation that after the administration of sufficient TLC the point might penetrate through the enlarged authorial ego into the residual node of good sense. Good financial sense.

David, sweetheart, we've always put our cards on the table, you and I. Face up, yes. Your latest is…OK David breathe deeply. Yes, that's it. Your latest…that is DYING TO KILL is… well lacks just a little of the sparkle of…. Oh dear, never mind I'll get a dustpan later. Just don't tread the fragments into the carpet. Your latest is not wholly…It is rather a… Well it just needs something to get it to fly off the shelves.'

'Oh, and what may I ask…?'

'Well, I have had the pleasure of reading Vina's…'

'Yes, I'm sorry Sam. I should never have let you see it. But Vina would go on at me so.'

'Well, David, of course you are right. THE DARWIN FACTOR

is not a work of transcendent genius, but it will sell...sell in sufficient numbers for...'

'And what publisher were you thinking of approaching with..'

'Yours of course.'

'Absolutely not. Terminally no. Whatever her faults, the faults of her book, I won't have Vina humiliated by that thug..'

'But David, Goran loves it. At the moment of speaking, there is only one thing Goran loves more...'

Apart from his Aston Martin, his goldfish and his fifteen percent share of my gross income, thought David Cameron. But all that could be forgiven if Goran were gagging for his book.

'David the one thing Goran loves just now more than THE DARWIN FACTOR is IN IT.'

'IN IT?'

'Your younger son's first novel. Experiences of a young middleclass Englishman in the death zones of the World. Stream of consciousness, river of pain, ocean of truth. It's a blockbuster waiting to be born, David.'

In the end, at the subcutaneous level at least, David Cameron had been brought to believe that the only way, Waverley, his publisher of twenty years, would take on DYING TO KILL was if it were done in conjunction with the launch of his wife's first novel and of the incipient blockbuster of his just seventeen and lucky to be alive younger son.

Finally, David Cameron had even tried to persuade Goran to sell the three books exclusively as a package.

'OK Cameron, we can do it, but only as a special offer. Knock a couple of quid off if they buy all three. Ok three quid. But I have to offer the books individually as well.'

The biggest fight had been about the format of the signing itself. The minders of the leaders of the political parties in Britain could not have squabbled more over the setup of their television debates than did loving husband and father, loyal wife and devoted son over the format of their book launch. In the end it was, left to right as you look at them, David, Vina and Felix. Arabia Felix as the press was already calling him. David had of course wanted himself, the patriarch, in the middle, as if sponsoring his family in their uncertain first steps into the world of published fiction. But he had allowed himself to be bulldozed.

He had, though, saved himself from total embarrassment, which even Goran could see was best avoided. The eager public were forced to form one line and to move along from David to Davina to Felix. Six quid off the package, Goran finally agreed. But then there were the critics.

They could not be made to line up, though they did read all three books. And on the principle that a bad review is more satisfying to write that a good one, David got twice the column inches, or broadcast media minutes, of the other two. Factor of ten for twitter. Most of it excoriating. Some of it obscene...and very personal. Trolls. Fuckers. Still good or bad it was the exposure that mattered, he supposed.

On the other hand, or was it the same hand, Vina was BBC2's Woman of the Week and IN IT was rumoured to be coming out in time for the Christmas market as a video game.

5

Double First

The morning after the book signing, David was slightly hung over, Vina was sleeping in and Felix was at his screen waiting for the inconvenient seconds to hurry by. Then at last a triumphant cry of 'Gotcha' from downstairs penetrated to the parental bedroom.

Over an extended and messy breakfast all was revealed. As David had reluctantly come to expect, his insufferable son had got all his A*s, History, Maths, Further Maths. Only Furthermost Maths was missing. But then that had been a joke, hadn't it?

'So, what are you going to do now, dear,' said Vina, failing to conceal a yawn. More a reflection of the champagne of the night before than indifference to her son's future.

'Well, as I told Dad before my gap year, I applied to Oxford and Cambridge. Back then I had to forge the school's letter of recommendation. Had I actually applied back then they would have said I was too young. But now I've met the conditions for both universities.'

'That's nice dear. So, which one have you decided on?'

'Dad, what you have got lathered on that piece of toast could feed a family of five for a week in a Syrian refugee camp.'

David tried to think how Manny Kant would handle such offspring. A slug between the eyes would not be in character, for Manny never handled firearms except when invited to shoot on the noble estate of one of his Oligarch friends. Better birth control probably.

'As to universities, Dad, what would you advise?' Wide eyed innocence from Felix trapped David into taking the question seriously.

'The buildings are better at Cambridge and undergraduate life is probably more fun,' David said at length. And it's further away, though this he did not say.

'Somehow I've always had a soft spot for Oxford,' said Vina, getting up to make more coffee. She had received her mediocre degree from Cambridge, for which she had since always harboured a visceral hatred.

'Well as it happens, I can make you both happy. I've accepted both.'

Gaping silence from the parents.

'That's it. PPE, Philosophy, Politics and Economics if you prefer, at Oxford. Moral Sciences, History and Economics if you like, at Cambridge. The only rule I'd be breaking is required residence during term time, and frankly these days who's going to check up on that? Of course, it does mean two sets of fees but I'm sure you'll be cool with that, what with the boost to sales IN IT will give your own books, Dad.'

'You are already far richer than I am, Felix. Why don't you pay your own sodding fees?'

'No, that would never do. All the other kids' parents will be paying for them, or grandparents or the Government. Certainly not themselves. I don't want to stand out. It might give me a complex or something.'

'But you will stand out anyway, dear. Because of the instant fame of your book.'

'Not necessarily, Mum. Cameron is a common name. For instance, I share it with the Prime Minister's children. Naturally I'm going to say a different Felix Cameron wrote IN IT. In fact, at the College, at the Colleges, I'm thinking of disguising myself a little. Call myself David Cameron at Cambridge. It is my second name after all. And at Oxford, Andrew Cameron, which in case you'd forgotten, is my first name. Felix is only my third you know and after it's all a bit of a give-away. Regarded in a certain light it's a bit soppy too.'

'And the news pictures and visual media interviews?'

'I've already told Sam voice only. Nothing visual. I may even have my words voiced by an actor. Obviously because it might be dangerous for me to be recognised after what I got up to over there. They might try to assassinate me. Blow up the house.'

'Oh, might they? I'd better look at the insurance policy.'

'Or move out. Like me.'

'And tell me on which unfortunate colleges are you going to inflict your multi-nominal self?'

'Jesus Christ's Oxford. And St. Sebastian's Cambridge. Weren't you at Jesus Christ's, Dad?

'No. Simple Jesus sufficed for me.'

'Which reminds me.'

Felix pulls from his pocket his iPhone and brings up Google Maps. He studies the screen closely for a minute or so.

'There is one other thing Dad. I'll have to get a fast car, to get to and fro between Oxford to Cambridge. Might make a nice pressy for my seventeenth. That's the big one really. Threshold of life. Nothing comes close till one's seventieth. You know, three score years and ten. Another threshold of life. Only that one is on the way to the check out.'

6

Cabbages and Queens

Luke Cameron stubbed out his half-smoked cigarette on a dustbin lid, relieved himself in the alley and got himself back in the line before Chef could have noticed his absence.

The origins of the word 'chef' have nothing to do with food and everything to do with being in charge. The El Jefe, the boss. If you had access to fine ingredients, had watched a bit of telly with attention and were quick on the uptake, being a sous chef in a starred restaurant kitchen was not so hard. But organising twenty or so headstrong workers to put a pitch perfect dish in front of seventy expensive palates every lunchtime and every evening took a rare talent. Natural sadism mixed with instinctive ability to give orders as if you were certain they would be obeyed. It was such a position that Luke Cameron coveted more than anything in the world.

'Sis', as that annoying insect Felix Cameron had insisted on and persisted in calling her virtually since his birth, was now

Second Lieutenant Alicia Cameron of the Scottish Regiment, on secondment to Military Intelligence, which had infiltrated her into a training barracks as an enlisted person.

In the gender-blind army, Everbright had been in the past a source of worry to the General Staff and of scandal to any right-thinking person. More to the point it had been a source among new recruits of apparent suicides, mostly women. And a reputation for sadism persisted among the NCOs, mostly men.

Alicia was nearly six feet tall in her kaki socks, lean like a Texas Ranger, with the face of a cherub. Some people might describe Alicia as a feminist. But that was not true in any self-conscious way. It was just that she wanted more than anything in the world to command men.

7

Double Life

The trouble with being seventeen, exceptionally clever, wonderfully articulate and an undergraduate at both our ancient universities at once is knowing what to do first. Ideas crowded in the mind of Felix Cameron like playgoers jostling to escape from a burning building. They tended to get jammed together in the doorway of the mind and in consequence perish before they can be acted upon.

He sat alone in his room, one of his rooms, failing to prioritise. Paralyzed with the thought that if he seized one opportunity another more glittering prize might be passing him by on the other side. What to do?

It had all seemed so easy back in the day. Get brilliant marks at school. Get into Oxford, and if Oxford why not Cambridge too. Scare the parents shitless by pretending to spend his gap year in one or more war zones. Terminally get up Dad's nose by writing a brilliant first novel based on his much hyped, much invented experiences in those supposed war zones. Felix Cameron might not be very brave or very honest, but he was a scrupulous researcher, so the factual detail of IN IT was immaculate.

But all that rush had evaporated by the third week of term, or was it the fourth? It depended on where he was. Very Einstein. He got up to look out of the window. The top of one of the pinnacles of King's College Chapel, so Cambridge. Since then, he had been paralysed by indecision. Unable to work. Unable to play. Do something. List your priorities. So first decide your goals. Those endangered throwbacks, pencil and paper.

What did he want above everything? He wanted to be taken notice of, to be famous, to be first. First at what. Well at his age maybe to be first was to be youngest. The youngest person to climb K2, second highest peak on the planet and not called the Killer Peak for nothing. Certainly not the walk in the park Everest had become since they had installed ladders and fixed ropes pretty much to the summit. One problem. His fear of heights. Toys of desperation. Something else then.

Youngest writer, youngest director, auteur, of a major film. Palm d'Or, Golden Bear, Oscar. Do a treatment. Based, of course, on IN IT. Expensive? All that action stuff. CGI, a couple of hundred mil for starters. No one was going to give a kid wet behind the ears that kind of budget, however notorious his first novel.

An idea for his half-finished essay on Charlemagne's Empire and the European Union. Both perished/will perish for the same reason. The atavistic need of peoples to be French or German or whatever was and is greater than the manifest advantage of sticking together. Shit. Stop buggering about. Get back to the film. The essay he could wing in the daylight hour.

Film, movie...budget. Ah that's it. IN IT elaborated by honesty. 'I was never there.' The film tells the tale of a young man who faked it, war, suffering, blood and guts, the whole caboodle. Took in the publishing world. Set the thing in Oxford and Cambridge at both of which our hero is an undergraduate, and the British Library, where he did his research. Plus, newsreels. TV footage. U-tube grabs. Whatever.

Voice of warning. Don't label yourself a cheat and a liar. Could come back to haunt. OK then double bluff. Story line is that IN IT was all faked, till the last fifteen minutes when it emerges, tender scene with girlfriend/boyfriend (ambiguity should scoop both the straight and gay markets), that the hero suffers post-traumatic stress disorder which could only have been brought about by prolonged personal exposure to actual war rather than to back numbers of the ECONOMIST. The hero puts it about that he faked it all in order to protect the innocent.

So, at the height of his reputation Felix wins a Nobel Prize for his portrayal of the victims of war. But the Literature Committee of the Nobel comes to blows with the Peace Prize Committee as to which prize should be offered to Felix. Clash of dates between the Nobel in Stockholm, or is it Oslo, and the Golden Bear in Berlin. 'Get me on the first plane....' Felix wakes with a start. It can't be daylight already.

He taps his ever-wakeful screen. Timetable for the new day. First check which new day it is. OK Tuesday in Cambridge. Checks his satnav app.

'You are at present on the third floor of St. Sebastian's College, Cambridge.'

Back to the timetable. History tutorial at four in the afternoon. Relax. Leisurely shower. Leisurely breakfast. Hey what's this? An intruding timetable for his Oxford day. Philosophy tutorial at eleven this am. Shit. Current time at Greenwich this cold but sunny autumn morning. Five and twenty minutes to ten. Fuck, bugger.

Reminder flashing in the sidebar. 'Your car is currently parked in Jesus Lane and has four parking tickets. Expect a municipally instructed privatised tow truck, concession held by the X Man on Staircase XXIII, before noon.' Fuck, bugger, shit.

Cigarette. 'I don't smoke. I will not smoke....' His hand trembles, as he shakes the already open pack to release... No, shower and go. Make it by eleven. Essay unwritten. Grab half-finished history essay and pretend to read in the Oxford tutorial while making up the philosophy. How would the later Wittgenstein, he of the PHILOSOPHICAL IINVESTIGATIONS, have regarded his earlier self, the one who wrote the TRACTATUS which the Investigations wholly contradicts?

Felix drives top down to wake himself up, one handed, as he scrolls through Wikipedia's take on the earlier and the later Wittgenstein. Great Tom at Christ Church is sounding eleven, at least he assumes it's eleven, as he drives into the centre of the Oxford. No time to park. Fake a breakdown. Red triangle out of the boot. Repair truck app. on screen. At ten past eleven, breathless, he is sitting opposite Annie Fritzweiler in her rooms in college. No one at Jesus Christ's had read a word of any philosopher since Thomas Aquinas, until this academic year when the College had somehow persuaded Annie Fritzweiler to accept a Fellowship.

He has sensed in the couple of weeks that he had been coming to see her that Annie has developed a liking for him. Rather in the way Tommy used to like him. But then Tommy had only a Porsche. Annie has something far more exciting. A bed in the next room. And why would she wear trousers as tight as that, as thin as that, on this fine but chilly late autumn morning, if she didn't at some point...So why not now?

Annie sits deep in her armchair, a small, determined figure, short fair hair, as if she is driving her car. She must be at least in her mid-forties in a tense, preserved sort of way. But this just fuels Felix's imagination.

'You are no doubt a clever young man Andrew...' She interrupts him half a minute into reading his essay. That voice, the Germanic inflections of which send his pulses racing. 'But I am really not qualified to comment on your views on

Charlemagne and the European Union.'

Shit. Where is his mind this morning? Well, mainly assisting Annie Fritzweiler in the careful removal of her gauze tight...

'So, have you anything to say about Wittgenstein? If not, perhaps we could...'

She is standing over him now. And he is looking up now into her pale blue eyes, the colour of...whatever is the name of that flower? She is looking down at him, an enigma, but maybe a willing one. Her lipstick so pink is yet so understated as to be...He inhales her perfume, smoky yet...

'If not, we could perhaps call it a day. I'll give you one more chance, this time next week. If you fail me then, Andrew, you can go elsewhere for instruction. The reading list is on my web site. "Unfairness." It is of this that I want you to write.'

Felix can think of only one thing that is unfair. That Annie Fritzweiler does not at all appear to return his aching desire for her. As he reaches the bottom of her staircase, he is conscious of flushing many shades pinker than Annie's lipstick. In an attempt to change his mood, he hops steps and jumps across the quad and gains the shelter of the JCR.

Relaxing in there with a coffee, he is able to put a better construction on events. All may not be lost. In Annie's severe words it is possible to read a message beyond the literal. With the help of his built-in double entendre reader, Felix, Andrew as he is known here, is able to perk up considerably.

Shit, his car. He calls Mighty Man Motors of Oxford and Abingdon. Yes, they have the car. Checked it thoroughly... 'That'll be three hundred pounds sir, before VAT. No, we can't find anything wrong. Plus, a tow fee of a further three hundred and fifty, plus paying the illegal parking fine of a hundred and eighty...and you can pick up the car any time before five today. Pleasure to do business with you sir.'

'Pleasure is all mine,' he mumbles.

'Oh, and one other thing sir.' He is beginning to tire of the subservient Thames Valley whine, 'we would also be collecting your accumulated Cambridge parking fines...yes, sir, on behalf of our associate X Man Motors of Cambridge and Royston. They have the enforcement concession from the Cambridge City Council.'

'So, what is that altogether?' he forces himself to ask.

'One thousand and ninety-six pounds exactly. Could I just verify your card number, sir...yes, that'll do nicely.'

Oh well, thinks Felix, consider the Air Miles. But what was it he was supposed to be thinking of? Ah, his film. First step call Sam, mistress of the film rights deal, as well as perhaps of his Dad. No, on second thoughts, his father would have neither the good taste nor the get up and go. And if he did, Sammy has better options, like her good- looking husband.

He leaves a voice message for her to call back. Felix scrolls numbers aimlessly. Mildly surprised to find Annie

Fritzweiler's. Mark of favour that she gave it to him or just practical necessity in the fast-moving world of the modern tutorial? Well, why not?

'It's Andy, Andrew Cameron. Yes, the one who confused Charlemagne with Wittgenstein just now. I'm sure it happens all the time.'

He is inclined to smile at his wit until he remembers that Annie has no detectable sense of humour.

'I wonder if lunch might make up for...

'No Andrew, I may not take lunch today.'

Interesting.

'May one inquire Annie...?'

Well, she does like him, doesn't she?

'Annie, what....'

'Andrew, I am at this moment entertaining my lover. So please call me only after the passing of one hour.'

Gob smacked really doesn't capture it. Or perhaps Annie does have a sense of humour after all. Either way he can't stop thinking about her until it is almost too late to retrieve his car and make it back to Cambridge for his five o'clock with Johnny Pebbledash, a young don who thinks he is cleverer than any undergraduate. We'll see about that, thinks Felix, changing identity as effortlessly as he changes gear, back to David Cameron junior, Cambridge undergraduate in history and economics.

On and off as he eats up seventy or so miles back to Cambridge, Felix rehearses what he will pretend to read to Johnny and laughs to himself about Charlemagne's German name, Karl the Grocer, or der Grosse, if one is being literal and German, like Annie.

8

Family Affair

'Surely, David, when the authorities say they don't pay ransoms that is just for public consumption.'

'I'm sorry David, it's not just for public consumption. It's for your consumption and my consumption, for public consumption and for private consumption. I know it sounds heartless, and in the particular case it is. But believe me, David, if it got out that we do pay, even in very particular cases, we'd have many more cases of kidnap. Not to mention the unfairness of it.'

If one can convey a sympathetic shrug over a landline, the Prime Minister managed it.

'Look David, I have to go. But call me again, on my private line day or night if there are any developments at your end or there is anything you think we *can* do. And of course, we'll be in touch as soon as the nationwide search turns up anything,

anything at all. We'll leave no stone un-turned, you can be assured of that. Tell Davina all our thoughts are with you all at this trying time in all your lives.'

'Thank you, David. I do appreciate all you've said.'

Phones were gently put down in North Oxfordshire and in Berkshire, for the Prime Minister was at his constituency home and the novelist at his, as he is about to learn, now soon to be vacated, sole home. There were, no doubt, some advantages of being on first name terms with the Prime Minister but at that moment the novelist could not for the life of him think of one.

'He says there is nothing he can do on the ransom front. But he is hopeful that the nationwide search will turn up something soon. No, he says there is nothing for us to do.'

'Well why don't we just pay it, David? They can't actually stop us, can they?'

'Davina it may have escaped your notice, but I don't happen to have ten million pounds lying around. Unless Felix had more under the floorboards than...'

'That is not remotely funny, David. Of course, we have ten million pounds, it's all around us.'

David Cameron stares at his wife. A phantasmagoric ten million pounds present in the ether? Perhaps she'd snapped, lost it. With the strain of the last few hours that would be entirely understandable.

'I think Dad,' said Alicia starring down at him in her stocking feet, 'that what Mum means is that you could sell the house.'

'But we live in the house. Well, OK you don't any longer. You live in some army hut in Surrey, but your mother and I...'

'And you could too Dad, if you had to. Well not an army hut, but for the sake of getting your son back, you could rough it just a little bit.'

David thought about Felix and was in two minds.

'Of course, we could, David,' said Davina furiously. 'There is no argument. We will pay the ransom. Let's call that number now. Where is it?'

'But the Government would make difficulties,' David murmured, making an orderly withdrawal to lower ground.

'They need never find out,' said Alicia. Her oath of allegiance after all had been to the Queen, not to whatever bunch of shysters and self-seekers might from time to time constitute her Government.

'Come on, what we need is some hot food inside us. None of us has eaten since breakfast.' For the outrage had been perpetrated just as the luncheon hors d'oeuvres were arriving. 'Then we can talk this thing out calmly, as a family.'

'Don't be stupid Luke, none of us is the least bit hungry,' snapped Alicia.

'Oh, and I thought an army marches on its stomach.'

'You must leave it to the authorities. There is no other sensible course.'

The whole Cameron clan turned to stare at the speaker. Who asked you? What's it to do with you anyway? Except, that is, for Luke Cameron who could only ponder what on earth you called that particular pale blue that was the colour of her eyes.

'Annie's right you know. She's a philosopher.'

Luke filled in while continuing to wrack his brains about that colour.

'And,' added Annie Fritzweiler, 'I have become quite fond of your son.'

As for a moment Luke toyed with the illusion that she meant him, it came to his mind. Periwinkle. Periwinkle blue. He'd even used that flower on occasion in a particularly pretentious dish where everyone effects to believe that it adds the flavour of the wild cliffs on which it grows. Which of course it doesn't.

'Who are you anyway? Why are you here?'

Vina's normal languorous good manners were evidently in shock, like the rest of her.

'My name, though we have been introduced Davina, is Annie Fritzweiler. I teach your younger son philosophy at Oxford, when he can be bothered to write the required essay. I am here because Felix invited me to the restaurant. In fact, he would brook no refusal.'

'But you can't be his…well his girlfriend.'

'If you mean his lover, of course I could be, Davina, but as it happens, I am not. Just a close friend. They do exist you know, close friends who are not lovers. Luke, if you wouldn't mind…'

He saw at once what she meant. Within a minute each person in the room had a glass of schnapps in front of them. Within another minute every person in the room had drained their glass and had a refill, along with a more sympathetic image of Annie Fritzweiler.

'Perhaps we might all sit down. Round the dining room table might be best. May I now tell you what I observed and what conclusions I draw?'

Taking silence for assent, Annie briefly recapitulated the shocking events to which they had all been witness but a few hours before. But after Annie had spoken, some of the family wondered if they had been there at all.

9

Kidnap

The second week of December. A light dusting of snow on the gardens outside in the hazy midday sunlight. Inside, in the dining room of one of the finest restaurants in the country, a roaring log fire, good cheer and keen appetites.

Quite what they were celebrating it was hard to say. Perhaps just the fact that Felix Cameron, aka Andrew Cameron, aka David Cameron junior, thoughtless son, indifferent sibling and cosmic smart ass, had invited everyone and by implication undertaken to pay. Though events were quickly to render the latter an empty promise.

If there was to be an extravagant celebration, then the only place to hold it was the renowned restaurant where Luke Cameron, Felix's older brother, was a sous chef. And it was only a few miles outside Oxford.

An initial toast had been drunk, to them all being for once

gathered together. They had just sat down to await the first course when the sound of shattering glass made them all look up. Not a sound as if some unfortunate waiter had dropped a tray of glasses, but as if several people were wrecking the place with baseball bats, which as it turned out, they were.

In a few seconds they were in the dining room, hooded, masked and smashing their bats down on the tables. All the diners, rigid with fear. Having effectively destroyed the table settings, shouting incoherently all the time, they dragged Felix to his feet and propelled him before them out of the restaurant and into a huge SUV which stood blocking the entrance to the property. Its plates had been masked.

Alicia acted fast, but not as fast as Luke from the kitchen who charged the retreating group with a carving knife. He received for his pains a numbing blow to the wrist. Alicia, catching up, was flung to the ground to lie in the exhaust trail of the vehicle as its huge tires tore at the gravel, gripped and were gone.

As brother and sister returned indoors, phones were being yelled into, texted through, twittered at and generally being put through their paces.

Then abruptly and for a moment there was silence. In the flattened wreckage of the Cameron family table at the centre of the restaurant, one item only remained standing. A stiffened piece of card with the crest of Oxford University at its head, facing the place where David Cameron had been seated. Printed in appallingly legible copperplate, the words spelled out: 'Ten Million Pounds. Await instructions.'

Abruptly pandemonium broke out once more. In four minutes the first squad car arrived. In ten the place was surrounded by police. A helicopter overhead. Roadblocks hastily assembled on all routes out of the place. Nothing. Nothing then and nothing in the four hours since then, during which the daylight had begun to seep away and with it the chance of finding the kidnap gang quickly.

So far so baffling.

'So how many of them did you count?' Annie in command. No one opposing her.

'A dozen at least,' cried Davina. 'Black of course. Muslims terrorists. So, we know what they will do with my son.'

She shook afresh with sobs.

'It's OK Mum,' murmured Luke, which of course it wasn't, but what is one to say?

'Not so many,' said Alicia, coming as she was intended to out of her shock. 'Six at most.'

'Yeh, thereabouts,' Luke agreed. 'Yes, probably black though they were pretty well covered.' David simply had no opinion. Things like this never happened, not even in his books, where the bad guys were far too well-mannered for such vandalism.

'Actually,' said Annie, very low key, 'there were three of them and all of them were white.'

'How can you possibly know that?'

'Three because I counted them. White because however well covered they were, when you are smashing up a place, your jacket tends to pull back from your gloves exposing your wrist. So, assuming that's a good indicator of what colour they are all over, they were white.'

'You are a very cool customer, Dr Fritzweiler,' said David Cameron, impressed but not quite believing. 'How come?'

'My name, David, is Annie. I'm a philosopher. That is my work. A key element of modern philosophy is to be as accurate as possible in your observations, as well as clear as possible in your thinking.'

Somehow David fancied there was more to it than that, but he contented himself with saying: 'How about the driver of the vehicle.'

'Yes. I'm sure the engine was running when I chased them towards their vehicle. So, there must have been a driver,' said Alicia, who had got closest to the SUV. And I didn't hear them start the engine when they got back in. So, Annie, four then?'

'Probably, yes,' said Annie. 'It's unlikely they would have left the engine running without a driver in place.'

Luke, with unquestioning belief in Annie's higher powers.

'What do you think happened to them? I mean the police were on to it more or less at once. How come they slipped thru the net?'

'There's an aerodrome at Windrush, within five miles of the restaurant...'

'Come on Annie. They couldn't have got away by air. They would have to have filed a flight plan in advance, and air traffic would have notified the authorities at the first sign of anything irregular.'

David was confident on subjects which he had researched for his fiction. But Annie very quietly but distinctly dismissed his learning.

'It's a disused aerodrome. So, no air traffic. In fact, no anything. Of course, it is a risk landing and taking off on a runway that is not maintained but with a light aircraft in decent visibility...'

'How come you know all this?'

Davina not yet pacified or reconciled as to Annie's bone fides.

'Because, Davina, my lover was a recreational flyer. He has used that runway a couple of times over the years.'

Luke's heart sank through the floor. Then although he was a

cook not a philosopher, he registered some hope in the tense change.

'Was? Has he given it up?'

'In a manner of speaking. He was killed...'

'Where? How?'

'Attempting a landing at Windrush.'

'When?'

From Annie a sad smile. 'Last week.'

Silence in the room. The moral centre of gravity has shifted decisively in favour of Annie Fritzweiler.

'Of course, I told the police all this when they questioned me. The helicopters were on to it quite fast, but a light aircraft would easily outrun a helicopter.

'The RAF at Brize Norton was scrambled, if that's the word for hauling guys out of the pub, orange juice only of course. Our friends with the baseball bats would have had at least an hour's start on them. By that time, they probably would have landed again. Both because of the likelihood of pursuit and because they are certainly using abandoned airstrips, for the reason you correctly identified David, so they need clear daylight. No chance of an instrument landing. That of course means that there are probably five of them, counting the pilot of the plane. If, that is, the pilot is in fact more than an outsider hired to do this particular flight, no questions asked, at ten times the normal rate.'

'So, since you know so much…I'm sorry Annie, I didn't mean it quite like that…' Vina coming back to her normal self. 'Where do you think my son might be?'

'I do not know Davina. On the basis of the available evidence, the answer to your question is anywhere within a radius of three hundred miles.'

'So, Ireland, Europe?'

'It is possible, but it is more likely that it is somewhere closer, if I'm right about them using abandoned aerodromes. My sense is this is a small operation.'

'With a big appetite for cash.'

David looked quickly at Vina but even if she heard him, she did not react.

'I suppose,' David set out further on his fragile branch, 'Felix could have staged the whole thing himself. I mean as a sort of cosmic prank. Just to show that he could?'

Vina was caught between loathing for her husband and wishing that what he had said was true, so she said nothing.

All eyes on Annie. She shrugged.

'You all know him better than I do.'

'I wonder,' David thinking half out loud, 'if that is true.'

10

King Lear

After Annie Fritzweiler has left to drive back to Oxford, the energy goes out of proceedings. They are all or course exhausted.

'Sleep on it,' Annie has advised. 'We'll talk in the morning.'

They have all pressed her to stay the night, even Vina, but she has insisted that she has commitments in Oxford.

David Cameron, failing to sleep. Sleeper's block not unlike writer's block. He pads around the house. It's a nice house. A very nice house. And it suits him, suits them, very well. Less than an hour from central London, half an hour from Oxford, set in a hollow of the Downs.

He'd never imagined leaving. Yet now he would probably have to make a fire sale, for the sake of a son who seemed to have been put on earth with the sole purpose of causing grief to his father. Yes, it was all too likely that Felix had staged the kidnap himself. What a poker game. After a long night, the suggestion of dawn. Felix on the other side of the table with all ten million smackers worth of chips. Loser pays for breakfast.

Another nasty thought comes to the novelist, as he eases open the back door to stare up at the stars. Full house tonight. As a boy he could name the constellations, but that was all gone now, like so much else of life.

The nasty thought. Might this not be a test? How much do you love me? Enough to give up your comfortable lifestyle and financial security, to rely as you did when you were thirty years younger on the ingenuity of your pen and the fickleness of the public. Felix, Lear's youngest daughter to the life. And the answer was that his mother loved him just that much, though David doubted she had really taken in what it would mean for her day-to-day life.

A terraced house in a less salubrious part of Swindon. No more holidays in the Barbados or Tuscany. No further skiing in Zermatt or St. Anton. Forget the chic hairdresser and all body therapist. No more top of the range restaurants. And no top of the range friends either. Not that they would drop her. It would simply be too embarrassing to be unable to keep up. The list of all the things they would not now be able to do was endless.

Worse, there was small prospect of any of those things returning. His powers and his reputation seeming to be competing over which would win the race to the bottom.

Of course, if Felix really had set the whole thing up himself, presumably he would return the money, when he'd enjoyed his little joke sufficiently. But then again perhaps he wouldn't. One never knew where one was with Felix. And anyway, their very nice house would be gone.

But what if it weren't Felix at all. Just a hardened gang of toughs who wanted the money. These hostage exchange things were fraught with danger. Especially when done without the approval of the authorities. Things might well end up with Felix dead and himself with no money. Or it could be worse. For reasons of deceiving the police, members of the immediate family were sometimes involved in handing over the money. He himself might end up dead.

But wait a minute. That was ridiculous. We were talking ten million pounds here. No way that that could be got into a suitcase, or even a whole suite of luggage. No, we were talking instantaneous transfers to dubious intermediaries, banks in the Caymans or Liechtenstein. It was almost bound to go wrong. He would gently explain this to Vina in the morning. If they were destined to lose Felix, better to keep their money. Wealth could to an extent assuage the grief of loss whereas poverty would only make it more acute.

But there was another, more hopeful aspect. He would check with Sam in the morning. How much did Felix's earnings from IN IT and its spin offs amount to now? Perhaps they could use Felix's own money to buy him back. And then again surely ransom payments were tax deductible. After all, the fact of the ransom payment could be well documented.

Wondrous how a little starlight could illuminate intricate moral issues, even if one could not now recall the names of the galaxies. Lear should have tried it, but then in his crisis the stars were presumably nowhere visible through the tempest. Lear aside, David Cameron definitely felt more cheerful after communing with the constellations.

There was of course the question Annie Fritzweiler had asked as he had shown her out last evening.

'Why you, David? If it is not Andrew's joke, a very silly joke if it is, then who hates you enough to do this thing to you?

Of course, like all successful figures in the literary world there were many who loathed him. Perhaps there were a few who had genuine grievances against him. But none of them had sufficient venom to pull something like this. Or if they did, none of them had the initiative or organising nous to carry it off, of that he was completely sure. No, it must just be random if it were not Felix.

Occupied with his thoughts, David had not noticed how far he had wandered across the lawn and away from the kitchen door. Or how cold it was. Now he registered both.

As he made to hurry back inside, a ghostly swathed figure emerged from the house. His heart leapt in his throat. But of course, it was just Vina in her white robe. She gestured at him like the mad woman she had perhaps become.

'Why the hell are you out here, David? I've been searching for you all over the house. It's them… They've sent an email. They want to set up the exchange of the money for Felix.'

He begins to run across the lawn towards her.

'No need to run. We don't want you having a heart attack until we've got Felix back.'

11

Contact

It's three in the morning. All four of them are clustered round Vina's laptop, starring at the screen. A heading and a list of bullet points. The heading is 'Felix'.

Vina excited. 'We should tell the authorities at once. They can put a trace on the sender.'

Her children put her straight. 'Mum, they've most likely hacked into some innocent person's computer. It's that they are using. There is not a hope of putting a trace on the hackers.'

'Perhaps not so innocent,' murmurs David. 'The message is from Felix's own computer.'

'That signifies nothing Dad,' says Alicia, impatient of previous generation's ignorance. 'It's the list of demands that is important. Look Dad, isn't that interesting?'

'It's not interesting, it's criminal extortion, that's what it is. An attack on basic freedoms.'

'On your money you mean. But look what they want. They want you to give the money to two named charities.'

David, who is a minor figure in the charity world, raising money and so on, recognises the names. Small but certainly all kosher. One is to do with elephants. The other with the aged. Ah, they turn out to be elephants too. Aged elephants.

Alicia is still reading from the screen.

"All bets are off, though, if you reveal, even to the recipients in confidence, the real reason for the bequests."

'And look there are is an attachment. Click on that Luke.'

Access to the web sites of three well known house agents who have clients on their books who are looking for a house just like the Cameron place.

'That's a nice touch, Dad. Look they've listed out your assets for you with estimated values.'

David thinks but does not say: inside job; Felix for sure. But the kidnappers could of course just have beaten the information out of his son.

Alicia continues reading.

'"House on a quick sale basis, eight million. Surrender value of your private pension one and a half million. Sale of shares, half a million. Odds and sods half a million."'

'Odds and sods?'

'Your Ferrari, Mum's Mercedes and that dubious Degas in the dining room. They are apparently assuming we can't authenticate it.'

'That's ten and a half million. The price has gone up!' exclaims David Cameron, starring over Alicia's shoulder at the screen in shock.

'Yeh. They explain that in the last bullet point. It's to cover their own expenses,' says Luke

Amateurs. Why didn't they think of that to start with? Again, it speaks of Felix.

'So, don't you see, Dad, there is no issue with a handover, because there is no handover of money. Just payment to two unimpeachable charities on a verifiable basis.'

It's of no consequence, thinks David Cameron, or very little. Of course, it's nice that all his money will be going to elephants and so on but just the same they are stealing all his money, and with it the life he and Davina have come to enjoy and depend on.

'But Dad, this is serious. In the line before they say that you should not delay since with each day that passes Felix's life will become "less endurable."'

A half-suppressed sob from Vina.

'Curious language for a kidnapper to use. "Less endurable."'

'Never mind that, there's another message. Yes, it's from them. But it says nothing. Oh, it's a video attachment.'

They are, all four, riveted to the screen as a grainy black and white image comes up. A bare room, a bare table and upright wooden chair on which sits a figure in a torn T-shirt and jeans. Bare feet. It shivers uncontrollably. No doubt of it. It is Felix. Low voice, barely audible, barely recognisable as belonging to Felix.

'Please hurry. Give them what they want. Whatever it is. Please, please, please. Please God give them what they want. I'm so cold, so hungry, and....they beat me this evening... my head. There may be permanent damage. If it goes on, I may never be able to realise my full potential. And they...they did other things to me.' Felix's voice rises several octaves. 'Noooo, please, not that again.'

A look of terror and the screen goes blank.

Vina is silently weeping. Luke is looking sober. Alicia is bearing all with fortitude. David, well David is now sure beyond any doubt that Felix has set up the whole thing himself.

Furtively, he closes the door of his study, checks to make sure the Degas is still in its place, for since Luke moved to live at the restaurant, David has removed the painting from the dining room. After all, the only pictures Vina looks at are in glossy magazines.

He places a call. It's barely dawn, but Sam answers at once. After all what are agents for but to be at one's beck and call. Anyway, at this time of year it's the start of the working day. He relates recent developments and his own opinion that the whole thing has been set up by Felix himself. Be that as it may he has to go along with raising the ransom money because otherwise Vina will go off her rocker and do serious damage to someone, aka him.

'Actually, what I was wondering Sam, was how much Felix's earnings from that dreadful book amount to. I mean as of whenever you last looked.'

'Strictly speaking, in fact speaking in any way, David, I can't tell you. Felix is my client, just as you are, and I owe a duty of confidentiality to him as much as to you.'

'But Sam, I thought, in the circumstances…'

'I can see, David, that the circumstances are very distressing for you all, but I can't see how that is relevant…'

'Well, I was thinking one might use Felix's accumulated funds, which one assumes are in a pretty liquid form, to pay, that is to contribute, even on a temporary basis to, the ransom money required.'

'David stop right there. Felix's earnings go into a trust. The trust is tightly drawn with very limited objects, which are basically to attend to Felix's reasonable material needs.'

'Who are the trustees?'

'Me and a lawyer called...'

'A lawyer called Tommy. I should have guessed. But you must have some discretion. And paying a ransom to free Felix from some gruesome captivity by terrorists surely qualifies as meeting his material needs.'

'You should talk to Tommy, David. In fact, I was about to call her. Hold on, if she's there I'll patch you in.'

In a moment Tommy is on.

'David, I'm so sorry for you all. It must be terrible.'

David agrees that there is no other word for it. Terrible sums it up nicely.

'But Tommy, if I may call you that...well, I mean, Sam was saying that the trust allows you and she to make payments for Felix's material welfare. Doesn't releasing him from the hands of vicious kidnappers qualify as...?'

'Well, David, naturally no one envisaged this contingency

when the trust was drawn up, but I think you would find that a court would hold that disbursements could be made in connection with a kidnapping...' Sigh of relief. '...but only after other avenues had been exhausted.' Relief evaporates like the morning dew.

'You mean me?'

'Well David as you have just told me that the kidnappers' demands were addressed to you, so yes, I suppose I do mean you.'

'No chance of a loan?'

'No David, I'm afraid the trust deed forbids in terms any lending of the monies in the trust.'

'Well Tommy, you've been most...well helpful is the word I suppose. Thank you, and you too, Sam. I'll chew on this and come back to you.'

'Anything we can do.'

It seems to David as if the two women say this in chorus.

'But I wouldn't get your hopes up too much.'

'Probably the best way, David,' Sam still on the line, 'is just to realise your assets as quickly as you can. After all that beautiful house of yours must be worth a pretty penny, especially in today's market.'

12

Fire Sale

Emerging from his study, David Cameron finds himself face to face with a small group of people. Vina effects introductions. They go over his head, except that the two flushed, prosperous looking men in their forties are from the very up market, local estate agent, Hampton & Pym. The blond, thuggish looking man in his fifties is certainly Russian and a potential buyer of their house. As he shakes treacherous hands his whole being revolts against the idea of giving up his home to these people.

The Russian is asking if he can take pictures for his wife back in St. Petersburg. Sadly, she cannot be with him today. No, no it will not be necessary for her to view the house in person. Yes, yes, he wants to make a quick decision. Of course, a cash sale. The only truck he has with banks is to own one.

Sergei, David catches the name on the third time of asking, looks down his nose at these people. Obviously, they are in trouble of some kind. Obviously desperate for cash. If he signs a contract for sale with them before he leaves, and gets friends to fix it so that surveys are done in two days (they can take three months in this part of the country with the level of sales running as high as it is), he can get a million off the offer price, he is sure.

Vina leads Sergei off for a photo shoot of the house. Fortunately, or unfortunately, the sun is shining, so it looks at its winter best, with a dusting of snow on roofs and gardens.

David excuses himself from the company of Messrs Hampton and Pym, and walks out into the fresh, cold air of his large front garden.

Across the lawn he catches sight of the compact figure of Dr Annie Fritzweiler. She is coming towards the house but not looking at him. Rather, in common with most of the population of the planet these days, her attention is fixed on the smart phone nestled in her hand. This gives David the opportunity to study her as she approaches.

Tight, faded blue jeans, pushed into brown boots which come half-way up her calves, a jacket in a lighter blue, to match the colour of her eyes, perhaps. She is certainly trim. And she has brushed her short hair nicely. He sees now that it is not exactly blond, but a mixture of more or less light browns. Fair would capture it. She is not exactly pretty, but he doesn't want to look at anything else.

Annie is only a few yards away when she notices him, and

waves at him with the hand which holds the phone.

'Have you seen this? It's just been posted.'

She lets him look over her shoulder. Fucking hell. This changes everything. It is the video of Felix as victim, under duress, begging for his family to get him released. It's just gone viral.

'This, changes everything,' he exclaims.

'Yes, I think it does, David. The question is in what way does it change everything? More pressure on you to come up with the money certainly.'

He leads the way into the house, the kitchen door, and fires up the espresso machine.

'And how are the family this morning?'

'Oh, tickety boo,' he says. 'Alicia and Luke are in the dining room seeing how they can make a quick sale of all my assets add up to ten and a half million pounds. Davina is three quarters of the way to selling our family home to some Russian hood.'

'He is not a hood, David.'

Davina angry in the doorway of their kitchen. Well, probably it's more than half Sergei's kitchen already. Davina rubs it in.

'Sergei is a distinguished Professor of International Law at the Institute of Culture and Political Science in St. Petersburg. And yes, he does want to buy the house.'

'That is correct, Mr. Cameron. I can have the whole proceeds in your hands within days. Hampton and Pym were suggesting eight million, eight hundred and eighty-eight thousand, eight hundred and eighty-eight pounds. But as I explained to them that number is of no consequence to me as I am not Chinese. I will pay seven million, nine hundred and ninety-nine thousand, nine hundred and ninety-nine pounds, in cash within a week. That is by next Friday. If not all the surveys are completed by then, I will assume the risk and pay you anyway. It is all in this document, Mr. Cameron. Perhaps you would like to read.'

David takes the proffered paper and pretends to read. But his eyes will not focus. Probably because he has not put on his glasses.

The Russian then catches sight of Annie, for the first time, it seems.

'This is a very pleasant surprise, Dr Fritzweiler. Was it in Berlin where last we met? At that Conference on Russo-German cultural stereotypes?'

'It is pleasant also to see you again, Professor Dzhugashvili.'

Dzhugashvili. That doesn't sound quite Russian, thinks David. But somehow familiar. Georgian? Bloody hell, wasn't that the real name of Joseph Stalin? Stalin being a nom de guerre.

'Not related, I assume,' murmurs David, half hoping not to be heard.

On the other side of the kitchen table, Sergei explodes with laughter.

'Quite right, Mr. Cameron.'

Though whether that means Sergei is or is not related to the old Soviet monster is never clear.

'For that David, I will round up my offer to eight million.'

And he laughs again as if it is the funniest thing he has heard since Boris Yeltsin handed him the concession to sell Bulgarian yoghurt in all the Russian lands. The concession has been the foundation of all his subsequent fortune.

Seeing his joke has not gone down well, Sergei walks round the table and puts a large arm round the novelist's shoulder.

'Look, David, eight million quids. Sure, you could get a bit more if you hang on for three or four months, for the spring weather. But by that time the bad guys would have handed your son's head to your wife on a Christmas turkey dish.'

There is a gasp of total horror from across the table.

'I am sorry Madame Cameron, but we must face facts, or we don't survive. Your son, Felix is it, doesn't survive.'

A croak in Davina's throat.

'David, what he says is right. Speed is everything. Sergei yes, we accept.'

'Thank you, Madame. But I'm afraid I must hear it from your husband also. Then we can shake hands on it now and here. Then things are as good as if the ink were dry already.'

David Cameron looks as if he will kill someone. Certainly, he doesn't look as if he is about to shake hands.

A quiet voice of command in a storm.

'David, let us go somewhere to be private and discuss this matter rationally. Please excuse us Davina, Professor Dzhugashvili.'

David follows the German woman out of the kitchen into a passage.

'Is there a bathroom I might use?'

'Of course, let me show you.' He leads the way up a flight of stairs. The house is a bit of a rabbit warren but that is one of the things he likes about it. He opens the door for her. 'I'll wait for you out here.'

'No, no, David. Come in and lock the door. We need to speak without distraction. While I relieve myself, I can explain.'

Unselfconsciously, Annie wriggles down her tight jeans and sits down on the lavatory. It seems as if she really does not intend this to be a step forward in a seduction sequence. But he is not sure if her intention is exactly relevant at this moment

'I told you yesterday that you should follow the instructions of the Government, not to pay the ransom.'

While she is speaking, her gaze is fixed on the small patch of floor in front of her small feet. He on the other hand cannot tear his eyes away from her exposed thighs.

'Exactly, Annie. So, I'll just tell Sergei it's been a big mistake. We are not selling the house...'

'No David. If you do that it will get back to the kidnappers, you may be sure. And we cannot predict what they may then do to your son.'

'Assuming it is not all Felix's joke.'

'Yes, assuming it is not all the joke of Felix. It may be, David. But David, are you willing to wager your son's life on the mere possibility that it is?'

Put like that David is silent. Annie continues to sit where she is though she seems to have finished relieving herself. Now she looks directly at him.

'What I suggest, is that you go along with the ransom process. Accept Sergei's offer. Get Christie's or someone to value your painting. Get valuations for your other assets.'

'Oh, Alicia and Luke are well into that already. But, Annie, what about the Government?'

'That is a point, yes, David. You are intimate with the Prime Minister, are you not?'

'What? Oh, I see what you mean. Well, I mean, I've met him and so on.'

'And he has spoken to you personally about this affair of Felix?'

She looks up at him questioning. *Have you enjoyed the sight of my thighs enough for the moment?*

'He gave me his private line to call if…'

'Well call it. Now. Explain that you plan to go along with the ransom process at this point but that you will keep his people closely in touch with events. But David, this is important, do not give the Prime Minister any detail of where we suspect the kidnappers may have taken Felix nor of the content of the emails.'

Her gaze is so insistent that he at once agrees.

She eases her knickers and jeans back on and flushes the loo.

'David, one thing is puzzling to me.'

'Yes, Annie.'

'How is it that a man of long experience of life, such as you yourself are, can become physically aroused by the sight of a woman of forty-nine sitting on a lavatory?'

There is no good answer to that. He simply stares into her light blue eyes looking back at him in the bathroom mirror as she washes and dries her hands and flicks her hair into place. Perhaps after all it is a very pale blond.

'Well?'

She turns to look at him directly now. A slight smile, anticipating.

'I suppose, Annie,' says David Cameron slowly, 'it's because it's you.'

'Yes, I thought that might be the case,' says Annie. 'Which makes it quite interesting to me, from a philosophical point of view.'

'Worth investigating further?'

Annie's expression is enigmatic.

'Perhaps David, but not now. Perhaps later, should time become available.'

13

Preparing to Pay

The man who answers the Prime Minister's personal line, if it is his personal line, agrees that David should play along with the kidnappers for now. It may even be acceptable to pay the ransom if the money really is going to various charities.

'Yes, keep in touch.'

So, when he goes downstairs, he shakes the dubious hand of the dubious Russian and with his help scans the proffered contract into his computer to email to his solicitor and to Annie. Eight million smackers in the bank, good as. Vina even gives him a peck on the lips.

'I knew you'd see sense, David.'

Alicia and Luke have finished their estimates, as far as they can.

The cars are a disappointment. The Ferrari is not a desirable model. Bit of a lemon, actually.

The shares turn out to be worth only four hundred thousand. David authorises his broker to make an immediate sale anyway. Well, why not show willing, buy time.

Cashing in his private pension will take a little longer but the Scottish Widows confirms an estimate of a million seven hundred thousand, which is gratifying.

All now rests on the alleged Degas. Unsurprisingly it's a study of a young girl from the Corps du Ballet of the Paris Opera. A woman from Christie's, or is it Sotheby's, will be there at three.

Annie's presence, so resented by the family eighteen hours before now seems to act like balm on them all. She even chats to Vina about the merits of various sorts of body rub, of the kind she, Vina, will never again be able to afford once the ransom is paid. If the ransom is paid.

David retreats to his study to speak to his agent once more.

'Just a quick one, Sam. How are the revenues from Vina's book doing?'

'Has she asked you to ask me?'

'Well, no, but...'

'Well, then the same answer applies as for Felix. Get her to call me herself if she's up to it. I can tell you, though, David that her royalties to date look as if they may be significant if not substantial.'

'And what does that mean in ballpark numbers.'

'I've told you, David, I can't say any more. One thing though that might cheer you up a bit. Now that Felix's kidnap is out in the open…yes, I've seen the video…simply dreadful, unspeakable….'

'So, you think it is genuine then? Not just Felix having a joke at everyone's expense.'

'David even you can't think that. No, that kid was scared out of his wits.'

'So, what's the news of good cheer, Sam?'

'It seems ghoulish to say it in the circumstances, but the wide publicity the kidnap case is now attracting means that your own book sales will probably rise substantially.'

'My book sales?'

'Those of all three of you. But yes, David, even yours, though less than those of Felix and Davina of course.'

'Of course.'

'Oh, and that PR girl you asked for to deal with the press is on her way. Should be with you shortly after lunch. In the meantime, probably best to say nothing to them, the press, if you can manage it.'

'Of course. Well thank you Sam.'

As his hand grasps the nicely fashioned handle of the solid mahogany door of his study, the edge of the door strikes him in the face as someone pushes it open hard from the outside.

'Is there any blood?' David is holding his nose tenderly.

'No, should there be?' Annie Fritzweiler is unimpressed. 'I came to find you, David, because the press is trying to get into the house through the window of the downstairs bathroom.'

'What did you say Annie? What the hell is that noise?'

She is shouting above the roar as a press helicopter carefully settles its undercarriage in the middle of David Cameron's front lawn.

14

The Theory of Fairness

'Well Andrew, have you managed to write for me an essay on the topic on which I asked you to write for this week.'

Annie is seated in her customary position deep in her chair. She is of course wearing trousers. Quite tight.

'Yes, Annie…'

Her stare is so withering that he corrects himself at once.

'Yes, Dr Fritzweiler.'

Seeking to recover the high ground.

'Actually, I am rather pleased with my effort.'

'Andrew, that is scarcely relevant. What is in point is whether I am pleased with your effort.'

She reads the hurt and confusion in his face and offers him a crumb of comfort.

'Since I am your tutor, and for the hour we are together each week your instructor, it is correct that you address me by my academic title. If outside the hour of instruction, you wish for example to invite me to dinner or to try to make love to me, then addressing me by my first name is arguably more appropriate. The matter you see, Andrew, is situational. Perhaps your essay will uncover for me whether you think moral decisions, like those of correct manners, are situational or whether they depend on independent principle.'

Felix's pulses are racing at the mere mention on Annie's lips that he might try to make love to her.

'On what topic, Andrew, have you written?'

'As you told me, fairness.'

'Very well then.'

Felix Cameron, unaccustomed to being nervous, stutters to a start with Plato and Aristotle. After all, did not everything in Western philosophy start with Plato and Aristotle? But Annie is having none of it.

'Andrew, in this room we are dealing with philosophy, with live thinking, not with the history of dead ideas. References to the philosophers of the past are relevant only in as far as you compare or better contrast your own ideas with them.'

Felix discards the next two pages of his essay. For once he has done a thorough job of researching the philosophy topic and to make time has winged it with Johnny Pebbledash in his history tutorial back in Cambridge.

'Utilitarianism,' Felix looks up anxiously at his tutor, but her face gives nothing away, 'might be thought to encompass fairness in its analysis of the greatest good for the greatest number. In fact, this is the very point at which the whole Utilitarian project comes to grief.'

The philosopher's argot is beginning to come naturally to Felix.

'For there is no mechanism in Utilitarianism to forbid oppression of a minority if in consequence thereof the majority derives greater satisfaction. This is self-evidently contrary to fairness.'

Felix looks up. No, it's alright, Annie is not going to rebuke him. Get on then.

'David Hume, the great empiricist, is in a difficulty with moral argument as he believes nothing to be real except to the extent it presents itself to our senses in a way that can be verified. Hume manages to concede that justice, which for many of the pre-twentieth century philosophers includes fairness, should be pursued to the extent it protects property and preserves order in society. But Hume is not really comfortable with statements about what should happen, since they cannot be derived only from what has happened. Since he seems unable fully to persuade himself, it is no surprise that he fails to persuade us.'

Annie frowns slightly.

'Are you losing your way here, Andrew, in the dexterity of your prose?'

He moves quickly on to the foot of the mountain that is Immanuel Kant.

'Kant purports to be a game changer.'

Annie perhaps wonders if the sage of Konigsberg, who took each day exactly the same measured walk and never left his hometown, would recognise the ideas of a game or of a change. But she sees what Felix is getting at and lets it go.

'He does not rely on the artificial notion of a social contract or on declaring fairness to be moral to the extent it assists attainment of some other convenient state of affairs. Kant maintains that justice, fairness, is an absolute, a 'categorical imperative', to be pursued regardless of consequences. There is one innate human right only. To do what one wills consistently with the freedom of everyone else to do the same. So far so fair.'

But, as it turns out, Felix Cameron is not impressed by such magisterial absolutes.

'As in so much of Kant,' though how would he know, having merely read forty pages of derivative material on the internet, 'there is a lack of clarity, of specificity, when it comes to practical questions, such as how wealth should be distributed between individuals. Indeed, on any practical, moral question.'

Annie leans forward with her knees together, concentrating.

'So, Andrew, why is it exactly that you dismiss Kant's Categorical Imperative? That we can know by reason alone what is the right thing to do and that we must do it?'

'Because it is simply not clear how Kant derives moral proposition from reason only.'

Annie nods for him to continue. Having spent much too much of her previous life in Germany lecturing on Kant she agrees with this. But she isn't going to tell him that. Not yet anyway.

'Kant is famously difficult,' Felix continues. 'But this is not because he is intellectually challenging, though he may be, but because he is unclear. The point of philosophy is to be clear. To the extent that Kant cannot be understood by an exceptionally intelligent and reasonably diligent undergraduate at one of our ancient universities, he is a poor philosopher.'

He looks at Annie for applause. She does indeed approve the thrust of his point, but she deplores his exhibitionist way of expressing it.

'"Exceptionally intelligent and reasonably diligent", are these terms intended to be self-referential, Andrew?' Annie asks, frowning slightly at him.

Felix feels discomforted rather than endorsed because he thinks Annie is laughing at him.

'So, Andrew are any of what the world takes to be the great philosophers of help in coming at the fairness question?'

If anyone might be, it will be John Rawls, whose Theory of Justice has defined the fairness debate among philosophers for the last half century.

15

The Practice of Fairness

For Rawls, justice is fairness. He starts with the assertion that basic liberties belong to all and that inequalities, even those of wealth, are justified only if everyone is made better off thereby.

Rawls dramatises the power of his argument by his 'veil of ignorance' construction. He postulates that each member of society should behave as if they did not know what position in the society they would fill, honoured judge or despised criminal, wealthy banker or distressed pauper. Rawls believes that such a system would tend to be egalitarian, fair in a common-sense way. Since most people are risk averse and would rather avoid the high chance of a miserable fate as an unsubsidised pauper than rely on the small chance that they would enjoy unrestricted wealth as a tax-sheltered banker. Justice, says Rawls, is not reducible to utility.

'What then is your conclusion on Rawls?' asks Annie, as

Andrew rests for a moment on his assumed laurels.

'Nice try but no cigar.'

'And the absence of this cigar, why is that?'

'It's obvious. Of course, because his theory cannot be applied. Aspects of utilitarianism and some of the propositions of Karl Marx contribute to real political programs today. But Rawls falls on his face as soon as he steps outside the schoolroom.'

'So, what Andrew is your own solution to the question of how we are to know what is fair and how we are to bring such a state of affairs more nearly about?'

Felix Cameron drops the pages of his essay neatly on the floor beside him and moves into his carefully rehearsed denouement.

'Well, Dr Fritzweiler, Rawls is right about two important things. First, the proposition that all individuals must at the outset be assumed equal. Whilst we cannot prove this in any mathematical sense of proof, it is intuitively so persuasive that we feel compelled to accept it.'

'And why is that?'

'For the same reason that we accept the axioms of Euclid? Fundamental equality of individuals is the "straight line is the shortest distance between two points" of moral philosophy.'

'Philosophical analysis does not generally get very far by use of analogy,' she says, but he is sure she is impressed. As if to confirm this for the young man, Annie permits herself the ghost of a smile.

'And what, Andrew, is the second thing?'

Felix is disconcerted for a moment.

'Second thing?'

'You mentioned two important things about which Rawls is correct.'

'Oh of course. Crucially Rawls deals with society, not the individual. So, when it comes to extending Rawls to the practical world, he has given us the hint. That we can use the instruments of society to bring about the reality of equality.'

'It sounds, Andrew, as if you meant a police force?'

'Well, a degree of compulsion, yes. If we do not deal with the question of how the propositions of moral theory, fairness in this case, can be applied in practice, we do only half the job. That is what Rawls has done, half his own job. I intend at least to sketch out how the second half can and should be done.'

'I am eager to hear what you have to say of this.'

'But I.... I thought I would only have an hour and so...'

Annie laughs.

'Very well we may address application of fairness next time. As it happens, we have already overrun the hour. However, our discussion may continue until the arrival of the colleague I am expecting.'

Felix beams.

'Andrew, I like your essay for one reason.' She leans back in her chair, her legs now apart. 'It keeps its foot on the ground. That is to say it keeps in mind that philosophy, if it is to be anything but a mind game, must articulate with reality.'

Felix beams some more.

'On the other hand, your essay is deficient in a number of respects.'

Felix wonders which method of doing away with himself would be quickest. The gas fire in his room? Annie continues her careful demolition of his ego.

'Your essay spends time on the irrelevancies of philosophers who are not much to do with the present debate on fairness. It uses the devices of literary showmanship to hide the fact that you have produced no single idea of your own in your essay. It is true that you seem to have understood well enough why the contributions of major philosophers to the fairness question are irrelevant to us today and you have shown a sufficient grasp of the essence of John Rawls's position. But, as my colleagues here would tend to put it, your effort merits no more than a Beta Plus.'

Felix's whole being revolts against the suggestion that he is mediocre. He gathers up his papers and prepares to flee. But Annie is not yet finished with him.

'Your recognition that essential to a valid theory of fairness is how it is to be applied in practice to an extent redeems you. This is so even though you have failed to give any account of how this might work. On the other hand, the analogy you make between the Principle of Fairness and the Axiom of Euclid is illuminating. So perhaps Alpha double minus.'

He likes the sound of an evaluation containing an alpha. But Annie continues.

'As I mentioned, I am at this moment expecting a colleague, a psychologist. He and I are planning some observations of controlled situations in the real world in the application of a theory of fairness. I think this might interest you if you can spare a few minutes.'

Felix can spare a universe of time if it is to be spent in the company of Annie Fritzweiler. Perhaps his undeclared campaign to get Annie to go to bed with him might yet be capable of rehabilitation.

Not so fast young man, for Annie is not nearly finished with his moral education.

A firm knock on the door and a muscular, fit looking man in his early forties is leaning down to kiss Annie in a practised sort of way. He shakes Andrew's hand. Andrew is almost oppressed by the psychologist's large physical presence.

'Andrew, this is Dr Gregory Halberstadt, the psychologist of whom I spoke.'

'But you should call me Greg,' says a friendly Australian voice, 'Do I gather we may be going to do some work together?'

Annie is now speaking into her phone, though neither of the men heard it ring. Finishing, she interrupts them.

'That was the Master. It seems he wants to discuss Crowd Sourcing for financing the new SCR. I'm sorry but I have to go across to the Lodgings. I shall be perhaps twenty minutes. There are some beers in the fridge in the other room, Greg. Oh, and as I said, do remain, Andrew, if you wish.'

16

Pencil and Paper

The family sits round the table. It's come to Jesus time. Alicia has the list.

'OK Dad, it's very straightforward, but there's a problem.'

'Oh yes, and what is that?'

'It doesn't add up. You simply don't have quite enough money to get Felix freed, Dad.'

'Perhaps we could reduce the charitable donations a bit. You know feed the elephants twice a day instead of three times.'

'That is simply not funny, David.'

Davina is in no mood to see the amusing side of anything. She is still haunted by Sergei Dzhugashvili's image of her son's head on a Christmas turkey platter. Somehow it seems so much more real when uttered by someone who might be a descendant of Joseph Stalin.

'Mum's right Dad. This is not a time for negotiation. We just have to find a way to pay.'

'All right Alicia, why don't you spell out where we stand?'

'OK. You've shaken hands with Sergei on the sale of the house. Since they were retained by Sergei there is no agent's commission for you to pay. There is no capital gains tax to pay since it's your main residence.'

'If, Alicia you mean it's my home, our home, that's right.'

'So, eight million for the house. The shares fetched four hundred thousand, give or take. Surrender value of the pension, one million seven hundred thousand. It's an estimate but the company seemed pretty comfortable with it.'

'They might be comfortable with it, but what am I going to live on in my old age?'

'Dad, please be serious.'

'I rather thought I was being.'

'OK. Eight plus point four plus one point seven is ten point one million. The cars another hundred thousand or so, making ten point two million. So, we are three hundred thousand pounds short.'

'So, it's all down to the Degas?' says Luke. 'I always rather liked that painting. Why did you move it to your study, by the way, Dad?''

'Because, Luke, I like it too. And since you moved out, only I look at it. Anyway, I thought we were going to get a valuation this afternoon.'

'Yes, she's been and gone,' says Luke. 'As she pointed out it would take months to get it into an auction, even if it is genuine. So, what Eng Ling suggested...'

'A Chinese expert on French Impressionism?'

'That's right, Dad. The Chinese are the biggest buyers of the stuff these days and it seems they feel more comfortable getting the low down from one of their own. Anyway, Eng Ling was very helpful. She said that if it's genuine, she might be able to find a private buyer for a quick sale,' Luke continues.

'Quick sale. Sounds like a rip off to me. Just like the house. Perhaps I should have offered it to Sergei.'

'Dad if it's genuine, we won't be counting the pennies. It will pay the whole cost of the ransom and much more.'

The phone is ringing, somewhere in the house. 'That's probably Eng Ling now, 'says Luke. 'I asked her to get back to us as soon as she could with a preliminary view on authenticity.'

There is no extension in the dining room. When his novels were the hottest thing in town, David Cameron affected not to like being interrupted at dinner by constant phone calls from agents and journalists, so he had it removed.

Luke goes out to answer the phone. He's gone what seems to be an age. Round the dining table they fall silent, somehow unable to continue the discussion without him. Alicia still has the list of values. But all that shows is that they need more money. The Degas is their last hope.

At last Luke is back. His face tells the story. Then he spells it out.

'Fake. Not a doubt. Lucky to get five thousand pounds for it. Still, I rather like it though,' Luke adds.

Alicia and Davina look daggers at him.

'So, David, what the hell are we going to do now?'

He thinks of saying, 'You could sell your jewellery, darling,' when he remembers that she does not have any. Always been against it on principle. Some principle or other.

Then the obvious strikes him.

'Vina, Sam told me this morning that the royalties from your book...'

'If you mean THE DARWIN FACTOR then say THE DARWIN

FACTOR, David.'

'From THE DARWIN FACTOR then, the royalties look as if they may be significant...'

'You've been prying into *my* affairs with *my* agent?'

'Don't worry Davina, she wouldn't tell me a number. But it's obviously substantial. Enough to make up the shortfall in the ransom money for Felix I'd wager.'

'You think you are going to use my money to.... That's despicable, David. What the hell do you think I'm going to live on after the divorce?'

Divorce? Not for the first time recently, David Cameron, has a sense of fences being jumped, when he had not even realised he had entered a steeplechase.

'You don't think I'm going to continue to live with you when you move into some slum terrace in Swindon do you? After the way you have behaved over our son?'

The way he has behaved. Stumping up ten million pounds plus. Bringing himself to the brink of bankruptcy. In his shock at the pure unreason of it all, there is only one thing he can think to say.

'What about me, Davina?'

'Oh, you'll be alright. You always are alright. Your novels

might not be much good these days. After all they never really were. But there'll always be a market for them. Among the poor sods who still recognise the name on the cover and are too gaga to mind what's inside.'

'I think,' says Alicia, the calm of her voice belied by the wild look she exchanges with Luke, 'that we should go over the assets again. We need to get to ten and a half million pounds. We need to be able to pay that to the charities by Friday of next week or we simply have no idea what they will do to Felix.'

Davina has got up from the table apparently to make tea. Luke gets up to join her.

'It's all right, Mum, let me do that.'

'Where is Annie Fritzweiler,' asks David suddenly.

Luke has failed to take the familiar large earthenware family teapot from his mother's hands for the good reason that she has thrown it at her husband's head.

17

How Hard Can It Be?

'Look on the bright side, Dad, it might have been full of hot tea. And it might have hit you between the eyes, instead of glancing off your bald patch.'

'It still hurts like hell. Where's your mother? Do you think I should have her sectioned?'

'Alicia's putting her to bed. She'll be fine after a good sleep.'

'Fine as in ready to have another go, you mean?'

'Another go at you? No, of course not. That was just a spur of the moment thing. Repressed jealousy I shouldn't wonder. You know, when you mentioned Annie Fritzweiler's name.'

'But there's nothing between us.'

'Of course, there isn't Dad. She's much too young for you. It's obvious to anyone that what Annie needs is a virile younger man.'

'Obvious is it?' says David.

He thinks that young men, even virile ones, shouldn't go counting their chickens where Annie Fritzweiler is concerned. David's mobile has been ringing. After a bit Luke locates it in his father's shirt pocket.

'It's Goran, Dad. Shall I get him to call back?'

'No, no. Give me that thing.'

He gives his publisher what he has learnt to call, much against his better judgement, a heads up. Goran is all solicitation, until they come to the point.

'Three hundred thousand? A loan? Of course, in the old days, Cameron when you were selling millions, I'd not have hesitated. But to be frank...' A Goran Lefkovitch strong point, being frank. 'To be frank, I'm not sure when I see it back. And the Americans won't like it. Can't afford to go against them. Things are a bit iffy just now, Cameron, with the Americans. Know what I'm saying here?'

The Americans are the bosses of the huge media conglomerate which owns the nominally independent Waverly Press. And things with the Americans have been iffy since the day they bought Waverly and made Goran a rich man in the process. Even so David would have pressed Goran for the three hundred thousand pounds were it not for the fact that he could not put up with a diatribe of at least thirty minutes about the injustices done to his native land and how every spare penny of his income goes to support....

David rings off. Luke is thinking hard, but thinking has not always been Luke's strong suit.

'You could sell a kidney or a bit of your liver. Well, no, I suppose you couldn't. There's a timing issue and anyway it wouldn't look good. Besides trading in organs is probably illegal here.'

It's probably Luke's line of work that makes him think in terms of offal.

David is dying to call Annie to ask her advice on laying his hands on three hundred thousand pounds, but he feels compelled to hear out his son's fanciful ideas.

'But you've got tons of rich and powerful friends, Dad. Surely one of them could help.'

This idea isn't so much fanciful as out of date. There was, for example, Amir Khan, who is practically a neighbour of theirs just across the county boundary in Oxfordshire. A hedge fund manager of legendary proportions, Amir had ceased to return David's calls since David had revealed in his blockbuster, HEDGED IN, a couple of Amir's practices that were not strictly in accordance with the letter of the law. Similarly, Fritz Fassenbacher, the model for FF in WHITE

OUT, David Cameron's novel of high-pressure professional skiing, had taken it amiss when David had made his character gay.

And there had been others.

Whilst he had regretted the loss of these friendships, David had always felt that such personal sacrifices were more than justified in the cause of literature. Still now it was certainly inconvenient to have lost his access to the world of wealth, where three hundred thousand pounds was a rounding error.

'I'm not sure they'd want to, Luke. The world can be very fickle, cruel even.'

The spool of ideas in his son's brain seems to have run out. Time to call Annie.

'Look Luke, probably better if I make this call in private, if that's OK.'

'Oh, right Dad.' Luke melts away.

Quite why he has asked his son to leave, or indeed quite why a philosopher would have instant access to three hundred thousand pounds was not clear to David. But philosophers deal in ideas, don't they? Perhaps Annie would have a good one.

No answer from her office. David tries her mobile. She comes on just before the call trips to her message service.

'Oh, David, yes. I really can't talk now. A crisis. Well, it's all a crisis, isn't it?'

He describes how he had narrowly escaped death at the hands of the family teapot.

'Yes, that does sound quite serious. Look David, would you mind coming over here. No, no, in my rooms at the College. I'll leave word at the Lodge that you are to be shown up.'

Forty minutes' drive, in traffic, but still.

He is sitting where Felix had sat, or any other student of Annie's come to that.

'It is occasionally inconvenient not to be rich,' she says. 'Most of the time I feel quite content with my situation, but occasionally....and it is usually in connection with helping a friend, I feel that money would make life more convenient.'

'You don't happen to know anyone, Annie...?'

'No David, I do not move in such roundabouts...ah, such circles. I really cannot be of help in this matter of money I'm afraid. You should have told me what you wanted to discuss, and I could have saved you a journey.'

'But Annie, you seemed to be in a meeting or something.'

It seems that the philosopher smiles at the recollection.

'Yes David, a sort of a meeting, a very small one. But now you are here. Let us discuss things. Will you have a drink?'

He will. He brings her up to date. Vina driven to the edge of madness by anxiety for Felix and rage against himself. Alicia and Luke wracking his assets to shake out an extra three hundred thousand. But the Degas a dead loss. No answer in sight.

'So, what is it you think yourself, David?'

'I think Felix, Andrew if you prefer, arranged the whole thing himself.'

'What motive would he have for doing that, David?'

'To torture me. To make some point about my moral fallibility. I don't know. But I'm sure he is a least a willing agent in this kidnap facade, if not the instigator.'

Annie leans towards him, her knees together, both hands pushed down between her thighs. As ever she wears trousers, quite tight. Does she even own a skirt?

'But does that make sense, David? He must know that it would most likely cause more suffering to his mother than to you. Even if we postulate some Oedipus complex or some other basis of resentment towards you, still why would he wish to cause such grief to his mother?'

David is silent. He cannot think of a good answer, but Annie is ready with a helping hand.

'Of course, you know your son many times better than I, but an outsider can sometimes see things concealed by their very familiarity from those closest to a person. I have seen Andrew every week this term, for an hour for his philosophy tutorial. He seems to me to be a person overdeveloped in his mental capacities but somewhat stunted in his emotional growth.'

'That could well be true, but...?'

'He is fascinated by intellectual problems. But he seems crucially to lack emotional intelligence, the ability to credit others as human individuals in their own right. To empathise, if you will. Yet he in no way shows a tendency toward Asperger's Syndrome, or even to shyness. To the contrary, he is extremely sociable, fearless in the company of others. Perhaps fearless altogether. I do not here speak of physical courage, David. You understand me?'

'If you could perhaps illustrate.'

This man is, or was, a bestselling novelist, thinks Annie. How could one achieve that and be obtuse to such an extent as to the workings of the human personality? But then she has read only a couple of his books. Perhaps such psychological stupidity is just what is required to succeed with his sort of book.

'In the last two weeks I...please do excuse me David, my phone...Oh hello yes of course...No, on no account do that.

You want to keep them all on your side at this point. No, no, not at all. Please call at any time. I'm sorry David. Just some College business. As I was about to say, at his last tutorial, Andrew…I still think of him as Andrew if you don't mind… and I have been discussing theories of moral philosophy. Normal curriculum stuff. But I have noted that Andrew seems particularly interested in the way one might test various hypotheses in practice. In real personal or societal situations. I do wonder, David, if you might not be right and Andrew took it into his head to try an experiment of his own? Hard as it may be to believe, he might have had no glimmer of the pain he would cause his family.'

'I see, Annie. He wanted to see if I, if the family as a whole, would act morally in a kidnap situation? That is, if one could work out what was the moral thing to do in such a situation. But Annie, what should we do, what should I do, at this moment?'

'A simple-minded view, David, might be to save one's son. Whatever it took. Even if one suspected that the kidnap was faked, as you apparently do, you cannot I suppose be sure. One would not want to be wrong in such a situation.'

Annie is just playing back to him the thoughts he has had a hundred times. That have been discussed a dozen times in family conferences. But on Annie's lips, muted brick red lipstick today, which really goes better with her complexion than pink, these ideas seem like new minted wisdom.

But Annie has things to do and places to go.

'I would offer you another drink, but I suppose you can't because of driving. And I'm sorry but I do have some commitments this evening which I really cannot break. I have to prepare, you see.'

He thanks her effusively. Then gets up. She offers him her cheek to kiss. Then she stares at him.

'David, what is it you need? Three hundred thousand pounds? Didn't you tell me that your wife's novel had obtained large advances? Would that be enough to...?'

He explains Davina's reaction that she would need that money to keep up even a semblance of her lifestyle after their, previously unmentioned, divorce.

'How interesting,' Annie murmurs, to herself rather than to him. 'And Andrew's own proceeds are embargoed by the lawyers I suppose?'

But now it is evident that her mind has moved elsewhere and that she wants him gone.

As he starts off down her staircase, she drops one last piece of wisdom down the stairwell after him.

'You could, David, try crowd sourcing. Only there's not much time left, is there?'

As he pauses on the stairs, thinking to seek clarification, he hears her door slam shut above him.

18

Whose Idea Was It Anyway?

Events have moved on by the time he gets home. Such is the press vehicles and those of idle onlookers in their lane that he has to park in the village and walk the rest of the way to the house. Alicia greets him in the garden with the latest disaster.

'I'd better warn you, Dad. Mum has got it into her head that you have a flat in London in which you entertained a string of girls.'

'A string of girls?' Like polo ponies he can't help thinking.

'Well over the years, you know. So, if you were just to sell that flat then Felix could be back with us tomorrow.'

'But you know that's nonsense, Ali.' Luke strolls across the grass with them. It's a gorgeous winter's day, barely above freezing but not a cloud in the sky. 'You both know that.'

'We don't know anything, Dad. Until recently we were children. And since then, we've both lived away from home.'

He recalls that from time to time the idea of a small flat in London had occurred to him, though without the girls of course. Vina had always said that that would be disruptive of the family. Anyway, the whole point of living so comfortably close to London was that they could do without a flat in town.

Of course, with hindsight, buying a flat in central London five or ten years ago would have been a brilliant investment. No problem with unexpected expenses like an outrageous ransom demand for one's younger son. And who knows perhaps having one or two girls on the side up there might have prevented their marriage from getting into such disrepair. Perhaps.

'Of course, Dad, we take your word for it,' says Luke. 'But really, Dad, it might be best if you moved out for a while.'

'Oh, to my flat in London?'

Alicia gives him a tight, this is no time for silly jokes, smile.

'The point is Dad, if in her present state Mum saw you, I don't know what she'd do.'

'But Alicia, that's absurd. This house has eight bedrooms. Why don't I just move into the M4 room?'

It was the one room in the house where through some trick

of local topology one could hear the distant roar of traffic on the motorway from London to the West.

'I seem to remember it has a fairly sturdy bolt on the door.'

'Well Dad, don't say we didn't warn you. Oh, and you should know that while you were away...Where were you anyway? Mum gave a press conference.'

'With Ali and me as a sort of chorus,' Luke chimes in.

'You know the sort of thing Dad, tearful mother appealing to the kidnappers to release her dear son, family holding strong together.'

'But I wasn't there,' David protests in spite of himself.

'Frankly, Dad, I think that's what made it work. You would just have confused matters by saying that Felix might have organised it himself.'

'Of course, I wouldn't. Anyway, it's true. He probably did organise it himself.'

'The PR girl,' says Luke, 'wanted Mum to give an exclusive to one of the Sundays, but it wasn't nearly enough money to make up the shortfall in the ransom. The problem is Felix is not yet famous enough...I mean apart from being kidnapped... and you are yesterday's man, Dad. Anyway, I had the idea of calling Annie Fritzweiler, and she said on no account to give an exclusive. Much better to have the whole press on your side, Annie said.'

So that is what Annie's phone call had been about. A matter of College business, indeed.

'Look Dad, the coast is clear for the moment. Mum is resting in her room after her ordeal with the press. So, come in and eat something. You can see Mum's press conference on the telly. The news channels have highlights on a repeating spool at the moment,' Luke adds.

'And then Dad, I really think you ought to go up and stay put in the M4 room,' Alicia says. 'There's a shower up there, isn't there? We'll bring food up to you from time to time when Mum's not around.'

'Look, Alicia, Luke, I'm not going to live like a fugitive in my own house. This nonsense has got to stop.'

But it is he who stops, dead in his tracks. His wife of thirty years looms across the living room on the huge screen, more than life size. Her blond hair is streaked with grey, her face haggard but brave without make-up...Don't be daft. She's on television. Of course, they would apply make-up. To make her look haggard but brave.

'Even now at this late hour, even after so much suffering, please, please, whoever you are, release my son. Take the money. It's all the money we have. Even though it's not quite as much as you want. We know that you have good intentions because you want to use the ransom to help charities, elephants and...'

She breaks down but, after a few endless seconds, is able to resume.

'So please out of the goodness of your heart, let my son go. We won't let the police come after you, not if you give us back our Felix. So please, please, please call me on the number on the screen. It's my personal number. The police cannot intercept it. Anyway, I know you will use a prepaid mobile that cannot be traced. But please, however you do it, get in touch and we will give you, the charities, all our money. Every penny we have. Just give us back....'

'Is there much more of this?' asks David, despairingly.

'The TV people thought it was great. And even the police seemed to think it might do some good.'

'What on earth good can it do, Luke? Suddenly put a bunch of ruthless toughs in touch with their touchy-feely selves, so that they let Felix go? Always assuming...'

'Yes, we know what you think, Dad. The point the police make is that it might jog someone's memory. If Felix is being held in captivity against his will, someone somewhere may have noticed something out of the ordinary. His picture is on every television screen in the land and across every national newspaper.'

'Wait a minute. Didn't the police object to your mother giving her private line and trying to cut them out of the ransom process?'

'Mum insisted, and even the forces of the law are not inclined to argue with a woman at the end of her tether,' Luke adds.

'No, I don't suppose the police wanted to be attacked with the family teapot,' murmurs David. 'Anyway, the publicity is going to blow Felix's Oxbridge cover. Although of course he'll be leaving anyway since we can't anymore afford the fees.'

'That's if he survives, Dad,' says Alicia.

But that stale and painful debate is curtailed by a call on David's mobile.

'What do you mean? No, I never read my books after the proof stage. Yes, certainly I wrote a novel entitled THE RIGHTEOUS AND THE DAMNED. Yes, it is about kidnapping. *It's about kidnapping!*'

Bloody hell, he'd completely forgotten.

'You mean, you think Felix...ah not necessarily Felix. His kidnappers, got the idea *from my book*?!'

It seems a few minutes on Google has given Annie Fritzweiler a good idea. Perhaps even the right idea.

The phone is still clamped to his ear. David runs to the study. He may not read his own books after he's finished writing them, but he preserves them all. Pristine and unread but all signed by the author. They stand in their first edition covers in case posterity might later take an interest. They have their own glass case, where they are arranged in the order of their publication. He tugs open the sliding glass doors, stiff with lack of use.

'UP AGAINST IT, THE FIRE AND THE BRIMSTONE, MIDNIGHT IN MOSCOW, IN BROAD DAYLIGHT...ah here it is. THE RIGHTEOUS AND THE DAMNED. It comes back to him. A kidnapping, not for money or for a specific political cause, but as a way of inducing moral behaviour by an egregious tycoon whose eldest son Manny Kant has abducted for the purpose. And Manny has demanded the ransom money be paid to charities of his choice.

'Annie? Are you still there? Yes, I've got it. But what do you think it means? The kidnappers are unlikely to hurt Felix, since they are the good guys. Or they see themselves as such?'

He listens attentively.

'But Annie isn't this consistent with the idea that Felix set the whole thing up himself?'

'But what difference does it make if you're not sure? And you can never be sure.'

'I see. Make contact with the kidnappers, even if they turn

out to be just Felix, yes. Get a message to them. So, if they want to talk, they will know how to contact me privately. No of course I won't mention this to Davina. Yes Annie. We'll try it. And Annie, thank you sweetheart.'

19

Extraction

Luke had been right. Davina's television performance had jogged someone's memory. Someone who preferred to communicate to the family rather than the police. A map reference, but no hint of the caller's identity, supplied.

'The idea of a light aircraft taking Felix and the kidnappers somewhere else by plane from Windrush turns out to have been a blind, if it's right. It all speaks to Felix as organiser of the whole thing.'

'But it's not conclusive,' says Alicia.

'I'll call Annie...'

'No Dad. Can't you see if you keep involving Annie it just makes the situation with Mum worse. Better idea. I'll call Jeremy. I should have done it before.'

Jeremy Wingate Grey is Alicia's boyfriend. Recently promoted Captain of Infantry, decorated veteran of two tours in Afghanistan. A young man for whom putting his own life repeatedly at risk in order to take the lives of the Queen's enemies is apparently essential to his tranquillity of mind. Where Alicia is considered and sensible, Jeremy is unreflective and impulsive. In fact, a complete cowboy. But Alicia has fallen under his spell.

'He's on his way.' Alicia is visibly excited. 'He has a plan.'

As the day declines into winter darkness, the trucks of satellite TV pack up and move out. They've got all they are going to get they reckon and besides, a major political story just has broken. It's now too cold for sightseers too, who anyway came mainly to see the TV operation. So, Jeremy in his old-style Land Rover is able to sweep up the Cameron drive unimpeded. Alicia, Luke and David crowd into the hall to greet him. Davina is still tranquilised upstairs.

Jeremy brings with him a plan for immediate action and two handguns. The action, he says, is to 'extract' Felix from his kidnappers. The guns, he says, are legally registered as recreational weapons since he belongs to a gun club. In which case they ought to be under lock and key at that gun club, thinks David.

Manny Kant, David Cameron's regular hero, handled firearms only in the last resort and then only with extreme distaste. Even so, David knows enough to see that Jeremy's weapons are heavy calibre special forces' issue.

Jeremy holds out one of the pistols to Alicia. She hesitates.

'Your brother's life and sanity are in danger. The safest way with a kidnap situation is to go in with maximum force and credibility. Shock and awe.'

She accepts the weapon.

David thinks about voicing one of the hundred objections which flood his brain but recognises that he is outgunned.

'Alicia told me we have a map reference for the place they are holding Felix.'

'It could be a hoax...or a trap,' says Luke, who does not altogether warm to his prospective brother-in-law's tendency to assume command at all times over all things.

'Let me see the message.'

'It was a voice call,' says Alicia. 'On Mum's mobile, which I've taken charge of while she's under the weather. Muffled voice. Couldn't even tell if it was a man or a woman.'

Jeremy is dismissive.

'If it's a hoax, what have we lost? Good practice for the real thing. If it's a trap, I think we will be equal to most things.'

He grins boyishly and sticks his gun into the pocket of his camouflage jacket, where it sags.

20

The Boundaries of Philosophy

Greg continues to speak about their experiment. How he helps Annie with certain practical issues. Without looking at the screen of his phone, which remains in his pocket, he enters and sends a text message. He gets what must be a reply almost instantaneously.

'Excuse me, Andrew, this could be important.'

He gets up and walks out onto the staircase, out of Felix's earshot. On his return Felix asks the obvious question.

'Was it?'

Greg has put Andrew almost too much at his ease.

'Was it what…important? Ah, in a way yes. I'm sorry to say I will have to curtail our little chat, Andrew. But no doubt we'll meet again soon. By the way, you should probably wait for

Annie, Dr Fritzweiler. Germans can be a touch on the formal side sometimes, can't they?'

Andrew gets up from his chair in order to shake the psychologist's hand, and again is overwhelmed by Greg's sheer physical presence. He feels like the little boy that perhaps he still is.

Greg gone. Andrew wanders round Annie's room, but there is nothing of interest. He wonders about the bedroom but doesn't quite dare.

His sense of physical inferiority quickly ebbs. He remembers a newspaper story he once read about the renowned French Existentialist philosopher and writer Jean Paul Sartre. Sartre was small of stature and as ugly as a toad, but his intellectual brilliance, or his reputation for such, had women and girls climbing over each other to share his bed. And here at Oxford, with Annie Fritzweiler, it was surely mind rather than body that finally counted. And he has the two qualities that will work with Annie. He is sure of it. Intellectual brilliance and almost total self-belief. He will put them to the test as soon as she returns. At that moment, in fact.

'Oh Andrew, has Dr Halberstadt gone? I'm sorry to have left you on your own. Would you like a glass of wine? I myself hate beer, especially Australian beer.'

'Annie, may I ask you something?'

She remains standing, looking at him carefully.

'Annie, do you go to bed with, with Dr Halberstadt?'

She laughs, in surprise, in amusement, he cannot tell.

'Not that it's any of your business, but the answer is no, never.'

She answers the impertinence because she is quite happy to have this information broadcast round the College. Her supposed liaison with Greg Halberstadt is not helpful to her standing in the place.

'He is homosexual, you see...gay.'

Well, that adds credibility to her declaration.

'But why are you interested?'

He tells her.

'But Andrew, to be physically intimate with you is not my desire. You are still more of a boy than a man. Rather puny in fact. And in any case, isn't it rather unnatural that you would feel sexual desire for a woman of my age?'

Still perhaps in the circumstances, she should play along with Andrew's fantasies. She continues to stand facing him, but crosses one leg over the other. She knows that he will be conscious of the tightness of her jeans over her groin. Andrew sits down, staring up at her.

'Let me explain matters to you, Annie.'

She seems to be all ears.

'First you deceive yourself in thinking you don't want me. It is just that you are shy because your own body may show signs of age. But Annie this is what I want.'

'Fascinating,' she murmurs.

'I can enjoy the perfect body of a nineteen-year-old any night of the week.'

Well Andrew is cute in a teenage idol sort of a way, she supposes.

'But sex is only interesting when there is a fascinating person reacting inside the body of the other.'

'The fascinating ghost in the aging machine,' she murmurs, adverting to the philosophical doctrine of the separation of mind and body. In spite of herself she is rather impressed.

'Then, I have the energy of youth. So, I can always satisfy you, however many times...however demanding you may be.'

She utters a slight sound which could be a snort.

'Is there more of this? You are becoming somewhat prolix, my dear Andrew. Quite like a German man.'

'No, I think that is all for the moment.'

'Well, Andrew, thank you for being frank. I will give careful thought to what you have said if you devote yourself to building up your body so that you will appear to me more of a man. But may we now return to the experiment, about which Dr Halberstadt was perhaps speaking to you, concerning how in practice we might change a person's actions to conform more to what he says are his moral principles, about fairness for example?'

'All right,' Andrew says, wondering how they have veered so quickly away from the course he had set toward Annie's bed.

His tutor continues.

'Your essay stated, I think, that you agreed with Rawls that equality, including in a general way equality of wealth, is a given moral truth. Of course, it may be varied in practice if all others are thereby benefited, but I suppose we might be safe in saying that in general at least the degree of inequalities of wealth that exist in rich countries today are morally unacceptable.

Felix nods. His eyes not leaving Annie's thighs as she stands over him.

'We might further say that especially egregious is the wealth of those who have done nothing to earn it or who have earned it without providing anything of value to others. And who do not intend to give the bulk of it away to causes helpful to the poor and distressed.'

'Yes of course,' says Felix.

He feels that all this is a bit elementary. But he has done enough philosophy by now to realise that this is how it often goes. A series of mundane propositions followed by a sudden plunge into a conceptual Olympiad.

'Now it might be objected to our procedure that those who do not accept Rawls's basic axiom of fairness should not be compelled to follow it.'

'But I thought Rawls's fairness proposition was something that in its nature is true, even if others disagree with it? Like the propositions of Euclid?'

'Yes, Andrew, Rawls might very well want to say that. And we might want to follow him in saying it. But we have to do a bit more analysis to convince ourselves of the security of this position. Let us start with the easier case where the subject actually agrees with Rawls, or something approximating to that.'

'But how would we know what a banker or whatever thought about it? I mean the only people who talk in public about such stuff are really politicians and they are mostly hypocrites, liars.'

'Yes,' says Annie, 'but there is at least one class of cases where we may be secure in thinking we have access to the subject's true thoughts, because he has deliberately published them for their own sake.'

'Oh, like writers?'

'Precisely yes, Andrew, writers.'

Her body still has his rapt attention. She hopes her words do too.

'Let us take the example of a novel published a few years ago entitled THE RIGHTEOUS AND THE DAMNED. I wonder if you've read it, Andrew.'

The title seems familiar to him, but he can't immediately place it. Annie gives him time. Let him get as far as he can on his own. But the self-confessed, extremely intelligent undergraduate cannot manage it on his own.

'The author,' says Annie, 'is a quite well-known novelist called David Cameron. The same surname as that of yourself and of the Prime Minister.'

'He's my Dad. But what he writes is crap.'

'I'm sorry Andrew, I did not know that. That he was your father.'

'Why should you? As I say, it's inchoate crap. Not your sort of thing at all, Annie, Dr Fritzweiler.'

'It may be nonsense to you, Andrew, but your father took the proposition of fairness seriously enough to write a forward to his novel in which he sets out his own view of fairness. Quite like that of Rawls's as I recall.'

'Oh yes, now I remember. It's about kidnapping. Dad's hero, Manny Kant...silly name...gets the rich guy to give over all his fortune to charity by holding the guy's son to ransom.'

Though Felix would not be seen dead reading one of his father's novels today, when he was twelve or thirteen, at the time when THE RIGHTEOUS AND THE DAMNED first came out, he had quite enjoyed it.

'Oh yes,' says Annie, 'I remember the plot, now you speak of it, for I do read such things now and then. Where was the kidnapping actually carried out in your father's book? Do you recall Andrew?'

'The changing room at a polo club, wasn't it?' he says. 'Or somewhere equally daft. A posh restaurant?'

'I actually found it quite convincing, Andrew. But in reality, to carry out Rawls's program in practice, in a single case anyway, there is no need to make a real kidnapping. After all, such a thing would be illegal.'

'But how would you do that legally? You'd need a victim whom you can abduct, or you have achieved no threat against the guy's nearest and dearest. The kidnapped guy's father in my Dad's novel.'

'What if the kidnap victim was himself in sympathy with the Rawls project?'

Annie reckons she has finally caught Andrew's interest.

'Oh yes, if the victim voluntarily cooperates then there is no crime. I see. And as long as whoever the ransom demand is meant for assumes it's a real kidnapping, then he will most likely pay up.'

He stares at Annie in admiration, and this time not just for her body.

'You are not quite right, Andrew. There is no crime of kidnapping because the victim volunteers to cooperate. But perhaps to demand money of the victim's father that is still a crime. Even if there is no actual kidnap. But I wonder if there may be a way to avoid that.'

Annie waits for the superior intelligence of her student to arrive at the solution.

'I've got it, Annie. If the victim himself is the channel to demand money from his father. There might still be a crime but the victim's father, or at least his mother, in the relief of getting him back will surely not allow a prosecution.'

'Andrew, yes, I think that may be correct. Now to revert to my question, where would be a good place to stage such a fake kidnapping, Andrew? Where do people go where they are most off their guard? At home?'

'No, too many alarms and stuff. At least we do, at home.'

'Where then? In surroundings in which he feels secure. A restaurant perhaps?'

'That's it, Annie, a posh restaurant. Like the one just outside Oxford where my brother works.'

'Yes,' says Annie. 'Andrew, you must excuse me for a moment. It has become urgent that I relieve myself. I will be absent for a moment only.'

When she returns, she wonders if she has overdone things.

21

Two Hawks Circling a Full Moon

It is eight thirty on a cold winter's morning and it is beginning to get light. Captain Jeremy Wingate Grey of the Foot Guards is under police guard and being prepped for surgery. Second Lieutenant Alicia Cameron of the Scottish Regiment has just reached home, battered, bruised and exhausted after her narrow escape. If it is an escape. There is no sign of Felix. It is almost as bad as it can get.

Shivering with cold and fear, Alicia gives her account to Luke.

With the help of the GPS on his phone, she and Jeremy had located, easily enough, the farmhouse indicated by the anonymous map reference. At least Jeremy seemed to think it was easy. Based on her own mobile GPS, Alicia had a nagging concern that the house, a field's breadth behind the target, as in Jeremy's mind it had become, might be the right one. But Jeremy insisted his was the correct reading as his phone was army issue and army checked. And, after all, Jeremy had done this stuff twice before, in the hell hole of Helmand. For one such operation he had been decorated.

What the dashing young Captain of Infantry had neglected to mention was that on both previous occasions the targeting was in the hands of specialists in contact remotely with drones in the sky above the target and with the operations group on the ground.

'OK Captain you're good to go. And good luck.'

They let the car glide to a stop in a lane a hundred and fifty yards away from the farmhouse. It's three thirty-seven in the morning according to both their watches. They get out without locking the car, since they don't have the key, and move in on the target at a slow lope. Across two fields and the dark back of a house presents itself. Jeremy checks the GPS on his phone. Alicia stares at her own GPS, which still it seems to her indicates that the house beyond this one may be the right one. She holds up the phone to Jeremy. He hardly glances at it before stuffing it into one of the capacious pockets of his army trousers.

She feels sick to her stomach. Natural anxiety before an operation or outright fear that they have the wrong place. There is an electric fence. But it's only two strands to prevent cattle straying. The two warriors easily slip under it, roll over a five barred gate and are running single file toward a door in the back wall of the house, Jeremy in the lead. The back door is outlined by the electric light from inside.

'OK Captain, you're good to go. And good luck.'

Well, he hears it in his head anyway.

Jeremy kicks the door, but it does not give way. Then several things happen in quick succession. A rooster crows thinking no doubt that the invaders herald an early dawn and breakfast. Two Rottweilers race round the corner of the house and start to tear at Alicia's clothing. Jeremy sets a small explosive against the door jamb and flattens himself against the wall, Alicia instinctively following. A flash and a muffled bang and the door swings wide. The dogs cower back in fear.

A roar of fury from inside. 'Be on the phone this minute Mabel. They're back.'

Jeremy tosses two stun grenades into the kitchen and fires his pistol twice into the ceiling as he charges in. The man, the farmer he supposes in the couple of seconds remaining to him, rises from the chair at the end of the kitchen table and fires both barrels of his shot gun into the lower part of Jeremy's body.

Jeremy is screaming, rolling on the floor in pain. Police sirens sound from not far away.

Alicia has a choice. She makes it in an instant and is gone the way they came. The dogs give half-hearted chase but are happy to see her gone. She can feel the electricity burn her shoulders as she blunders through the cattle fence. The voltage is not enough to do real damage, though. She sprints across the two fields between her and the car. Drops from the final gate into the lane and falls awkwardly on the tarmac of the road. As she gets up, she is horrified to see two police uniforms approaching her. She turns and runs away from them, blindly down the middle of the lane, her fear suppressing the pain from the ankle.

Even with her injury the rangy soldier is more than a match for the Constables. Sense returns to her when she can no longer see the police in pursuit. An all points alert will have gone out for her.

'Shit, get off the road.'

So, she drags her injured foot across more fields. Even without her GPS, which, like Jeremy, is missing in action, her sense of direction is good enough to get her going towards home. But it's ten miles, even as the crow flies, and the injured soldier staggers and crawls rather than flies. Whenever she has to cross a road, she listens carefully for traffic before making a painful dash for it. At last, a break. A last hedge and she is on the Downs. Here, even with her gammy ankle, she can make much better progress.

Alicia gives up any pretence of hiding and marches and limps by turns, like any early morning walker who has twisted her ankle. In the darkness of the early winter morning she meets three fellow walkers, two of whom ask after her injury. She just smiles bravely and hurries on. Alicia does not see these people as the kindly, concerned dog walkers they are but as witnesses for the prosecution.

As she gets near their village she slows down. Here, a few people might recognise her, though she is an infrequent visitor to the parental home. Even so, she decides the best policy is to go straight through the village. To her horror, she spots a police car by the village green. Before she can turn aside a Constable is asking if she's seen anything suspicious. It seems a car is missing from outside the Church. Of course, it is. She and Jeremy stole it, thinking to return it under cover of darkness before it was missed.

'You look as if you've been in the wars, Miss, if you don't mind me saying so. Sure, you don't need a hand?'

It seems that he will insist of giving her a lift.

'No thank you, Constable. I was looking at two hawks circling the full moon, the first rays of the sun catching the underside of their wings. I just blundered into a ditch. I'll be fine. I'm nearly home anyway.'

Just dumb luck, but he doesn't ask where home is. It doesn't enter his head, it seems, that she, a well-spoken, young women, dishevelled as she might be, could possibly be the suspected woman terrorist presently sought across three counties.

'Well just go up and have a thorough shower. Then get into bed. I'll bring you some breakfast and then have a look at your ankle. Ten to one it's the last you'll hear of it unless that boyfriend of yours blabs.'

'e won't,' says Alicia, though actually she is far from sure.

e, after all, left him to his fate without a moment's sitation. But then, what could she have done for him with lower body full of shotgun pellets fired at close range. She s lucky not to have caught a blast in the face as she came ough the door. But then, it was some residual fear that situation was all wrong that had made her hang back and t had saved her.

m is still asleep,' her brother continues. 'Still on those e tranquilisers. Obviously, we say nothing to her about

Dad?'

ot seen him this morning. Maybe he's taken our advice rt about lying low. But if and when he appears, I think etter tell him. From what you say, the police have got y, so on the assumption he keeps stum, we need to work tory. Dad is after all supposed to be good at that. And ws'...and this is the killer...'that you and Jeremy set ether last night with malice aforethought.'

all she can say. She starts to crawl up the stairs. He etter than to try and help her. She turns back on the ir. 'And Luke, thank you, sweetheart. You were right 3 about Jeremy. Tell me when Dad shows up.'

22

Full Disclosure

'Tench,' the man says, 'like the fish in the river. Not Trench like a hole in the ground.'

He has made this introduction hundreds of times before, so he no longer gets exasperated. Even so perhaps he should have chosen a line of work in which he had less regular contact with the public.

'Detective Inspector Tench. And this is Detective Sergeant Smogulecki. That's...' And he spells out the Polish consonants. '...pronounced, in his anglicised version, SMOG-UL-ECK-I'

What a pair. Half the time for interviews must be taken up with making introductions.

'We are making inquiries...' The detective is from South and West of here, real West Country, Somerset or Devon. '...

in connection with an incident in the early hours of this morning at a farmhouse near the abandoned airfield at Windrush. Perhaps you know it...the airfield?'

Alicia sees the eyes of the Polish DS narrow as she makes a note. It was a good question and Alicia reckons she would have given herself away somehow.

After her long, hot shower Alicia had felt much more herself, so had come downstairs to have breakfast. Luke had cooked, traditional English, but with the freshest local ingredients stripped of anything unhealthy. David had joined them, ravenous from writing the first fluent eight hundred words for many months. It's an ill wind....

So, they hash it out, the three of them, over the hash. What is to be their story when, as he undoubtedly will, an Inspector calls? OK, says David, follow the golden rule. Tell the truth except for the minimum deviation you have to make to protect the guilty.

First seize the high ground. Yes, we are the family of the kidnap victim for whom police forces nationwide are searching. That's right, Felix Cameron. His mother is asleep upstairs, heavily tranquillised after her courageous television appeal. Is there anything you can tell us? No, no, of course, not your department. And so, to business but with the upper hand in hand.

So yes, Jeremy was, I suppose you would say, Alicia's

boyfriend. No, no, nothing permanent, just one of those temporary relationships that...well, you know how it is. Yes, Jeremy was here last night with some crazy plan. They all, well actually only Luke, but who's to know differently, tried to persuade Jeremy against it, but he just took off. Armed? They debate this. Should they admit to knowing Jeremy was armed? Armed to the teeth, actually.

'And I still have this,' adds Alicia shyly, laying on the kitchen table the heavy-duty army pistol Jeremy gave her. Panic round the table. 'Why the hell didn't you throw it in a hedge, drop it in a pond. Why on earth bring it back here?'

She can't think of a single reason. OK face facts. It's here and it must disappear pronto. Bury it in the garden, in the laundry cupboard. No, hide it in plain sight. Put it in David's book display case. A first physical exhibit. Manny Kant's actual weapon. Except Manny almost never used a weapon and certainly not a clunky, state of the art piece of ironmongery that could blow a hole through a man at one hundred paces. The pressure builds with the family's panic. What the hell to do? The police may arrive at any moment. Another round of low fat, organically hand-reared bacon for anyone? Shut the fuck up, Luke, about food. This is life and death. Food too, thinks Luke but shuts the fuck up anyway.

'I'm just going to pop into the study for a moment,' says David standing up. 'Just to look up something.'

Doesn't he know that these days you look up everything on your smart phone? In any case his children see through him, in chorus.

'No, Dad, absolutely no. You can't go running to her every time you...'

But who has a better idea? David repairs to his study anyway. What's so secret? He's going to ask her advice on dealing with the police not to have telephone sex...isn't he?

David is back in a few minutes.

'Annie says, first up-front volunteer possession of the gun and ammunition and hand them over to the police. Ali you must admit you went with Jeremy, in order to restrain him if you like, but that proved impossible. Yes, you see now you should have called the police at once, but you were half accepting, as Jeremy led you to believe, that this was a covertly authorised operation to extract Felix. And, most important of all, she says. Call the police now and own up to everything.'

'OK I'll do it,' Luke says. But even as he picks up the phone there is a heavy knock at the front door.

Introductions are finally at an end.

'I would like to say something, before you go on,' says Alicia.

And, as Annie Fritzweiler has advised, she proceeds to tell everything, not forgetting to hand over the handgun. The police look at each other as if they have never seen one of these before, as indeed they haven't. DS Smogulecki is just double bagging it in plastic when it goes off, blowing a hole in the kitchen door, not to speak of two plastic bags.

'Oh, didn't I mention it was loaded, primed and on a hair trigger setting? Well, no, because I didn't bloody well know myself,' says Alicia.

Shit, she had been carrying it all night in her waist band. It could have gone off at any time, most likely blowing her leg off or worse.

'Better check, Detective Sergeant,' says Inspector Tench, apparently unmoved, 'it didn't do damage outside.'

The DS is gone in a flash, partly to check but mainly to be sick.

No one appears to have been killed or maimed. There is a lot of back garden out there before you hit the dense thicket that marks the end of the Cameron property. Beyond that, the emptiness of the Downs. By the time the DS returns, Alicia is typing a statement on her laptop, Luke is making tea and Tench is tucking into some hand fed bacon with a mound of very organic vegetables of various sorts. DS Smogulecki wanly accepts a glass of tap water.

'Oh, Smogulecki we'd better let them know to call off the search for the young woman spotted running away just at the back of the Windrush farmhouse last night. That was you, I suppose, Ms Cameron?'

Alicia looks over her screen at the detective and nods.

'Thank you. Best to put it in your statement if you haven't already,' he adds before returning to more serious matters on his plate.

David has disappeared, to his study, where he is on the phone. Not to Annie this time, but to his agent. An article, five thousand words, covering recent events. From, as it were, the front line. Yes, doable says Sam. She means saleable to a quality newspaper or magazine. If you are sure you want to do it. Under your by-line?

Why not? Well, you know best. Or even if you don't, there is still twenty percent commission to consider. This with a view to a series of pieces as the kidnap develops. The Inside Story. After all, before all this novel writing nonsense diverted him, he was a news correspondent. His true vocation. Yes, at last, he's back in the game and on his game. For the first time for a long time David Cameron feels energetic and in control.

He calls Annie and fixes lunch at the best Oxford restaurant he can think of. Not, of course, the one where Luke works and from which Felix was kidnapped. That really would be too tasteless.

The detectives are wrapping up and DI Tench is wiping his lips with an over-used piece of tissue.

'That will be all for now. I should warn you, Miss Cameron, that there may be consequences, serious consequences. So, you need to stay in the vicinity and hand over your passport. The rest of you...' This seems to mean Luke and his absent father. '...I'd be obliged if you give the police advance warning if you plan to leave the district for any length of time. We may need to take statements from you also.'

Alicia stands nonplussed. The relaxed manner of DI Tench, and his acceptance of Luke's breakfast, has made her think she was off the hook. But, of course, aiding and abetting an armed attack in the middle of the night on a peaceful farmhouse is not the sort of thing that can be glossed over. It at least demands its day in court.

'Your passport, Miss, if you please. And you may want to let me look at your statement, before you sign it. Thank you.'

Alicia is suddenly all action. Her ankle forgotten, she tears up the stairs, throws everything out of her drawers and cupboards in her frantic search, before locating her passport on top of her bedside table.

Eventually the detectives are satisfied. Alicia has handed over her passport, signed her statement and given it back to Tench after making a copy.

The back door closes. Luke says furiously: 'And he didn't even thank for the breakfast.' Just as the back door reopens to disclose DI Tench's slow features.

'And Mr. Cameron, my thanks to you for the breakfast. Best I've had for many a long while.' He ponders. 'Perhaps ever.'

'Why did you even offer him breakfast?' says Alicia, as the back door closes again. 'That awful man is going to see that I'm prosecuted. I'll lose my army commission.'

She bursts into tears and sobs into the kitchen table, as if she is about to lose the thing dearest to her in the world, as indeed it is.

Luke does not know what to do. He hasn't seen his sister in tears since she was four years old. Eventually Alicia stands up again. 'One thing though, Luke. Before they put me in prison, I'm going to put a stop to this nonsense between Dad and that Fritzweiler woman. She's breaking up our family.'

Alicia has stormed out before Luke can urge restraint based on the periwinkle colour of Annie's eyes.

'Give me the telephone, Dad.'

Alicia has stormed into the study as angrily as she stormed out of the kitchen. Amazed, David surrenders the phone to her.

'Listen, Dr, Professor Fritzweiler, if that is what your name is, you are not to contact my father ever again. Is that clear. Nor accept any calls from him.'

'Ali, this is Sam. Who is Dr Professor Fritzweiler when she's at home?'

But Alicia is spared the challenging task of explaining because

Luke is standing in the doorway.

'Since no one else seemed interested I thought I'd better check Mum's laptop. There's another message.'

'From them?'

'From them. They remind us that today is Thursday and if the full ten and a half million isn't paid by close of business tomorrow, things will get very nasty for Felix.'

'Is there another video.'

'No,' says Luke. 'Just audio. A scream.'

23

An Offer Not to Be Refused

Davina is back in control. And Sergei is back in their kitchen. David is in the kitchen too. But only because he came in to make himself a cup of coffee and found himself surrounded and outnumbered.

Sergei is serious, solicitous.

'Mr. Cameron, your wife is explaining the problems with your situation. It is perhaps worse now than when we are last speaking. The deadline to pay the full amount of the money is tomorrow. There is in your bank already the full amount of the price for this house. But you, you are still three hundred big ones short. And you have exhausted all streets to get the money.'

'Avenues,' says David, irrationally irritated.

'You attempt to rescue your son, without consulting your

wife...I consult my wife about all my decisions...and that has been a terrible mistake. Most likely it has angered the bad guys. That scream on the last message.'

The expected sob from Davina does not come. This morning she is pale, in control, business-like.

'This three hundred thousands of pounds. It's not a big sum.' Hopes in the kitchen soar...'But it's not a small sum either.'... and plummet. 'No one would give such a sum. Even to your best friend. And guys in a bad fix such as you, such guys find they no longer have best friends. Am I right here, David?'

Goran himself could not have put it better, David thinks. These Slavs do have a talent for zeroing in on bad news and re-writing it in letters ten feet high.

'But David, there may just be a way,' Sergei continues. 'Your wife, you know your wife...' Sergei gestures across the room as if introducing them for the first time. 'Your wife she is a most persuasive woman. A beautiful woman and a persuasive woman.'

In a moment he is going to tell me I am the luckiest man alive, thinks David. But he has underestimated Sergei.

'You, David, are not the luckiest man alive. You are the luckiest man alive or dead, the luckiest man who has ever lived, to have such a wife.'

David looks across at Davina. She might not quite meet

Sergei's spec, but she is looking remarkably attractive this morning. The new mask of pale suffering suits her, as do the several pounds in weight the agony of the last few days have cost her.

'Look David, I am absolutely not a rich man. Ah, the helicopter...'

For the first time, David glances through the kitchen window where the machine's rotor blades continue to revolve slowly in the pale morning sunshine. How could he not have heard the deafening noise of the thing landing on his lawn? Perhaps the odd aural ecology of the M4 room where he's been holed up since the detectives left earlier that morning.

'The helicopter is only on daily rental. So, I can get fast between the deals I need to make to keep the bear from my door.'

The Russian laughs self-deprecatingly at his all but perfect command of the English idiom. But Davina can stand the circumlocutions of her friend and admirer no longer.

'What Sergei wants to say, David, is that he will lend us the three hundred thousand.'

'Your beautiful wife says it so much better than the clumsy fellow that is me could say it. I wish I could give it to you, David. But I just work for other guys, mean guys, who don't know what giving is.'

Definitely, David thinks, Sergei and Goran, brothers under the skin. Maybe they belong to the same bunch of thugs. But Sergei is still speaking.

'But I have to ask you to sign this loan agreement. Sorry, David but it is necessary.'

This time David finds his glasses and reads the five pages carefully. On page two he sits down at the kitchen table. By page four he is ready to screw the thing up and throw it into the flames of the Aga. The terms amount to indentured labour.

All his earnings, from whatever source are garnished to be used first and exclusively to pay off debt and interest on the loan as fast as may be possible. There is to be a charge, in fact the charge document is attached, over the rights to all his books and any films, recordings, adaptations and so on not already subject to pre-emption. There is a floating charge on all his liquid assets. Not too onerous, that one, as there are no assets left. Or there soon won't be. The loan is to be repaid, come what may, on the expiration of three years. The interest rate is twenty per cent per annum, and there is a front-end fee of ten per cent. Realistically enough the front-end fee is rolled into the loan, making it three hundred and thirty thousand pounds.

'But we need the money now,' says David, at the end of his third reading, interrupting the intense, whispered conversation into which, on the far side of the room, Davina and Sergei have sunk. 'We need a solicitor to make the charges effective.'

'No problem,' says Sergei. 'My pilot. He is a qualified solicitor. He realises he needs another qualification for when his eyes or his nerves become too bad to fly. There's a lot of downtime flying a helicopter and if you're a guy who looks to the future you use it to study something. In his case it's the law, I think. I'll get him.'

Sergei opens the back door and gestures. The pilot gets down and comes over, without removing his dark glasses.

David shakes hands.

'And you are a qualified solicitor?'

The pilot is chewing gum. David can see the wet gum rolling around in the interior of the guy's mouth as he opens it to answer.

'Yeh, whatever.'

David realises that there is no point in asking for time for his own solicitor to review the documents. It would be in Sergei's interest for them to be well drafted. His solicitor would merely charge him a couple of thousand pounds he doesn't have to point out the obvious. That the terms are insanely onerous on David to the point where he is almost bound to be quickly in breach. But so what, in his situation? Well, only that he will be living in one room in Swindon, existing on pizza and cocoa, and working full time and forever for the

Russian.

But Annie? Surely, he can ask for an hour while he scans in the documents for Annie and gets her take on them.

'I think there will be no need for that, David.' What a complete shit the man is. Not even to give him that. 'For I can see Dr Fritzweiler walking across the lawn towards your house now.'

24

Philosophical Advice

David meets her halfway across the lawn, in the shadow of the rotor blades. Annie is well wrapped up. Her black boots come up to somewhere short of her knees. Her black coat falls to the top of her calves.

'I am on my way to a meeting in London. I thought I should drop in for a moment to see how things are.'

He tells her how things are.

Her welcome in the kitchen is unexpectedly warm. Sergei comes forward and kisses her on both cheeks.

'Such a pleasure again so soon, Dr Fritzweiler.'

Even Davina is amiable. She hardly raises an eyebrow as David guides Annie to the study.

Annie allows David to help with her coat. He lays it on the couch. She sits at his desk rapidly to read Sergei's documents.

What he has not anticipated was that under her coat she is wearing a black skirt which shows off a discrete element of thigh when she sits down. He draws a chair up to sit at right angles to her.

She smiles, vaguely conscious of his gaze. It occurs to him that she is tensing her legs. When she has finished reading, she flicks back and forth to check one thing or another, but then quickly lays the documents down on the desk.

She says nothing he doesn't know already.

'It seems to be well drafted. Of course, that is in Sergei's favour. It is extremely onerous. But what choice do you have?'

'You mean I have to sign it as it stands.'

'If you want to stand any chance of getting your son back in one piece, yes. And, I'm sorry to put it like this David, if whatever happens, you want to be seen to have done all you could. Yes, you have to sign.'

'Oh, you mean even if it turns out badly the family won't blame me...'

'I wouldn't go that far, David, no. But at least you will have done the one big thing in your power. Made all the sacrifice you could. Now David, I must go. And you have a lot to do. Making sure the money goes to the right charities in the right amounts. And that they make the appropriate announcements, so the kidnappers are convinced. And get your PR person to get you all the media she can. It will help keep the kidnappers honest. By the way, how are you supposed to make the half million payment to the kidnappers you mentioned to me. For their expenses wasn't it?'

'Felix's internet account. After all, they still have control of him. Their last act will be to make him give them that money, I suppose. And, of course, Sergei will disburse the loan proceeds directly to the charities.'

'They won't have told you,' Annie asks, 'where Felix will be released?'

'No, nothing.'

'Don't worry about that. They can't really tell you, can they? For fear of giving away something about themselves or even risking capture.'

'Annie,'...He is still staring at her legs as he says this. She has swivelled in the desk chair to face him now. '...how will they make sure Felix doesn't give their game away? You know when he comes back.'

David is conscious again that Annie is very tense, though she continues to speak calmly enough.

'Well, that depends on how good they were at disorienting Felix and not giving clues to their identities while he was with them, so that he knows nothing of value he can tell you or the police.'

'Yes, of course.'

'And now I really must go.'

She stands up. Facing her, he puts his hands on her upper arms, as if he would kiss her formally on either cheek.

She looks up at him. Yes, he is a good-looking man, strong from his regular exercise. He makes the most of himself with expensive but under-stated grooming and an exact amount of aftershave, or whatever it is. His thrillers, the two or three she sampled anyway, may be psychologically naive in places, but they are well structured. To write such a book, and he has written thirteen or fourteen of them, is a real achievement. Not a man to be scorned, even if he does on occasion seem unequal to the problems which presently confront him.

If this man were now to embrace her tightly and kiss her on the lips, she may not want to resist him. She thinks of the couch behind her. How stupid could she be? She thought she was just exciting him, to influence him better, but actually she has merely excited herself.

But her face does not give her away. She laughs.

'I really have to go, David.'

'Annie, before you go, may I ask you something?'

'If it's quick.'

'Why are you so tense?'

'Oh, you have noticed that have you? Because, I was wondering if you would try to detain me, here on the study carpet for example. And if...' She half smiles. '...I would try to resist you if you did.'

As he digests this, she slips from his hands and walks quickly past him, to open the door. But there she turns back.

'Look,' she says very quietly but very distinctly, 'as I drive to London now, I have to think about my meeting. And in the next few hours you have a lot to do with the mechanics of paying the ransom, the TV and so on. But when I'm free of the traffic on my way back, I'll call you from the car. About eight, I should think.'

She pauses, her coat now slung over her shoulders, her legs slightly apart. He wants her desperately, but Davina is waiting in the kitchen for him to sign Sergei's paper which will spare their son's life.

'No, don't show me out. You're needed elsewhere at the moment. But when I call you this evening we'll see where we go from there.'

He wonders if her words can possibly mean what he thinks

they mean, or does she merely mean the next actions in the kidnap saga. He watches her from the study window as she runs across his lawn to her car, clutching her coat around her. Then he turns away to respond to Davina's calling from the kitchen.

25

Release

At eight o'clock in the evening he can stand it no longer. Everything has been done. All the various payments have been made and acknowledged as received. Even Felix's internet banking service has acknowledged that the five hundred thousand pounds of expense for the kidnappers has gone through.

The elephants, or rather their minders on their behalf, have made televised statements of gratitude for the astonishingly generous gifts from the Cameron family. David and Davina have given a joint and smiling statement on Skype to the BBC, ITV News and Sky.

Always admired the amazing work done for elephants, David contrives to say. It is elephants not chimps that are our nearest kin in the animal kingdom. Not of course in an evolutionary sense but in a shared sense of family and importance of memory. David's creative powers begin to fail him as he tries to express further his intense feeling for the pachyderms. But the interview is time limited and the broadcasters seem delighted with what he's already said.

David admits that he has given away all his money, every scrap. It feels so good. To be free of possessions. And to have to accept the challenge again to use his creative skills to build a new and simpler life. No more the deadening routine of just repeating the same safe dreary stuff in order to ensure enough cash flow to maintain their ridiculously expensive and deeply unsatisfying lifestyle. His only regret is that it took such suffering on the part of his younger son, and such, ah, such radical action by those who took Felix, to make him, David Cameron, see the error of his ways. To follow literally the course of charity he has so often urged on others.

'Let us all behave more nearly according to what we truly believe, rather than allowing the materialist world to make hypocrites of us.'

It is, David feels, a sentence to treasure, even if the sentiments it represents are almost entirely false.

Right at the end of the last interview, Alicia is able to pass a note to her mother, and Davina is just able to hold back her tears in order to announce it to the nation.

'We've just heard. Felix will be home with us this evening, by nine o'clock.'

Not a dry eye in the house, or in many houses round the

country.

Many people, it seems are inspired by the actions of David and Davina Cameron, even though one or two spoilsports on twitter rub in the point that none of this would have happened but for the kidnappers. Offers of financial help to the Camerons flood in. The Prime Minister feels moved to make a statement, praising his namesake, and asking that food parcels and cheques go to the Berkshire Camerons rather than to their North Oxfordshire namesakes. The Prime Minister then feels constrained to call his novelist alter ego to congratulate him.

'We must have you and Davina over to Chequers one weekend. The diary is endless of course, but perhaps in May or June next year. Felix too, of course. The Office will be in touch. And David, absolutely jolly good show. In a darkening world this sort of thing gives a lift to all our spirits.'

The Prime Minister has already used this last phrase in his public statement from the steps of Downing Street. It's not a bad phrase though. Good enough for a repeat or two.

Even Sergei has been stirred by the public mood. No need for the Camerons to think about moving out, at least not for a couple of months. If his contractors can just have access... Nothing major. After all, he bought the place because he likes it how it is.

Davina, Alicia and Luke are in the kitchen drinking tea. David puts his head round the door and excuses himself. He is hardly acknowledged. Well, some things haven't changed.

Warm waterproof jacket, trainers, hands in pockets since he can't find his gloves, he strides out along the lanes. There's already a frost. Nothing from Annie. Vibration in his pocket. Annie at last. But no, it's just Felix. Felix!

His son has been dropped off at the roundabout a mile or so North of the village. He should be at home in twenty minutes. No, no point getting the car out. They'd be sure to miss him. Yes, better tell the family. He doesn't want his mother having a fainting fit when he strolls across the threshold. No, he's fine. Oh, you're out walking. OK see you in a while.

David calls Luke and passes on the glad tidings. Luke promises to do what he can to contrive a soft landing. Yes, in a way better if his father stays out for a bit, if that's OK. Well, is it OK? It's already eight thirty and no word from Annie. And he's getting cold.

As he walks quickly clear off the village, he sees a dark figure, walking equally quickly, in the other direction. Felix. He is sure the boy has seen him. But both of them pass by on the other side.

In another minute his phone rings again. He is so sure it's Annie that his hand is shaking as he presses answer. But it's only Luke again.

'Hey, Dad, you'll never believe it but Elephants Like Us have just put out a statement saying they have received another four hundred and sixty thousand pounds. You'll never guess from who.'

'From *whom*, and by the way it's *has* just put out a statement', he stops himself saying, and instead admits that he will never in a month of Sundays guess.

'Authorised by Felix's computer. In other words, the kidnappers. Maybe they are good guys after all.'

David expresses himself suitably amazed, which he is. The remaining forty thousand pounds could be the actual scale of their expenses. So, no profit. What the hell are they up to? Why do they care if they look good or not?

'And there's more,' says Luke. 'Elephants Like Us say that the kidnappers have told them…yeh, via Felix's computer, sure…that they did it, the kidnapping, to take a first step to make people more in touch with their actual moral feelings. Got to go. Felix has just arrived. He looks great.'

David can imagine the scene at home. The fatted calf, postponing its own slaughter, gets up on its hind hooves to embrace Felix.

But there are two realities that do not change. He has been forced to give away all his money in so public a way that there is no possibility of getting any of it back, by a subsequent quiet appeal to the charities. And it's cold enough to freeze your nuts off. On which cue Annie finally calls him. She'll pick him up by the Church in the centre of the village in five minutes. It takes him ten minutes, partly running, partly getting lost in the dark, to get back to the village.

He sees her car at once. It's the only one showing any lights. He opens the passenger door and gets in.

'Where the hell have you been?'

She looks stunning but she is seriously angry. She resists his attempt to kiss her.

'I just came to see if everything went well, with the payments and the media.'

'Look Annie, I have to go, Felix has just got home.'

'Of course, he has. What did you expect? What possible motive would those guys have had for double crossing you? They've got everything they wanted. More, given the unexpected quantity of media. Obviously, it was never about the money. They've even given most of their expenses money to the elephant people.'

Suddenly there is a doubt. Well not really. Obviously, she heard it on the car radio, though the radio is not on now. But she sees his eyes move for a moment to the radio and then back to her face.

'I heard it on the radio driving over here.'

Too quick, David wonders. Nonsense. Like so much else it's all in his head.

'I'll drop you,' she says, turning the car tightly and driving the hundred yards or so to the bottom of David's long drive.

He wants desperately to kiss her before he gets out, but he cannot risk another snub. As he is about to close the car door behind him, she leans over and speaks quietly.

'I'll be home in twenty minutes. Showered and in bed in forty. If you want to call me then you can. Only don't leave it too late.'

No choice, she thinks as she pulls quickly away. Now she has to make a permanent ally of him, as well as of his smart ass of a son, whatever it takes.

26

Cold Comfort Farm

'So, Mr. Llewellyn Davis, you were in a manner of speaking expecting them?'

'Not in a manner of speaking, Mr. Trench, I was sure as you're sitting there on my kitchen chair that they'd be back. Tried it on before, hadn't they?'

'What exactly had they tried on before, Mr. Llewellyn Davis? And by the way it's Tench like the fish in the river, not Trench like the hole in the ground. And it's Detective Inspector.'

'Oh, is it now? Well come to that it's Llewellyn Davies pronounced with a zed not Davis pronounced with a...'

'My apologies, sir. Now if you could answer my...'

'They'd been in on my ewes. Just last week it was. But I was out there before they could load the stock and let them have it with both barrels. I couldn't see a blind thing in the dark, but it was enough to send them about their business. Of course, what they were really after was Cyrus the Great.'

'Ah yes,' murmurs DI Tench. He has come across quite a few first- class nutters in the course of his work in this neck of the woods.

'Cyrus the Great, that's my prize ram. Got five thousand living offspring round the world.'

'Busy boy,' says Tench.

'Of course, most of that was done with AI, Artificial Insemination. They freeze a load of Cyrus's best stuff, fill a big syringe with it, shove it up the ewe's....'

'So, it's a gang of sheep rustlers?' says the DI quickly interrupting the agri-business specifics. 'Did you report this first incident to the police?'

Tench of course knows that he did, which is why after Captain Jeremy Wingate Grey, MC and bar, charged into the Llewellyn Davies kitchen the police were on their way within seconds of the farmer firing his shot gun.

'Your lads got here in double quick time I'll say that for them. Glad of it I was, what with that bandit rolling around on my floor, squealing like a stuck pig. If he wants to play soldiers, he should join the real army.'

'Well, Mr. Llewellyn Davies that is rather what I wanted to talk to you about. Your victim, Jeremy Wingate Grey is in fact a serving officer in the Guards. To be frank with you, sir, we find ourselves in rather a ticklish situation.'

'Look I'm all for the army. Brave boys, and girls too, now I believe, doing their bit. And look, unlike some, I'm all for giving them terrorists hell where ever they are in the world. There's too much pussy footing around in my opinion. We got all that fire power, especially the Yanks, but don't use a fraction of it for fear of this and that. You can't make a decent omelette, you know, without breaking a basket full of eggs.

Tench sniffs the air as if there might be a suggestion of breakfast in the air though it's not at all the time of day for it. All he gets is thick strong farmhouse tea plonked down before him by Mabel.

'I'm obliged to you Mrs.....'

'But Detective Inspector if that is what you are, why did you say that young thug is a victim? Self-defence pure and simple it was.'

'Yes of course, Mr. Llewellyn Davies. We'll come back to that in a moment.'

'Speaking of that, have you charged that young thug who came in here with his guns blazing yet? Scared Mabel near to death I can tell you. Don't suppose he really wanted to murder us. Kidnap more like till we handed over Cyrus. But in the heat of the moment who's to know?'

The tea is a whole lot better than he gets at the station, which brings him back to the point. Detective Inspector Tench is not often in the presence of the Chief Constable, a person five ranks above him. And never before in the company of a Deputy Assistant Commissioner from Scotland Yard, a woman at that, and some senior officer from the Army's Household Division. The formation which includes Jeremy Wingate Grey's regiment.

Having heard his patriotic sentiments and detected some nervousness on the part of the farmer with regard to what might be seen as his over-reaction with the shotgun, Tench decides to play it straight with him. Lay things out the way the Brass laid them out for him.

'As I was saying, Mr. Llewellyn Davies, we've got here a ticklish situation. First of all, there is your own situation. Clearly you were defending yourself and yours.

'And Cyrus.'

'Of course, Cyrus. Every right-thinking householder would, I'm sure, applaud your actions in the circumstances. However, the law in this area is a bit unclear. To get directly to the point, if we prosecute your attacker, his defence counsel might try to say that you used unreasonable force against him. He is, you know, in quite a bad way in the hospital.'

'Well, he shouldn't come barging in here with all guns blazing like...',

'Look I entirely understand that, sir, but it is right that I point out to you the situation, in law if you follow me. And there's another thing.'

'All seems very straightforward to me. That young thug comes charging in here...'

'Yes, yes, sir. As I told you just now, that the young thug as you call him is Captain Jeremy Wingate Grey of the Foot Guards. Decorated twice for gallantry in Afghanistan, you know Helmand Province, the worst place out there so they say. Now in this case Captain Wingate Grey was on a mission to extract a kidnap victim. You may have read about it in the papers. Felix Cameron it is. No, no, nothing to do with the Prime Minister. The son of the prominent thriller writer. Same name, you know.'

But the farmer is not a reader of David Cameron's books, any more than is Tench himself. DS Smogulecki has read a couple though and pronounced them testosterone-fuelled crap.

'The point here is that Captain Wingate Grey, the one you shot at close range, was attempting to carry out a vital mission. To save a young man with most of his life before him who otherwise might have died at the hands of vicious kidnappers.'

The farmer, most of whose life is behind him, looks unimpressed.

'So, why'd he come barging in here then with all guns blazing...?'

'A very unfortunate mistake in targeting. We now believe the kidnap victim was being held in the house directly behind yours.'

'This is the kid who's just been released? It was all on the telly just before you came. Still is, come to that.'

Tench turns and sees what he has not noticed before, a television set high up on the wall behind him. It's showing a re-run of the David and Davina interview, though the sound is turned off.

'Yes, always thought it a bit fishy that place behind us. Been empty since Giles Crisp had to give up, after the last foot and mouth. Took all his money it did. Government compensation went only to pay his debts. Dead now, poor bugger. Dead with the misery of it. His missus too.'

'You didn't think to notify the police that there was something fishy when the place was suddenly occupied again after all this time?'

'Folks keep to themselves round here. Whoever they were in that place, they obviously weren't after Cyrus. No place to hide him over there.'

Clearly Llewellyn Davies's view of his public responsibility for safety of the realm begins and ends with his prize ram.

'The thing is that Captain Wingate Grey, the man you shot, is a by way of being a national hero. The kind of man the army needs to carry out the sort of military actions you were speaking of so warmly just now.'

'Now don't you go trying to twist my words to mean something I didn't say.'

Tench is not sure where he had gone wrong, but he decides to press on and try to press home the advantage he has somehow lost with what should be for any sane person the clinching point.

'Look Mr. Llewellyn Davies, what it amounts to is this. The totally uncalled for and very frightening attack on you and your wife was an awful mistake. No harm was done...'

The farmer looks up at his ceiling still showing the impact of Jeremy's heavy calibre weaponry.

'As to any physical damage or mental distress that may have been caused, I'm sure the Army would be more than happy to compensate you.'

'So come to your point, Inspector. I haven't got all day and all night. There's sheep to be seen to. Soon be lambing again. Up all night and every night then most likely, the missus and me.'

'The point is sir, if we can let bygones be bygones and take no action against Captain Wingate Grey or against you...'

'Me!

'You sir, because a Court might feel that you fired your shotgun recklessly, causing grievous bodily harm. You might even have killed the man.'

The farmer ponders this.

'Give me a day or so, Inspector. Come back this time on Monday.'

As he drove away from the farm, Tench feels resentment. Why had he been set up in this way by the Brass? Why couldn't they do their own bloody sweet-talking? He was a detective, solving crimes, not saving other people's asses. Asses that probably didn't deserve to be saved at that. And he was going now to have to go directly to the Chief Constable's office to report.

But the Chief is emollient.

'No, no. Yes, yes. I'm sure he'll come round. Good show Tench, good show. We are all grateful to you, you know. And now I'm delighted to tell you that we are going to put you in sole charge of tracking down the kidnappers. They may be enjoying a certain vogue in the left-wing press at present, but the bulk of the public will want them caught and punished. Just because this case ended happily doesn't mean that they all will. Kidnapping is a grave crime. Find them, Tench. Find them.'

Back at his desk, what the Detective Inspector finds is that all his other cases had been re-assigned and that Smogulecki alone has been detailed to assist him with the kidnap investigation. But if, as the Chief Constable said, it was such a big deal, why was the Met not deployed, with their infinitely greater resources? Why just DS Smogulecki and himself? Because the authorities don't really want these kidnappers caught? But perhaps he and DS Smogulecki will show them a thing or two, thinks Tench, gagging on the police tea.

Meanwhile, Captain Jeremy Wingate Grey, in intensive care and slightly delusional with fever, is turning over and over in his mind who could have betrayed his operation.

At the same time, Second Lieutenant Alicia Cameron, on compassionate leave because of her brother's kidnap, has heard nothing. Nothing from the police and nothing from her regiment. It rather takes the edge off the family celebration for Felix's safe return.

27

The Younger Son's Tale

'No really, Mum, I'm not that hungry,' Felix is saying as David comes through the kitchen door.

His family are all sitting round the rustic kitchen table with champagne.

'No, they fed me OK. Simple of course, but they told me I ate what they ate. Only water to drink,' adds Felix setting his champagne glass aside.

With a novelist's eye, David notices that Davina has finished her champagne, Alicia hasn't touched hers and Luke is sipping at his, assessing the supermarket quality. He walks unheard behind Davina, stretches to pick up the bottle from the middle of the table and refills her glass. He thinks about pouring one for himself but decides that it doesn't sit well with the new austerity.

'Of course, they couldn't let me eat with them because they had to conceal their identities,' Felix continues.

'Well, I'm certainly glad to have you home in one piece,' says his father, who has returned to stand at the entrance to the kitchen, still unnoticed, or at least unacknowledged.

'Oh, Dad. There you are. I gather it cost you rather a lot.'

'Everything.'

'David for heaven's sake. The boy has just this moment set foot inside the house.'

Davina is already angry. The makings are all here of a terminal family row. Terminal for the family that is. But David has no intention of letting that happen. At least not yet.

'It's all right Mum. Well Dad, I can do my bit,' says Felix. 'You know, to put the family finances back on an even keel.'

David is still sometimes able to convince himself that there is a bundle of money to be had for optioning Felix's war novel. For a film, for a video game? And David still clings to the thought that, if not untold wealth, then a substantial sum in large denominations lies hidden under various floorboards of the family home, beyond the reach of Sergei's awful contract. For he is certainly going to make sure that Felix disgorges that money before Sergei assumes occupation, and even before he sends in his workmen.

'What had you in mind?' David asks.

'I think I've just about made my point with simultaneous residence at Oxford and at Cambridge. And Johnny Pebbledash has been becoming a bit of a pain about the essays I haven't written. So, I won't go up to Cambridge when the Lent Term starts in January. That will save you seven or eight thousand a term in fees and expenses.'

'Felix, has no one told you? I have no money whatever, skint, cleaned out, bust, with precious little prospect of earning any. On Monday I intend to sign on at the Job Centre in Reading. So, I will not be paying your fees or your expenses at either Cambridge or Oxford.'

'Look, Dad, I do understand. It must have been a tremendous shock for you and for the whole family, this ransom thing.'

'But nothing compared to your suffering, darling,' Davina comes in, after swallowing half of her refill.

'I think from my savings,' Felix goes on, 'I could just about afford to support myself at Oxford till the summer. Give you time to get back on an even keel, so you could start paying again in the Michaelmas Term. Does that sound fair, Dad?'

'Felix, please get it into your head that I am never again going to be in a position to support you financially. In any event I thought the rapidly accumulating royalties from your book..'

'You mean IN IT?'

'Yes, I mean that. I thought the royalties, option fees, whatever they were, would be such as to be able to keep you in whatever style of life you choose. The rest of the family too, if you were to be so liberal.'

'Whatever gave you that idea, Dad? You didn't actually take seriously all that hype that Goran and Sammy were pumping out. One or two publishers and film producers considered the thing for a week or two. OK, I got a bit of media but when it came down to it, I was a complete unknown, right? A one in a thousand punt. So, in the end none of them did take an option, which as you will know, Dad, is where the real money is.'

'Would you mind, Felix, telling us how much money you have, now? Just roughly you know?'

'David, for heaven's sake, the boy has only just...'

'Yes, I know, Davina. Only just set foot. But this is rather important, from the point of view of the whole family.'

A few hidden assumptions there, but damn it he wants to know. And Felix is quite happy to tell him, it seems.

'Well before I was so cruelly taken from you all, when I last checked my net worth amounted to twenty-five thousand three hundred pounds. And that includes what's under the floorboards in this house. Take fifteen thousand out for my fees and living expenses at Oxford for two terms and that leaves ten thousand give or take. I probably should keep that for contingencies. You know spending money over Christmas and the summer, any trips that come up, that sort of thing. So, I'm afraid, Dad, I can't be of much help as far as the family finances are concerned. Beyond not going back up to Cambridge, that is.'

David thinks that is probably true. Between crises, he's been digging around with whatever industry contacts he has left, and it seems that, after an initial flurry of excitement in the press, IN IT has disappeared more or less without trace. It certainly doesn't seem to be on anyone's Christmas list.

'Of course, IN IT may turn out to be a sleeper,' adds Felix, trying perhaps to look on the bright side. 'You know redis-covered fifty years hence and proclaimed a masterpiece.'

David no longer considers things that may happen fifty years hence and is pretty bored with anything beyond next week.

'So, Felix, have you told the family the gripping tale of your adventures?'

'Of course, he hasn't,' snaps Davina pouring herself a third glass. 'The poor boy has only just arrived. And immediately you go badgering him with all sorts of irrelevant....'

Luke silently goes to the fridge and without fuss removes and opens another bottle of Krug. 'Shit,' thinks David. Seventy pounds a bottle in the local supermarket. Nearer a hundred and ten from his wine merchant in St. James's.

'And,' adds Davina, staring at her husband, 'I don't want to hear a word about your scandalous idea that Felix set up the whole thing himself.'

Felix grins delightedly.

'Did you think that, Dad? Really? That's great. I only wish I'd thought of it myself. It would have made things a whole lot easier.'

David admires his son's quickness of mind and acting ability. After all, didn't he always take the big part in productions at school? Hamlet in Hamlet, Widow Twankey in Aladdin and so on. David is now finally sure that Felix was at least complicit in his abduction and in the ransom demand.

'So, tell us what happened?' says Luke, having re-filled Davina's glass, and for form's sake his own, and having returned the bottle to the fridge.

'Are you sitting comfortably,' says Felix, delighted to have an audience again. 'Then I'll begin.'

He starts at the beginning, the restaurant raid. He was slightly injured, a nosebleed actually, but nothing serious. Just shock and fear. They blindfolded and handcuffed him, forcing him to lie prone on the back seat of the huge off roader covered with a rough blanket. From the start he realised resistance was pointless and decided to go along with whatever they asked. Hence the videos, the scream and so on.

That was all fake in the sense that he was not tortured. But it was genuine in the sense that his abductors told him they would torture him, water boarding and male rape were mentioned, if he didn't act his part and act it well. And he believed them completely.

No, he never saw the faces of any of the gang. In his hearing they hardly talked among themselves. They took turns in giving him his instructions. Broken English, mid-European accents, but their meaning was always terribly clear. He couldn't tell if the accents were faked or real.

He got regular meals. Variants of the All-Day Breakfast, with scalding hot strong tea and water when he wanted it. He had his own flushing loo. Surprisingly, it was en suite. No bucket in the corner for him. But his feet were shackled... 'A nice Guantanamo touch that.'...at all times. He could shuffle to the lavatory whenever he wanted and could shower. But there were metal grills on the windows. Through the windows he could see nothing in daylight, just hedges and trees and not a single light at night. He had no idea where he was. In the bedroom, a single bed, quite comfortable, but no other furniture. They told him they'd beat shit out of him if he shouted for help or for anything else.

They kept his door locked. He could sometimes hear talking in an adjacent room. But couldn't make out any words. He couldn't even be sure if the language spoken was English though he assumed it was not. Sometimes he caught the sound of a TV or video.

The kidnappers? Four of them. No names given. Always when he saw them, as in the restaurant, in black clothes and black masks. All four looked strong and fit. In the house they sometimes wore T-shirts. Somewhere between twenty and forty, but he couldn't be sure. All men, yes.

Educated? Professional thugs? He really wasn't sure. Quite smart, one or two of them, at least he thought so. No, nothing specific, just an impression. No, not regular heavies from off the street, he would have said.

Did he know they were demanding a ransom?

Yes, of course they told him.

Did he know the ransom was to go to charities, for elephants?

Yes, they made a point of telling him that. No, they never responded to his questions. Once they hit him when he wouldn't shut up. After that he shut up.

And the final payment, of four hundred and sixty thousand pounds, from his internet account?

Yes, they said forty thousand would cover the expenses of the operation. They didn't want to make a profit. They needed him to authorise the payment, passwords and so on. So, he did.

'After all, if they were telling me the truth, and it certainly looked like it from that last payment, I couldn't see what they were doing was so wrong.'

'Not see that it was wrong!' David has gone from nought to apoplexy in two seconds. 'Felix, they robbed me of all my money. My lifetime's earnings. Ten and a half million pounds! So, I've had to sell...'

'We have,' put in Davina, asserting the rights of an erstwhile co-owner.

'So, we have had to sell the house. They have taken absolutely everything. Do you understand that, Felix? I barely own the shirt on my back.'

'Actually Dad,' says Luke, 'you don't own that. It's subject to Sergei's floating charge.'

'That's right, Luke. They robbed me of all my money plus three hundred thousand pounds I didn't have, and which was lent to me on the most usurious terms by some Russian hood...' A glance at Davina. '...some kind Russian man who has bought this beautiful house at a fire sale price and now owns me like a slave. And you can sit there saying that you can't see that what the kidnappers did was wrong, Felix?'

The house phone is ringing. Alicia goes out to take the call.

'I suppose, Dad, it depends on whether your range of reference is limited to yourself or whether it encompasses society as a whole.'

Escalation of conflict between father and younger son is pre-empted by Alicia coming back to announce that DI Trench of the local constabulary wonders if it would be convenient to talk to Felix tomorrow at some time. And then to the rest of them.

Felix is eager to oblige. OK then, eleven o'clock. Allow for a leisurely family breakfast. Oh, why not make it ten and invite him to breakfast, says Luke. And Detective Sergeant Smogulecki too? Oh yes, why not? The more the merrier.

As David thinks about taking his leave of the family for the night, he realises that it is now too late to call Annie.

28

She

In the event, Tench declines the offer of breakfast, with profound regret. But he has had to agree with DS Smogulecki that it would set the wrong tone. Of course, publicly the Cameron family are not suspected of anything. How can they be? They are obvious victims. But there is some ambiguity in Felix's role in the kidnapping. Tease that out and who knows where it will lead.

The police interview of Felix follows closely what he has told his family, without David's theatricalities about stealing all his money. But Tench has those to look forward to when he interviews David separately in the afternoon.

The detectives of course go over things more carefully than did the family in their son's initial torrent of words. They ask several times what he noticed about his kidnappers. Tench takes particular note that Felix put on an act, albeit under apparent duress, in the video and the audio. There was no actual torture.

'What would be the point of actually being tortured,' asks Felix in response to the detective's scepticism. 'I have an exceptionally vivid imagination so I was able fully to internalise what it would feel like. Worse than the real thing in some ways.'

Tench lets that go.

The detectives then focus particularly on the conversations with and between the kidnappers. If there is to be a clue to their identity it will most likely be there. After all the farmhouse where Felix was held, the one next door to the Llewellyn Davies farm as Alicia had suspected, has already been gone over by the Scene of Crime people. No fingerprints of course. Possible DNA. But for that to be of any value they need to find suspects.

'I know this is getting boring, Felix, but try to remember.'

'I remember perfectly. I have a near photographic memory.'

Is there an audio equivalent of that, Tench wonders?

'The one time they hit you?' Smogulecki comes in.

'Yeh, when I was giving them a bit of lip. Persisting in asking questions.'

'How many of them in the room?'

'Two. There were always two. They were clearing away my third All Day Breakfast of the day.' Felix here pauses to explain.

Smogulecki allows the suggestion of a smile.

'What did you say when they hit you?'

'"Shit, that hurt." Something like that.'

'And what did they say. There was the one who hit you and another one in the room, yes?'

'Yes. The one who hit me said. "Well shut up with the damn questions then."'

'And the other one, did he say anything?'

'No, I don't think so. Maybe he mumbled something to the other guy as they went out.'

Tench leans forward across the table, all ears. But he knows better than to interrupt his colleague. She is doing a nice job.

'Mumbled what?' says the Polish DS gently. 'Try to remember.'

Photographically, thinks Tench, ungenerously.

Smogulecki smiles. It is, so it seems to Felix, a beautiful smile. Perhaps because she has not smiled at all during the whole two hours of the interview. Perhaps because he has seen no one smile since he was abducted, except his mother when he came home, and she was sobbing at the same time. So, Felix tries, hard.

'OK. The other one, the one who didn't hit me, may have said something like, "Don't do it again. He doesn't like it." Something like that.'

'Isn't that an odd thing to say, Felix? Of course, you didn't like being hit. No one would.'

'Or perhaps "he" referred to someone else?' says Tench very quietly. 'Someone who was not there but who was in charge?'

The police let the silence hang. Then Tench again.

'Did the kidnappers ever refer to a "he" at any other time?'

But Felix is thinking about something else, not paying attention to the DI's question.

'Perhaps it was "*She* doesn't like it." Yes definitely, it was "she"', he says at length.

Smogulecki cannot help a second smile as they wrap up the interview with Felix's account of his release near his home.

29

Television News

They take a break for a late lunch. This time Tench does not resist Luke's invitation. After all, the village is too snooty to allow even a cafe. There is a high-end restaurant, but it is way beyond any police expense budget and besides it opens only in the evenings. To show disapproval of her boss, Smogulecki goes outside for a smoke. But when she comes back in, she eats like the rest of them, heartily.

As in so many domestic kitchens around the country, where the family spends most of its time, the television is on at all times. In the Camerons' case, this is to catch further news on the kidnap investigation. Though since the investigation is having lunch with them, this is fairly pointless. Not that Felix has left the top of the news agenda. But in the absence of hard news, the television newsrooms are reduced, as so often, to soliciting the endless opinions of experts.

On a possible terrorist angle: would the gang be likely to

be connected to ISIS or Al Qaida? On the psychology of the victim: how might an experience like this change someone's personality? On the medical impact of abduction: does being kidnapped increase the risk of cancer or heart disease? In consequence of this mostly meaningless babble, and in deference to their visitors, the TV in the Cameron kitchen has the sound turned down almost to nothing.

It's Alicia who is the first to notice. She comes in very late for late lunch, having failed once more to get any information on where she stands from the regiment. The Major with whom she speaks at the regimental barracks near Edinburgh won't even acknowledge Jeremy's escapade.

'No, Second Lieutenant Cameron, we're lacking information on anything of that kind. I'll advise you though to say nothing at all to the press or to anyone of what you may know or think you know.'

'The police?' Alicia asks. 'If they ask.'

'The English police?' The Major chews on that one for a while. 'Well supposing them to be the legally constituted authority where you are just now, you'd best be co-operative to the extent necessary...No, no, lassie, there's no need for you to be fussing your head about getting back to barracks any time soon. Indefinite compassionate leave we have you down for, in the matter of the kidnapping of your brother. Terrible thing, kidnapping. Please give your father and mother the regiment's condolences.'

'But he's just been released, unharmed,' says Alicia. 'He's not dead or anything.'

'There's a blessing in a wicked world. But you'll be needed all the more at home I'm thinking. No occasion to worry. We'll be in contact, Second Lieutenant, as soon as there's any change in the situation.'

As Alicia enters the kitchen, she glances up automatically at the screen.

'I'm sure I've met that woman, recently, round here.'

Luke comes to the table with a large serving dish with a view to distributing second helpings where wanted. In response to his sister's comment, he glances up routinely at the screen and nearly drops the dish. In the event he leaves the dish on the end of the table, tantalizingly out of polite range of the long arm of the law. Where, DI Tench wonders, has he gone wrong? They all seemed to be getting on so well together. Even Smogulecki had thawed a bit, chatting to Luke about Polish cooking.

When Tench turns to see what the fuss is about, he cannot see the screen. His view is obstructed by three large male backs. Well two large and one smaller back. The Cameron males are all standing in front of the screen, eyes fixed front.

Tench, in the way of duty and when it seems no more food will be forthcoming immediately, gets up and joins the Camerons. He remains mystified. Someone has found the remote among the food and turned the sound up.

Some woman with a foreign accent is giving an interview about Felix's kidnapping. Well of course anything of this kind is bound to be interesting for the family. But their concentration seems unusual.

Something about the psychological effect? No, not that. It's the moral issue that is being discussed. Is it ever justified to break the law to cause a good effect? In this case, was it justified to abduct Felix in order to redistribute his father's wealth to worthy charities? Something the novelist has often advocated in public and in the abstract but never to any great degree done. Not only to redistribute wealth, but to force an end to hypocrisy, to set an example for others to follow voluntarily, as in the aftermath of the kidnapping of Felix, some are already doing.

David and his sons seem to be in a state of suppressed excitement, but none of them is saying very much. Not commenting on the discussion going on above their heads as one might normally do of a topic that seized your attention. Finally, DS Smogulecki is at Tench's elbow to whisper enlightenment.

'I think it's that they all fancy her, though I can't for the life of me see why.'

'Nor can I, Detective Sergeant.'

She's nicely got up for the TV lights, but has an unremarkable, un-expressive face. The camera reverts from time to time to her legs, as TV studio cameras do when the subject is a woman who has crossed her legs, so her knees are visible. Nothing special there either, is the judgement of the detectives. But Smogulecki is undoubtedly right about the Cameron father and sons.

Eventually the interview is over. The three men, two men and a boy as Annie might have put it, return to the table. But there are still no seconds, for the three of them now debate the merits of what Annie has been saying. It gives them an excuse to talk about her, which when one has fallen head over heels for someone, is a temptation that is hard to resist, as Smogulecki points out to her boss, sotto voce.

30

Situation Management (1)

'Can you come over here? I'm working in my room in College. Yes, I know the Christmas vacation has started but that doesn't mean I have any less to do. Research, endless administration.'

'OK. As soon as I'm finished with DI Tench.'

'Perhaps as soon as he is finished with you,' she says. 'Call me as you leave.'

'You took your time. I have a meeting at five.'

She invites him to sit on the easy chair by her desk.

'Actually, Annie, it was Tench who took his time. I can't understand what he wants with me. I told him the facts of the kidnap from the family's point of view, and the process of paying the ransom. But he kept going over the same ground. It's as if he thought I had something to do with the kidnapping.'

'Perhaps he does,' said Annie, smiling slightly and pushing back her chair from the desk so she can cross her legs more conveniently. 'Did my name come up by any chance, in your conversation with Tench?'

'Of course not. No reason it should, was there?'

'None at all. But since I seem to have become involved, as someone the media call on for what they call expert comment on the moral angle, it's perhaps better if you continue to say nothing about conversations between us. That way any personal relationship which may develop between us in future will not be affected by media inquisitiveness or by the police investigation.'

'Of course. I understand. But how is it Annie that you've suddenly become a media pundit on my son's kidnap?'

She laughs in the way she sometimes does. Half amused, half embarrassed.

'It's my area of research, David. You did Philosophy, Politics and Economics here, didn't you? I mean years ago?'

'Three decades or so, certainly. But how do you know that?'

'Perhaps Andrew, Felix, as I shall now have to remember to call him, perhaps Felix mentioned it. More likely I just read it somewhere. You are quite famous after all, David.'

'Oh well yes, in some sense.'

'Well from the time you were reading PPE here, do you remember the name John Rawls?'

Yes, he does. He is even able, after wracking his brain for a few moments, to come up with a passable outline of Rawls's big idea on reconciling an increased degree of social and economic fairness with individual freedom.

'Alpha plus,' she says, laughing again. 'Well I am one of a handful of people at Oxford, philosophers and psychologists, who are working on seeing if Rawls's general idea can be developed so it has real life application. I'm nominally head the research effort, so if the media rang up the University Press Office, my name would come up naturally. And just because I am pursuing this area of research, I also don't neglect opportunities to bring my name to a wider public. It helps with getting research grants for one thing. And it may give a wider audience for the book I'm writing. If it ever comes out.'

'Very impressive, Annie. I couldn't really follow exactly what you were saying on TV, because the sound was turned off until Alicia happened to notice it was you on the screen. We were having the police investigators to lunch at the time.'

'I'll send you the link, so you can review my interview at your leisure. But in essence I just tried to put the issue raised by

Felix's kidnap and your payment of the ransom as clearly and fairly as possible. Trying to take the emotion out of the situation.'

David thinks that it is all very well for Annie Fritzweiler to play the detached observer, but he has lost ten and a half million pounds, all that he owned in the world. But then he thinks how very exciting it is to be able to have a sight of her legs, or at least her knees between the hem of her grey skirt and her black boots. And he does not fail to observe that she is showing a certain amount of cleavage above her tight orange top.

She smiles vaguely, as if reading his mind, and continues to ask him in detail about Tench's investigation. Annie seems to have forgotten about her five o'clock meeting. It's really a bit like being interviewed by the police again. Very precise, coming back and back to clarify points that are not quite clear.

'Sergei's loan, you did not mention that to the police?'

'No, I thought it…I don't know. It seemed somehow jarring.'

'Not good for your image perhaps. Well let's hope Sergei won't mention it either if the police get as far as interviewing him. Perhaps not so good for his image either.'

Eventually, Annie seems content. It has become dark outside while they've been talking. In a couple of weeks, it will be the winter solstice and a few days after that Christmas, as the earth prepares to reawaken for another year. David surprises himself with the speculation that in the New Year perhaps his career will take off again on the basis of renewed inspiration. And that this new inspiration will be provided in large measure by the woman now sitting in front of him.

As she shows him out, accepting his kiss on either cheek but resisting a hug, she asks about his plans for Christmas.

'Your friend Sergei Dzhugashvili has said we can stay in the house until at least the end of February.'

'Yes, Sergei may seem a bit sinister until you get to know him. But for a Russian he's really a fairly nice guy. I used to see a lot of him when I was in Germany. But,' she adds, sensing David's unease, 'that was a long time ago.'

'Well,' David continues, 'I suppose I'll have to be with the family during the so-called festive season, drinking cheap wine and making the best of things. And getting down to writing the series of articles I've been commissioned to write about the kidnapping. Might pay for a few groceries I suppose. What about you?'

'Oh, family and friends in Germany. They make quite a big thing of it over there. But we'll see each other before I have to leave. End of next week. Take care, David. And let's be discrete. Best for everyone concerned. And the only way you and I might be able to take things forward.'

When David gets back to his car, a third hand micro into which he fits only with discomfort, he finds the windscreen festooned with parking tickets, as is usual on his visits to Annie in Oxford. Previously he didn't count the cost of parking for a couple of hours or more in the half hour limited spaces, along the wide road opposite St. Johns. But now he is conscious of every penny. He must google Oxford car parks when he gets back. Or he could borrow Felix's car, and let him pay the parking fines. But one thing he is not going to give up however constrained his finances, is visiting Annie, as often as she will see him.

31

Situation Management (2)

'Can you come over here? I think it would be useful if we could meet before Christmas.'

They huddle on high stools drawn close together in the bar of the Oxford Union. The place may be world famous, where the global great and good are delighted to accept invitations to speak in student debates. Where students who fancy themselves future prime ministers of somewhere or rather are groomed and tested in the cut and thrust of ideas. All well and good but the bar menu is very limited.

It does, though, fit the bill in this case because it is the cheapest place in Oxford. Felix bought himself a life membership at the start of his first term, those few short weeks ago, when money seemed to grow on the otherwise bare trees in the quads of Oxford Colleges.

Outside, it is bone chillingly cold with that sort of damp cold that is only found in the Thames Valley. Annie Fritzweiler is in faded blue jeans, tucked into calf length brown boots, and a dark blue ski jacket. She is still shivering from her short walk from College. Felix is still shivering from his rather longer walk from an underground car park near Nuffield College. Perhaps he should have continued at Cambridge rather than Oxford. Stupid. No Annie at Cambridge. And anyway, in Cambridge the winter winds come uninterrupted from Siberia.

'Better to keep to Andrew, Andrew. That way you won't confuse the College authorities and it will be easier for me to remember.'

Annie laughs in that way she has, at the same time amused and self-deprecating. The way that charms David Cameron and his younger son so much.

'Of course. Anyway, Andrew is just as much my name as Felix,' Felix says.

Numbed fingers round mugs of horribly sweet hot chocolate. Thawing.

'You looked super on TV the other day,' he begins.

'What did you think of what I said?'

'Agreed with every word of course.'

'What a good student,' she laughs.

'Actually, I got into terrible trouble with my Dad when I said it was hard not to admire the kidnappers for their effort to redistribute wealth from a rich individual to very deserving charities. Particularly in a case like my Dad's where the individual in question has gone round shooting his mouth off about how wealth should be redistributed but taken minimal steps to bring it about in his own case. Anyway, he got in a terrible strop.'

Thawed. Annie slides off her coat and Andrew goes to hang it up along with his own.

'That's understandable, I suppose. We all tend to get especially angry where we recognise that we are at fault and suffering justly. But Andrew, are you able to speak about the details of the kidnapping yet?'

Now it's his turn to laugh.

'I've already told the family. Then the police in excruciating detail. So, I think I can tell you the essentials without having a nervous breakdown. That is, as long as I may look at you while I'm doing it.'

She swivels to face him on her stool, presses her knees together and waits for him to begin. But quickly she interrupts him.

'Andrew, as you go along, do you think you could tell me about the questions the police asked you, the things they seemed to be especially interested in? They would most likely have an instinct for what is important in trying to catch the thugs who seized you. That's the key thing after all.'

'But I thought you said on TV that in this case the kidnappers were justified, because their actions taken as a whole did good.'

'I did not say that.'

Annie angry for a moment at his sloppy attention to her words. But in a second, she is calm again.

'What I said was that that was the question about which we all have to come to our own conclusion. On the one side kidnapping would tend to lead to unnecessary suffering and ultimately a breakdown of law and order if not checked by process of law. On the other hand, in a case such as yours seems to be, where the kidnappers behaved reasonably to their victim...' Andrew nods. '...and where the redistribution of resources they brought about would be seen by many as right, in this particular case the kidnappers on balance may have done right. Here what is moral may be what most people think is moral in the circumstances.'

'That's what I thought, Dr Fritzweiler. So?'

She laughs.

'Annie is fine outside our tutorials.'

She lets her left-hand rest lightly on her knee.

'Annie,' he repeats, because he likes the sound of it as he looks at her.

She continues.

'But Andrew, your abductors need to be caught if possible so that the case, with all the facts put before us by the forensic process of English justice, can be judged by informed public opinion.'

'But whatever public opinion says, the court may send the guys to prison.'

'Quite right, Andrew, there is a minimum tariff set in statute for kidnapping, so the court would have no choice. But the court could recommend exercise of the Royal Prerogative of mercy, actually exercised at the direction of the Government, to have the kidnappers released at once. The Government would be sure to be sensitive to public opinion at such a time.'

Andrew grins.

'All helpful to your work on applying to the real world the public morality theory of John Rawls?'

'Well John Rawls as modified in light of the practicalities by me and my colleagues, but in essence yes, Andrew. But do continue your account of the abduction.'

So, he does, until he gets almost to the end of his story.

The cops were very interested in what the guys, the kidnappers, said to each other immediately after one of them hit me because I was asking too many questions.'

'I hope you weren't badly hurt, Andrew?'

'It was painful at the time, but nothing broken.'

'In what was it that the detective, Detective Inspector Tench was it, was so interested?'

'It was both of them. In fact, it was the woman DS, Smogulecki, if I've got that right, who started it.'

'And what were you able to tell them?'

'That the second guy, the one who hadn't hit me said something like, "Don't do that. He doesn't like it." But then the cops said that sounded odd because if "he" was me then of course nobody likes being hit by some heavy. Tench was going on about some idea of his own, but I was thinking "he" isn't right. It sounded more like "she". "She wouldn't like it." Though to be honest the words were quite indistinct and may have been something else altogether.'

If an expression of alarm passes across Annie's face, it is gone so fast that Andrew immediately thinks he dreamed it. But then he wonders if he did not.

But Annie is again in complete command.

'What else?'

'Nothing really.'

'How about your release?'

'They just drove me, blindfolded of course, and told me to get out of the car when they stopped. It took me a minute or so, standing there in the cold, to work out how to take off my blind fold. Then I saw where I was. About a mile from my house as it turned out, my parents' house. The car had gone before I'd got the blindfold off. Anyway, they'd probably masked the car plates, so I couldn't get a number. I called Dad, who was out walking...actually I saw him a few minutes later heading away from our village. I'm sure he saw me, so I pretended I didn't see him.'

'I think I can understand both of you,' she says, climbing off her stool and looking for her coat.

32

Closer to Home

Smogulecki greets her in German. Anne Fritzweiler replies in English.

'Since we are in England.'

DI Tench, having no other option, identifies himself in English. Annie remembers to allow the detective to go through his fish in the river not hole in the ground routine, though she'd heard it twice before. Once from David Cameron, in exasperation. And again, from Andrew Cameron, who had acted Tench's part so as to make her laugh out loud. The original seems a bit colourless compared to Andrew's version.

Smogulecki, speaking now in English, takes the lead in questioning.

'Thank you, Dr Fritzweiler, for seeing us so close to the

holiday.'

'Yes, I'm leaving in half an hour.'

'Oh, going home to your family for Christmas?'

DS Smogulecki makes a note of her contact details in Germany, though surely her mobile phone number is all the police need.

'I grew up on the coast near Stettin,' the Polish woman says. She uses the old German form of the name rather than the Polish, Szczecin. Put the subject at her ease, or unease, as the case may be.

Yes, thinks Annie, further to the East across the border from where I grew up in the GDR, East Germany. Along that grey flat Baltic coast, empty and dead except for a couple of months in summer. There in the years before the fall of the Berlin Wall pale faced, exhausted workers came to pretend to enjoy themselves. But she does not respond to this attempt by her interrogator to form a bond of fellow feeling. She, after all, has been a Stasi informer, like many people in the GDR, and knows this game of old.

They go through the drill. Yes, she is Andrew's tutor in philosophy. Felix, yes. He calls himself Andrew at Oxford. Felix had invited her to the restaurant celebration, at which he was kidnapped. That is how she got to know the Cameron family.

'Alicia Cameron, seemed impressed that you had observed the kidnappers to calmly and accurately, while the rest of them came up with descriptions of the event which turned out to be wildly and variously inaccurate,' says Smogulecki.

The detectives wait for her to speak, but she does not oblige. For heaven's sake I have a plane to catch. Let's stop playing these childish games.

'I suppose we were wondering, Dr Fritzweiler,' Tench joining in the questioning for the first time, 'how you were able to be so calm in such a frightening situation?'

'I assure you I wasn't calm. I was frightened to death the kidnappers would attack us, me, with their baseball bats. But I am a professional philosopher, trained not only to think clearly but to observe accurately. It has become second nature for me.'

'How would you describe your relations with the Cameron family? In the days after the abduction of Felix, or Andrew if you prefer.' It's Smogulecki again.

'Cordial. They were naturally emotionally distressed, and they seemed grateful to have an outsider to help them think clearly about the situation and what was best to do.'

'With which of the family did you have most to do?'

'David Cameron sought my advice more often than any of the others. I found that quite natural that as head of the family he would be the one to consult me. To be honest, I don't think I had any ideas that the family had not thought of for itself. But just having confirmation from an outsider that they were doing the sensible thing was helpful to them, I think.'

'In our conversation with her, we formed the impression that Mrs. Cameron seemed not to warm to you so much?'

'I don't know. I saw little of her. I believe she was sedated much of the time. Certainly, she seemed hit harder than any of the others. Natural in a mother no doubt.'

'Did David Cameron ever discuss with you the idea that Felix may have been complicit in his own abduction?'

'Yes. I understood why he might think that. Certain things could be seen as pointing that way. But I told David Cameron consistently that unless he was sure of that, which in the nature of things he could not be, he should act as if Felix were completely a victim and that the kidnappers might carry out their various threats to harm him.'

'So, you didn't encourage David Cameron in his idea of Felix's complicity?'

'No.'

'Dr Fritzweiler, are you and David Cameron friends?'

'Yes, I think we could be so described.'

'Lovers?'

'No.'

'You don't seem surprised or insulted by the question?'

'You have a job to do. I don't have time to understand why you ask me what you ask me. Or why you are questioning me at all. I'm just trying to answer your questions straightforwardly. And catch my plane to Berlin.'

'As indeed you are doing, Dr Fritzweiler.'

The soft cop, with his soft West Country vowels is emollient. But then it's the Detective Sergeant again.

'Not only Davina, Mrs. Cameron, told us that she thought you and David Cameron were having an affair, but their daughter, Alicia, also.'

'That is their speculation?'

'Yes, Dr Fritzweiler, speculation,' confirms Tench.

'But I am in a position to say definitely,' says Annie, 'that we weren't. And we weren't and we aren't. And for the record I am divorced and not currently in a relationship. Will that do?'

She smiles wearily at the two policemen.

'Just for the record...' It's Smogulecki and it's definitely not just for the record. 'Who was it you were married to?'

They know. And even if they don't yet know they will find out sooner or later. She smiles, even more wearily, at Smogulecki.

'It was before the Berlin Wall fell, when I lived in East Germany. His name is Sergei Dzhugashvili.'

'Same name as the well-known oligarch?' says D I Tench, affecting bemusement.

'Same man,' says Annie Fritzweiler, very quietly.

If the detectives think this is a game changer, they don't show it, and simply continue as if nothing of significance had been said.

'Just one more thing if we may, Dr Fritzweiler,' purrs Tench. 'In our interview with him, Felix mentioned that he overheard one of his kidnappers say to another, that "she" wouldn't like the fact that one of them had hit Felix.'

'So?'

'It might imply that there was someone other than the gang of four men who held Felix, someone who was not there, someone from whom the gang accepted orders, someone who was a woman.'

The format Bertrand Russell's theory of definite descriptions. That a name corresponds to a series of descriptive propositions which together uniquely define the object or person named, thinks Annie. In this case the corresponding name in the detectives' minds is of course her own.

'You are wasted as a policeman, Detective Inspector' she says. 'You should have been a philosopher.'

Speaking as an expert on terrorism, do you have any comment on this "she"?

Smogulecki interrupting the love in.

'If I were I might, but since I am merely trained in moral philosophy, I have no comment. And now may I go?'

But DS Smogulecki has a further question.

'Have you seen either David Cameron or Felix Cameron since Felix's release? And did either of them speak to you of the matter just mentioned by DI Tench.'

'Both and both,' says Annie, getting up and going to open the door for the detectives. 'I'm happy to answer any further questions you may have, but I really will miss my plane if you don't go now.'

Tench is effusive in his thanks. Smogulecki wishes her a happy Christmas, in German.

Sergei Dzhugashvili has sent to Annie Fritzweiler a crate of Krug and a very large tub of extinct Iranian caviar. She falls over them as she rushes out of her room. Her carry on makes its own way down the staircase. The strap of her shoulder bag makes an effort to strangle her. Her hand is grazed. She swears comprehensively in German, the original language of swearing, and feels better. Down two flights to the front quad. Then she trails her recaptured carry-on through the unforgiving damp sand of the quad to the Porter's Lodge. Here she prints an address and telephone number on a pad of College notepaper there provided.

She tries to attract the attention of the Porter himself. No messing with his flunkies. But he is engaged with a self-confident young man who is obviously rich and evidently foreign.

She rummages in her bag and brings out two crisp new notes, fifties, which she crackles together. She had intended to give him only one of the notes, but it's Christmas and more urgently she doesn't want to be kept waiting by the Porter's long conference with the young man. He excuses himself elaborately and comes over. He takes the letterhead on which she's written the address for delivery of the champagne and caviar.

'The Prime Minister? So, you are acquainted, Dr Fritzweiler?'

'The thriller writer. Please don't make a mistake.'

'Certainly not, Dr Fritzweiler. It will be with the greatest pleasure.'

With one hand he waves away an underling, who has picked up Annie's case to carry it out to the taxi, and with the other causes the two fifties to disappear like a conjuring trick. The Head Porter takes the case himself.

He helps her into the taxi.

'And a Very Merry Christmas to you, Dr Fritzweiler.'

Annie has plenty of time to catch her plane, since she was already packed and had only half a dozen brief emails to send, before she left. She had deliberately exaggerated the pressure of time to the police. But on the subsequent train ride from Berlin to the Baltic coast, as she stares out at the grey, dead fields, she wonders if, after all, detectives are cleverer than philosophers.

The two detectives stare through the windscreen of their car at the bare trees and the rising afternoon mist, which will soon envelop them. Neither speaks until Smogulecki breaks the silence.

'Well, sir, do you think I was so off beam in suggesting she may be involved in it?'

Tench takes time to reply, suppressing the thought of the lunch they have missed before he is able to focus.

'She's better looking than she seemed on TV, don't you think,

Detective Sergeant?'

Smogulecki is impatient.

'Do you think, sir, that she might be involved...in organising the abduction?'

'I think, Smogulecki, that you could be right, but it remains a long shot. She told us nothing to support your idea. In fact, you were embarked on a complete fishing expedition and she would have been within her rights to refuse to answer any of it.'

'Oh, she's too shrewd to do that, sir. Go along with the police at every stage however unreasonable they are. It was standard procedure in the GDR, the old East Germany where Annie Fritzweiler grew up. She's an old hand. I checked up with the Berlin Documentation Office. They were most helpful. Did you know that she was a Stasi informer?'

'As was everyone else, weren't they?' says Tench.

33

Chief's Powwow

In the dreary days between Christmas and New Year, virtually the whole country was away or sunk in a food and drink induced coma. But in the case of the kidnapping of Andrew David Felix Cameron, the need to make a strategic decision could be postponed no longer.

The place judged most likely not to be found out by such members of the press who might still be free of a hangover and at work was the County police headquarters where the investigation was centred. Something about hiding a leaf in a tree, the Chief Constable had said.

In addition to the Chief Constable himself, who had assumed personal overall charge of the kidnap investigation, there were gathered a Commander from SOECC, the Metropolitan Police Specialist, Organised and Economic Crime branch which included a Kidnap Unit, the Lieutenant Colonel then acting in command of Jeremy Wingate Grey's Guards battalion, one of the deputies to the Director of Public Prosecutions, a senior official from the Cabinet Office and a Minister of State from the Home Office.

'Minister would you care to....'

And the Minister naturally assumed the chairmanship of the meeting.

'If I might suggest, Minister,' the Chief Constable continues, 'that we might proceed by setting out the question that needs urgently to be resolved by this meeting, and then go round the table to get the views of each of the interested parties. Key information regarding the case is contained in the five-page memo...' Here holding up a copy of the memo. '...a numbered copy of which has been made available to everyone here.

'A senior officer from Alicia Cameron's Scottish regiment is available on the phone should we need to consult him. My officers leading the day-to-day investigation are available downstairs should we need any further information.'

'Thank you, Chief Constable,' murmurs the Minister, who has had been asked to attend the meeting because his home is in the County. He has received less than two hours' notice of the event and not read the paper.

'Well then, perhaps Chief Constable, you could set out the background and the matters for decision at this meeting.'

'Delighted, Minister.'

The Chief efficiently sets out the salient facts of the kidnapping, including the payment of the ransom to charity on the direction of the kidnappers and the release unharmed of Felix.

'In a nutshell,' the Chief Constable continues, 'the question before us is whether considerations of public policy are such that we should drop the investigation into the kidnapping of Felix Cameron, or whether such investigation should continue on the basis of the resources of the Metropolitan Police which would normally be deployed in such a case. There is a possible middle ground, which we have adopted up to now, of restricting the investigation to two of my officers without wider support.'

'I see, so that we would be able to say the investigation is ongoing although actually there would be very little chance of finding anything,' says the Minister. 'You're wasted in the police force, Chief Constable.'

The Chief thinks so too.

'What on earth would be the grounds for not pursuing this case with vigour? It is surely agreed the kidnapping is among the most serious of crimes,' says the Commander from SOECC, visibly straining at her leash.

'I must say at first sight, I agree,' adds the Deputy DPP. 'Surely the normal form would be to catch these chaps if we can and then decide on all the facts then available whether to prosecute?'

'Thereby spending as much public money for as little effect as possible,' says the Minister, beginning to warm to his role. 'And I would suggest to you, Commander, that before you press your argument any further that you take account of the likely reductions in manpower in your branch consequent on expected further Home Office cuts. Now, who would like to put the argument for dropping the case?'

'Well, Minister,' the Cabinet Office official to the rescue.

People tended to pay attention when he spoke since the Cabinet Office was thought of as a proxy for the Prime Minister.

'Whilst normally my Department would be eager that any matter of law and order be vigorously pursued, we understand that the Army is anxious to avoid any public exposure of serving officers. Especially in this case where one of the officers who was involved, if only tangentially, has been decorated for gallantry. Is that correct Colonel?'

'Twice,' says the Colonel, 'twice decorated. Newspaper Johnnies wrote him up a bit after his first MC, you know. Good for morale out there. In Afghanistan you know.'

'So, Colonel, you would favour dropping the investigation?' The Minister of State making sure.

'Yes Minister, helpful to the Regiment, you know. Up to now Captain Wingate Grey's wholly unauthorised operation in connection with the kidnapping has not got into the newspapers.'

'How did you manage that?' asks the Minister, whose department like several others has been plagued by recent unauthorised leaks of embarrassing information.

'Normal procedure,' the Colonel continues, 'to welcome our man back into the battalion when he's fit again, a slight slap on the wrist, nothing on his record you know, and carry on as if no harm has been done.'

'And indeed, no harm was done,' adds the Chief Constable.

'Except apparently to Farmer Giles's ceiling,' says the Deputy DPP, referring to the memo in front of him. 'The Army would be OK with paying compensation, Colonel?'

'Regimental funds very tight.'

'We'll take that as a "yes",' says the Minister. 'That all seems satisfactory then. No need to go further into the substance is there? Shall we just go round the table again to take a vote on it?'

The Minister, who has a lunch to go to, thinks he can see in front of him a three or four to one majority in favour of dropping things, SOECC having been steered into at least abstaining.

'At least, Minister,' pleads the Deputy DPP, 'let us hear the views of the officers actually investigating matters. I think you said they were available to us, Chief? And could we get some more coffee while we are waiting for them to arrive?'

'In that case, a doughnut might not come amiss either for those of us who've had no breakfast,' adds the Minister.

The Chief, though not best pleased, cannot but agree to so reasonable a request from so influential a source and makes the call.

34

High Policy, Low Morals

'Detective Inspector Tench and Detective Sergeant Smogulecki.'

The Chief Constable makes the introductions.

'Thank you for being available to us,' starts off the Deputy DPP. 'We've been briefed on the major points of the case so there is no need to go over those. From you we would just like an assessment of your progress towards catching the kidnappers and your understanding of their motives for an operation from which they appear not to have benefitted personally. Detective Inspector.'

'Well, sir, to be truthful we have no direct leads to the kidnappers. No clues were found in the house where the victim was held and in our intensive interviews of Felix Cameron, he was able to give us nothing of value. He said there were four kidnappers, and they spoke with mid-European accents, but he couldn't tell if they were faked or not.'

'Yes, that is in the memo your Chief Constable has given us,' murmurs the Deputy DPP. 'And is it your judgement that Felix Cameron was being entirely straightforward with you? I ask only because in the memo there is some suggestion that Felix could have been complicit in his own kidnapping.'

'We can't be sure sir, but it seemed to us that he was being honest with us and doing his best to recollect matters that might be helpful to us.'

'There is in the memo a reference to Felix mentioning a possible fifth person, a "she" who might be involved. Have you been able to make any progress with that?'

'To be frank, we have not, sir.'

'May I say something, sir?'

The Chief Constable looks discomforted, DI Tench bemused. The other members of the meeting look interested.

'Yes, Detective Sergeant,' says the Deputy DPP.

'DI Tench thinks this of no significance but I think it worth mentioning to you.'

'Well?'

'We interviewed Felix's philosophy tutor at Oxford, Dr Annie

Fritzweiler. She seems to be close to Felix and a particular friend of Mr. David Cameron....'

'The prominent novelist and Felix's father,' says the Chief as if no one in the meeting ever watched television news, let alone read their numbered copy of the briefing paper. 'Not, of course, the Prime Minister.'

There is a suggestion of nervous laughter round the table.

'Dr Fritzweiler was helpful to the family during their kidnap ordeal,' adds Smogulecki.

'Very well Detective Sergeant, but I'm not following your point, I'm afraid,' says the Deputy DPP with a suggestion of irritation.

'I think it possible that Dr Fritzweiler is the "she" referred to by the kidnappers.'

'You mean that she was the master mind of the kidnapping?' says the Cabinet Office official, incredulous but alert.

'Or at least was involved in some way,' says Smogulecki

'I think, DS Smogulecki, that what you have said is completely unsupported by evidence?'

The Chief Constable is visibly annoyed and actually angry.

'The evidence is circumstantial,' concedes Smogulecki, 'but

I think, taken together with the Russian connection, it is a lead worth following up.'

The table is in uproar.

'What Russian connection?' demands the Chief, blindsided and furious. 'I was not told of any Russian connection.'

'Perhaps we should hear about it now,' says the Deputy DPP.

Smogulecki explains.

'Over the Christmas holiday, I have been going over the transcripts of the interviews we conducted with the Cameron family. There is reference there to the fact that eight million of the ten and a half million of the money for the ransom came from David and Davina Cameron selling their house. The sale went through unusually quickly. Within a week in fact. Just in time to meet the kidnappers' deadline.'

'I'm still not following the relevance of all this, Detective Sergeant.'

'Nor me,' says the Minister, who five minutes earlier had thought himself well on his way to pre-lunch aperitifs with his county neighbours.

'The point, sir, is that the buyer is Russian. You will recall that Felix Cameron mentioned that his kidnappers spoke with mid-European accents. Perhaps those accents were Russian. And perhaps the kidnappers worked for Sergei Dzhugashvili.'

'Who the devil...?

'The buyer at a fire sale price of the Cameron house? I follow,' says the Deputy DPP. 'But it's a bit thin, isn't it, Detective Sergeant?'

'Thin, it's transparent nonsense.' The Chief Constable is angry again.

The Deputy DPP ignores the Chief's discomfort.

'Perhaps worth a couple of minutes of thought though, Chief, eh? So, Detective Sergeant, your idea is that the Russian buyer of the Cameron house, with the help of Felix's philosophy tutor at Oxford, set up the kidnapping in order to save some amount of money in buying the Cameron house. That really is a bit farfetched, isn't it, Detective Sergeant?'

'The saving the Russian buyer, Sergei Dzhugashvili, made, compared to an estimated normal market price, was at least a million pounds,' Smogulecki persists. 'The cost of the kidnapping was forty thousand pounds.'

'Even so, the risk of being caught?'

'Perhaps not so high, for someone resident in Russia.'

'How about someone resident in Oxford?' murmurs the man from the Cabinet Office.

The SOECC Commander sees a new opportunity to press

her point of view, public expenditure cuts or no public expenditure cuts.

'After all, apart from the Detective Sergeant's interesting thesis, the police have expressed themselves baffled up to now,' says the Commander. 'This is our one lead.'

'This so-called connection between the Russian buyer and the Oxford tutor, that's pure fabrication, Detective Sergeant,' snaps the Chief.

'Not exactly, sir. Annie Fritzweiler and Sergei Dzhugashvili were friends, perhaps close friends, from a long time ago when Annie Fritzweiler lived in East Germany, before the fall of the Berlin Wall.'

'A long time ago.'

The Chief Constable stretches his scepticism.

'Not entirely, sir,' says DS Smogulecki. 'According to Alicia Cameron, no to Davina Cameron, Dzhugashvili and Fritzweiler had met much more recently, in Berlin, and perhaps in other places.'

'This may be all fantastic nonsense,' says the Deputy DPP looking round the table at each of the participants in turn, 'or at least completely circumstantial, but we can't entirely rule it out, can we?'

The question sinks into all of them.

'What is your opinion, DI Tench?'

'Exactly what you say, sir. All the evidence is circumstantial, it's probably nonsense, but we can't rule it out. And sir, we haven't ruled it out. DS Smogulecki and I are continuing with our inquiries. Some help from the Met though, would not come amiss at this stage.'

'There you have it, Minister,' says the Deputy DPP. 'Do we dare let this go? If we call off the investigation now, perhaps in the not so far in the future, our failure to pursue things may come to be seen as a cover up.'

"Cover up" does it. The words ring like a fire bell in the night with all senior Government officials. There have been just too many cover ups, alleged or admitted, in the recent past. The public, forget the public, the Prime Minister, is fed up with such incompetence and worse. But the Home Office Minister and the Cabinet Office man are not able to able quite to let go of the need to save public money.

'If I may sum up,' ventures the Home Office Minister. He has got the hang of things now. 'The good Detective Sergeant has drawn to our attention a possible line of enquiry. Even she,' he smiles on Smogulecki, 'would not claim it was the most likely explanation for the kidnapping, but the consensus round the table seems to be that we should not ignore it.'

He pauses briefly to allow any dissent, but even the Chief Constable is quiet.

'So, if I might suggest, perhaps Chief Constable you could instruct DI Tench and his excellent Detective Sergeant to continue to pursue matters, in just the way you have so wisely organised things to date. But, if at any time your two officers feel they need specialist support, over a particular matter, let them by all means apply to SOECC. What I have in mind is help with contacting foreign authorities, specialist analysis, that kind of thing. No boots on the ground though.' He laughs, but everyone round the table knows what that means. 'Would that be all right, Commander?'

The Commander nods.

'So, Chief Constable, if you could prepare a note of the meeting. Just a one pager on the conclusions. No need for any detail on the discussion or any mention of who said what. You know the sort of thing. So, I think, Chief, all that remains is to thank you for your hospitality and to thank all of you for your attendance in the middle of the holiday.'

The Minister gets up, and although he is dying to be gone, goes round the room shaking hands with each participant in turn, and bestowing words of appreciation and encouragement on the detectives. Then he is gone to his luncheon and, he hopes, a very good Burgundy. It has after all been in the end a satisfactory morning's work.

'Damn it, we have that Scotsman still hanging around waiting for a phone call,' says the Chief Constable, still irritated at being blindsided by his Detective Sergeant, who is now of course untouchable. She has received the personal blessing of a Home Office Minister.

'Attend to that myself,' says the Colonel of the Guards. 'Reinstate our respective officers when the time seems right. No proceedings against.'

'I wouldn't do that just yet, Colonel,' says the Cabinet Office man, who can't entirely resist a little teasing of the Army. 'Let the two officers in question remain on indefinite leave. And let the police and the politicians have their head. Then we'll see what they've turned up in a month or so. In any case your man is still laid up, no? '

His day is made when the Colonel salutes him.

35

A Cold Time

It's snowing, it's cold and it's the start of Hilary Term at the University. The snow is mean, thin stuff, which will soon melt to slush in the streets of Oxford, making walking an unpleasant as well as a treacherous experience. The cold is the kind that seeps into your bones and stays there. Annie Fritzweiler shivers in her chilly rooms and wishes she were at home, in her warm, properly insulated flat, some way up the Banbury Road. She's been working in her flat for most of the vacation since she got back from Germany. Now she has to be in her rooms in College since a string of students will soon start to arrive for their first tutorials of the new term.

Annie has a mountain of work pending. Peer review articles to read, research grant applications to make, requests from students for letters of recommendation to decide on, and arrangements to make for the planned Moral Philosophy Conference which the College will be hosting in the Long Vac., University-speak for the summer holidays. Her German soul revolts against the backlog. She wants always to be on top of things.

One thing she is most definitely not on top of is the continuing police investigation into the kidnapping of Andrew Cameron, as he styles himself at Oxford. Following her interview with DI Tench and DS Smogulecki, just before Christmas, she received a brief email from Smogulecki to the effect that the detectives would want to interview her again and would be in touch. No details or likely time frame. The delay is, she thinks, deliberate. To make her nervous. If so, it has succeeded.

In fact, the delay in setting up a second round of interviews has not been planned. As soon as he had returned from the meeting in the office of the Chief Constable at County Police Headquarters, where he was confirmed as Officer-in-charge of the kidnap investigation, DI Tench has gone sick. Something he ate? Something he caught? Something more serious? After three days he is taken to hospital where he spends New Year's Eve and dreams intermittently of Luke Cameron's food.

Hovering between sickness and hunger, it comes to Tench that, in all her diligence and energy, Smogulecki may have missed an obvious point. But before the point is secured in his mind, the Detective Inspector drifts off again into sleep.

DS Smogulecki seems never to be ill. In her boss's absence she ploughs through the records of all the interviews undertaken by police into the Cameron kidnapping, and then ploughs through them again. She makes use of the Metropolitan Police SOECC connection, recently approved by the powers that be, and finds encouragement and cooperation. Smogulecki draws neat charts of connections between possible suspects. She makes lists of points. She looks at things one way and then another. By the time Tench returns to duty, she is ready.

First, re-interview Annie Fritzweiler. She slides a list of questions across the table to her boss. Tench reads slowly and then re-reads even more slowly.

'OK Smogulecki. You really think she's involved, don't you?'

'Don't you sir, in your heart of hearts?'

Next, make arrangements to interview Sergei Dzhugashvili. The DS has already established the Russian's address and that he divides his time between London and St. Petersburg.

'Why in heaven's name?'

'Because the kidnappers were his people.'

'There is not a shred of evidence, Detective Sergeant.'

'It's the only hypothesis we have come up with on the identity of the kidnappers,' insists Smogulecki.

'And there are probably political sensitivities. Isn't he quite prominent, this Russian?'

'That's for the brass to consider, sir. Our job is just to solve the case.'

'Or not,' murmurs Tench.

He continues to review Smogulecki's note.

'Then interview all the Camerons again?'

The DS nods.

'And Dr Gregory Halberstadt. Who is he?'

'A colleague of Fritzweiler's, much involved in her research effort to apply ideas of fairness to real life situations.'

Smogulecki quotes the last few words from a description, available on the University website, of the work of Annie Fritzweiler's team.

'Sounds barmy to me,' says Tench.

'It's a University project, sir.'

'Then the abortive rescue angle,' Smogulecki continues. 'The farmer you talked to...'

Tench smacks his forehead with the palm of his hand.

'Everything alright, sir?'

'I was supposed to go and see Llewellyn Davies to make sure he wasn't going to press charges against that bloody Guards officer.'

'Jeremy Wingate Grey?'

'That's the name. Went clean out of my mind it did. Remind me to ring Llewellyn Davies as soon as we're finished with this.'

'Will do. This Wingate Grey might be able to tell us something germane to the kidnap. Then I thought, sir, as background, I could go and see David Cameron's agent and his publisher. I could do those on my own, sir.'

'If you really think so, Detective Sergeant. I suppose the Chief has given us a fairly free hand.'

As his Detective Sergeant makes to bustle off to set up interviews, Tench calls her back.

'I wonder, Detective Sergeant, if we should just take a moment to think about what we actually know. Do sit down, Detective Sergeant.'

Tench sits down too. He invites the DS to start.

'One, Felix Cameron was kidnapped from the Oxford restaurant.'

'I'm not sure, Detective Sergeant. I think what we know is

that four persons smashed a lot of glassware in the restaurant and that Felix went away with them.'

'Against his will. He was abducted by them.'

'Apparently abducted. He may have gone with them voluntarily, by prior arrangement.'

'Felix had injuries,' the DS objects.

'Only a nose bleed? After the gang left with Felix there is no evidence of their further involvement. All the ransom demands and threats came via Felix himself. So, he could have originated all of them.'

'Implausible.'

'Not necessarily. What could be hard for a jury to swallow, Detective Sergeant, is that an unconnected gang motivated by greed would demand that ten million pounds odd be given to charity, leaving only forty thousand pounds for themselves. On the other hand, if the whole thing was set up by Felix, forty thousand could be a reasonable fee, or a bit of play acting in a restaurant.'

'Felix is only seventeen.' Smogulecki now begins to see the way her boss's train of thought could fit in with her own conviction. 'He couldn't possibly have organised the whole thing himself. If you are right, sir, that's where Annie Fritzweiler fits in.'

'Perhaps, Smogulecki, perhaps. But we have no evidence for that.'

'But only Felix could provide such evidence and he was so much under her influence that he wouldn't.'

'Let's just stick to facts for the moment. For the period he was missing, Felix was somewhere. We need to find out where that was. And we haven't found the car, the SUV the gang used to escape from the restaurant. Why wasn't it found?'

But Smogulecki can think of only one thing.

'Whether there was a real abduction or not, the key is Annie Fritzweiler. Let's interrogate her again.'

'Let's first try and find some evidence, Smogulecki. You could take a look at this Gregory Halberstadt. There may be something there.'

'And what will you be doing, sir?'

'I? I will be thinking, about Annie Fritzweiler.'

Also, in the first week of the Oxford term, his publisher calls David Cameron in a state of high excitement.

'Hey Cameron. That you man? You OK? You don't sound so good.'

'It's hunger, Goran. Since I've got nothing coming in, we can't afford to buy food.'

'Sounds bad, Cameron, very bad. How so?'

'I think it's because my publisher doesn't send me any royalties. I assume that is because there are no royalties?'

'Hey man, forget that shit. Have I got news for you? I just got the flash estimates for the Christmas sales. Even myself I had to read them twice. I've always had faith in you, David man, even in the darkest hour.'

'Oh yes, I remember,' says David, recalling that in their last conversation his publisher warned him that he was about to be dropped from Waverley's list.

'Got to make room for younger talent, Cameron. Know what I'm saying here. Tough but it's the way of the world.'

But today, Goran flatly denies that any such conversation could ever have taken place.

'Come on man, guess where you are in the flash estimates list.' David resists the temptation. 'Only bloody number three, man.'

'Say that again Goran.'

So, Goran gleefully repeats.

'But Goran it could be a blip, right, or a misprint, or any number of....'

'Such things, Cameron, they happen only in books.' Inevitably he laughs at his own wit. 'Look man, if this goes on, and I'd bet my grandmother to a packet of crisps that it will, you'll be back earning over half a mil. a year. Ok that's gross but enough to keep you in the style.... We must do lunch, Cameron.'

'Hold on a minute, Goran. Where do Davina and Felix figure on the list?'

'Lost without trace, Cameron. I mean without trace. You expect it with first timers. Know what I mean? But for your name they wouldn't have been published at all. But the old pro, he's showing them all the way home.'

David takes a second to realise his publisher is speaking of him.

'Lunch Cameron, Claridges, Savoy River Room, whatever you want. Or there's some new Ecuadorian in Hoxton. Charges more than El Bulli did in its prime, so it's said.' He laughs. 'You remember the time we took a private plane down there, to El Bulli, just up the coast from Barcelona, just for lunch, to celebrate the film deal on your kidnap book? Those were the good times, Cameron. Maybe they are coming back, your good times.'

'Yes, I recall. The film was never made, and the restaurant

was shut. But Goran before we get too carried away....'

'Oh, and Cameron, be a pal, will you? Pass on the bad news about the DARWIN FACTOR shit to the missus, will you? Women can be a bit emotional about this type of thing. As for young Felix, likewise. Best coming from the father this kind of thing. Boy has his whole life before him, right? I should use that approach. Never fails I find.'

Goran is gone. David calls his agent to make sure he's not hallucinating, or Goran isn't. But Sam confirms.

'Of course, we can't be sure it's a firm trend until we get the three-month figures in April. But the Christmas ones are the key. I wouldn't have any worries.'

'That's a relief to hear, Sam.'

'David, could I just say something which Goran mentioned to me? I think the old reprobate may have a point. He's got a wonderful reading intelligence, despite the fact that he is incapable of speaking a single proper English sentence.'

'OK.'

Although it is to Samantha's Roedean accent he is listening, all he can hear are Goran's gravel tones.

'What these numbers are showing, Sammy honey, is that Cameron's true talent is in the writing of unadulterated crap. You see what happened to his wife when she comes over all profound in that DARWIN FACTOR shit. People have had it with serious by the time they leave their office each day or for holidays, right? They want escape, sometimes a laugh in the belly. You know what I'm saying here, Sam?'

'Goran I so do.'

'Maybe because he knew he was losing his public with his last book or two, he went all the way down the market in THE AVENGING ANGEL. And you know what? It worked. Sammy, somehow, you've got to stop him going back to that intellectual horseshit he used to write. Might have worked back in the day when people had energy left at the end of the workday. But now we're all working like slaves. Am I right here, Sammy?'

'You are so right here Goran.'

'Whatever, keep the bugger down in the gutter for the next one. Promise me, Sammy.'

'I will do what I can, Goran, do what I can.'

'You know what they say, Sammy my sweet, we are all in the gutter but some of us are looking at the stars.'

'Well not all of us Goran. Only Oscar Wilde.'

But Goran has already put the phone down. From where does he come up with these slightly off-centre mots justes, she wonders? A dozen years ago he was a shepherd somewhere in the Balkans, or so he would have you believe.

36

Spooked

The detectives seem put out when Annie tells them she isn't free to see them until the following Saturday. Her calendar is full of tutorials and start of term admin meetings. She thinks it best to see them in her College rooms. As before, it's Smogulecki who starts the questioning.

'Thank you for seeing us again.'

Annie says nothing.

'We've been going over our notes of evidence and come across one or two discrepancies you might be able to help us with.'

'Oh yes.'

'In the immediate aftermath of the kidnapping, it was puzzling to know how the gang could have escaped the initial search for them, as a lot of manpower was deployed very quickly. The police...'

The Detective Sergeant speaks of the police as an agency a million miles removed from herself and DI Tench.

'...the police then worked on the assumption that the kidnap gang may have taken a light aircraft from the disused aerodrome at Windrush, quite close to the scene of the abduction.'

'Oh yes.'

'On examination, the only person to have mentioned the Windrush scenario was you. And yet we subsequently found that Windrush was never a possibility since the surface of the runway there is too decayed.'

'I was trying to be helpful to the police in the immediate aftermath. I had no idea of the conditions at Windrush. I assumed the police would check before they committed resources to following up the idea.'

'But later that day of the kidnapping, you told the Cameron family that your lover, a recreational flyer you said, had made two landings recently at Windrush. Indeed, you said he had been killed the previous week attempting another.'

'Look, Detective Sergeant, what I said directly to the police was merely an idea that occurred to me at the time. I said nothing about the condition of the runway because I had no cause to know. It was not my responsibility what use your colleagues chose to make of my suggestion.'

'So, you did not intend to mislead the officers to whom you spoke?' says DI Tench quietly.

'No. Nor would any reasonable person think that I did so.'

'Yes, we can see that, Dr Fritzweiler. But when you spoke to the Cameron family, you did imply that the runway at Windrush was fit for a light aircraft to land and take-off? You must have known that such a suggestion might get back to the police. Incidentally, we can find no record of a recent crash at Windrush.'

'Detective Inspector, my priority at the time of which you speak was to stop the Cameron family falling apart, as a family and individually, because of the shock of their son's kidnap. To do this I used a recognised psychological technique of gaining their sympathy by suggesting that I had suffered recent misfortune as great as their own. In fact, I do have a friend who is a recreational flyer, but he has never been my lover, was not killed at Windrush and as far as I know never made any attempt to land there.'

'So, it was a ruse?' suggests the Detective Inspector, with the suggestion of a smile. He can't help liking this woman, kidnapping mastermind though she might just be.

'Yes, a ruse that I considered then and consider now to be justified by the circumstances. It never occurred to me that it would go back to the police, still less that they would in any way act on it.'

'Do we have further questions for Dr Fritzweiler?' asks Tench with a note of reproach to his Detective Sergeant.

'Not on that topic,' concedes Smogulecki.

'Any other topic?' asks Annie.

She wonders if she should show the detectives the door, as is her right. No, don't be provoked. Show you'll go the extra mile to be cooperative.

'Well yes, actually,' says Tench, almost shyly.

Annie finds him quite appealing, but she recognises that just because of that he could be far more dangerous to her than Smogulecki. The Detective Sergeant asks if she may use the washroom. Obviously, this is a device to allow the detective to snoop around in Annie's adjoining bedroom, the door to which is firmly closed. Annie directs the Detective Sergeant to the shared student facility outside on the staircase.

'We understand you know Sergei Dzhugashvili, the Russian gentleman who recently bought the Cameron family house?' Tench in the absence of his DS.

'Yes, I met him at the Cameron place, and I've run across him sometimes at academic conferences in Europe. And I was married to him before the fall of the Berlin Wall.'

If Tench is surprised he does not show it.

'And divorced?'

'Yes, Detective Inspector, and divorced.'

'Which was when?'

'The divorce? I can't recall exactly but certainly within the year following the fall of the Berlin Wall. A quarter of a century ago that is.'

Smogulecki is back. She has scarcely had time to relieve herself. She quickly cottons on to the conversation, Tench continuing.

'Why did you divorce him?'

'Because he deserted me and went back to Russia. The Soviet Union as it then still was.'

'That must have been a great shock for you?'

'Everything at that time was a shock for all of us. The world was turned upside-down. But it turned out all right. I found myself living in a democratic country, the unified Germany, instead of a totalitarian hell hole where we went in daily fear of arrest and torture. In the new Germany I was able to pursue my career, without interference from the authorities.

'Your former husband, what was his job while you were married to him?' Tench asks this as if it is just another item on his list.

'He was attached to the Russian Embassy in Berlin. The embassy to the GDR, East Germany. He was also a well-regarded academic.'

Annie pauses, weighing the course of the conversation. She remembers the Documentation Centre in Berlin and assumes they are pretty free with their information to overseas official bodies, like the British police.

'I believe he did some intelligence work for the Soviet Government. Yes, before you ask Detective Sergeant, he was a spy.'

The detectives don't seem too astonished. But then who would be given the circumstances?

'Did you help him in his spying?'

'Only as far as any wife might help her husband in whatever job he might have. Occasionally making travel bookings for him, that sort of thing. I was a student in East Berlin. I was not a spy. I had no connection with Moscow or with the Russian Embassy. Do you have any more questions only I have a lot of work to do?'

'No, Dr Fritzweiler, that will be all for now,' says Tench getting up. 'We are due to call on your colleague, Dr Gregory Halberstadt. Would you be so kind as to point out his room to us?'

'I'll come down with you. I think I'll get some lunch in Hall.'

Annie leads them down the narrow stone staircase, which twists down to the quad. DI Trench can more and more see her appeal to the Cameron males. Nicely groomed, short not quite blond hair, a taut neat body. He can feel Smogulecki's contempt hot on the back of his neck. Annie points across the quad.

'Over there. It's the same floor as mine.'

'So, you can wave across to each other?' suggests Smogulecki.

'We don't do much of that,' Annie says, smiling tightly. 'Are you likely to need to talk to me again?'

'Yes,' says Smogulecki. 'At the station.'

The two detectives set off across the quad, carefully obeying the injunction not to walk on the grass, though at this time of year there is precious little of that.

Annie, abruptly changing her mind and her direction, goes back up her staircase. Smogulecki has seriously frightened her. "At the police station." That is code for arrest. But what the hell have they got on her? Who has been saying what to them? If it's all bluff, the detectives are carrying it off pretty well.

Shit, she has a student at noon, no two. Two women, whom she suspects of being lovers, though she has less evidence than the detectives have against her.

37

Another Mind

When, later in the afternoon, Felix comes for his tutorial, she is surprised by the change in him. Physically he is much the same. Still appealing in a teenage idol sort of way. And still weedy. But his attitude has been transformed.

She has moved the topic of his essay away from the dangerous ground of the Rawls project. This despite saying, when they met at the end of the previous term, that they would explore applications of it further. Instead, she has asked him to write on the Other Minds problem. Though it turns out that this too is germane to the present situation.

It's a good essay. He has done the reading. He reaches a conclusion which is at variance to the view she holds. But nothing wrong with that. Annie believes that the real value of philosophy, as taught and practised in the English-speaking countries, is in undergraduate teaching. Preparing the minds of students, the better to wrestle with the conundrums of the real world. Any conclusions in philosophy are at best a way station to a different set of conclusions in the future. As an advanced research topic, it is mostly a waste of time. No actual progress in the subject has been made since the early part of the twentieth century, with the occasional exception, like Rawls's work On Justice. And she hopes, her own project on Rawlsian fairness.

'So, Andrew, you conclude that the privileged access one has to one's own mind, you cannot replicate for the minds of others. You go further and claim that you have no basis for asserting that other minds exist.'

'For the reasons set out in my essay that seems fairly clear. All you have to go on as far as the minds of others are concerned is the way the persons putatively possessing them behave. One is then only entitled to say that patterns of behaviour occur in other individuals but not that they possess self-conscious minds in the way you yourself do.'

'Why is it not legitimate to infer the existence of the mind of another from the actions that the other takes, including what they say and how they look? If they behave quite like you do, is it not most reasonable to assume that they have self-conscious minds as you do?'

'But' insists Andrew, 'we cannot be sure. It remains an inference. This is proved by the fact that sometimes we are wrong about what is in the mind of another person. I can never be wrong about what is in my mind, unless I'm delusional for some reason.'

Now that he is applying his whole attention to the essay topic, and has abandoned his exhibitionist attempt of the Michaelmas term to be a Cambridge undergraduate at the same time as doing PPE at Oxford, the quality of his intelligence is properly shown in his work. Annie is impressed. But she is not yet satisfied that this new Andrew Cameron has sufficiently discarded his old arrogance to tell him so.

'Andrew, would you not concede that a philosophical position such as the one you are taking fails to give a proper account of reality as we perceive it in practice? Have you read Quine on this topic?'

'No, but if he says what you just suggested, he is full of it.'

Annie laughs and is glad she has not praised him.

'Please be less demotic Andrew, and more analytical?'

'Well Quine, is that it, Quine is just plain wrong.'

'And you are not troubled by the fact that your position may lead to Solipsism, the view that the external world, the world outside ourselves, cannot be known? May be assumed not to exist independently of oneself?'

'Well, alright, there are different levels of reality. I am most certain of what is in my own mind. Less certain of the world immediately about me in daily life. And less sure again of things like the nature of the universe.'

'But my dear Andrew, that is approximately what Quine holds.'

'So, Quine agreed with me all along.'

She laughs, and he laughs seeing she is poking fun at his arrogance.

'Andrew we must end there, for the hour is passed. But that last discussion was a genuine philosophical argument in which you thought standing up. On your feet. You should show me more of that side of you, now that apparently you have decided to take the subject seriously.'

'Since the tutorial hour is over, does that mean that I may stop calling you Dr Fritzweiler, Dr Fritzweiler?'

'Yes, "Annie" is OK now.'

'Are you expecting another student?'

'No, you are the last of the day.'

'That's good, because I have something to say to you, Annie.'

'And I to you, Andrew. But please, you may speak first.'

'I have been profoundly changed by my kidnapping, Annie.'

'It appears so to me, Andrew.'

'I have come to value other people more....'

She wonders if he is conscious of the apparent irony of this juxtaposed with his just stated position on Other Minds, but then it is a rare philosopher who behaves consistently with his own theory.

'...And I've come to realise that though I may be cleverer than average undergraduate, there is probably nothing particularly special about me. Rather than posturing all the time as I did last term, I have decided to live real life to the full, each day. It is no good making grandiose plans for the future when one does not know what will happen next week.'

'Carpe diem,' says Annie. She can't tell where this is going exactly, but she has an uneasy feeling that it involves herself in a starring role.

'When I told you last term that I desired you sexually, Annie, you told me that I did not attract you. And you said that you would not even consider going to bed with me unless I became physically much more muscular.'

'Yes, I remember.'

'Well, I see now that what you said was an obvious device to make sure I could never sleep with you. Whatever I do I am never going to be like that guy Otto who lives a couple of floors above you. You must know him, the oarsman.'

'Yes, I know. I can assure you, Andrew that I do not desire

Otto, even though he is a strong, blond German man. And he, I'm very sure hardly notices me beyond greeting me formally whenever we see each other.'

'Actually, that's not true Annie. As it happens, I've spoken to him a few times and he told me that whenever he passes you on the staircase, he gets a...that is, that he feels desire for you.'

'That is most surprising, if true, but it in no way changes my view of him.'

'Well, that clears one thing out of the way. Look, Annie, what I want to tell you is that I have to have you, now. Live life to the fullest each day. No nonsense about building up my body. I mean I'll do my best but even without that I'm sure I can satisfy you sexually. But you have to give me a chance, at least one chance.'

'Andrew, I do not have to give you a chance, as you put it. Sex between two people, morally requires the consent of both. And I do not at present consent to have sex with you, Andrew. I am flattered that you think about me in that way, but I simply do not feel the same. That is the end of this conversation.'

But an increasing sense of foreboding tells her that it will not be the end. For she has now understood, what till now was a puzzle, that the reason that Andrew spoke to the police of a "she" who could have been directing the kidnapping was to have something to hold over her.

In a moment he is going to tell me that, she thinks. And in a moment, he does.

'I don't like to do it like this, Annie, because I have such overwhelming feelings for you. But I am so desperate, and I can see no other way to change your mind. So, Annie could you please lead the way into your bedroom next door.'

She is horrified, though she knows she shouldn't be. It's just a teenage crush run way out of control. Andrew cannot see the normal social limits that govern the behaviour of most people. So, she replies calmly enough.

'Even were I inclined to give in to your blackmail, Andrew, which I am not, you must understand that having sex with an unwilling partner is profoundly unsatisfying to oneself.'

'How would you know, Annie, since you are not a man?'

At this stage she has no energy to go further in arguing with him. Though in the back of her mind she acknowledges that his approach is at least consistent with the idea that whether the minds of others exist is unknowable. One of the less pleasant moral consequences of that position is that others may not be valued equally with oneself.

Well, she must explain to him, in terms even an Other Mind can accept, why, on purely practical grounds, his attempt at blackmail won't work.

'Andrew, what you are trying to do simply won't work. It

is already too late. You have done the biggest damage you can do by mentioning that "she". The detectives are now convinced that I am "she" and they will persist until they find evidence or have to invent it.'

'But if you cooperate, I can tell the police that I was wrong about "she". It was "he", or I never heard anything.'

'Oh yes, so how will you explain your mistake, Andrew? Even if you can think of something, and after all we both know that you were actually mistaken, they won't believe you. On the strength of what you told them the detectives have already made certain false connections which they won't relinquish now whatever you may now say to them. I am not saying that they will ever get a conviction in the English courts. But if they decide to pursue their so-called case against me, then over the months and years while they try to make their case, they may make my life intolerable and my job untenable.'

For the first time since Annie has met him, Andrew is speechless. Annie believes that the mention of "she" by Andrew to the detectives gives them only a basis for interrogating her and for seeking further evidence against her. It surely cannot constitute on its own enough to charge her with a crime. But she blesses her luck that, what Andrew apparently has not realised is that he knows something further which really might be fatal to her with the detectives.

'I must now consider, Andrew, whether to report this outrage...'

He seems genuinely puzzled.

'The outrage of trying to blackmail me, Andrew, into granting sexual favours to you. Report you to the College authorities. Should I decide to do so, you will undoubtedly be sent down at once and debarred from re-entering this University, and effectively any University of standing in the English-speaking world.'

'But it's your word against mine.'

'You are an undergraduate in bad standing with the University, since your parallel residence in Cambridge was in breach of University statutes. I am a tenured Fellow of this College and a University Lecturer. Which of us do you imagine will be believed, Andrew?'

'But you wouldn't destroy my academic career, my life? I could turn out to be brilliant, make a contribution.'

'That, Andrew, is a point. But I may decide that your offence is so grave that I have no choice but to report you. In the meantime, it is obvious that I should not continue to act as your tutor in philosophy. I will find someone else to teach you. It is a great pity for today for the first time I thought you might turn out to be an excellent student. Perhaps the best in philosophy in the College in your year. Now please leave me and do not return. I will notify you in writing if I decide to report your conduct to the authorities.'

He leaves, without a word, without hope. As the door closes

Annie Fritzweiler picks up the phone and calls the Tutor in Law at the College, Martin Peters. He is a man of her own age with whom she thinks she should become better acquainted.

38

The Hounds of Spring

The following day, Oxford is transformed. The hounds of spring appear to be on winter's traces, in that ungainly but oddly memorable metaphor of Swinburne's. The temperature has risen twenty degrees. In place of the stinging flurries of sleet, a gentle breeze blows up the Banbury Road from the South. And Annie Fritzweiler has a date for lunch.

It's a Saturday, so she can spend the morning at home and make a leisurely toilette. Annie knows she shouldn't, but the mood of the day is such that she dresses in what she knows will please her guest. Her long mirror reflects back to her an image which she feels sufficiently suitable to her age. It's just the effect on her guest that could be inappropriate.

Annie is early at the new bistro, the signboard of which proclaims it to be The Bistro. It is only ten minutes' walk from her flat. The place opened only a couple of weeks previously, in defiance of the cold New Year. It's small, barely twenty covers, and has a very limited menu. In fact, you eat what the chef has decided to cook that day. The place is already filling up by the time they arrive: her vodka martini and her guest. She extricates herself from behind her corner table so he can more conveniently kiss her. She is at once aware that her dress choice has worked but is still unsure whether it was wise.

Annie catches the waiter's eye. Yes, we are ready now and ravenous. And yes, we'll have a bottle of the house red, claimed to be a cut above the average, according to the slight menu. But first we will have a glass each of very cold Sancerre, as the menu recommends, to go with the starter.

In light of his then apparently dire financial situation, she has persuaded David Cameron to cancel the best restaurant in Oxford, to which he had in a previous life invited her, in favour of this untried bistro. She has insisted that she will pay. To her surprise he looks very well. That expression of constant stress and confusion has been replaced by a new confidence, which she has not seen before and which she finds appealing. It would, she feels sure, have been a very happy lunch were it not for what she has to tell him.

But before she can open her mouth, he cannot resist starting on his own affairs. Annie laughs in astonishment as he describes the Christmas flash sales estimates. His imitations of Goran are almost up to his son's standard. And his compliments of her appearance are rather more elegant than those of his son. It's one of the things she likes about him that by wearing nice, but perfectly ordinary clothes, she appears to be able to drive him into a state of excitement. It surely speaks to his good taste.

Adding to the mood and to the premature spring weather, the new chef has done his guests proud. In such circumstances it should be easy to forget one's troubles. But once she has sufficiently congratulated David on his return to literary success, she forces herself to return to the matters that press on her mind.

Annie thinks she probably will tell David the whole thing. He is, after all, a man of the world. Perhaps he really could give her some perspective and, more importantly, support her evidence to the police in one or two critical areas.

But David interrupts her before she has begun.

'I can tell you have something serious to say, Annie. But the day is so beautiful, and you look so nice, let us postpone serious matters for a few minutes at least.'

Annie notes that it is the day that is asserted to be definitely beautiful, she merely seems to be nice. She can't help it, this analysing of words. It's an occupational hazard. But she is happy to begin on the starter before her serious topics.

David Cameron had resolved to distance himself from Annie in order to respond more whole heartedly to his wife's new pale, slim look, brought on by her son's kidnapping and return, and her new-found devotion to his own needs. This in turn supported by the Christmas book sales flash estimate.

He finds that his resolution has not survived thirty seconds in Annie's company. But why? Objectively considered there is nothing special about Annie Fritzweiler. But in affairs of the heart, for what does objectivity count?

They pick up their wine, touch glasses, and drink. He looks into her wide-open periwinkle blue eyes and smiles. She is all his. He is almost sure. After all Annie has been loyal to him throughout the kidnap crisis, whereas his wife of thirty something years was half way to the divorce court when she heard the propaganda of the professionals that her first book was a winner and his last a catastrophe.

As knives slice delicately into the dish before them, David Cameron opens the conversation.

'You know, Annie, I think his kidnap did Felix good. He's sobered right down. Might make something of himself now, with your help, my sweet.'

'From what I can see, he might fall off the rails.'

Annie rebukes herself silently. Let us enjoy the start of the meal at least. They chew, consider, and chew some more in companionable silence.

'What exactly do you mean, Annie, about Felix going off the rails?'

'David, this seared foie gras is absolutely scrumptious.'

'Yes, but I don't eat foie gras, in principle,' says the novelist absently finishing the last morsel on his plate. 'Annie, you remember the charities to which I was forced to give all my money?'

She does.

'Elephants Are Us and Elephant Emergency...are merging. Throwing a big party at the Savoy. I'm invited guest of honour,' he adds bemused. 'I wonder if it's quite appropriate for them to be using my money to fund a free flow of champagne. Do you think I should go?'

'Make your excuses, I should,' says Annie. 'Speaking of excuses, I suddenly need to go to the loo. I won't be a moment.'

She sets aside her napkin, uncrosses her legs and carefully gets up. She is conscious of his eyes on her as she expected. Be nice to him, she thinks, and put him in a sympathetic mood to hear her story. No heads turn as she walks the length of the place, but she knows David Cameron's gaze is on her every step of the way.

She doesn't actually need to relieve herself, but like someone in a spy novel thinks she should go through the motions. Her East German upbringing, she reflects. On emerging, she checks her make-up in the rather inadequate mirror provided, before walking slowly back to the table.

Within a couple of minutes, the main course arrives. It is the new chef's piece de resistance. Though in the moment before tasting, Annie has no idea what it is.

Red wine is poured exactly on time. She certainly knows what that is, sniffs, sips and approves.

But Annie thinks matters can wait no longer, or, before they get into it, she will be forced to invite him back to her flat and she knows to what that will lead. And it is not the time for that, if ever.

'Were you aware, David, that your son had become fixated on me, sexually?'

He is hardly surprised. He is totally electrocuted with shock.

'But he's only a kid, a puny little squirt. You must be mistaken.'

'David, I know when someone is trying to get into my knickers, especially if the method employed is blackmail.'

She describes the conversation with him after his last tutorial with her, earlier in the week.

David can't credit it. Some mistake. He couldn't have meant it. A poor joke misunderstood. Finally, he is brought to believe what she is telling him. His fury with his son is without bounds.

'You and the College should prosecute him, Annie.'

Annie describes what she is thinking of doing.

'But that would destroy his whole future. He could be a brilliant, writer, thinker, anything. Annie, you can't destroy all that promise.

'A moment ago, you wanted me to prosecute him.'

'It's a foul thing to have attempted. But Annie, to destroy the boy's future before it has begun?'

'Perhaps you would have preferred me to give in to his blackmail.'

'To sleep with him? No, of course not. The idea is absurd. But Annie, the police would never believe all that nonsense, not in a month of Sundays.'

'But David they do believe it. At least they want to believe it. As soon as Andrew mentioned "she" to the detectives, they seem to have formed the unshakeable belief that I am "she". They were desperate for a lead, and since they had no other, I did very well.'

'But you are nothing to do with it.' She can see his mind working. 'Nothing at all. I mean, are you Annie?'

It depends what you mean by 'nothing at all', she thinks.

'Of course not, David. The only point of possible contact with the kidnapping is the coincidence that in our tutorial a few days before, we did discuss the idea of whether there were circumstances in which it would be just to coerce wealthy people to give away their money in order to increase economic fairness.'

'Oh, you mean like my being forced to give away all my money to elephants in order to get Felix back?'

Even in the grim circumstances, Annie laughs. It's the elephants that does it.

'Yes, but of course not that. But more generally devising methods to coerce rich people into giving away their money or some of it to those in greater need. In other words, methods of putting the Rawlsian project of fairness into practice. Kidnapping as a method of coercion was mentioned in that context. But it was just a bizarre coincidence with Andrew's subsequent actual kidnapping.'

She wonders if David believes that is all there was to it. Or is a doubt even now seeping into his mind? She seeks to scotch such a thing.

'Felix has tried to destroy me, and he may have succeeded, whatever I do. David, do you still think as you were inclined to during the kidnapping itself, that Felix organised it himself, or was at least complicit? I mean he had read your novel in which a similar event takes place.'

'Oh yes, THE RIGHTEOUS AND THE DAMNED.'

'And my tutorial may have revived the idea in his mind. Then relations between you and him have not been so easy lately, have they?'

'That is certainly true, though better since he's returned. As I said he is much less full of himself than before. I suppose because of that I now rather think he was not implicated in organising the kidnapping. But Annie, even if Felix did intend to force you to have sex with him, he is not capable of such a thing. I mean physically he is no colossus.'

'The point of the disclosure threat obviously is that no force is necessary. I was supposed to be so terrified by the consequences of not going along with him that he could count on passive submission.'

The thought of what Andrew might have imagined he could make her passively submit to makes Annie shiver.

In the concentration of the moment the Chef's piece de resistance has been cut into but not tasted. Knives and forks lie askew. The conversation is so intense, each staring into the other's eyes as if to read truth or intention there, that neither notices the Chef has arrived at their table expecting to gather further plaudits, as is his due.

But what the Chef sees exceeds his worst nightmare. A woman with periwinkle blue eyes and an immaculately tailored older man completely taken up with each other. The best dish of his career lying ignored and scorned before them, displaced by what he is sure is their mutual regard. There is only one thing to do and Luke Cameron does it. He picks up David Cameron's untouched plate and brings it down with all his might on the top of his father's head.

39

Two Into One Doesn't Go

Annie follows Luke into the broom cupboard that serves as his kitchen, calms him with a kiss on the cheek and helps to get the dessert service back on course. She then goes to clean up the mess Luke has made on their table.

The mess Luke has made of the bald area on top of his father's head, hardly healed from his mother's efforts with the family teapot, is cleaned up to the best of his rather poorly remembered skills by the University's Joseph Lister Professor of Infectious Diseases, who happened to be lunching with his wife two tables away.

When the restaurant can safely be left in the hands of Luke's assistant and when David feels he can safely walk a short distance, Annie invites both men back to her flat. There is nowhere else. At least, thinks Annie, this afternoon she is safe from being seduced.

David, of course, has other ideas.

'Well Luke, I'm feeling much better. I think we can let you go back The Bistro now.'

Luke gets up uncertainly, looking at Annie.

'Luke, I wonder if you would be very kind and make us coffee. There's a machine in the kitchen, but I've never properly got the hang of it.'

She leads him into the kitchen, pulling the door shut behind her, and gets out the coffee beans and milk. Then she watches him prepare the coffee, with her back against the kitchen door.

'What do you prefer, um...?'

He's too in awe of her even to use her name.

'Please call me Annie. And I'll have double espresso please.'

'I'll do yours last, Annie. That way it will still be at its best when you drink it.'

He bends to his task and Annie watches him carefully, though whether only to learn how better to make coffee is not clear. She's hardly noticed him before. They've exchanged barely half a dozen words. Now she registers that he is much the best looking of the Cameron family. Medium height with a moderate muscularity which speaks of the gym, but somehow not the supplement-fuelled body building she associates with homosexual men. No, she's very clear on that score. She fancies she can feel waves of lust coming off him.

What Luke sees when he looks up from his task is a woman of five foot two, nicely done fair hair falling to just short of her shoulders. Little make up and only a thin line of red lipstick to deflect from the appearance of her forty something years. Trim body. She stands leaning against the kitchen door, one leg flexed so the base of her foot presses against it. Her orange top discloses a pleasant amount of cleavage. Her grey skirt, falling just short of her knees suggests strong thighs. Her elegant brown boots come half-way up her calves. He wants only to take her in his arms. The rest of the world, the rest of time, can go to hell. She smiles.

'I think that one may be ready, Luke.'

'Oh yes, of course. I can't imagine what I was thinking of.'

'Perhaps me,' she murmurs in a voice low enough that you might be in doubt that she had actually spoken.

Annie loves this game. Although she knows she shouldn't, she sometimes plays it with her students. Of course, it can have bad consequences, as with Felix.

'The lunch was the best I've had anywhere in recent memory,' she says, more clearly.

'But you hardly ate it.'

'We ate the starter. It's just that we got on to the unfortunate events surrounding your brother before the entree arrived. My fault I'm afraid. Don't worry I will come back to have it next time you make it.'

The three coffees are ready. Luke puts them on a tray.

'There's a bottle of schnapps in the cupboard directly above your head. Perhaps you could pour three glasses.'

She comes over to him as if to take the tray and looks up into his face. Oddly it's not her periwinkle blue eyes of which he is conscious at that moment, but the fact that she is reaching up to kiss him lightly on the lips and to murmur: 'I'm sorry Luke.'

As she had perhaps intended, Luke cannot help himself. He pulls her tightly against him, kisses the side of her neck and slides one hand up her thigh. She sighs deep in her being and whispers to him.

'Luke, not now. Your father will be fretting.'

And indeed, a moment later the kitchen door opens and David is inquiring if everything is alright.

'I was about to seduce your good-looking son,' she says by way of explanation. 'But perhaps it would be better that we should first have coffee and schnapps.'

David might have taken that for a pleasantry were it not for the fact that he notices that Annie's skirt is caught up slightly on one side.

In the living room, they sit, father and son, at either end of the couch on which Annie sometimes lies full length to think, and sometimes to sleep. She sits facing them, on a small chair, her knees nicely together.

Now Annie is all business.

For Luke's benefit, she goes over the ground of Felix's attempt to blackmail her and of the apparent certainty in the minds of the detectives that she is the "she" mentioned between two of his kidnappers, half overheard, or perhaps not overheard at all, by Felix. She takes a risk and tells them everything the police have said. But then it's not much of a risk since she assumes the Cameron family will all be re-interviewed by the detectives and they will trail everything they think they know about her as bait. 'Just for the record, could you confirm that...?'

David pounces on what is for him the point of interest.

'So, Annie, the police think there is a connection between you and Sergei Dzhugashvili?'

'There is a connection. I do see him from time to time at academic conferences. Amazingly he finds time to be a serious international law professor as well as an Oligarch.'

'He told me he was only a hired hand,' says David.

'That is the sort of thing he would say, yes David.'

'But Annie, the fact that you are fellow academics is hardly a basis for...'

'The police were more interested in the fact that I was once married to him, many years ago, before the Berlin Wall fell, when I was living in Eastern Germany.'

'So how is that relevant?'

'It isn't David. It's just that the police have no other leads. That is, they have no leads at all. So, on the basis of imagination and perhaps DS Smogulecki's suspicion of Russians from her early life in Poland, they have come up with the idea that the kidnappers were Russian hard men of Sergei's. The sort of guys an Oligarch would naturally have hanging around, or so they imagine. It would also tend to explain how the gang disappeared so completely. Returned to Russia, no questions asked, immediately on releasing Felix.'

'But there is absolutely no evidence, Annie?'

'None. But they've been told to find the kidnappers. So, they feel they have to try anything, however wild.'

'But popular opinion turns out to be rather in favour of the kidnappers. Apparently, the British public approves of all my money being taken away.'

'That's because you gave those stupid speeches,' Luke intervenes, 'about how it was immoral that the rich didn't give up of at least some of their wealth to help the poor. And you said if they wouldn't do it voluntarily then they should be made to. And you wrote a novel in which the hero kidnaps the son of rich family to force them to surrender their wealth in order to get their son back. That's right, isn't it, Dad? As I remember it, your book was all in favour of the kidnappers.'

'Luke, none of that justifies blackmailing me to force me to give away....'

'I suppose...,' Annie intervenes to divert things away from further violence between father and son. 'I suppose public opinion is rather fickle and in future there might be questions to the authorities why they didn't make a proper investigation. Certainly, from the detectives I got the feeling they were under a lot of pressure to crack the case. You do say "crack" don't you?'

She smiles at Luke, but it is David who quickly replies.

'Yes Annie. "Crack" is quite idiomatic. But the police case is dead ended. Or do you think your ex will want to take the opportunity pin the blame on you for some reason? Are you on bad terms?'

'Not that I know of. We're quite friendly all things considered, though neither of us likes to be reminded of the fact that we were once married to the other. I suppose I can trust you both not to mention it.'

'Absolutely, Annie,' says Luke.

'But the police know,' objects David. 'How is that Annie?'

'Oh, if you have the right credentials, if you are the British police, then the Documentation Centre in Berlin will tell you anything you want to know about what went on in the GDR, East Germany, before nineteen ninety.'

'It seems to me that you have nothing to worry about, my sweet,' says David. 'Since you were not involved in the kidnapping, Annie, if Sergei plays it straight and denies any involvement...'

'At least any involvement by me,' says Annie carefully. 'We have to remember, somebody actually did kidnap Felix, whether with his cooperation or not. We all saw the gang smash up the restaurant and take him away. I suppose the rest of the kidnap story Felix might have contrived by himself, without assistance, but it's a bit unlikely, isn't it, even for Felix?'

'Couldn't Felix have left the restaurant with the kidnappers voluntarily?'

'Yes, David, that is possible. But Felix could not have smashed up the restaurant. We all saw the gang do that.'

But still David and Luke both seem convinced that somehow Felix might have contrived the gang's action, Annie is happy to note.

David resumes.

'If Sergei Dzhugashvili denies your involvement and no doubt his own, then the police are back to square one, aren't they?'

Would that they were, thinks Annie. She is not yet quite ready to tell David and Luke absolutely the whole story. But David is now studying his expensive looking watch.

'Actually, sad to say, I'd better be getting back.'

David has told Davina, in her new attention to all his concerns, that he has lunch in Oxford with a publishing connection. Even if he leaves now, it will be four thirty before he gets back home. Much later than that would strain the credibility of the bonhomie of even the longest business lunch.

'But Dad, you're hardly fit to drive.' Luke glances at his Swatch. 'At a stretch I can leave it till five thirty to get back to The Bistro. And you are hardly in a state to go on the back of my motorbike, so I'll drive you in your car.'

'But how will you get back for five thirty, Luke?' asks Annie. 'You drive David's car, Luke, and I'll follow in my car to bring you back here. I've nothing on until the evening.'

Both men look surprised. David concerned and Luke pleased. So, Annie goes round to the back of the huge Victorian house, which was recently converted into flats, including hers, to get her car. It's much colder than earlier and Annie suddenly wants a loo. However, everyone is in a hurry now, so she decides to hold on.

She drives the two men the short distance down the Banbury Road to where, after merging with the Woodstock Road, it widens by St. John's to permit car parking on the further side of the road and in the middle. Then she waits while Luke clears the parking tickets and flyers from the windscreen of his father's car. She notices that on the strength of the Christmas flash sales estimates, David has exchanged his micro for a large Mercedes. Then they are off, in convoy.

On arrival, Annie parks discreetly at the bottom of the Camerons' very long drive. The urge to relieve herself is greater now. Of course, she could ask to go in and use a loo in the house. But she does not want, at least at this moment, to complicate David's life more than necessary.

Within a minute, Luke comes running down the drive. He climbs in beside her and she sets off back on the road across the Downs on which they have come. It's already beginning to get dark, but there is little traffic.

Annie drives as fast as she dares, but it's no good.

'Dad was pretty pissed off that you were driving me back to Oxford. Is there something between you?'

'Of course not. Not as far as I'm concerned. Your father will no doubt speak for himself. Luke, I'm sorry, but I'm going to have to stop for a moment.'

She bumps the car carefully onto the verge, where the grass is billiard table smooth from the attentions of the sheep. She turns off the car lights, gets out and goes round to Luke's side of the car. She reckons it is just about dark enough. Anyway, there is no choice.

Luke has got out also, with a flashlight he has found under his seat. He points it at the ground so Annie can find a place free of sheep droppings. Then he stands a few feet away from her, on guard. Annie pushes her knickers down over her thighs and squats. The shock of the cold coming up from the ground a few inches below her stops her for a moment, but then it's OK. The beam from the flashlight reflects off her knees. Luke can probably see between her thighs, she thinks.

'Luke, turn it off.'

He does so. She is shivering by the time she has finished. At least the cold may cool Luke's ardour. Annie stands up. Her knickers are wet so, no help for it, she pulls them off over her boots. They both get in the car and she drives carefully back onto the road surface and then fast, on towards Oxford. If they can make it to the suburbs, she reckons she is safe. But perhaps not. She reckons Luke has had an erection since shortly after they left his parent's village.

It's not so much the idea of allowing Luke to have his way with her that she hates. It's that she doesn't want to be a mere repository for the urgent detritus of male lust. Even if she has been the active cause of it.

They are abruptly on the Banbury Road.

'Left here,' he says 'and just a couple of hundred yards down on the left.'

She draws the car to a halt just beyond the restaurant. It's twenty to six and it's unnaturally dark. For some reason the streetlights have not come on. An electrical fault or Oxford City Council saving money. Luke tries to embrace her despite the inconvenience of the gear leaver.

'Annie, I'm so sorry but I have everything in the world tied up in this little place. The little money I had, professional reputation, all my hopes. And then there are the guys who put up the finance. I just can't not get everything perfect for every service.'

It takes Annie a moment or two to understand. He is apologising to her for not, well for not servicing her, because he is needed to prep for dinner in the bistro. Food before sex.

Several thoughts go through her mind.

First that he is a very good looking and probably, given the right circumstances, charming young man. His assumption might naturally be that a woman in this sort of situation would desire him. Especially, a woman of forty-nine, who has virtually given herself to him in her own kitchen, with his father in the next room.

Then that he is a very responsible young man not to give in

to the imperatives of desire when he has a business to get off the ground.

And finally, that she wants him terribly.

'Luke,' she says below a whisper. 'Luke come round when you're done with service. However late it is.'

But he merely brushes her lips with his own and is gone.

Slowly she makes a three-point turn and slowly she drives back to her flat. She parks and walks round to the main entrance, fumbling for her keys. She is about to unlock the front door when a voice halts her.

'Dr Fritzweiler, we wonder if you could spare us a few minutes.'

It is Tench and Smogulecki. They loom out of the darkness.

'Down at the station, if you wouldn't mind. You see we have had a very interesting conversation with Mr. Sergei Dzhugashvili.'

But all Annie can think of at that moment is that she is not wearing any knickers.

40

Annie and the Detectives

She negotiates with the detectives for a few minutes to go up to her flat. There she packs an overnight bag which the detectives have suggested she may need. Then she takes a shower, which the detectives have not suggested she needs. But after all, are they going to stop her? The detectives sit in her living room, at either end of her couch, waiting.

From the bathroom, leaving the shower running, she calls her new friend, Martin Peters, the Law Fellow at her College. Her experience of human rights was in a country where such things scarcely existed, so in this country she is a bit at sea. Peters says that she should on no account go to the police station, unless they have a warrant for her arrest. In that case she should demand that they go nowhere until her solicitor has reviewed the warrant. He will get a pal, a criminal defence solicitor to come to her house now. This woman knows the ropes of police procedure much better than he. In the interim she should say nothing to the police.

On emergence from the shower, she tells this to the detectives. She is wearing a bath robe. A nice touch of defiance she thinks, but one to which they probably can't object. She sits opposite them, in her small chair. They look at each other. Smogulecki shrugs.

'Perhaps on reflection there is no need to drag you down to the station at this time of night,' DI Tench begins.

Annie looks at her watch and smiles. It's only six thirty.

'Professor Dzhugashvili...' What has the poor man done in life to deserve these alien tongue twisters, Dzhugashvili and Smogulecki? '...Professor Dzhugashvili....Well to cut a longish story short...'

'Why don't you call him Sergei?' says Annie. 'I do. You'll find it easier.'

Tench frowns. But he is not diverted.

'Professor Dzhugashvili told us that you had asked him about supplying men to carry out the kidnap of Felix Cameron. As he was a friend of yours and generally in sympathy with your, may we say, somewhat advanced views on public morality, he gave you a contact which might meet your needs.'

The pause goes on forever. Annie cannot believe she's just heard. She feels the need to be sick, but forces herself to be still. Eventually Tench again.

'We wondered, Dr Fritzweiler, if you would care to comment.'

Yes, she would care to comment. What the hell does Sergei think he is up to? She'll have his balls for this.

'No.'

'No, what, Dr Fritzweiler?'

'No, I wouldn't care to comment, at least until I have legal advice and possibly not then.'

'Come now Dr Fritzweiler, it looks rather black against you for you not to answer a key question like this. Almost suggests as if you were unable to answer without incriminating yourself,' DS Smogulecki insists.

'Dr Fritzweiler, this is not a formal police interview.' DI Tench, emollient as ever. 'Nothing is being recorded.'

Except in your minds, and immediately afterwards in your notebooks, thinks Annie.

'You have no need to have legal representation in attendance at an interview like this. Little more than a friendly chat. What we all want is to get at the truth, isn't that so? So, we can be out of your hair as soon as possible.' Smogulecki's version of trying to be sympathetic?

'You, Detective Sergeant, have no right to question me.'

She is tempted to throw them out, which Martin Peters has told her she is entitled to do, unless they show her this supposed warrant and it is valid. She will if this solicitor does not show up in the next ten minutes. But she wants to see the police given their marching orders by someone who knows what he is talking about.

They sit in silence. From time to time the detectives seek at least to revive the conversation.

Smogulecki. 'May I have a glass of water?'

Annie: 'No.'

Smogulecki. 'May I use your washroom?'

Annie. 'No. There is a public facility at the bottom of the Banbury Road.'

Annie knows, as many an undergraduate with drink taken has discovered to his or her cost that the Banbury Road public lavatory is shut and padlocked after dark. The image of DS Smogulecki relieving herself in the gutter under the windows of Balliol College rather appeals to Annie, but she knows that the Polish woman has no actual need of a loo.

The entry buzzer goes off. In a couple of minutes an out-of-breath, overweight woman in her forties is in Annie's living room, dripping on her Persian rug. Unnoticed by Annie or by the detectives, there has been a cloud burst over Oxford, improbably enough given the cold, clear evening of an hour or so earlier.

Annie guides her visitor to a safer piece of floor, takes her sodden coat and gives her a towel to wipe herself off.

Somewhat recovered, the criminal solicitor introduces herself to Annie. Priti Patel. She does not introduce herself to the police since it at once becomes apparent that they are the best of friends.

'Marie, good to see you. Tench, you old rogue, trying to rough up my client in the comfort of her own home? Annie, any chance of a coffee?'

Annie ignores the last remark. It's a long time since she read Franz Kafka's THE TRIAL, which in any case was not really approved reading in the GDR, but she can recall no scene in that novel as Kafkaesque as what is going on in her living room now.

'OK, anyone like to fill me in? Martin was only able to give me the merest outline on the phone. The important thing was to get round here pronto and stop you two beating my client black and blue, he said. By the way Annie, it's a hundred and fifty an hour if that's all right. Because its weekend and after six. Only ninety an hour in office hours. Modest enough I think you'll agree?'

Annie resists the temptation to burst into tears. Instead, she gives a brief, lucid account of her questioning by the police, including their account of Felix's kidnapping.

The detectives have nothing to add except persiflage, save for one thing.

'We've been trying to deal with Dr Fritzweiler in as friendly and informal a way as possible.'

'Pull the other one, Tench.'

Annie wonders if DI Tench is like that old detective on TV years ago. She used to watch it in the unified Germany on some late-night channel. The one who was always addressed by his surname because he was ashamed of his Christian name, or something like that.

'You heard what my client said,' Priti continues. 'You've been worrying at her, like a dog with a bone, because unlike a dog you've got no lead.'

She laughs heartily at this though no one else even raises a smile.

'But Priti, we have a lead.'

And Tench tells her about their interview of Sergei, the one element Annie left out of her summary.

'OK people. You must let me speak to my client. You two go back to your homes, if you have any. Annie and I will chew the fat for a bit. I'll be in touch on Monday. How's that?'

The detectives seem to feel they have no choice but to agree.

As they close Annie's front door behind them, Priti plonks herself down in the middle of Annie's couch.

'I don't think they even had a warrant. And I don't think I could fit in that chair. Now Annie, tell me about this Sergei Dzhugashvili. No, my love, don't do that. Go and make us both a cup of coffee and if you've got any biscuits...? That bugger Martin tore me away from my family dinner table. You'd have thought your house was on fire the way he went on.'

So, Annie goes to make coffee. On her return the solicitor has got out a legal pad, a ballpoint and has switched her mobile phone to audio record. At the back of her cupboard Annie has found an unopened but long past sell-by-date packet of chocolate biscuits. She has shaken half of them out on a plate and now nervously puts the plate down in front of Priti.

'Annie, that fact summary you gave just now was absolutely wizard. Not a lawyer in a thousand could have done it as well. What do you do in life? A philosopher! Oh yes Martin said you were a colleague. I always wondered what they did.'

'It's all about being clear,' says Annie. 'At least in my view it is. Then applying that clarity to various areas of human experience. In my case ethics, or more precisely the application of various theories of morality to public life. Hence my interest in the Cameron kidnapping. There the kidnappers appear to have taken nothing for themselves but forced David Cameron to give away the whole of his assets to charity.'

'Oh yes, it was on TV a lot recently, wasn't it? Anyway Annie, best I take a few personal details if that's OK. Do you mind if I record? More chance I get things right that way. So, you're a German citizen? But you intend to stay indefinitely in the UK.'

'I have a tenured Fellowship at my College here.'

'And which College? Right. My daughter's there now as it happens, Sandra Patel. Doing law, of course. Place of birth. Germany, of course. East eh? Date of birth? So, you'll be, what, forty-nine? Honestly Annie, I'd never have guessed. How do you do it? Though now I look at you closely, your face is quite lined. One advantage we Indians have. We may get to be fat as pigs, some of us, but we tend not to show so many wrinkles.'

Priti bursts out laughing, through a mouthful of chocolate biscuit.

'These are scrumptious by the way. You don't eat them? I suppose that is why you look the way you do, and I look the way I do. OK my love, that's enough about you. Oh, one more, marital status. Divorced. Fine. Half my clients seem to be these days.'

Annie is not sure she is comforted by this. A good proportion of Priti's clients presumably are criminals.

'We've got that out of the way. No chance of a refresh?'

Annie takes the plate, goes to the kitchen and empties the remaining chocolate biscuits on to it. On return, it is at last business.

'Tell me about this Sergei Dzhugashvili....'

So, she does.

'What he says about you asking for men to carry out the kidnap, is that correct or not?'

Annie hesitates.

'Look, Annie my love, we can do this one of two ways. You can tell me the whole truth, all of it. Or you can lie selectively. I've defended many clients successfully who lied through their teeth. I could see it, the prosecution and the Judge could see it, but not the Jury.'

'I was rather hoping this wouldn't come to Court.'

'Quite right, Annie my sweet. And I'll do my damnedest to make sure it doesn't. Actually, it's usually better if you tell me the truth.'

'Usually?'

'Ah that's the philosopher in you. What of course I should have said was that it was probably better. It's probably better if you tell me the truth since then I know where the elephant traps lie. If you decide to do that, it will be entirely between us. Well, in practice my secretary has to know. But she's been with me for half a century. Seems like that anyway. And whilst she is a great worker, stays to all hours and so on, she doesn't understand one end of a legal sentence from the other. That way I don't have to cut off her ears at the start of each case.'

A great guffaw and another spray of chocolate biscuit crumbs. Annie smiles weakly.

'Look my sweet, you don't have to decide now, about telling the whole truth. You could phone a friend. Sleep on it overnight. We could even do all this first thing Monday morning, if you prefer. Though I did say I'd get back to that bugger Tench on Monday. You should watch out for him you know. That Smogulecki's full of sound and fury but most of it signifies nothing.'

'Rather what I thought,' says Annie. 'Macbeth isn't it,' she adds, 'sound and fury?'

'Search me, Annie. I pick up this nonsense from being around the Courts all day. Don't know why I do it. Don't need the money. My husband makes a fortune out of his corner shops.'

Annie tries to look impressed.

'He does have a hundred and fifty of them.'

Another guffaw, though minor. Why, Annie wonders, does this woman laugh only when her mouth is full of chocolate biscuit.

'Priti Ps they're called. Mainly in the Midlands,' Annie's lawyer adds. 'It would be better though if we decided things now. Sorry, there's me rabbiting on, confusing you. Better if we decided how much of the truth you're going to tell me.'

'It's not a question of that, Ms. Patel. In order to give you the full picture, I need to understand something first. To do that I need, as you put it, to phone a friend.'

'This Sergei Dzhugashvili I suppose. Sounds like a good idea, to get your story straight between you. All right Annie, Mr. Patel will be happy I'm not too late. Saturday nights is when we do it you see. That and Wednesdays. Regular as clockwork. Not bad for a man of seventy. And then I get a bit on the side now and then. You'd be surprised the men who get turned on by us fatties.'

Annie isn't so much surprised as comprehensively gob smacked. Twice a week and the odd bit on the side. She can barely remember the last time she slept with a man.

The solicitor heaves herself up and Annie accompanies her to the door.

'Look Annie, Dr Fritzweiler, I'm sorry if I put you off. It's just the way I am. Helps me to get along with all the odds and sods I have to deal with in a day's work. If you have doubts about me, talk to Martin. He could get you someone else, but he wouldn't have recommended me to you if he didn't think

I was the best.'

'Look, Ms Patel, Priti, thank you so much for coming out on a Saturday night at such short notice. I'm sorry if I've been ungracious. It's just a shock. All of it.'

'Annie, you are a sweet woman. Call me as soon as you can. At home tomorrow, Sunday, would be best. You've got my mobile. I'll keep it on for you.'

As she listens to the Indian woman heavily descending the two flights of stairs to the ground floor, she thinks that probably she is in good hands, jolly good hands. Now what she has to do is get hold of Sergei Dzhugashvili and try to work out what species of game he is playing.

41

St. James's Park

Getting hold of Sergei is not so hard. What is hard to well-nigh impossible is to get hold of Sergei quickly. Oligarchs may be available on demand to their squeeze of the moment, to people to whom they owe a debt of any kind and to the Kremlin if they are in good standing there. But to no one else, no one else at all, normally speaking.

In the past Annie would go through the International Law Department at his Institute in St. Petersburg but it's midnight there now and a weekend. Anyway, the average response time using that route is at least a week. She has a day. She wracks her brain. An inspiration. Wildly unlikely but just possible.

'Davina, Davina Cameron? It's Annie Fritzweiler.'

Annie is not entirely sure of her welcome, but Davina is all smiles, or whatever corresponds for the telephone. After all she's got her son back, now on best behaviour after the shock of his kidnapping. And she's got her lifestyle back if the Christmas sales flash stats are right.

'Annie; you were so helpful to us during the crisis. Then we seemed to see you all the time and now when everything is fine again, we never see you. Come for lunch...Ah term time... You don't know whether you're coming or going. I know the feeling....'

Like hell she does, thinks Annie.

'All right, we'll be patient and wait till the vacation. Then you can come to Monday lunch and see Felix and Luke. The Bistro is closed on Mondays you see. But I expect you see Felix all the time in College...Oh I see, you're not teaching him this term.'

Annie makes a firm resolution not to be available in the Easter vacation. Perhaps she'll go skiing, if she can find anyone to go skiing with. Since Davina is in such a good mood, Annie asks her where the family is moving to, come March.

'Oh, nowhere we hope. We are negotiating with Sergei to rent the house back. Apparently, his wife has changed her mind. Doesn't want to live in England. Too cold or wet or something. Did you ever hear such nonsense?'

'Davina, I was wondering if by any unlikely chance you might have a direct contact number for Sergei....Oh marvellous....'

What's going on there, Annie can't help but wonder. Davina puts Annie on hold while she scrolls through her phone numbers. Annie prays the housewife knows how to get herself back on the line. She need not have worried.

'Wonderful....Right, that's his UK mobile? And for Russia? Wonderful. Thank you, Davina. Yes, see you soon. Sorry to have bothered you.'

Heart in her mouth she calls the London mobile.

'Yes.' No doubt of Sergei's gruff tones. 'Dr Fritzweiler, how pleasant is this surprise on a dull Saturday evening.'

No reason to mess about. She begins to explain her situation. In less than ten seconds he cuts her off.

'Dr Fritzweiler, this topic is not convenient for a telephone discussion.'

Annie catches the tone of conversation that Sergei wants to adopt. In case anyone is hacking into his phone this evening. As if they would dare.

'But it is rather pressing...' He doesn't know the word. '... urgent, Professor.'

'Ah yes. A meeting in London on next Tuesday is maybe possible.'

'That may be too late, Professor. Can you do it tomorrow?

Please Professor, I really need your advice immediately, really.'

'Very difficult, Dr Fritzweiler.'

He is obviously weighing how much trouble she can make for him if this all goes to Court. He doesn't need her to explain the peril in which she stands. And in consequence of which, the peril in which he may stand.

'All right. St. James's Park for a coffee. There's a place at the end where are all those British Government buildings. Eight o'clock. I am embroiled for the rest of the day.'

Presumably he means "engaged", thinks Annie. Although knowing Sergei he may well mean "embroiled". She prays there is a train that will get her from Oxford to Paddington by seven thirty on a Sunday. Otherwise, she is going to have to drive and face a huge West End parking charge.

She decides to drive anyway. With the weather as dramatically changeable as it has recently been, she thinks it wise to bring a change of clothes. In any case, she won't be long with Sergei and the roads early on a Sunday morning will be as clear as they ever are on the western approaches to London.

Annie is early but she sees him at once, sprawled on a chair in the cafe, no shirt, gazing through dark glasses at the ornamental ducks. Automatically she looks for the members of his protection, but there are a lot of people about on this early sunny Sunday morning and she cannot spot them. What she can see is more of Sergei's body than she's seen since they shared a bed together all those years ago in Berlin. He's obvious just finished his Sunday morning run. She wishes she'd known. Then, she could have brought her own gear and tested whether she was as fit as he. But he does look good. She of course means fit. She thinks.

'Annie, do sit down my love.'

A bit of a change from the formal tone he adopted yesterday on the telephone. Perhaps it's the sunshine that's got to him.

'No actually sitting down is not preferred. Let us walk together, you and me, in the sunshine. Like in the old time in the Tiergarten.'

She falls into step. Yes, she remembers only too well their times together in the Tiergarten, the great sprawling public park just to the West of the Brandenburg Gate in Berlin. At that time, it was in West Berlin. Sergei was attached to the Russian embassy to the GDR and not only was able to travel easily to the West but to procure a pass for his then wife. This even though Annie was a citizen of East Germany. It's not the walks Annie remembers so much as the fact that he used to have her under the trees, oblivious of passers-by. She wonders if she has ever again enjoyed such physical pleasure. But this is not the Tiergarten in the summer 1988, but St James's Park in the false spring of now.

'So, Dr Fritzweiler, the police have made a call on you. And exactly what did they say to you, these British detectives?'

She tells him. They are walking anti-clockwise round the park, between Horse Guards Parade and the Foreign Office at one end and Buckingham Palace at the other.

'Your British police they are not so exact, even in the words of their own language.'

'What did you say to them, Sergei, in your own exact words?'

'But Dr Fritzweiler I should first tell you how lovely you are looking in this surprising London sunshine.' He laughs. 'Just like in the old time.'

She remembers only too well. In another park, under other, German, trees, he would strip off all his clothes. He loved to be naked in the sunshine. Was that a thing with Russian men? And with West Germans of both sexes once they got into the park it seemed. The sun seemed to compel them to dispense with their clothes, however shapely or un-shapely. Annie just couldn't do it. She used to wear a simple short dress, which no doubt Sergei had bought for her in the West. He respected her modesty but contrived to ravish her all the same.

With a shock she realises she is wearing something like that short dress, now. Sergei, bare-chested and in his brief shorts is as close to naked as he can properly be in a small English park already crowded with people. He sees it too.

'Shall we, Dr Fritzweiler, lie together under those trees as in the old time?'

It is a moment before she understands that he is serious. Does she have a choice?

'It is more convenient for a private conversation, is it not?'

He guides her by the shoulders to a spot up towards the top of a bank on the edge of the park, near Birdcage Walk. Across from this lies the Guards' Barracks. She thinks she has identified his protection now. A man and a woman, about to sit down on the grass not too far away, managing by their presence to create a small area of privacy for Sergei and Annie.

They lie down, facing each other, almost touching. He reaches for her and gently moves her body against his. She thinks he is about to kiss the side of her neck, but it's not that. He is whispering into her ear.

'Annie, what I told them, your British police, was that we had discussed how a kidnap might be done. This was to see if it would work, your idea about forcing Cameron to part with his little fortune for charitable purposes. Just an example of your general idea, this Cameron business, yes? But all very much in theory, no?'

'Sergei, it was your conversation. You tell me. The big thing is whether you said you gave me a contact for the kidnappers. That is what kills me with them, Sergei.'

'Of course, I did not. It is rubbish what they say to you.'

She heaves a huge sigh of relief. She trusts him, if not absolutely, a lot more than those hyenas Tench and Smogulecki.

'Will you repeat that it's rubbish if they question you again?'

'If I must do it to save you from inconvenience, Annie, yes. But only if the conditions are very discrete. Everything must be very discrete. At a place, and time of my choosing. OK Annie?'

'OK Sergei. May I call you again?'

'Of course. But there's a new number. It's good to change every so often. This will get me wherever I am in the world.'

He recites it to her. She recites it back. Now she will remember it. She's always had that ability.

'And yes, my love, for you I will always pick up.'

'Will you be in London for the rest of this week?'

'For you my love I am always in London. Ah, we Russians are so poetic. But yes, to speak without poetry, yes.'

'Tell me Sergei, why did you even agree to speak to the British police at all? I'm sure you have official connections which you could use to stop such harassment of an important foreign resident in London?'

'Ah my love, you understand so little. This other Cameron,

yes, the one who is Prime Minister in this country, he seems to have changed the attitude of his Government, you know in a way that is not so obvious. Before, we...' She assumes he means "we Oligarchs". '...we could disregard the British law, if we were moderate, discrete. Not murder in the street you understand. But now things are more delicate. I must not lose my right to be in this country. It would be too inconvenient, for business. Besides I like it here. And you are here, Annie Fritzweiler.'

She can now feel him against her thigh. Impossible.

Then she sees it. On one side the trunks of two massive trees shelter them. Between them and Birdcage Walk they are sheltered by the rise of the ground. And on the side with an open view of the park, shielding them from public gaze, four substantial figures, three men and a woman now stand close together with their backs to the couple. The full protection.

She is frightened. By Sergei. By what he might do. By her own physical desire.

'Sergei, tell me a secret. Are you having an affair with Davina, David Cameron's wife?'

It works. He laughs and relaxes his hold on her.

'An affair, by no means. But these last days, since the kidnap and return of her son she has become more attractive. And she is, I think, very excited by me. But no, I want to be friends with her because she might be useful. Don't be like a jealous woman, Annie, and don't ask me more.'

Now he kisses her.

'Directly speaking, I want to have sex with you, Annie Fritzweiler. Here and now. But in this crowded little park, this crowded little island?'

'In any case there is your beautiful wife, Sergei?'

'Ah, my beautiful wife. We can go to my house, but she is there, in front of her mirror. Always in front of her mirror. Do you know Annie for a man what is the most boring thing in this world? It is, night after night, to have sex with a beautiful woman. And this one she is not only beautiful, she is connected. So, what to do?'

He means, she supposes, that it would be too "inconvenient" to leave her.

'And now we are here, Annie Fritzweiler, with a problem and an opportunity. In the old days you were quite skilful in such matters.' He ponders his problem. 'Ah, but of course. We go over the road into Green Park and walk up there to the Ritz Hotel. For me they are happy to make ready a room.

He gets up and makes to pull her to her feet. But at that moment a heavy shadow passes across Annie's face. She looks up through the trees at the dark cloud that has that moment appeared above them. Then it's raining, hard. Not English rain. It is a monsoon. Everywhere people are running for cover. Annie and Sergei run too.

Reaching the Mall, they exchange a few hasty words, reaffirming his commitment to help her. Then he is off running towards Buckingham Palace and beyond to Belgravia and his mansion, his protection at his heals. She wonders if just possibly the protection is the gang of four, Felix's kidnappers. There is the woman, but Felix could have been mistaken, or lying.

The protection is evidently relaxed. If they were concerned, one of them would run ahead. If they were frightened, they would run in tight formation round their man. All the members of the protection detail are a head taller than Sergei. It is remarkably difficult, even for a marksman, to kill a subject surrounded by such a tight formation, running.

Annie starts to run too, across the Mall, closed to traffic because it's Sunday, past St. James's Palace, where even the ceremonial guard has taken cover, towards where she has parked her car off Piccadilly. Out of breath, she stops running. No point. She is anyway soaked to the skin. Annie walks quickly, lengthening her stride to the most the hem of her short dress will allow. She is conscious that the rain has pasted her dress to every contour of her body.

She has a change of clothes in the car. But on reaching the car she finds the prospect of changing too daunting. So, soaking as she is, she pulls out and sets off back to Oxford. She takes the A40, less likely to be congested than the motorway.

Now she remembers, Luke did not come round last night, after things at the restaurant had finished. When Priti Patel had left…Priti Patel, she must call her as soon as she gets back. She had felt suddenly exhausted, had taken a hot shower and collapsed into bed, dead to the world until her alarm roused her next morning in time to get on the road to see Sergei.

Annie knows she shouldn't be doing this. It's pathetic. Worse, it's not likely to be effective. But she can't stop herself from pulling into the next lay-by and digging her phone out from her bag.

She scrolls through nineteen messages, mostly University stuff, nothing that can't wait. Then she notices the missed calls. Three, from a number she recognises. The calls are timed at 00-43, 00-44 and 00-58 that morning.

42

Shades of the Prison House

Annie calls Priti only for her good news to be met by bad. The police have decided to charge Annie and Felix jointly.

Annie does not need her solicitor to explain the cleverness of this. It speaks of an urgent powwow with some panjandrum representing the Director of Public Prosecutions. Or perhaps the artfulness of Tench himself. Or the sheer machine-gun-them-in-the-streets mentality of Smogulecki. Probably a combination of all three.

Priti Patel explains to Annie the danger to her inherent in the change of police tactics. Now, if Sergei and Felix refuse to incriminate Annie in the matter of arranging the kidnapping, they will prosecute Felix at least, along with Annie, for conspiracy to defraud David Cameron. Defraud him of substantially all his fortune by causing him falsely to believe that only by giving this amount to charity could he hope to have his son released from captivity by his kidnappers. That threat alone may get Felix to change his mind about testifying against Annie. For this to stick the police don't even need to prove there was actually a kidnapping. Just that Annie and Felix conspired to cause David Cameron to believe that there had been a kidnapping.

On the conspiracy to defraud scenario, the police would recognise that they were unable to prove that Annie arranged the kidnapping. Instead, they would attempt to convince a jury that Felix cooperated with the kidnappers to convince David Cameron that he, Felix, had been abducted and would only be released if his father paid a ruinous ransom to the specified charities. This, the police would contend, had been done under Annie's influence and direction.

'But that's ridiculous,' Annie shouts at the phone. 'It's a fantasy, this influence. And anyway, how can they show Felix cooperated?'

'Conspiracy is a tricky area,' Priti explains. 'I've already spoken to Martin Peters. I think it's best if he and I come round to see you this afternoon and hash things out with you. Don't worry, my sweet. With a legal team like us you should be safe as houses.'

Annie heaves a sigh. Having failed to get Luke on the phone from the lay-by on the A40, he's already prepping for Sunday lunch at the Bistro, she had resolved to go round there in the afternoon when he will have a few hours break before they start on dinner.

'OK,' she says. Her reluctance is all too plain.

'Got a hot date, eh Annie? Love in the afternoon? But being ready for Tench and Smogulecki on Monday is even more important than getting your rocks off, my love.'

'Bring your own biscuits,' snaps Annie. 'I've run out.'

Annie serves only coffee. She feels the schnapps would not help the situation. Surely things have not got to the drowning of sorrows stage. Before Martin Peters can begin, Annie begins. She doesn't want to stop the police prosecution only to find that her legal fees have bankrupted her.

'Nothing Annie. I believe it to be unethical to charge a colleague.'

'Just as well,' Priti comes in helpfully, 'because you wouldn't be able to afford him, Annie. He charges ten times what I do, and gets away with it, lucky bastard. No, I mean it Annie. A thousand pounds an hour.'

'It's seven hundred and fifty at present,' says Martin, not a man to leave a false impression if he can help it.

'But Martin, how can I repay you?'

'Actually Annie, there is something you can do for me. It's been in my mind for some time, but I've never quite dared to approach you about it. But we can speak of it later.'

The two lawyers are huddled together in the middle of Annie's couch, so they can share papers. At last Martin begins on Annie's case.

'Normally Criminal Conspiracy is hard for the Prosecution to prove. But it is a nightmare also for the Defence, for two reasons. First, juries easily become confused and can convict in face of the evidence, or more likely lack of evidence.'

'Why?'

Annie hates this talk of juries. Hasn't Priti more or less promised her that it won't come to that? A public prosecution, even if she were ultimately acquitted, would be the end of her career in England and probably everywhere else too.

'Because, Annie, it is easy for juries to misunderstand the Judge's directions and well-nigh impossible for the Judge to declare a mistrial on the only grounds open to him that no jury in its right mind could have reached such a verdict. That of course assumes that the Prosecution is able to put forward some respectable evidence and that they get the law right.'

Annie tries to concentrate, putting aside all memories of being tightly embraced by Luke.

'The second reason for the Defence to be concerned,' Martin Peters continues, 'is that the offence itself is not exactly clear. Where there is no direct evidence of what words passed between conspirators, to what extent can such words be inferred from subsequent actions?'

You tell me, thinks Annie.

'It's not clear,' Martin concludes.

'We know you are a bloody academic lawyer, Martin. Sorry Annie.'

Annie can't tell whether her solicitor is apologising for the imprecation or the aspersion against academics.

'But it would be easier for your client, Martin, and certainly for a simple practice solicitor like me if you used the example of this case.'

Priti mouths the word "p-l-a-t-e" to Annie, who goes and gets a large one. By the time she comes back into the living room, her solicitor has extracted from her bag a huge value pack of chocolate biscuits the contents of which she empties onto the plate and at once begins to munch.

'Very well,' Martin continues. 'In this case the police are alleging that Annie here conspired with Felix Cameron to defraud Felix's father, David Cameron. So, what do they say? That Annie influenced Felix to carry out a practical demonstration of how redistribution of wealth could be carried out by means of criminal threat. Annie and perhaps her colleague, Gregory Halberstadt, aided Felix in creating the false impression that he had been kidnapped against his will and that his life was in danger.

'But someone procured the gang to smash up the restaurant

from which Felix was taken,' says Priti, interrupting her eating. 'There's no getting away from that.'

'Yes, Priti, but on this alternative we are assuming that the police have given up their attempt to discover anything about the gang. On this view, the reason that the police search for the gang, throughout the duration of the supposed kidnapping, proved fruitless was that from day one they were back in Russia. There was no kidnapping.'

'OK, Martin, and what about the original allegation? That Felix was an innocent victim and that Annie organised the kidnapping?' demands Priti.

'Surely,' says Annie, 'the police have to decide which offence they think was committed before they bring a prosecution?'

'Actually, they don't, Annie. There is an established tradition in Common Law of presenting alternative, even contradictory fact scenarios.'

'If you don't like apple pie with cream, perhaps you'll enjoy black current tart, with ice cream,' Priti suggests.

'I suggest that we now go over the facts of the case, to see how we best should react to the alternative police allegations,' Martin Peters continues.

'Before you get into all that, could you excuse us for a moment, Martin?'

Priti leads Annie into the kitchen. The kitchen where the day before, it seems hardly possible, she kissed Luke lightly on the lips and he took her in his arms.

'Have you decided how much of the truth to tell me, Annie? And, of course, Martin. Whatever you tell us, we are not bound to present in evidence. We can suppress or invent in whatever way seems best from your point of view.'

Annie notes the lack of clarity, which she takes to be deliberate, as to who is to decide what is best from her point of view. But she lets it go for now. Buoyed by the confidence of that morning's conversation with Sergei, Annie has decided to tell the whole truth. At least that is what she tells her solicitor. Priti is not deceived. She laughs.

'As I'm sure you appreciate, Annie, there is no way for Martin and me to know if you actually are telling us the truth, unless you are tripped up by your own lies. But no matter. We will take what you say as gospel. OK, we had better not keep the great scholar waiting any longer.'

She moves to lead the way back into the living room, but Annie says: 'Give me a moment, Priti.'

As the door closes, Annie calls Luke's mobile and prays. A prayer answered. He comes on just before his message service is about to cut in. A prayer denied. He at once recognises her voice and cuts the line.

Cursing herself, Annie returns to the lawyers in the living

room. After all, without them she doesn't have a future life let alone a prospective love affair.

'Are you OK, Annie?'

She nods. Martin Peters is a kind man, sensitive to the mood of his client.

'All right give us the facts of the case.'

So, Annie goes through it, with the efficiency and lucidity for which she is known.

Yes, she and Felix discussed ways in which the rich might be compelled in individual cases to do the morally right thing and give away their wealth to the benefit of the general good. This included a theoretical discussion of the pros and cons of kidnapping.

Yes, her colleague the psychologist Greg Halberstadt, had been involved in this project and had met Felix.

Yes, she had discussed the matter with her academic acquaintance, Professor Sergei Dzhugashvili of the St. Petersburg Institute of Culture and Politics. How such a thing might be arranged, but purely from an academic standpoint. Crucially Sergei had not given her a contact with men who might act as kidnappers, nor had she sought such. If necessary, Sergei will confirm this to the police directly.

Yes, she believed that Felix had been abducted from the

restaurant against his will.

No, despite pondering the matter for many hours, she had no idea of the motives or identities of the men who kidnapped Felix.

Yes, it was logically possible that the gang of four had only been involved in the abduction of Felix and not in his subsequent captivity or the ransom demands, since all contact with the gang could have been fabricated by Felix. In that case it would seem most likely that that Felix had organised matters and had carried out the whole exercise by himself. His motive would have been to spite his father, with whom she had been led to understand, he was not on good terms.

How would she characterise the police case against her? As entirely circumstantial. The reason, she thought, that they were pursuing it was that they were under enormous pressure to find the perpetrators and had no other idea where to look.

Why then had they looked in her direction? Simply because of the coincidence that she had introduced a discussion of the practical application of the idea of fairness promoted by the American philosopher John Rawls into a tutorial with Felix only a matter of days before his abduction. That, and the fact that she was an academic acquaintance, yes perhaps one might say a friend, of Professor Sergei Dzhugashvili, a Russian oligarch.

'Is there any other kind?' asked Priti Patel, bored with not being able to open her mouth for ten minutes, except to put a biscuit into it.

'And that's all?' Peters confirms. 'Thank you, Annie, that is very clear. If we may now go to a few questions of detail that Priti and I may have?'

'Yes, if I may first go to the loo?'

Annie does not need to relieve herself. She needs again to try to reach Luke. But she goes and sits on the lavatory anyway. Again, the heritage of having been brought up in East Germany. Go through the motions in case someone is watching. This time there is no answer at all. She sends a message of grovelling apology from which she cannot keep a hint of desire.

On her return to the living room, they address the hard part. What to do?

Annie emphasises that the aim must be at all costs to get the police to drop the case, or cases. A prosecution, even if unsuccessful, would ruin her professionally and personally. Acquittal without a stain on one's character only works if you are a celebrity or if you had had no character to start with. Or, of course, both.

43

The Heart of Things

Priti Patel starts off.

'If the cops offer Felix immunity from prosecution, in return for his giving evidence against you....'

Annie is outraged.

'On what grounds, for heaven's sake?'

'On the grounds that they would allege that he was entirely under your influence. Because you were his instructor, he was in awe of you...'

'And, yes, he was obsessed with me. I see.'

'Sexually? Well,' Priti continues, 'if they do that, how bad could it be?'

'I'm sorry?'

'What is the worst he could plausibly say against you?'

'What are you implying? That Greg and I saw an opportunity, through Felix, to do some "live" research into redistribution, using David Cameron's fortune as the example.'

'That's it,' says Martin. 'Felix would say he was so in awe of you that he followed exactly your instructions. He was, in a fairly typical teenaged way, at odds with his father, for whom he had only contempt and saw your scheme as a way of getting "revenge" on him. The device of making the ransom demand exactly correspond to his father's net assets and of directing David to pay directly to those charities added piquancy.'

'And the plausibility that Felix was the instigator of his own kidnapping?' says Priti. 'But in the end the demand was a bit more than the amount of his assets?'

'Yes Priti. Felix must have forgotten that the kidnappers would need to be paid. He entirely over-estimated what they would cost, hence the extra payment at the end to Elephants Are Us. But how was he to know?'

'Does Felix have any evidence that you were in contact with the kidnappers?' Martin asks.

'No,' Annie snaps back, 'because I wasn't.'

'Quite sure Annie? It is better you tell us now.'

'I've told you and I won't tell you again, I did not have contact with the kidnap gang, none at all. And I did not organise the kidnapping in some indirect way. Is that clear?'

Annie is now conscious she has got up from her chair and is standing over her two lawyers, as far as a woman of five foot two can stand over two large people, and yelling.

'Very well, Annie, we won't mention it again.'

Martin Peters has remained calm in face of this barrage. Annie resumes her seat and crosses her legs angrily.

'So, the most Felix could do is to invent some story that connects you with the kidnappers?'

'He already has.'

'Of course, the supposed overheard conversation between two of the gang in which they mentioned that "she" would not be pleased if they used physical violence against Felix.

'That is why all this shit that I'm in,' snaps Annie, conscious that she is still speaking too loudly and not very grammatically.

'Why do you think Felix said that?' asks Martin.

'Either because genuinely he thought he heard what he said

he heard and was simply mistaken. More likely the police put weights on him...'

'Lent on him,' says Priti quietly.

'But most likely,' Annie is reluctant to say this but can see the lawyers can serve her best if she is frank with them, 'because he hoped to use that to force me to have sex with him.'

'I don't understand. Once he'd put it into the minds of the police, he effectively couldn't withdraw it.'

'That's right, Martin, but he didn't know that. He's only seventeen for heaven's sake.'

'That's the reason, isn't it, Annie?' says Priti. 'This thing about blackmailing you to have sex with him. The other possible reasons you gave us are not possible are they, because the sex thing is the reason. You and he had that conversation.'

Annie nods and flushes.

'Annie it's the filth you're supposed to mislead, not your own lawyers. No more of that please.'

'What is the situation between you and Felix now?' Martin inquires.

Annie explains to them her threat to make a formal complaint against him to the College authorities, which would undoubtedly lead to the immediate end of his Oxford career and probably of his career in any decent institution of higher learning.

'His father was desperately anxious that I should not make a formal report. As it happens, I have written such a report, but for now I've archived it. I've also told the Master of the College informally. Reluctantly he has accepted my approach. David perhaps has been moderately generous to the College in the past.'

'And what effect has this had on Felix?'

'I no longer teach him of course, but I hear that he is now a model student. His mother told me that he is greatly quietened down since his kidnap experience. No longer full of himself.'

'So, Annie, this might mean that Felix might not be swayed by the threat of prosecution to testify against you?'

Priti has lost interest in the chocolate biscuits in favour of Annie's case.

'He'd be in a difficult position, though,' says Martin. 'If he testifies against you, Annie, you could get him sent down for good. If he doesn't testify the police may prosecute him. To be honest I don't know how the College would react to the latter. It should of course stand by him, innocent until proved guilty and so on. Certainly, I would advise the Corporate Body, the Master and Fellows, to do so.'

'Can you tell him that, Martin?'

'You are correct, Annie, it would be good for him to know that. Let me consider modalities.'

'Oh, you mean how to do it?' says Priti. 'You bloody academics. Ivory tower doesn't do you justice.'

Priti is looking at the remaining biscuits but now she is thinking of the diabetes report buried somewhere deep in her chaotic bag.

'It's clear to me,' Martin Peters resuming, 'that if we could contrive for you, Annie, and Felix to tell the same story to would greatly strengthen our hand. Is there a way to achieve this, Annie? Through David Cameron?'

'I can try, but I'm not sure.'

Annie gets up. She now really does need to relieve herself. But Priti beats her to it.

'Oh good, toilet break time.'

'Martin, would you?'

'It has been rather a long afternoon. Thank you, Annie.'

While the host is uncomfortably waiting, she ponders exactly what she should say to David Cameron.

44

Turnaround

It has come to him deep in the night. Annie Fritzweiler is a two-timing bitch. He pads around the by-ways of the house thinking of what to do. Revenge. He pads some more. Means of revenge? Staring him in the face. His next novel.

Now, un-breakfasted in the early dawn, David Cameron sits in his writing room at the top of Sergei's house staring out at the slashing rain, the sodden garden and his near future.

Negotiations over a series of articles about the kidnapping have broken down. David is relieved. He has determined to write his next book in record time, to take advantage of the apparent runaway success of THE AVENGING ANGEL. In his new book he will say what he has to say about kidnapping, extortion and betrayal. And about Annie Fritzweiler.

In THE AVENGING ANGEL he had defied conventional wisdom and his advisors. First in getting rid early on of his long-term hero, Manny Kant, tortured on an open phone line to his niece and surrogate daughter, by the contractors of some apparently American security agency. There are so many.

Manny himself had long been a deniable freelance for various security services, but always working on the side of the truth and light. After all, this is fiction. Since there is obviously no remedy through process of law, his niece, herself a junior member of a security agency, decides that retribution must be delivered personally. Obviously not by Manny himself, now convalescent at the home of a friend on Cap Ferat. There perhaps his body and his dignity, which collapsed so piteously under moderate torture, may slowly mend. But in the meantime, Anke is ready to step into the breach.

Often using herself as bait, Anke executes her task with extreme violence, physical and psychological, which makes even the bad guys think twice. And which can only be driven by internal fires of hatred. Anke hates injustice of all kinds. But she also hates other things, starting with her father, Manny Kant's brother.

When the call comes in the late afternoon, David Cameron has just re-created Annie Fritzweiler as Annie Fassbinder. The black swan to Anke's white swan. Identical, except that the white swan has good intentions and the black swan evil.

In WHITE SWAN, BLACK SWAN, Annie Fassbinder, is just about to get into the bed with the son of her current lover. No writer's block in sight here. The story, driven by painfully actual events. David is reluctant to answer his phone whilst the words are flowing so easily, but he has been at it since the early morning and is tired. Just in time he answers.

'Dr Annie Fritzweiler. Are you calling to tell me you've just made out with my son, the stupid one?'

Annie had been prepared for coolness, even for a rebuke, but this was going to be harder than she had thought.

'Actually David, I called to ask how your head was.'

'It aches, what do you think?'

Actually, it doesn't. At least not after all the painkillers David has taken.

'I'm sorry, David. It was an uncalled-for thing to do.'

'Uncalled for. It was common assault, grievous bodily harm. I was thinking I would prosecute him, but then I thought the fault is really yours.'

'How is that, David?'

'Come on Annie you little...' He doesn't quite dare to say "bitch" or worse for in the back of his mind he still desires her and still nurses hope. 'You were having it away with Luke in your kitchen.'

'It's true that I embraced him and kissed him lightly on the lips. To comfort him, David. He was devastated by what he'd done and for destroying his own special dish.'

'How about his father's head?'

'I told you, he's wracked with regret, guilt, about you. He cannot forgive himself or even come to terms with it.'

'I'm sure you've been a great comfort, Annie?'

'Actually not. Since I dropped him off at the restaurant last afternoon after bringing you home, I've not seen him nor heard anything from him.'

'I suppose you'd exhausted each other shagging on the Downs on the way back from here?'

'Too cold,' Annie says, laughing in spite of herself. She can feel him reluctantly beginning to thaw. 'David are you awfully tied up tonight?'

'Yes.'

'I'd really like to see you, David. In the week it's so difficult. You know the pressure of the Oxford term. But I'm sorry, you have Davina. I spoke to her last night, as it happens. To get a phone number. For Sergei. Yes, that's the one. The guy who bought your house...Oh some academic matter. Davina was my last hope but amazingly Davina had his number.'

David is moved by this intelligence, she can tell. And she is believed. After all she knows he can go downstairs at once and ask Davina. So, Annie Fritzweiler did not have Sergei Dzhugashvili's number, but his own wife did. Interesting to a husband who was perhaps thinking of taking an interest in his wife again. But he is not to be won over so easily.

'Annie, I'm writing. Just now I am, as Goran my publisher would say, in the zone. I have to get on while I have inspiration.'

Annie can deal with this. Low voice.

'David, I could give you a little extra inspiration.'

'Well, I have been at it since dawn this morning. But you know I can't drive at present.'

'I will come over and pick you up.'

'I suppose there is that snooty place in the village. This time of year, it will probably be empty.'

'And closed,' suggests Annie. 'It's Sunday night. Look, it doesn't matter. I'll come and pick you up and we'll find somewhere.'

'Not the Bistro?'

'No, not there.'

They both laugh. Job done, or almost.

'I don't want to go far.'

'No problem. Anyway, I'll bring you back afterwards.'

'OK, shall we say eight o'clock at the bottom of the drive? And Annie....' Now he is almost shy. 'Wear something nice.'

Push over, thinks Annie turning back to the lawyers.

Seven o'clock in the evening. Annie opens a double-glazed window and closes it quickly. It is bitterly cold outside. Only someone who was desperate would go out voluntarily on a night like this. But Annie Fritzweiler is desperate.

A key decision. Something nice, David had said. She runs her fingers lightly over the clothes hanging in her closet. He undoubtedly is thinking in terms of a short skirt. She could never understand the preference most men seemed to have for that, when tight fitting jeans, say, would outline a woman's body with greater clarity. Take a chance then.

She pulls on a pair of blue jeans. Tight enough? She reviews the look in her long mirror. She crosses one leg over the other and admires the effect. A push-up bra. She doesn't really approve of this but needs must. A tight, orange top. She has several. No, she could not be mistaken for a whore. Too old, for one thing. She never wears much make-up, but she does put on more lipstick than normal. Brick red since it suits her. She combs her hair carefully. She should have had it cut for such an occasion, but obviously no time. It will have to do.

Annie pulls on her tan boots. Half calf length. Winds a scarf round her neck and pulls on her camel coat. Goes with the boots. She's already late. Never mind. She'll call when she gets close. She locks the door of her flat, runs lightly down the stairs of which Priti Patel made such heavy weather and bangs the communal outer door shut behind her, running round to the back of the building for her car. The cold takes her breath away, but then she hasn't bothered to do up her coat.

She is about to pull out onto the road when her mobile rings. Glancing at the screen, she has to take it. It's Priti saying that the interview with the police has to be at the police station. It will be formal, so lawyers present, and recorded. But her lawyers have won an important concession. It won't be at the Oxford City central police station, which is a zoo, where Annie would stand some chance of being recognised. Where a journalist might pick up a sniff. A leafy suburban police station has been agreed, way up the Banbury Road. Five in the afternoon, as late as the police would agree to. Annie to meet Priti and Martin Peters at the station at four thirty.

'Oh, and Annie, two other things. First, don't worry. Martin and I won't let those buggers get away with this phoney prosecution.'

'And the other one?'

'Bring David Cameron if you can. If you've got him on side.' Annie hesitates, uncertain. 'For heaven's sake, Annie, I don't have to draw pictures for you. If you have to, fuck the bastard tonight.'

Annie turns off her engine. After all she is a modern German woman and quite environmentally sensitive. She spends a few minutes sending messages cancelling the next afternoon's tutorials. Will reschedule for later in the term. That done she is on her way to possibly the most important meeting of her life.

The roads are empty, of course. She takes a chance that there is no black ice, a particular hazard since it is invisible day or night and drives for all she's worth.

As she drops down off the Downs into the Camerons' village, she has made up all her lost time. She douses her lights, except for side lights, as she approaches the bottom of the Cameron drive. But he's there already. In a Shetland sweater, leather jacket, cord trousers and a red ski hat. Normally so exact even about casual clothes, David, like many Englishmen, seems to feel that exceptionally cold weather gives him licence to dress in whatever eccentric combination of clothes seems warm. She's glad she has not dressed up and that she is wearing jeans.

'It's cold,' she says by way of explanation.

He is gallant.

'It will do very well.'

Perhaps he is just pleased to see her.

As they set off, she asks: 'Davina?'

'Out with her friends. Just to be on the safe side I said my old friend, your colleague, Jeffrey Cunliffe, had invited me to a Fellows Guest Night in Hall. That way Davina wouldn't have to prepare a meal for me. And that old bugger Cunliffe lies more easily than he tells the truth. As you know, he is the College Fellow in Politics.'

She smiles. He is in a good mood.

They are back in central Oxford in less than thirty minutes. There's a wine bar she knows, near the river. One of the few which serve food on a Sunday evening. A perfect place on a warm day in June. But on a freezing night in January there is only one other couple, and they are completely taken up with each other. Perfect, in fact.

The young waiter, must be a student, takes her coat and scarf. David carefully sits at an angle to her, rather than across from her. She orders modestly from the remembered menu. David orders an expensive bottle of red wine, Burgundy. She reckons he is capable of drinking all of that on his own. But she immediately forsakes her intention not to drink by ordering a glass of schnapps to give herself Dutch courage. David has a whisky and takes off his Shetland sweater.

After the drinks arrive and are sampled, Annie takes the initiative. In the car driving to David's house, she has decided to administer a slight shock, in an attempt to get things off on the right foot.

'What is it about you Cameron men that within a few minutes of being in my company, you all get a hard on for me? I can walk down the High in Oxford looking as sexy as I can manage, and not one head will turn. No surprise in that. As previously discussed, I'm nearly fifty years old and was never exactly one who looked.'

'A looker,' says David absently.

He is gazing intently at her. In admiration? Shocked? Appalled? She simply cannot tell.

'Annie, I told you.'

She ignores him.

'All right, I might have a certain attraction for young men, of my students' age say. You know there is a kind of pattern of young men falling for a woman in authority over them. A kind of physical urge to turn the tables. To make the boss submit.'

'Annie, stop. Take a breath. I told you once, only a few weeks ago it must have been, when we were together in that bathroom at the house. You asked why a man of the world like me would show physical excitement at the sight of a woman of forty-nine on the lavatory.'

'Oh yes, I remember. You said, "Because it's you, Annie." I thought that a rather good answer but requiring further explication.'

Annie is happy. They are back on the old footing. She at once launches into a summary of the situation with Felix, though of course he knows most of it, and of where she has got to with the police and her lawyers, which he doesn't know.

'So, you want me to support your case, and in particular to persuade Felix not to testify against you?'

Annie carefully gets up from the table and stands directly in front of him, crossing one leg over the other at the knee. In her tight jeans she is encouraging him to see the possibilities.

'What I want David for you to desire me. You don't have to fall in love with me. Just desire my body the way your two sons do. They do not interest me at all. But you? We could enjoy each other without lifetime commitment, I'm sure. No harm to Davina.'

It's of course a huge risk. He may just as well be put off by this explicitness in a woman as excited by it. But she has judged her man exactly.

He puts a hand on her thigh.

'Annie, I hope it's not just your perilous situation talking. But yes, to speak plainly, I want you more than any other thing in the world.'

They both know this is rubbish. But it serves the situation. She wants his help with the police. He wants just at this moment to get into her knickers. It is a deal of convenience.

She sits down, relieved. Their food arrives.

'David, we'd better eat.' Annie fills his wine glass and the waiter comes in time to fill hers. She asks for some tap water and fills both their glasses. The steak they've both ordered is not bad. Between carefully regarding her legs and her cleavage, he asks her various questions about the alternative police cases against her and about the lawyers' advice.

45

Whatever It Takes

They come to the end of the meal, and Annie empties the remains of the bottle into David's glass. She's drunk two glasses in addition to the schnapps, but she prays that tonight of all nights she won't be stopped by the police. Normally she never drinks if she has to drive afterwards. But tonight, she needed to be relaxed in order to be daring enough to say what she wanted to say. To do what she has decided to do.

David has a large brandy. She gets up and goes to the loo.

When she comes back, she says: 'We need to do something about Felix, tonight or tomorrow morning.'

'Nothing like striking while the iron is hot. I'll go over there now, to your College.' He tosses off the remainder of the brandy. 'Let me get the bill.'

'I've paid it already.'

He smiles at her. She really does want to get on with things, he is thinking.

'Thank you, Annie. That's very sweet of you. And thank you for a delightful and instructive evening. Let me just call to make sure Felix is there and able to receive us.'

He is. 'Better not with me,' she mouths. The new Felix is deep in his books and would be happy to see his father.

Outside they run to her car. It must now be two or three degrees below zero. There was little competition for parking spaces, so the car is close by.

She drives the few minutes it takes to the College, with completely empty roads. She has a permanent parking space in the car park by the covered market, just behind the College. The ultimate Fellow's perk. They run, hand in hand, to the College gates. The Porter salutes her.

'Brass monkey...' Just in time, he remembers his station in life. 'Very cold tonight, Dr Fritzweiler.' He doesn't bother to ask her to register her guest. Dr Fritzweiler is obviously entertaining a lover in her rooms tonight. Nothing in the Statutes of the College to forbid that. And discretion in a Head Porter tends to be rewarded sooner or later.

Annie however, has to introduce David as she does not know which room is Andrew's. Duly informed, she leads David there and points out her own staircase, just across the quad, just in case he's forgotten.

For forty minutes she frets alone in her room. At least while she is waiting, by means of her new gas fire, she is able to convert the place from an ice box to an almost cosy sitting room, with a warm bedroom conveniently beyond.

Then a soft tapping on her outer door. David is there and well pleased with himself. Felix is entirely onside. If by supporting Annie Fritzweiler's account of relevant events he can save his College career, he will of course do anything he can, including attending Annie's Monday afternoon interview at the police station and keeping to the script her lawyers will provide. Even if it means being prosecuted.

'He seemed more concerned about his College career than about his liberty,' says David, accepting a schnapps, since Annie has no brandy. 'Oh, and I introduced Felix on the phone to Martin Peters, whom I know well.'

Why, wonders Annie, did neither of them mention that to her before now?

'Martin says he will take a sworn deposition from Felix of what he wants him to say in evidence because he is concerned the police side may not let him speak tomorrow afternoon. After all, it will be the occasion when the police question you under caution, and supposedly that's all.'

She needs again to relieve herself. The tension, she supposes.

As soon as she comes back into the living-room he takes her

in his arms and kisses her. She really doesn't want to do this, but she knows she must, to keep David onside.

'Take it slowly, David.'

They have never slept together before. Potential pitfalls as well as potential delights. He is already releasing her belt and easing down her jeans. He helps her put back on her boots. This particular male fantasy Annie has never understood, despite reading a couple of academic articles about it in Germany.

Ah yes, he is well used to this. His manicured hands move sensitively over her skin. He stands her with her back to the wall, her legs slightly apart. She tenses her thighs as hard as she can and tries to think of Luke. She is shivering with anticipation, or is it apprehension.

It is not until she feels his tongue moving slowly up the inside of her thigh that he slithers to the floor and rolls over quite gently. He lies there as if sleeping. Her mobile is ringing in the pocket of her jeans. She pulls it out. It is Luke. He sounds terribly sorry, wants to come round. For a second, she is tempted to ask him to come over to her College rooms to help with his father, but she realises just in time that she cannot do that.

'Luke, there's an emergency. A real medical emergency. No, I really can't say more now. I'll call you, Luke darling.'

She calls the Porter. Fortunately, David is fully dressed. By the time the Porter arrives, so is she. She has also called Jeff Cunliffe to tell him the story she has concocted on the spur of the moment.

Mr. Cameron was taken ill after the Fellows dinner in Hall. In the quad on the way to Dr Cunliffe's rooms for a nightcap or two. Since Dr Cunliffe had imbibed and seeing lights on in Annie's rooms, he had called her to take David to hospital.

'Whereas the truth was that he was having his way with you in your room.' Cunliffe laughs softly. 'Enjoyed it did you?'

Her loathing almost gets the better of her. But her survival instincts are stronger.

'Nothing of that kind took place. We were discussing how to extricate David's son, Andrew, who is my student, from a difficulty he finds himself in.'

'Nothing, despite appearances? By the way Dr Fritzweiler, I mentioned to David that saying that he and I would be dining in Hall is not a very robust deception. If questioned no one who was there would be able to say they saw David. Accordingly, if challenged, we agreed that we would say we dined privately in my rooms.'

It is almost intolerable, Annie thinks, to be beholden to Cunliffe, to have to be grateful for correction of the, on reflection, obvious flaw in their alternative truth. But she has to think of David's home life. She has to think of her own survival. So, it had to be said.

'Yes of course, Jeff. Thank you. So obvious when one thinks of it.'

'Not at all, Annie. Glad to help you both.'

'Could you come and...?'

'Carry David downstairs to your car?' Again, Cunliffe laughs softly. Again, she longs to grind his balls under her heel.

David is showing signs of life, if not yet fully coherent. Annie dead eyes the Porter. Two fifties crackle in her hand. Then she is off and running for her car. When she returns, the Porter has already opened to their fullest extent the two massive gates of the College, so Annie can drive into the front quad right up to the bottom of her staircase. Cunliffe arrives and he and the Porter half carry, half drag David down the twisting staircase to the car.

Annie tells the Porter to call Davina, Mrs. Cameron. Then the Porter should call Felix and get him to go to the Infirmary. Another two crisp fifties crackle in her hand, and insistence in her gaze.

Felix will put two and two together, and draw heaven knows what conclusion. The accurate one she fears. But there is no help for it.

Then she drives with a semi-coherent David as fast as is safe to the Radcliffe Infirmary.

It's a rare slack night at A&E. The weather.

'But within an hour or so, Dr Fritzweiler, this place will be overrun with road accident victims. The ice you know.'

But within an hour or so the doctors have scanned David's head from various angles and pronounced it and him fit to go home. Further tests to follow, of course.

When they are about to leave, the Senior Registrar on duty comes over.

'Dr Fritzweiler?'

After all, the Hospital has a long-standing connection with the University. He takes her aside, speaking in the kind of lush British accent that, outside the better English public schools, survives only in the better public schools of the Sub-Continent.

'As my colleagues will have told you, we found nothing. Such black outs are not unknown but puzzling all the same. Mr. Cameron was not engaging in any vigorous physical activity at the time of the event? Nothing that would excite his heart rate exceptionally?'

Well only licking my...but best not to go there, even with this charming youngish man with his knowing eyes.

'Not as far as I know. He'd just finished dining with a colleague of mine in College.'

'Oh well, probably just the food and wine then,' says the doctor, not hiding his disbelief.

She smiles her thanks.

While David was being scanned, Annie had waited in Reception for Felix. Yes, it was a regular Fellows Guest Night in Hall. David was the guest of his old friend the Politics Fellow, Jeffrey Cunliffe, though in the end they thought better of the Guest Night and had a private dinner in Dr Cunliffe's rooms. As the two friends were leaving Jeff's rooms in College, David had collapsed in the quad. By chance she had been returning to her rooms and found Jeff Cunliffe trying to revive David. Since she happened to have her car in the car park adjacent to the College, Annie had volunteered to take David to A&E. The safest option because naturally Cunliffe had been drinking heavily.

Annie doesn't know if Felix believes her. He probably doesn't know himself. He looks distraught. She takes a risk and gives him a hug.

'I don't think it's too bad you know. Probably the stress of the last few weeks.'

When David is released, Annie carefully drives him to the family home. Felix has declined to go with them. A tutorial first thing in the morning. He will call himself a cab.

Davina is at the end of the drive, waiting anxiously in the cold. Out here it's several degrees colder than in central Oxford.

Davina is wrapped up like an Eskimo. She gets into the back of the car for the short ride to her front door and cannot thank Annie enough. First her son and now her husband. Annie resists all attempts to invite herself indoors. It's already after two in the morning and she has a full load of teaching tomorrow morning.

'But, Davina, call me at any time if there are any developments with David. If I don't hear from you, I'll call in the morning.'

Annie hugs Davina. Then she is gone. Again, she drives too fast, wondering if her luck will last forever. She needs it to.

46

Show Time

Annie is running fast but effortlessly through an inch or two of newly fallen powder. Across Christ Church Meadow, where in summer students lie with other students under the rustling leaves of huge oak trees. Today the bare branches of the trees stand out, black sentinels against the snow.

In her sights is a group of young men running in tight formation. Luke Cameron and his friends. Chasing behind her two men, running shoulder to shoulder. Seemingly older but very fit since they hold the pace without effort. Now Annie notches up the pace so she is gaining, little by little, on the tight group of young men. Now she can't be more than twenty metres behind, ten. In a moment she will be within touching distance of the formation, and of Luke.

Just then the group raises its running speed, seemingly without any trouble. But Annie is at once struggling with her breathing in the cold early morning air. What has until then been the exquisite pleasure of her running body perfectly in tune with the winter beauty all around her, is now an agony of cold air being drawn desperately into her lungs, too quickly, too deeply. She can't sustain it and falls off the pace.

Worse, the two older men behind are closing on her. Over her shoulder she can see now that they are David Cameron and Sergei Dzhugashvili. Shoulder to shoulder, they are churning the snow in their efforts to be the first to catch her. At all costs she must keep clear of them. She trips, staggers a few yards and trips again, crashing into the flowing water of the Isis at her right, made more turbid by skeins of dirty ice beginning to form on its surface. Then it's cold, awfully cold, and wet.

Annie wakes in her College rooms, wet with sweat, shivering with cold. As her eyes adjust to the pitch dark, she sees that this is because she turned off the gas fire before she went to bed at three o'clock and the duvet has slid off the top of her bed. She finds her robe and pulls it tight round her. She lights the gas. Coming back, still shivering, from the loo, she looks out at the quad. It's under an inch or two of snow.

Her body aches for a hot shower. But Annie knows better and stands under an icy, cold stream of water for four minutes, washing away the sweat and the fears of the night. By the end, if she doesn't die of heart failure brought on by the shock of hypothermia, she will feel a new woman, full of energy to take on the enemies of justice. Her enemies.

She doesn't die, but instead drinks three glasses of freezing tap water, straight off, makes herself coffee and turns on her desk light. Organise her thoughts for the day ahead. For her showdown with the forces of law and order.

Damn. She forgot to call Luke last night. Unforgivable not only because she desires him but because he needed, needs, to know about his father. She calls the number.

Eventually he answers. He listens in silence until she's finished. And then.

'Annie, do me a favour. I don't need you to call me when you happen not to be in bed with my father. I don't need you to be a go-between with my own family. And I do need some sleep if I'm going to put in the eighteen hours a day required to do my job. And Annie, get this. I don't need you in my life anymore.'

He rings off without waiting for her reply. Drawing strength from the mood brought on by her shower, Annie does not wilt under the onslaught of these home truths. She thinks he is desperately tired. She needs to explain to him the danger of prosecution she runs and why in consequence she has to be nice to his father for a while. Then all will come right she is sure. But that must wait.

Dismissing Luke from her mind for the moment, Annie considers how strong her position is opposite the police charges. It depends of course what her support actually says in the police interview that afternoon.

Felix Cameron. All reports suggest that Felix is genuinely

terrified of the prospect that his academic career would be grounded for ever if Annie chooses formally to report him to the College authorities for blackmail and sexual harassment. Yes, surely, he will keep to the script.

David Cameron. Until his unfortunate collapse, things seemed to be going better than ever between them. Of course, as Dr Faisal at the Radcliffe had said, it's hard to predict the consequences of blackouts, but by the time Annie had handed him over to Davina very early that morning he seemed almost his normal self. And in the few minutes before they reached his house, he seemed to have the story of what had happened last night, as opposed to what had actually happened, straight in his mind. So, all things considered, David should be solid.

Davina Cameron. Hard to be sure, but Annie Fritzweiler seemed to be the flavour of several months with her at the moment. Anyway, she ought to be a minor player in the story.

Greg Halberstadt. Annie has found time to give him his script and to make sure he understands the risks he faces if she were to be prosecuted. The last thing Greg wants is for his highly satisfactory arrangements in Oxford to be abruptly terminated by his deportation back to Australia in the leg irons of professional, and every other kind, of disgrace.

The Master of her College, has agreed to write a testimonial as to the respectability of Annie's academic research and the high esteem in which she is held both by the University Philosophy Faculty and by the College. Of course, the Master is unaware that his testimony may be used in connection with criminal proceedings.

Sergei Dzhugashvili. That is the hard one, since she has only a dim idea of what murky considerations might determine his response to the British police, irrespective of what he has said to her. But she fancies that she acquitted herself well in the park the previous day, as far as that went. Though how much of it was in her mind and how much actually in the park she was hard put to say. What she could say was that if supporting Annie Fritzweiler meant it less likely that his various boats would be rocked, he would be there for her.

At this point her bench of support is probably solid. But on the night, who's to say? Things outside her control, indeed outside her purview, might determine the outcome of the afternoon.

The Office of the Director of Public Prosecutions has the final say in whether major prosecutions in England and Wales should go ahead. Priti has told her that the DPP will be represented at the afternoon's meeting. So, what is crucial is what they will think after her interrogation by the detectives that afternoon and in particular after they have heard the legal arguments from Martin Peters.

And finally, though Annie hardly perceives this, it depends on the mood of the Establishment concerning the 'pro bono kidnapping' and on the competing attractions of having Sergei Dzhugashvili remain a resident of the UK or of deporting him back to Russia.

Two o'clock sharp and those reluctantly gathered in the Chief Constable's office, after a disagreeable sandwich lunch provided by the Constabulary, are eager to get on. Positions have changed since the meeting between Christmas and New Year.

The Chief Constable who had previously prevailed in urging a low key, that is to say cheap, investigation of the Felix Cameron kidnap, now wants the whole thing off his plate. The latest Home Office budget directive to police forces in England, has made the Chief think that sparing even two officers for the kidnap investigation is two too many. Also, he sees that the last month's statistics show that clear up rates in the County are falling. He had not realised how efficient Tench and Smogulecki were at getting confessions out of local villains, so he wants them back on the job. His job.

The Chief thinks that if Fritzweiler and perhaps others were prosecuted on the basis of the presently available evidence, then there would be no obligation to continue the present investigation and all future responsibility would fall on the DPP's Office. With luck the case might be moved to the Southwark Crown Court or even the Old Bailey, so he would not even have to provide policing to control the possible hordes of journalists at the trial. And of course, the public.

The senior official representing the DPP is still inclined to feel that the right thing to do is for the evidence against Annie Fritzweiler to be heard in a Court of Law. But he has come to recognise that the state of public opinion still strongly favours the kidnappers and the forced transfer of a rich man's assets to charity. Reflecting this, he sees the most likely outcome of a trial being failure to reach even a majority verdict, given the bias on any Jury is likely to be in favour of Annie. In other words, the facts of the case would be likely irrelevant to certain members of the Jury who would vote to acquit anyway.

There was also the matter of the long email analysing certain legal issues in the case, which Martin Peters has sent to the DPP on that Monday morning. Among other points, Peters has written that he would have with him at his client's formal interrogation a deposition, a statement sworn on oath before witnesses, by David Cameron.

In this Cameron will assert that, before he transferred his money to the two elephant charities, he had become convinced that, independently of the kidnapping, it was the right thing to do. Well but for the kidnap he might not have chosen elephants. But what Cameron will say is that he had given away his money voluntarily. This statement is consistent with the interview which David and Davina gave at the time to the major news channels in which David Cameron had said that he had come to see that giving away his money was the right thing to do.

If this were believed by a jury, the Prosecution was lost. There had been no crime because no ransom. The crime of taking Felix and holding him against his will might still be made to stand up, if the police thought they could scotch in the jury's minds the doubt that the holding against his will had been a contrivance of Felix.

But the police lack direct evidence that a kidnapping has actually taken place anywhere but in Felix's mind. The best they might do was to allege that Annie was an accessory before the fact in the criminal damage of the restaurant. Not worth the candle.

It would appear then that even on purely legal grounds the prosecution case might fail. And the last thing the Government and the DPP in particular want is for the Judge to halt the trial halfway through and dismiss the case on the grounds that the Prosecution did not have a case in law.

Just before his rushed departure from Downing Street, the Deputy Secretary at the Cabinet Office has received an ear bashing from the Minister of State at the Home Office. The import of the Minister's tirade was no embarrassment and no extra public expenditure. This translated to "drop the bloody case".' The Prime Minister's Director of Communications has said something along the same lines.

But there was one thing that gave the Deputy Secretary pause. Late the previous evening, under the cloak of darkness, a counter espionage officer with the ear of the Co-ordinator of the Security Services, had slipped into the Cabinet Office. He was there to remind the Cabinet Office that the Fritzweiler case could be an ideal pretext to get rid of Sergei Dzhugashvili from the UK, for good. It is not that Dzhugashvili has been shown to be doing anything inimical to the interests of the UK. It is far worse than that. British counter-intelligence simply does not know.

It is not until nearly six that evening, when darkness has already fallen outside, that the formal police interrogation begins. A plain table in the centre of the room. On one side Martin Peters, Priti Patel and Dr Annie Fritzweiler. On the other, the local Crown Prosecutor, Detective Inspector Tench and Detective Sergeant Smogulecki. All these declared their full names and official titles for the recording device, as was required by the rules of procedure. The time and date were recited by Smogulecki, who further stated that Dr Fritzweiler had not been charged with any offence and had submitted herself voluntarily to this interrogation.

Behind Annie and her lawyers sat David and Felix Cameron. Like the Camerons, Greg Halberstadt had provided a sworn deposition, of which Priti had provided copies to the police and their lawyer.

Martin Peters had got up at three o'clock that morning in the cold of the pitch dark and driven without regard for speed limits on an empty motorway through the recently fallen snow to the Belgravia mansion of Sergei Dzhugashvili. There he had joined the Russian and his protection in their regular morning run of six kilometres round Hyde Park. The only time in the twenty-four hours when, at least in winter, the Park was totally silent. Not even a single snort from the mounts of the Horse Guards in their barracks across the way, as the runners came back along Rotten Row, pushing hard for home. By this stage, Martin is fifty yards adrift and wallowing. The inside of his lungs burning with the huge drafts of cold air he is forced to try and take in.

Fortunately, the Russians are impressed anyway and wait for him so they can cross the road together at Hyde Park Corner.

The purpose of this early morning exertion was achieved when Sergei signed a half page typed statement, witnessed by Martin Peters, English Solicitor, and one of the Protection, identifying himself as a security advisor. And possibly, Peters reflects, Annie having shared the thought with him, one of Felix Cameron's kidnappers.

'We must do these things again, Martin,' said Sergei, escorting Martin to his car. 'I never know an Englishman who is such a good sporter.'

There was even a bear hug.

Martin is constrained to report these things to Annie that afternoon, in order to explain how he has obtained the statement signed by Sergei denying that Dr Annie Fritzweiler had asked him to provide, directly or indirectly, people to execute a kidnapping.

'You had said, Annie, that he was a runner. It was the only way I could think of just possibly to get his confidence.'

'How did you become so good?' Annie inquired. 'In running.'

'I was an athletics Blue. I ran against Cambridge when I was an undergraduate. If you reach that level of fitness in your youth it never entirely leaves you. And yes, I still do run occasionally, though the work and the family don't leave much time.'

'Would you allow me to join you sometimes? Though I'm sure you'd quickly leave me in the dust.'

'I think I would like that, Annie. It would make me get back to it properly if we had a regular date. I'm sorry, I meant....'

'No need to be sorry, Martin.'

'Now, Annie, we really must get back to the case.'

But the case was dissolving before their eyes. Having read the depositions of David and Felix Cameron and that of Greg Halberstadt, and the statement signed by Sergei Dzhugashvili, DI Tench could see none of them gave any quarter to the police case. Knowledge of anything that could amount to the suggestion of a crime by Annie Fritzweiler or by themselves was flatly and absolutely denied.

He has called his Chief Constable and conveyed his opinion that the police will get nowhere with their interrogation. To Tench's surprise, the Chief is all bonhomie.

'Much better to recognise when things are beyond us, Tench. We all did our best, especially you and your good Detective Sergeant. The Fritzweiler woman is most unlikely to go round the county kidnapping other rich individuals, eh Tench?'

The Detective Inspector had done his best to join in with the

Chief's laughter.

'No, no, much the best outcome. Now you and your DS can get back to your real work. We've been missing your effort here, you know. And good show, Tench. Good show.'

The delay in the start of the interrogation is caused by the police side conferring privately with the local Crown Prosecutor. Smogulecki burns with rage and frustration when told of Tench's feeling and the Chief Constable's reaction.

Dr Fritzweiler is told she is free to go. The police would consider further the position, but, without prejudice, Annie could expect the case against her would be dropped. A formal letter would follow.

And that was that.

Annie gets up from her chair and turns formally to thank David and Felix Cameron, sitting behind her. But she quickly excuses herself. She has other obligations tonight and anyway she can really only manage one Cameron at a time.

When Annie and her two lawyers walk outside there is no marching band or overjoyed crowd of supporters. Just cold air and a light sleet.

Conscious that Martin Peters has spent the last two and a half days working without sleep and with extraordinary ingenuity on her behalf Annie asks again how she can possibly repay him. Blinking in the streetlights behind his rimless glasses, Martin tells her. What he has had in mind for some time is a seminar in the Trinity (Oxford University speak for summer) Term, led jointly by Dr Fritzweiler and himself, in which the tools of analytic philosophy would be brought to bear on some critical issue of English law.

Priti Patel laughs out loud on the pavement.

'Martin you cold fish. I thought at least you were going to invite her to Monte Carlo for the weekend so you could have your wicked way with her.'

'As you know Priti, I am a family man....'

'Well, I'm a family woman, but....'

But even Priti realises she had better stop there.

Annie half-heartedly suggests at least a drink, but Martin and Priti have dinners and families to get back to. Food for thought there, thinks Annie, as she drives slowly down the Banbury road, back to her empty her flat.

Annie feels her life has been given back to her. But what life? Lonely meals at home. No one with whom to share the chores or domestic decisions, or even the profound relief of not being prosecuted.

That was one of the things that drew her to accept a Fellowship at an Oxford College. These days, if she feels the need of company on any day of the week, she can lunch or dine in Hall. The Fellows have welcomed her warmly, all but Jeff Cunliffe and one or two others. She may not turn heads in the High, but she is by some distance the most attractive of the scattering of women to be found at High Table. She always takes care about her appearance. Something not all women academics are known for, following no doubt in the footsteps of most academic men.

And in these enlightened times, as long as it is not a formal night, she can vary things by eating with the students, with whom she is generally popular, at one of the long tables and benches that stretch off into the distance at right angles to High Table.

As to chores, her efficiency is such as to make those less of a burden than if she had to share her flat with a partner or to hire someone to do the shopping and cleaning. And as to decisions, she much prefers to make her own without the need to take account of the desires of anyone else. It's only the difficulty of holidays which gives her pause. Somehow holidays are naturally designed for families or couples.

But tonight, she has no appetite for food and no energy to think of holidays or anything else in her life. All she can do is to manage to have a hot shower, before she collapses on her bed, dead to the world.

Annie Fritzweiler sleeps soundly, content in the knowledge that she is now safe from prosecution for any aspect of Andrew's kidnapping. But also, that she is safe from Andrew himself. The threat of his blackmail has vanished along with the risk of prosecution. And Annie still has in reserve the report on his attempt to blackmail her into having sex with him. Andrew is not going to stray far from the straight and narrow with that hanging over him.

47

Unforeseen

Ten o'clock, her first tutorial of the day. Twenty minutes in and her phone rings. She nearly doesn't answer it, especially as she notes it is the Master's number.

Could she spare him a moment? Not until four o'clock she couldn't. The tutorial traffic is backed up till then.

'That could be a shade too late, Dr Fritzweiler. If I may suggest that you crave the indulgence of your present student and excuse yourself for ten minutes. It is a matter of which, in your own interests, you need to be made aware as soon as may be.'

This is as close to a direct order as the Master ever approaches. She tells Joyce and Anthony to debate between them their differing views on What We Can Know until she returns.

'Try reach an agreed conclusion and be ready to present it to me in twenty minutes. No, I'll make up the time to you later in the term.'

Students who have had to take out loans to fund their tuition payments are often keen to get their money's worth, even if they can count the value of a tutorial only in minutes.

'Dr Fritzweiler, Annie, so glad you could spare me....'

The only advantage of a visit to the Master's Lodgings is that he serves the best coffee in the College, and within thirty seconds of sitting down in the Master's study, a College servant is setting down a cup of excellent espresso beside her.

The Master frowns at Annie's tight jeans. At least he thinks they are jeans. Irritated she crosses her legs.

Masters of Oxford Colleges come in two forms.

Successful academics raised to the purple by their colleagues, the other Fellows, by vote. This sometimes leads to bitterness within College with the supporters of losing candidates. But it does mean the College is run by someone who understands the issues.

The second kind of Master is an outsider, sometimes an academic but more often a recently retired senior figure from the public sector, Permanent Secretary of a major Government Department or Ambassador to a major country. Increasingly though, the criteria for appointment have been reduced to one. Who is likely to be able to raise the most money for the College? This is especially true for a middle ranking College such as Annie's which has inherited no large endowment in the way of St. John's or Christ Church, for example.

This Master is Sir Alexander Graham Burns, a former Permanent Secretary at the Home Office, the Department responsible among other things for the police and for controlling immigration. Unusually, he gets to the point at once.

'Dr Fritzweiler, you will recall the conversation we had, a week or two ago would it have been, about a student of yours, Andrew Cameron. Yes, yes, son of the novelist, just so.'

'Yes Master. You were most understanding.'

'I was Annie, perhaps too understanding. As you may remember I had my doubts at the time. But I allowed the power of your arguments, skilfully deployed I may say, to sway me.'

'Indeed, Master.'

Annie uncrosses her legs and drinks her coffee quickly. She does not like the sound of this at all.

'I was dining last evening with the College Visitor....Oh I forget, you are new to our quirks of governance. The Visitor is a distinguished figure from outside the College who occasionally pays us, as it might be, a visit. At base his function is to see that the College is being properly run, in accordance with its traditions and aspirations, if you follow me.

'Naturally, Master.'

'The Visitors at some Colleges treat their role as entirely formal and at best come and enjoy a good dinner once a year. Our Visitor is, if I may put it like this, made of sterner and more inquiring stuff. He's a self-made man, you know, a hugely successful entrepreneur.'

'I didn't,' says Annie. But it might help, she thinks, if you told me his name.

'He comes to us normally once a term and asks me and some of the senior Fellows if there is anything particularly on our minds here. Oh, didn't I say? Sir Siddhartha Mukherjee. He allows a few of us to call him Sir Sid, you know. He has done wonders for the College, absolute wonders.'

Annie can do the translation. He has donated a pile of money.

'Well over drinks last evening, he asked, as he customarily does, if there was anything in particular concerning me in connection with the running of the College. I must confess, Annie, that what you had told me about young Andrew Cameron then came to my mind. I explained to Sir Sid the facts of the case and that you had particularly requested that no action be taken as long as his conduct from now on were exemplary. This on the grounds, if I remember correctly, that this student was particularly gifted and had the possibility a great career before him. Bringing honour to the College and so on.'

'And, Master, that Andrew is emotionally very underdeveloped for his age.'

'Ah yes. I must tell you, Annie, that Sir Sid did not react well. Not well at all. He hails no doubt from a hard school. Harder than you or I can imagine, Annie.'

I wouldn't bet on that, thinks Annie, thinking of her struggles just to stay out of jail in the GDR.

'But Sir Sid is straight as a die, Annie, honest as the day is long.'

A short winter day in January, Annie can't stop herself from wondering. But the Master is getting to the point.

'I was, if I may so admit it, shown the error of my ways. In sum Annie, it has been decided that Andrew Cameron should be sent down with immediate effect and removed from the College and from the University rolls as soon as the formalities can be completed.'

'Master, may I speak?'

'No Dr Fritzweiler, you have spoken enough on this topic. You may however, as a courtesy, read the letter which I will this morning have delivered by hand to this student.'

The Master hands her a single sheet of College notepaper, his own signature appended.

'As you see Dr Fritzweiler, this is not for discussion. You are new to our ways. Though we all hope you may have a long and fruitful tenure here.'

Annie wonders if she should simply tear the page in half, from top to bottom. But what would that achieve except damage to herself and her cause?

Trying to keep her voice level, she says: 'Master, I shall appeal to the Fellows, as I believe is my right under the College Statutes in the case of a student who....'

'Dr Fritzweiler, by long custom disciplinary matters are delegated by the Fellows to a sub-committee of the Vice Master, the Senior Tutor, the Dean, the Bursar and myself. Late last night we met, by Skype...never say we don't move with the times here...since the Bursar is in Africa dealing with a particular project in which the College is interested. The decision was quick and unanimous.'

'I wonder if your proceedings are legal, however long the custom of which you speak. I shall investigate the matter further.'

She has no idea of her ground here. But in these circumstances, one must say something. At least one must if one is Annie Fritzweiler.

'Dr Fritzweiler I believe you have tutorial students to attend to. May I remind you that students are the life blood of this College? The justification for our somewhat privileged existence.'

Annie leaves the Lodgings without kissing the Master on the lips.

She strides back to her room and dismisses her students with the promise to re-schedule the whole tutorial. Annie then texts the students who are due to come next to her tutorial. Then she calls Martin Peters.

He sounds tired, tired of her and her troubles, and in the middle of a tutorial.

'Annie, in College matters it does no good to fight the powers that be, even if in strict logic or law or what have you, you might be right.'

He is about to ring off, when she manages to make her point.

'But don't you see, Martin, my case. Andrew Cameron... Felix...may change his mind. Go to the police.'

Martin grasps the point at once. In his mind, whether he realises it or not, he has become her champion. He will stand by her come what may.

'Where is your room, Annie? Staircase twenty-four? I'll be over as soon as I'm finished here.'

Martin does not say not to worry because, Annie assumes, there is something to worry about.

48

A Very Gentle Knight

An anxious twenty minutes later, Martin knocks on her door. In his hand is a single sheet of College notepaper.

'What's that?'

'The Master's letter to Andrew Cameron.'

'You got him to retract it?'

'No, I intercepted it before it reached Andrew.'

'Isn't that, I mean...? Anyway, the Master told me he was going to send it for delivery into hand of addressee only.'

'Annie, those of us who have been at this College for any length of time know that the College servants have fallen into somewhat lackadaisical ways. Not unreasonably since their average age must now be well over seventy. You told me that

Andrew's room is on the fifth floor. Faced with such effort of mountaineering, most College servants would simply leave the letter in the subject's pigeon hole.'

'Won't the Master find out?'

'Unlikely. He assumes that once he has issued an instruction it will be carried out to the letter. Never been known to check.'

'But Martin, given time, he may notice that Andrew is still here.'

'Well, given time the procedures for formally removing Andrew Cameron from the College and University rolls will work through of course. It is not my intention to destroy the letter. Merely to buy time to reason with the Master.'

Annie sits down. It's all too much.

'Martin, I did not find the Master at all reasonable. He forbade me to speak. Do sit down Martin.'

'Par for the course, I'm afraid, Annie.'

'So, what can we do?'

'It's really what I can do. Since I'm the only lawyer among the Fellows of this College, I have a rather privileged position with Sir Alexander. The man is preternaturally stingy, so taps me for all sorts of free legal advice. Of course, I tell him that before he takes any action, he must consult a specialist in the appropriate field. But I do as far as I can give him a general idea as to whether his notion of the moment is barmy or not.'

'And it sometimes is?'

'Almost always. Anyway, he will at least listen to me on legal questions. Before I came to see you, I had a quick look at the Statutes of the College. The Master's sub-committee on College discipline is indeed provided for, but the Statutes require this committee to report back to a full meeting of Fellows before action is taken.'

'Oh Martin, my great burden of unpaid obligation to you is about to get bigger. I'm not sure I can stand it. What can I do?'

'Start sketching out ideas for our joint seminar. But Annie let's not run ahead of ourselves. The Master may argue that in practice his sub-committee has always proceeded without reference back to the Fellows. That everyone is aware of this and so his action is justified by custom, precedent if you like. The problem with this from the Master's point of view is that, in law anyway, statute always overrides precedent.'

'So, you've solved it?'

Annie jumps up in excitement and looks down at him where he is sitting just in front of her.

'By no means Annie. Firstly, it's unclear if the College

is bound in its internal procedures to follow English Law. Secondly, even if we overcome that, we still have to convince a majority of the Fellows to support your position. Not as easy as all that since there are certainly drawbacks for a third party in opposing what Alexander wants, you know. He can be quite vindictive.'

'So, what should we do?'

'I'll help of course, but this one is mainly up to you, Annie. Your great clarity of mind and your, well charm, I suppose.'

Annie laughs.

'Yes, it probably is charm rather than clarity of mind, Martin. But do I have to go into all my filthy laundry in public?'

'Your laundry is merely dirty Annie, not filthy. And no, you don't need to explain the attempt to blackmail you in relation to the kidnap story. Just stick to sexual harassment. Indicate that Andrew threatened something which merited his being sent down, but for the sake of the student's future... A number of Fellows will be sympathetic to that line since they do actually care about their students. Oh, and Annie, there is a regular meeting of Fellows this Thursday evening.'

'OK I'll start with those who are in Hall for lunch.'

'Today is Tuesday,' Martin continues. 'If you contact the College Secretary by five o'clock this evening you can get your matter on the agenda.'

'Where would I be without you, Martin?'

'In a police cell,' he says. 'And I'll make an appointment for later today to see the Master. You know Annie, I don't think you will have so much trouble in charming a majority of the Fellows if you look to them as nice as you look to me now.'

Annie is now conscious of the intense gaze of his rimless glasses on her person. She wonders if he will kiss her as he leaves, but he just leaves. Perhaps a little pinker in the face than when he arrived.

49

Supporters' Club

Annie sits down and makes a list of the Fellows whom she feels are friendly towards her. Then she starts to make calls. There are forty- eight or nine Fellows at the College, so Annie quickly realises that even excluding those who are unlikely to support her whatever she says, such as the members of the Master's sub-committee, it is not feasible to canvass them all quickly enough.

So, she sends a personal email to all those she thinks could support her and invites them to a gathering in her rooms that evening at six to discuss a question of how the College should treat junior members, students, in any matter which could give rise to a permanent dismissal from the College and the University. A live case is before them at the moment. Deliberately she gives no further detail.

An inducement to attend, in addition to seeing justice done, is that decent wine will be served. Then she calls her staircase neighbour, Otto, who despite being in constant training for some athletic event or other, patronises Oxford's best wine merchant. She asks him to organise things for her. He is deferential enough to be delighted to oblige her. Or perhaps, after all, he quite likes her.

By six fifteen when she attempts to bring the meeting to order, her room, for she has wisely locked the bedroom, is overflowing. The atmosphere is more like that of a party than a meeting to discuss the lifetime fate of a student. Not to speak of the fate of herself. Although of course she nowhere refers to that.

Seeing that almost everyone in the room is taller than she, a few by a foot or more, she sees nothing for it but to climb onto her desk. This action alone commands attention and then silence. Annie blesses the fact that she is wearing trousers.

Over the next four minutes and without notes, Annie Fritzweiler sets out the facts and key decision criteria. She has reduced the latter to two only:

That disciplinary decisions affecting the long-term future of a student should be made by the Master and Fellows meeting together as is required by the College Statutes and not by a sub-committee of old men (remarkably, no single College office holder is a woman), out of touch since they seldom teach undergraduates;

That the case of Andrew Cameron, having been made urgent by the Master's decision, acting alone but for a handful of senior colleagues, should be reviewed and reversed by the meeting of Fellows to be held on the next ensuing Thursday.

Dr Martin Peters, Fellow in Law, then reports that in his meeting with the Master that afternoon, Sir Alexander had expressed himself perfectly amenable to the matter being referred for decision to a full meeting of Fellows.

A storm in a teacup, he had said. He would always have been open to changing his mind on this matter in light of the views of a majority of Fellows, had it been clearly explained to him by Dr Fritzweiler. There is general laughter at this in light of Annie's perfect clarity a few moments before in explaining her case.

Several Fellows make contributions, mostly supporting Annie's point of view, but two cautioning that mechanisms of governance that have served the College well over the years should not be lightly discarded.

As discussed with Martin, Annie does not ask for a vote. The mood in her favour is running strongly and with luck will continue to do so for the next forty-eight hours.

Only one anxiety comes to spoil Annie's triumph. At the back of the room, she sees Otto with a woman she assumes must be his girlfriend. Presumably having organised the wine, with enough glasses and snacks for a small army, Otto felt he had been implicitly invited. But if news of Andrew's issue, or even the fact that there now is an issue, gets back to Andrew, as it surely will once it is common knowledge among the junior members of the College, there is no knowing if Andrew might panic and react irrationally, disastrously.

When Annie brings the meeting to an end, even the quality of Otto's wine does not detain the academics long. In the short term of eight weeks which Oxford allows, like their students they are all furiously busy. The inevitable few stragglers Annie bribes to go by offering them a bottle each to take with them. All but one is not too abashed to accept it.

Annie's scout is on hand at once to clear up, in return for the inducement of one hundred pounds which she has offered. While cleaning up is going on, Martin takes a bottle of the best of the Bordeaux and invites Annie to his room.

He congratulates her. She tells him her anxiety.

'A good point Annie. I think you have to invite him to come and see you, now. This evening at least.'

'I'll go over to his room.'

'No, too importunate. It looks as if you were worried about something other than Andrew.'

'He knows that I am.'

'Give him a call now and get him to come over here.'

'All right. Yes, it is certainly better that we see him together. He might be too frightened to see me alone. Also, you add the gravitas of legal certainty.'

'If ever there were self-contradiction, Annie, it's "legal certainty".'

Ten minutes later, Andrew arrives. Annie asks him to sit down, but does not offer him a glass of wine. In fact, she had cleared the wine out of sight while Martin went to let him in.

They explain the confusion that has arisen and that the Master has agreed to revoke his expulsion depending on a decision by the full meeting of Fellows.

'It's good that that young man should understand in what jeopardy he stands if he tries to cross you, Annie,' Martin had said.

Annie explains that in the meeting just finished there was general support for retaining him as a member of the College as long as he continues to behave himself. Andrew however seizes on the possibility, however improbable, that the Fellows may decide to support the Master's original decision.

She cannot deny that such a possibility exists, but she and Martin emphasise that anything he might do prior to that decision would be disastrous for him.

He goes away unhappy and uncertain. Martin is confident that things will hold until after the meeting on Thursday. Annie is not so sure. After all, originally, she had told him that as long as he behaved himself nothing would happen to him. No mention of telling the Master informally.

'Why did you, Annie?'

'Tell the Master? In order to make sure of my credibility, should I have to use my nuclear deterrent at a later stage.'

'I wondered,' says Martin.

The mood of her triumph at the meeting has evaporated. She feels depressed and leaves to go back to her flat. What she is really worried about is not Andrew doing something stupid, but that Andrew will tell his father, which she is sure he will. And Annie cannot predict what lunatic impulse may enter the head of David Cameron. Though she has a pile of work, she thinks that she should find out. That very evening.

50

Making Things Right

She is not looking forward to the call. But it needs to be done. She can think of nothing but a straightforward approach. Here is where we are, David. The Fellows' meeting on Thursday will make it all right. Hang tightly. Is that what the English idiom is? Don't do anything rash. End of message.

Before she can rouse herself from the prone position into which she has fallen on her couch, her mobile rings. She gets up to answer it.

'Yes...Oh it's you David. Feeling...?'

Andrew has evidently been in contact with his father. David's stream of invective knocks her backwards, almost physically.

'You told me the fucking problem with Felix was fixed. And now? You're nothing but a cheap whore, Annie, only out for what you can get for yourself.'

When his initial anger is almost spent, her own anger takes over.

'You are an abusive and pathetic figure, David. You can't even service a woman properly. Nothing is more contemptible in a man than sexually to arouse a woman and then leave her in the trough. You only get a proper hardness in your pathetic books.'

Annie is conscious that behind her fury her English is collapsing around her, but she doesn't care. Then abruptly she is can think of nothing more. There ensues a long silence. At last, he says one soft word.

'Annie.'

And then it is all right again.

'Yes, we have to talk…Face to face is better…No, it is fine to come over here…No Davina will be fine with it. Now she's got her confidence back, not to speak of her son, she doesn't see you as any sort of competition.'

In spite of herself, Annie almost bridles at this.

'Anyway, she's best pals with that Russian of yours. Effects to say it's all in the cause of getting him to give us a long lease on soft terms but there seems to be more to it than that. Not that I care as long as I have you, Annie my love…Yes, come over now.'

So, she has a quick shower, changes, repairs her make-up, gets a coat and scarf, and climbs into her car for the now familiar run across the Downs.

Parking close to the house, Annie makes the short dash through the cold to the front door. It's open. David emerges from somewhere and hugs her.

'You're warm,' she says.

'Come into the kitchen for a moment.'

Davina is at the long, rough table which is scattered with books, newspapers, a couple of iPads and the remains of an early dinner. She gets up and embraces Annie, while continuing to chat into the phone. Annie is apparently not encouraged to linger, though Davina says: 'Don't allow that bear of a husband of mine let you freeze to death in his study.'

Two things are clear. As David had promised, his wife is entirely relaxed about David being alone with Annie. Neither David nor Felix have told Davina about the Master's action.

'Come and have some dinner when you're finished,' Davina says as Annie retreats, though no sign of preparation or even of leftovers is apparent.

They sit at an angle to each other in the study. Annie crosses her legs and sets out her stall. David asks the obvious question.

'But what if the Fellows meeting goes against you?'

'It won't. I've taken thorough soundings. More than half the voting Fellows were at my meeting, and the mood was strongly in my favour. Only two people expressed doubts. Anyway, Martin Peters is totally on side. He'll be at the Thursday meeting to back me up and to keep the Master under control.'

'This Peters chap? I've met him a number of times at College functions with my old friend Jeff Cunliffe...you know the Fellow in Politics. Got lots of kids, hasn't he? What's your connection with him?'

Annie explains, without making too much of Martin's decisive contribution both with the police and with the Master. If David is really so enamoured of her, she doesn't need to inflict on him any other source of jealousy. He seems to be happy that Sergei's interest in Davina removes the Russian from Annie's area of ambition.

As for Luke, David is now inclined to think that Annie's obvious eagerness to sleep with himself on the previous evening means that he was mistaken as to the strength of Annie's affection for Luke. Certainly, the plate full of dinner smashing down on his head indicated strong passion for Annie in his elder son. But on reflection he is inclined to think that whatever exactly happened between Annie and Luke in Annie's kitchen on Sunday afternoon, it was as Annie said, innocent. On her side at least.

Annie's explanation about her lawyer is enough to cross him off the list of potential spoilers. So, he has Annie all to himself, in his mind anyway.

'Annie, I think what you said yesterday evening, you know before my black out and so on, was exactly right. There is nothing to stop us having an affair. Certainly not Davina, as long as she doesn't think I'm going to leave her for you. That would cause her too much social embarrassment.'

Oh well, thinks Annie, that's all fine then. Just one problem. She's hasn't remotely fallen for David. But what does that matter to someone in her position. She needs more than ever to keep him on side and if that means allowing herself to be aroused by him from time to time, that's readily enough done.

'There's just one thing Annie. I can't imagine what possessed you to tell the Master about Felix's appalling behaviour? Since you had decided to protect him this time, conditional on his future good behaviour.'

She slowly uncrosses and re-crosses her legs. Tonight, she is wearing her black boots, a green top and the same grey skirt, which in her rush was all she could lay hands on. She can sense the desire slowly welling up in him

'In order to ensure my credibility, if I ever had to use my nuclear deterrent.'

'Of getting Felix expelled from the University and so destroying his future? Even so, was that really necessary? After all, if your deterrent failed and Felix did carry out his threat, what point would there be in using your power to destroy his future?'

'For a deterrent to work, one must believe that one would use it.'

'Not sure I follow. Anyway, didn't you run an awful risk if the Master turned out to be very hard line and insisted on Felix's expulsion?'

'Not really. I didn't tell the Master bluntly just like that. I led up to it gently with a hypothetical about how the College would deal with a case of sexual harassment by a junior member of the College against a member of the teaching staff. The Master indicated that he would be inclined very much to leave it up to the Fellow concerned to take the lead.'

'But, Annie, if the Master subsequently found out the true foulness of Felix's threat, might he not have adopted an intransigent attitude anyway?

'I did tell the Master that Felix's offence involved a threat disclosure of something personal which properly should be kept private, though of course I did not go into the detail of the blackmail. Surely you can see that was reasonable?'

David is wearing a new pink shirt, jeans and brown brogues. He smells, Annie admits to herself, rather acceptable.

'Well yes, I suppose I can see that. All right, topic closed.'

'And you'll make sure Felix does nothing rash between now and the Thursday meeting…or after it?'

'Yes Annie, I'll make sure. Now, what shall we do this evening?'

He smiles at her.

'Just one moment, David. I have something to ask.'

He sits back, indulgently. Anything I can tell you Annie. To you, I'm an open book.

'What about Davina, exactly?'

'Ah, as it happens, we had a heart to heart just before you arrived.'

51

Grown Up Conversation

'Oh Davina, Annie is coming over for a few minutes, if that's OK. Just to see how I am after last night.'

'Oh yes, she told me she might drop in. That makes it a good opportunity to say what I've been meaning to say to you, David, now things are all right again between us. To avoid misunderstanding in the future. Our marriage is completely solid, isn't it? What I'm going to say works only if you are sure it is.'

'Completely solid, Davina.'

He draws her to him but she resists.

'No David, listen to me carefully. As long as that is so, I am prepared to tolerate a little bit of latitude on your side.'

David pricks up his ears.

'It's inevitable at your time of life that you're going to be tempted and probably from time to time, give way. It's just a matter of your age and declining powers.'

David's ears flatten against the side of his head.

'I know that you and Annie Fritzweiler have something going on between you. That's been obvious for a while, however discrete you may think you have been. Whilst I can't say I like it, if it has to be somebody, better Annie than anyone else.

'Oh, but why should you think...?'

'Please David, no more pretence. It insults my intelligence and belittles you. As I said, better Annie than some twenty-year old undergraduate. She is at least somewhere close to your own age and is less likely to have her head turned. To mistake your philandering for anything more permanent.'

'Does Annie Fritzweiler have other un-dreamed of advantages?'

Davina grimaces but continues.

'Annie is, I think a nice, clean woman. Sensible within her limits. In her fashion she has been a good friend to this family, and to me, over Felix's event.'

Even now she cannot bring herself to call it a kidnapping. The image he supposes conjured by Sergei Dzhugashvili in this very kitchen of her son's head on a Christmas platter will not recede for a long time, if ever.

'As I say, Annie Fritzweiler is in many ways I'm sure, a decent woman. Her looks are nothing special to my eyes, but I can see she is attractive enough in her way. And if she's lonely, living by herself and so on, then I can see no great reason why, when you have nothing better to do, you and she shouldn't be of service to one another. But only occasionally, David. It must not become a regular thing.'

How exactly would we define 'regular' in this case wonders David, but remains silent?

'And David, you and she must be absolutely discrete. I do not want to be aware of when or where anything may take place or indeed if it takes place. I will not be humiliated or even embarrassed.'

'Understood, Davina.'

Beyond that David doesn't quite know how to react. He feels jumping for joy might not be quite in keeping. A pious speech granting Davina freedoms similar to those she has just given him would be too trite.

'But David, only Annie. All right? And do not let yourself fall for her. Remember she is five years older than I am. There is no need to say anything. I just hope this will work to solidify our marriage.'

"Solidify." That's exactly the right word in relation to their relationship, he feels. He nods and is sure looks embarrassed.

But his wife is embarrassed too. There is one other point, but she can't find words. He helps her out.

'It's OK Davina, I understand. Marriage is a two-way street.'

Davina seems relieved that he has understood. The doorbell.

'Oh, that will be Annie now?'

52

Storm in a Chafing Dish

Annie regards David. Her estimation of Davina's good sense has risen sharply in the last several minutes. And of David's too. And she gives him every credit for breaking the stalemate when their quarrel on the phone just now had deadlocked them in their mutual anger. Something she could not have brought herself to do.

He smiles at her.

'And now, Annie, what shall we do for the rest of the evening?'

He glances at the couch. Too short, she thinks. Not for her but for him. She casts her eyes modestly downwards and looks at the thick pile carpet. David gets up and takes both her hands as to pull her from her chair. The next dance? The next…?

'Wait, David, wait.'

She can tell he is very tense. The risks of discovery are exactly counterbalancing his now fierce desire for her. She needs to navigate carefully. They must not jeopardise Davina's surprising good will.

'It's OK David. What is it you want to do with me?'

He is the sort of man who knows how to arouse a woman. And after all she has not entirely forgotten how to excite a man. But they will be discrete so that if someone does come in, unexpectedly, they can break off at once and nothing will seem to be amiss.

So, his attack when it comes a minute or two latter, like that of a drowning man desperate to get on shore, takes her completely by surprise. He has her on the floor. She yells out. She does not know if it is with pain or surprise. What she does know is that it is only a few seconds after this that the door is flung wide. Luke stands in the doorway. Annie feels a complete sense of despair. Luke is evidently deeply upset.

'The Bistro. They closed it down this afternoon. They found a cockroach in a chafing dish.'

In less time than it takes to say "cockroach", Annie is standing up, her skirt smoothed, her bag on her shoulder, willing Luke not to pay regard to what he must have seen.

'Oh Luke, that is something awful.'

'It's for a full week, Annie.' He is almost sobbing. 'And

there's a bank payment due at the end of this week. I shan't be able to meet it.'

She is embracing him tightly. As a sister, a best friend, not a lover. 'Luke! Luke! Listen to me. It will be all right, I promise. If I have to, I'll give you the money myself.' But she has no idea how much it would be.

At last David has composed himself.

'Don't be silly. It's very sweet of Annie, but of course I'll help you out. Whatever you need. And first thing tomorrow you and I, Luke, will go and see the Oxford public health people. Very likely we can quickly sort this out.'

Annie has released Luke and melted into the wall paper. Davina is now in the doorway.

'It sounded as if someone was being murdered in here. Is everyone all right? Oh Luke. Nice to see you dear but shouldn't you be serving dinner at that Bistro of yours? Anyhow as long as everyone's OK....'

And Davina is no longer in the doorway.

'David, as I told you, I really must be going. I only came to make sure you were OK, after last night. There's a huge pile of things to I have to get through for tomorrow. Luke, I'll call you later to see if there's anything I can do. I mean it, Luke.'

And Annie is gone, scot free, without a glove being laid.

David doing exactly the right thing. Absolving Luke of responsibility for the cockroach. This is one of the few occasions when it's of more help to have the imagination of a thriller writer than the practical knowledge of a public health official.

'Have you had any competitors in recently? And no doubt you let them have a nose around the kitchen? Oh, my dear Luke. Obviously, one of these guys was sufficiently impressed by The Bistro to try to sabotage it. It doesn't take much insect life to get a restaurant closed down. And planting the little buggers is the work of a moment.'

Luke is almost ready to celebrate by the time father and son emerge from the study. David guides Luke to the kitchen, gets the one remaining champagne bottle out of the fridge and pours three glasses.

They toast new beginnings.

'Pity Annie couldn't have stayed,' says Luke after a couple of gulps of the yellow and delightful liquid, bubbles winking at the brim of all their glasses.

'Yes,' says David, with as heavy a heart as Luke's, 'it's a very great pity.'

Annie drives back to Oxford, as so often before, much too fast. All the way she curses herself. David was quite right earlier. She is a whore. The fact that he didn't actually succeed in penetrating her before her scream stopped him in his tracks was neither here nor there.

Back in her flat, she works her way through her pile of papers, not to speak of accumulated emails. From time to time she gets up to pace the room and swear at herself.

It's three in the morning by the time she calls a halt. By then she has formulated two absolute rules for herself. She will use her apparently enduring powers of attraction sparingly and only to the extent required to get the support she needs to stop Felix giving her away. And she will not again allow a man to sleep with her or even come close to doing so.

But if it becomes absolutely necessary to allow that, she will only do it in her rooms in College, where she cannot be ambushed and where a College servant will be there in the morning to make up the bed with clean sheets.

53

Good Fellowship

On Martin's advice, Annie spends a good part of the day when she is not actually teaching making sure those who came to the meeting in her rooms are still solid. All but those few dissenters. She reckons that even if all the other Fellows vote against her then she will still have a clear majority on Thursday evening. But not so clear that she can rest easy in her mind until the Thursday meeting is over. What she has learnt since coming to Oxford is that the unexpected happens unexpectedly often.

In consequence her administrative emails remain unanswered and her current research paper abandoned, for the moment.

Annie agonises over what to wear. There is normally only one Fellows' meeting a term, but the one that was due to take place in the previous term, Michaelmas, her first at Oxford, was cancelled for some reason. So, she really does not know the form.

In England, a few formal occasions still require a woman to wear a skirt, though not to show too much of her legs, obviously. In the end Annie wears a black skirt falling below her knees. She has had meetings in the Fellows room and remembers that the central heating doesn't work, so she wears her long black boots and a black leather jacket with a muted silk scarf. The overall effect is a bit sombre. It needs some jewellery. But since Annie isn't rich enough to afford real gems, she scorns to wear anything. Her lovers were not very generous in that area. When she had lovers.

She has made some headline notes of what she wants to say. But she is good at spontaneous speaking in public and the notes are only in case her mind goes blank at the start. After that she will be fine.

On account of her nerves, she starts down her staircase ten minutes too early. Realising this, she returns and scrolls rapidly through recent emails on her lap top to see if there is anything really urgent. There is, and in consequence of answering it, she has to run down the staircase and across the quad. Even so she enters the Fellows Room just behind the Master. Probably an unforgivable breach of College etiquette.

But he smiles at her indulgently and they go to find their respective seats, he at the head and she near the foot of the long table. While the table is settling down, Annie asks the College Secretary, who is taking the minutes, to exchange seats with her, so she is seated right at the very end of the table and able to look the Master straight in the eye, when she wears her glasses at least. Also, she can see, obliquely at least, all the other Fellows

More than an hour is taken up with housekeeping matters, but fortunately hers is the only issue of substance on the Agenda.

At last, the Master invites her to outline the facts of her case and the action or inaction she recommends.

Annie asks the Master's permission to stand to deliver her presentation. She speaks with her usual clarity and efficiency. Her German accent is more marked than usual, but that is all right she feels as long as she makes no grammatical errors.

First, she recites the motion before the meeting, that no disciplinary action be taken against Andrew David Felix Cameron, Junior Member of the College, in the matter of certain words uttered to his tutor in philosophy, Dr Annie Angela Fritzweiler. This to be conditional on his continued good behaviour and standing whilst he remains a Member of the College.

She carefully outlines and edits the words spoken. A threat to make certain disclosures of a private nature potentially damaging to Dr Fritzweiler's reputation.

A couple of the Fellows wonder if the meeting can make a proper judgement if the actual threats uttered by the student to Dr Fritzweiler are not disclosed.

Martin Peters makes the obvious point that disclosure of the private matter would defeat the object of suppressing the substance Andrew Cameron's threat.

When it is objected that the disclosure would remain private to those in the room, Martin, in his best courtroom manner, merely raises his eyes to the ceiling and wins his point to mild laughter.

'Could you tell us, Dr Fritzweiler,' the Fellow in Zoology, a woman widely spoken of in the College as Dr Zoo, asks, 'to what end these threats were uttered to you.'

'In order to induce me to engage in sexual intercourse with my student,' Annie replies.

Several of the Fellows look as if they would like to explore this further but none can quite think of a proper reason to do so.

'Dr Fritzweiler, one gathers from what you have said that there are particular reasons in this case for not taking action against the young man in question. May we know more of these reasons?'

Annie has taken the trouble to check up on Andrew's 'A' Level record. Perfect scores.

'Now in his second term,' Annie says, 'Andrew Cameron has shown the beginnings of promise in philosophy much greater than that of any other student I have taught here. Whilst one cannot be sure at this stage, I would conjecture that Andrew has the talent to have a career in philosophy and possibly to make a considerable contribution to the subject.'

'You mentioned something about his mental stability?'

For a moment Annie is angry. Why are supposedly highly intelligent people who are trained to think precisely not trained to listen with equal precision?

'No, Dr Quest, not instability. Lack of emotional development. If I may put it in everyday terms, emotionally Andrew is very young for his age, just as intellectually he is very advanced.'

'Dr Fritzweiler.'

It is David Cameron's boon companion, the Politics Fellow, Jeff Cunliffe.' Drunk or sober, it is impossible to tell.

'Dr Fritzweiler, I have sat at this table for more years than I care to remember and I can recall no single instant of a threat of the kind you have reported being uttered against a teaching Fellow of this College. You have been here barely more than a term and this happens. What is it about you, Dr Fritzweiler?'

Annie has rarely been so furious. What the hell is David's great pal up to? Various unpleasant possibilities churn through her mind. She is about to get to her feet to let fly at him, when Martin Peters rises from his place.

'Master, the tenor of Dr Cunliffe's question is unacceptable in this company and out of order in this meeting. I would ask him either to withdraw his question or to withdraw himself from the meeting.'

Whatever Sir Alexander Graham Burns actually thinks, he can see matters boiling over if this is allowed to go on.

'Dr Cunliffe you are to withdraw your question.'

'As my Master pleases, I withdraw it.'

'Dr Cunliffe, your attitude is not consonant with the seriousness of the matter under discussion. I would ask that you withdraw yourself.'

The word 'drunk' is clearly heard circulating round the table.

'It was ever thus, Master.'

He gets up from his chair which promptly falls over. Setting the chair carefully upright, Jeff Cunliffe makes to leave the room. As he passes Annie Fritzweiler on his way to the door, he utters one single and distinct word.

'Bitch.'

Annie does not think he is drunk. But she is very glad he is gone, and once again feels in the debt of Martin Peters.

'Well, if there are no other Fellows wishing to speak on

this matter,' the Master intones, 'before we put the motion standing under the name of Dr Annie Fritzweiler to a vote, I have a few words to say on the matter.

The Master remains seated to deliver his message.

'I do not urge my own opinion in this matter on the meeting. I wish only to report the view of the College Visitor, Sir Siddhartha Mukherjee. Sir Siddhartha will be known to many of you from his frequent visits to the College, but for those new to the College....'

The Master explains, as he has explained to Annie previously, the role of the Visitor, Sir Siddhartha's generally strict outlook in matters of College discipline and his substantial financial contributions to the College.

'Sir Siddhartha's most recent and largest contribution to the College has been to fund the four Fellowships the College has recently created, including, as it happens Dr Fritzweiler, your own. As you all know, the funding of a single Fellowship is an enormous financial commitment, but to fund four is an act of stupendous generosity. Now, of course, these Fellowships are all vested and so now beyond the control of the donor to revoke.'

Evidently the other three holders of the new Fellowships are as unaware as was Annie of the source of their funding. The Master senses the puzzlement.

'Yes, the four new Fellowships were funded by Sir Siddhartha's foundation. Sir Siddhartha's aim is to advance the teaching of the young in subjects relevant to today's world and to promote moral character.'

Annie wonders how on earth she could have become a recipient. But the Master is now well into his stride.

'On the advice of Dr Peters, on whom we all rely to keep the College from legal harm, I convened this meeting. Naturally I reported this to the Visitor. His very firm view was and is that Mr. Andrew Cameron's infraction should be dealt with by instant and permanent expulsion, no matter what extenuation Dr Fritzweiler or anyone else might pray in his aid.'

The room is completely attentive.

'Sir Siddhartha wanted to be here tonight. Of course, in a non-voting capacity. But important charitable matters have detained him in the United States. In light of this he has asked that, before a vote takes place, I report to this meeting the action he proposes to take should the meeting vote in favour of Dr Fritzweiler's motion.'

Now the attention in the room has become palpable anxiety. Reprisals by the College's biggest benefactor loom.

'Naturally, Sir Siddhartha and his foundation will honour all commitments thus far made to the College. But the programme we had agreed in outline with Sir Siddhartha of continuing to fund the College's growth, physically but more particularly by way of enhanced intellectual capital...'

More teachers and scholars, Annie translates, as well as more buildings.

'...that would not now go forward. Sir Siddhartha would sever all connection with this College and our hopes of being in future able to enter the top rank of Oxford Colleges, Christ Church, Merton, St. John's and so on, would be dashed for a generation, possibly for good.'

Colleagues cannot resist beginning to speculate with each other what it will mean for them. Sir Alexander calls the meeting to order.

'That is all I have to say. Before voting I urge you all to consider not only the situation of Mr. Andrew Cameron but the whole future of this College. In light of the new development which I have just explained, I proposed to adjourn the meeting until ten o'clock when the vote will take place without further debate. I hope the time thus provided will be well used by you all in due discussion and reflection.'

54

Counted Out

Ten minutes past ten and all the Fellows are assembled, including Jeff Cunliffe. Martin Peters raises a point of order that Dr Cunliffe having been duly removed from the meeting may not re-join it to vote. A brief but sharp debate ensues, in which Annie does not join. The Master asks the Senior Tutor to call the role of the Fellows. All are present, save one who is on sabbatical at New York University at the southern tip of the island of Manhattan. So those present and qualified to vote number forty-eight Fellows in all.

Martin Peters raises a further point order as to whether Jeff Cunliffe should be permitted to vote on whether he is to be excluded from the vote.

Three votes then follow, each following the same format. The Master calls on the Junior Fellow to count the show of hands and the College Secretary to tabulate them.

The Master intones: 'On the point of order number one standing in the name of Dr Martin Peters that Dr Jeffrey Harrison Cunliffe be excluded from voting on whether the said Dr Jeffrey Harrison Cunliffe be excluded from voting on Point of Order number two. Those in the affirmative.... Those to the contrary....'

The Junior Fellow and the College Secretary confer. The Junior Fellow carries a slip of paper the length of the table to the Master, who unfolds it and reads it out.

'Those in voting in the affirmative have it.'

So, Dr Cunliffe is excluded from voting on Point of Order number one, whether he should be permitted to vote on his own exclusion from the vote on the substantive issue.

And so, to the vote on Point of Order number two. The same procedure.

The Master: 'Those voting to the contrary have it.'

So, Dr Cunliffe is allowed to vote on the proposed expulsion of Andrew Cameron. Bad news for Annie and Martin Peters.

'On the motion standing in the name of Dr Annie Angela Fritzweiler,' the Master intones. 'Those in the Affirmative... Those to the Contrary...'

The Junior Fellow and the Secretary count and then count again. Annie wants to be sick. She can't tell which way it has gone. The Junior Fellow is in whispered conference with the Master at the head of the table. A recount. Finally, the Master is satisfied.

He announces a tie, twenty-four to twenty-four.

'In this situation I believe the College statutes are clear. Dr Peters? As Master of this College being in my right wits...' He pauses for any contrary voice to be heard. '...I have the right to break a tie by exercise of a second and casting vote.'

Even the poker-face features of Dr Martin Peters, veteran of more court verdicts than he can comfortably enumerate, cannot hide his anxiety.

It comes to Annie through her fear of what is about to happen that it is a long time since the Master has enjoyed himself quite so much.

'As Master of this College, being in my right wits, I cast my second vote to the contrary side.

'In consequence of this Mr. Andrew Cameron will be notified tomorrow that he is forthwith expelled and that there will be set in train by the College and the University authorities the process of barring him permanently from, respectively, the College and the University.'

Dr Martin Peters is again on his feet with a point of order.

'Very well, Dr Peters.'

The Master is close to exasperation, but he does not quite dare to defy as clever a lawyer as Peters has often proved himself to be, for fear of appearing a fool in retrospect.

'On a point of order Master, I think there is sufficient evidence that one of our number present and voting this evening was incapable of exercising the highest standard of judgement by reason of alcoholic intoxication.'

The Master is past the point of insisting on strict procedure.

'Dr Cunliffe, have you anything to say?'

'If the ladies present will excuse my freedom, Master, but Peters can suck my....'

The meeting is in uproar. Annie feels like bursting into tears. But then she feels Martin's arm squeezing her shoulders and whispering into her ear through her fine Baltic fair hair.

'Annie, during the recess before the vote I telephoned our friend Priti Patel and put in train certain arrangements. A bit desperate I'm afraid, but they might just do the trick.'

'May one know, Martin, of what you are talking?'

'In the course of her work in the criminal courts, Priti comes across some odd characters. One of these is a former police officer skilled in the administration of breath tests to detect alcohol. I remembered this when it appeared in the meeting that Cunliffe was grossly drunk. As he went out of here just now, he will have been detained by the College Bulldogs. Student disciplinary officers to you Dr Fritzweiler.'

Traditionally the Bulldogs were appointed by the University as a sort of private police force to ensure order amongst the student body. After they were abolished, certain Colleges found it useful to employ such officers directly.

'I knew what the College Bulldogs are,' says Annie stoutly.

'I've no doubt. The Bulldogs will have detained Dr Cunliffe on the pretext that he is not safe to cross the quad back to his room unassisted, and Priti's police friend will administer a breath test.'

'But where does that get us, Martin.'

'We should have the result with the next ten minutes. Let you and I entertain the Master till then, in case he takes it into his head to make his escape back to the Lodgings.'

But there is really no need for that since Sir Alexander Graham Burns is surrounded by six furious Fellows, four of them women, demanding that a way be found to remove Cunliffe from his Fellowship.

The Master is still surrounded when one of the Bulldogs, identifiable by their formal black clothes, black bowler hats and generally burly physique, brings Martin the breath test report.

'Thank you, Jackson. And Dr Cunliffe?'

'Alan's taking him back to his rooms to make sure nothing untoward befalls, sir.'

'Good work Jackson.'

'Come on Annie. Let's tell the Master the glad tidings that one of our number present and voting, was according to a police breath test intoxicated to the point where he was incapable of exercising the judgement necessary to drive a family car. So how one wonders can his vote, decisive in the future of a Junior Member of this College and apparently the future financial prospects of the College, be allowed to stand?'

They approach the still beleaguered Head of the College, who with relief gives them audience.

'Oh, don't go,' says Martin to the small crowd around Sir Alexander. 'This is pertinent to what you all were just discussing with the Master.'

He repeats to the Master the findings of the breath test. The Master nods slowly.

'What do you recommend, Dr Peters?'

'That you reconvene the Fellows meeting tomorrow, Friday, to declare Dr Cunliffe's votes tonight invalid by reason of his incapacity and to have the votes re-tabulated. There being then an odd number of votes cast, there will then be a clear result without the need of the Master's casting vote.'

'So, we will win?' Annie does not dare quite to say out loud.

'Yes, that would sound reasonable,' says the Master quite out loud.

Annie is abruptly alert. That highly ambiguous English 'would'. Is this a 'would but for...'?

The Master continues: 'Dr Murphy, could you spare us a moment?'

The Junior Fellow lays aside his copy of the College Statutes which has been left in each Fellow's place round the table and comes to join them.

'Tell us, Dr Murphy, on Dr Fritzweiler's motion concerning the fate of Mr. Andrew Cameron, on which hand did Dr Cunliffe cast his vote?'

'Oh no doubt of it, sir. With the Affirmatives. To drop any action to remove Mr. Cameron from the College.'

Annie in a low voice from which all hope has drained.

'So, if the Dr Cunliffe's vote is removed from the tabulation of votes it would mean that my motion is lost even without need of the Master's casting vote.'

55

Vice

One or two of the Fellows on whom Annie has been counting for support come up to her and confess that they changed their votes because of the threat that Sir Siddhartha's funding would be withdrawn from the College. More likely from specific projects or students in which or in whom they have an interest.

'It's all right,' she says in a voice heavy with lack of conviction.

Others slink away un-shriven.

To Annie it's all the same. It puts her back in the clutches of the police and destroys her future as surely as Andrew's future will shortly be destroyed.

'Annie, I am more sorry than I can say.'

'It's all right Martin. You did all you could. More than I could have expected.'

'Yes, I think I had every legal element covered. It was just that Sir Siddhartha's funding that sank us. I had no clue it was in the offing. Look Annie, I really have to get home. One of the kids has a fever.'

She doesn't care if he stays or goes. Awkwardly he takes his leave. After all they've been through together, they can scarcely shake hands but he doesn't feel a kiss or a hug would be well received at this moment. He walks heavily away across the empty quad. Snow is beginning to fall.

'Oh Martin.'

Her voice is like crystal in the cold, empty quad. He turns back to her.

'There is one more thing we can do.'

Hasn't he covered every angle? He walks back to her.

'I can withdraw my complaint against Andrew. At the moment as far as the Master is concerned it is oral only. So, if I write to him formally withdrawing the complaint, he has no basis for removing Andrew Cameron from the College. Isn't that right?'

'But Annie you can't do that. You will be defenceless against Andrew Cameron's blackmail.'

'Of course. But he won't carry out his threat to go to the police if I do what he wants.'

'Sleep with him?'

'I just need to get used to becoming a whore. I might be quite good at it. Good night Martin and thank you for all you've done.'

'Annie, no. I won't let you. I'll try to think of something.'

'You said it yourself, Martin, there is nothing more to think of. No, I'll deal with things myself from now on. Good night Martin. I hope your child will be all right.'

Annie turns away from him. The snow is beginning to lie now and her black boots make a black track in the pure white as she trudges back to her staircase.

Her phone is ringing. It's been ringing for some time. But she continues to ignore it. She can't face another blast of irrational abuse from David. She can't really face anything more tonight except the oblivion of sleep.

It's harder than ever, but she forces herself into the cold shower. She can't face a run this morning, though from what she can see from her windows, as the light slowly comes up, the world has turned pure white.

A quality of snow is that it disguises all ugliness, smooths away all sharp edges and surfaces of the world.

But soon it will begin to deteriorate. First in the streets with the first of the morning's traffic. Then in the quad as students make their reluctant ways to libraries, tutorials and lectures or back to their own rooms. Finally, out in the fields and on the bare trees as the winter sun makes the snow covering vanish as magically as it came. By the end of the day the world will have returned to its customary ugliness.

Annie's day, she feels, will be like that. Well, not quite like that as when she calls David, the tirade of fury and abuse would melt all the snow in Oxford at one go. For his appalling friend Jeff Cunliffe called him the previous evening to tell him that the Fellows meeting has voted down Annie's motion. So, Felix would be expelled from the college for good.

'I did as you asked, Dave, and voted for that kraut bitch's motion. But I'm afraid it wasn't enough. Sorry about your son. Tell him to have a stiff whiskey. I'm going to.'

'You fucking bitch, Annie. You assure me that you would protect Felix. And where the hell were you last night when I was trying to get hold of you?'

'I have protected him.'

And she tells him how she will do that at the cost of exposing herself to Andrew's desires. There is silence on the line and Annie thinks his fury must have brought on another collapse. But no, it is much more likely he is simply stuck for something to say. What can he say after all?

'Annie, this is an unspeakable outrage. Don't worry about anything. I'll tell Felix he is not to lay so much as a finger on you.'

'Yes do,' she says.

She knows it will do no good. Felix has little respect or affection for his father. He is on fire to possess her. No contest. And he doesn't really need his father's money, if there is any left. His talent and his relative penury would be enough to find money in one of the dark pools of funds that lurk around the University.

'Let me know, David.'

She calls Felix, Andrew. Be first with the good news. She reckons she has two or three hours to withdraw her complaint before the Master will have written and dispatched his letter reflecting vote of the Fellows' meeting the previous evening. There is no answer from Andrew or his room.

Annie has tutorials from ten. Undergraduates don't like getting up any earlier. Or they are still finishing, or starting, their essays in the mornings. But in the meantime, she can concentrate on nothing.

She gets dressed. In her green top and grey skirt. Unwashed but still serviceable. Pulls on her long black boots from where they lie at a crazy angle at the entrance to her bedroom. No tights. She wants to feel the freezing air on her legs. She shrugs on her camel coat, without doing it up, and runs lightly down the staircase to the quad. It's cold. She does up her coat and pulls up the collar.

Hands deep in the pockets of her coat. Out of the gates, up the narrow curving street in which the facade of her College stands and across the High, slithering where the first traffic of the day has crushed the new snow to ice. Down the lane between Oriel and the back of Christ Church, under a black wrought iron gateway and so to Christ Church meadow.

Of her decision she has no doubt. Anything is better than falling back into the hands of Tench and Smogulecki.

Whilst she believes both Priti and Martin when they tell her she is very unlikely in the end to be convicted of anything, they cannot hold out real hope that she will not be prosecuted and possibly held in custody for a time while she endures the long wait for her trial date. In the meantime, her Fellowship and her professional reputation will have gone up in smoke. Or is it flames, the English say? So, there is no alternative to surrendering to Andrew's demands.

She registers that she is getting cold and that time is getting on. So, she makes her shortest way back. In the lane, just before the College entrance, someone slips on the pavement behind her and cannot stop themselves from cannoning into her. She falls to the ground, on all fours.

The cause of her fall offers a hand and pulls her to her feet.

She looks up to thank him. It is Andrew Cameron.

56

Conditional Surrender

Oh well, why not now?

Annie takes him to the relative calm of the Senior Common Room. Guests who are Junior Members of the College are not allowed in there but at this hour, still before nine, the place is all but empty save for the intermittent appearance of a vacuum cleaner and its minder.

Annie leads the way to a remote corner of the large room. She orders a double espresso for herself and for him two croissants and an orange juice. Of course, as yet he knows nothing, she thinks. It's warm in here so she slips off her coat, crosses her legs and turns to her student.

'Andrew, I'm going to tell you something a bit alarming, but please wait until the end of my story before you say anything. At the end I promise you that you will get exactly what you want. OK?'

He nods, concentrating hard on her.

But as Annie has foreseen, it is only the unfamiliar dignity of their surroundings that stops him from crying out or breaking down when she tells him of the Fellows meeting of the previous evening and the consequent letter expelling him for good, which the Master is even now preparing.

A show of defiance, or the real thing? He speaks in a fierce undertone.

'I'll do what I said, Annie. As I told you I would.'

But the hopeless way in which he says this makes Annie suspect that actually he will do nothing. Not go to Tench and Smogulecki to deny his sworn deposition letting her out. However, it changes nothing for she cannot depend on him. That in the dark days to come he won't give way and go to the police.

Annie then tells him what she plans to do.

Andrew is nothing if not quick on the uptake.

'So, you're going irrevocably to give up your threat to have me thrown out. So, I could stay on at the College even if I tell the police what I know.'

She nods. Her pale blue eyes are unnaturally bright he thinks, since she is close to tears.

'Annie, the last thing in the world I want is to hurt you. But you know I just need you so. But Annie if you really don't want to....'

She thinks he might not even force her to have sex with him, at least for the next few days. But before long her image will so inflame his mind that he won't be able to resist. And the sooner they start the sooner he will outgrow her and find some girlfriend of his own age. Before the end of term perhaps. But the thing has to be faced. And done.

'It's all right Andrew. If this thing matters to you so much. I'm not going to tell you I like it, but I have reached the conclusion that it has to be done. So, let us try to remain friends.'

She can see the delight spread across his face. That one human being could have so much power to bring misery or happiness to another.

'Thank you, Dr Fritzweiler, thank you. You won't regret it. I'll go to weight lifting every day. Twice a day. I'll soon look like Otto. You'll see.'

In spite of herself Annie almost laughs. And how zany that when he was thinking of giving her up to the police, he called her 'Annie'. Now he is going to make love to her, he calls her 'Dr Fritzweiler'.

'Andrew, do you mind to eat up your croissants, since I must go in a moment to write to the Master withdrawing my complaint against you.'

As he chews furiously, for her news has made him suddenly hungry and he is naturally eager that she write her letter, she lays down some ground rules.

'You must be absolutely discrete, Andrew. Mention this to no one.'

Although she will have no power to enforce this, she thinks he will keep to it. Being with her will be too precious a thing for him to discuss with anyone else.

'I think it is best if you return to me for your weekly philosophy tutorial. I shall arrange it. Then you can have sex with me afterwards. This will prevent anyone else finding out by accident. And Andrew, do not press me to do it with you more than that single time each week. All right?'

'Yes of course, Dr Fritzweiler.'

She suspects he will keep to this too. Partly out of early repletion and partly since he is so in awe of her.

'And Andrew. Nothing out of the ordinary. Nothing deviant. I will grant you as long as you need each week, but the only things you can do with me are to caress me gently and to insert your stiffened cock into me until such time as you are able to ejaculate or you lose your erection. Since I'm sure you don't want to hurt me, this must also be gentle. Is that understood?'

Her explicit words have caused him to go a much brighter pink than the lipstick she occasionally uses. But he manages to reply.

'Absolutely, yes, yes of course, Dr Fritzweiler.'

'One last thing on your side, Andrew. Should you suspect I am attracted to another man, or even that I am having an affair, you are not to protest. After all, this is most unlikely to be anything but your imagination. And it will in no way affect our arrangement.'

'Of course, Dr Fritzweiler.'

The knowledge that he is going to have her is all consuming. He would have agreed to anything. But still, she thinks, he will play by her rules. He is, after all, basically a nice boy.

'Do you have anything to say to me, Andrew?'

'Thank you, thank you....'

She cuts him off.

'Andrew, my meaning is in connection with our forthcoming sexual activity. Do you have any comments or requests in relation to the ground rules I have just set out? Just think carefully for a moment. And do finish your last croissant if you want to.'

His reply eventually comes through heroic efforts to chew

through the last croissant. But she can't make out what he means. Having swallowed and drunk some orange juice, he tries again but she can see he is too shy to ask her explicitly. She guesses what he means though.

'Can I have an orgasm whilst you are servicing me...having sex with me? Is that what you mean?'

He nods gratefully.

'That is up to you. How much you arouse and stimulate me. I will play my part. But, Andrew, may I suggest that you spend some time before next week, when we will resume our tutorials, reviewing the internet under headings having to do with women's sexuality, the process of their arousal and so on. With this knowledge you will be much more likely to get pleasure from me. As well, perhaps, as giving some pleasure to me.'

'Dr Fritzweiler, can we do it, can I have my first tutorial with you, this coming Monday?'

'I think that Fridays would be best. It would give you more time to write a good essay.'

'And to check the internet on the points you mentioned?'

'Yes. But you must not allow your enthusiasm for my body deflect from the improvement of your mind.'

She cannot help but smile, almost, at his delight.

As they walk out of the SCR, a tall gaunt man addresses her. A Nordic accent.

'You are Dr Annie Fritzweiler, are you not?'

This must be the Visiting Professorial Research Fellow in the Icelandic Sagas, about whom all Fellows have received an email. Nordstrom is he called? Danish or Norwegian she fancies. Since as far as she knows, no one in the College has the slightest interest in the Sagas, she wonders how he has come to be amongst them.

'Dr Fritzweiler, could I prevail upon you to grant me an hour or two of your time. I have one or two difficult points of philosophy in relation to the Sagas, on which I would value your opinion.'

Scholars in other disciplines, especially foreign scholars, often have no idea what philosophers in the English tradition do. But she agrees and says she will send him an email suggesting some times.

'By the way, Dr Fritzweiler, I assume this young man is an undergraduate?'

Annie introduces them.

'It was my understanding that Junior Members of the College are not permitted in the Senior Common Room.'

Annie resists the temptation to ask to see his College accreditation. Instead, she takes a leaf from the Master's book.

'Professor Nordstrom, it may take you a few weeks to get used to some of our little ways in this College, where some rules are, by tradition, never observed.'

'Ah tradition. How well I understand. The Sagas are almost entirely based on tradition.'

In the quad, Annie and Andrew part company. He detains her briefly.

'Dr Fritzweiler. Please don't worry. I'm sure I will be able to make you enjoy it.'

57

Scuppering the Master

Back in her rooms, without removing her coat Annie types and prints her single page letter to the Master, under the heading Mr. Andrew Cameron: Withdrawal of Oral Complaint. She proofreads it, though she knows there are no errors, then walks with it over to the Lodgings.

When she states her business, she is admitted at once to the Presence, which is in its study in shirtsleeves. His typing is as ponderous as Annie's is fluent.

'I think I can save you the trouble, Master.'

Sir Alexander rises from his chair at once, thinking she is offering to type to his dictation.

'My secretary has been held up by the weather, you know. Most inconvenient. But thank you Dr Fritzweiler.'

Annie hands him her letter and sits at his computer. She swivels the chair and crosses her legs as she watches the Master read and read again her one pager.

He can obviously read what Annie has written there, and understand intellectually that this completely undercuts the basis of his intended expulsion of Andrew Cameron. But in the core of his being he just cannot absorb or accept it.

'Dr Fritzweiler, it is impossible for you to do this.'

'But it is done, Master.'

'Your change of mind is so radical as to cast doubt on whether you are in your right mind.'

'I am willing to submit my mind to testing, Master, if you are.'

'But how…?'

'On reflection last night after the Fellows meeting, I came to see that Andrew Cameron's words to me, which at the time I took as a threat, may have been intended as playful. Not to be taken literally. In such cases the benefit of the doubt must always lie with the accused, the student. Dr Peters will doubtless confirm this if you care to call him.'

The woman has obviously set this up with Peters, thinks Sir Alexander, so there would be no point in speaking to him. In fact, Annie hasn't spoken to Martin since bidding him a frosty goodnight on the last evening.

'You realise, Dr Fritzweiler, the consequences of this for Sir Siddhartha's funding? Sir Sid will suspect jiggery pokery. He may well sustain his threat to withdraw all future funding for the College.'

'How odd, Master. Withdraw his intended funding by reason of the absence of blackmail or of sexual harassment by a member of the undergraduate body of the College?'

'You may go, Dr Fritzweiler.'

But Annie continues to sit gently swinging back and forth on the Master's swivel chair.

'Not, Master, until you confirm to me that you recognise that it would now be grossly improper for you to write to Andrew Cameron purporting to expel him from the College and the University.'

Sir Alexander Graham Burns stands to his full, burley height. Like some giant College Bulldog in shirtsleeves and red braces.

But faced with Annie Fritzweiler's attractive knees, he finds himself at a loss. After a few seconds of indecision comes the concession.

'Of course, Dr Fritweiler, it would be apparent to a three-year old that after what you have done, I cannot write in such terms to Andrew Cameron. Now I am sure the College expects you to be about its business.'

'Not until ten o'clock as it happens, Master.'

She slowly uncrosses her legs, showing an unnecessary amount of thigh in the process. But one must take one's petty revenges as and when opportunities present themselves.

58

Wise Counsel

The day after her SCR conversation with Andrew is a Saturday. No students, so she can get on with clearing some of the backlog of work that has built up during the last exacting days.

Crossing the quad from the main Gate to her staircase she catches sight of a pretty blond girl whom she's noticed a few times before. She must live on a nearby staircase. She is carrying a large container of instant coffee, a student staple.

'Dr Fritzweiler?'

The girl is in front of her. Close up she is certainly very pretty, but in a baby doll sort of way that Annie does not find attractive.

'You must be frightfully busy but could I take a few moments of your time?'

'Yes,' says Annie, 'and yes.'

The girl looks puzzled.

'Yes, I'm busy but yes I can spare you a few moments. Why don't you come up?'

Annie leads the way up her staircase to her rooms.

'Gosh,' says the girl.

English public school, thinks Annie from her accent and self-confidence, doing a soft option like French and Spanish.

'I didn't know that some tutors have bedrooms. Mine doesn't.'

Annie goes to close the door into the bedroom while the girl says her name is Polly Philips, in her third year, doing physics. Without conviction Annie offers the girl something to drink but she quickly shakes her head and gets down to business.

'You are Andrew Cameron's tutor, aren't you?'

'In philosophy, yes.'

'Andrew and I are friends, close friends I would say. No there is nothing between us. He is a bit of a dish, but he's not interested in me. Anyway, I have enough going on in my life without that.'

It surprises Annie, that part about the 'dish'. But it encourages her too. He should find it easy enough to find a girlfriend once he has got over his infatuation with her.

'Apparently Andrew has fallen for some older woman in Oxford. Nothing to do with the University I gather.'

'How much older?'

'Heaps. Thirty-five or something. She is married so of course in principle not interested in Andrew. Except that, he told me last night when he dropped in, that recently she seems to be thawing towards him. Probably some problem in her marriage.'

Well Andrew, Annie supposes, deserves good marks for dissembling. Or, the thought strikes her, perhaps Polly does.

'But now Andrew has a problem. I say you don't mind me telling you all this, do you? It's just that I've become very fond of Andrew and I don't like to see him unhappy that way. And you know him and have a lot more experience of life than I do....'

Annie wonders if that is true.

'Go on, Polly.'

'...and I really feel I ought to tell someone. Especially as his problem has sort of become my problem too. Frankly I don't know what I should do. Of course, he'd kill me if he knew that I'd gone behind his back, especially to you.'

Annie is not sure. But Polly seems genuine in her anxiety and from her own point of view Annie reckons more information is better than less.

'Why don't you go on Polly and I'll stop you if I think it's becoming inappropriate.'

'Well, Dr Fritzweiler, the thing is Andrew wants more than anything in the world to have sex with this woman. He's obviously obsessed with her. But he is desperate not to disappoint her. You know because he's so inexperienced.'

'What do you mean exactly by inexperienced?'

'Never done it. Not properly anyway. But he knows that I've done it lots of times. It's the school I went to. Run like a nunnery so of course at every opportunity we just went mad. Well, you know. I hate to think of it now.'

'And you're a very pretty girl.'

'Well thanks. But you know sometimes that is more of a curse than a blessing.'

Annie knows what is coming but she encourages Polly to tell her.

'So, Andrew wants me to give him practical tips. Of course, it will end up with him shagging me. That's OK I suppose. I don't have a regular boyfriend at present. But I've just sort of lost my moral compass. Would it be good for Andrew? Would it really be OK for me? I mean I'm fond of him and so on but… .'

For a moment Annie can see only one thing. If this girl has sex with Andrew, he might well fall for her. Then her own problem will be at an end. But she realises that she has responsibilities to third parties here. She has, perhaps stupidly, allowed Polly to confide in her. Annie owes the girl an objective answer. After all, she smiles to herself, she is the College tutor in Moral Philosophy.

'Polly, there is of course no right answer here. Before I tell you my opinion, and that is all it will be, let me ask you some more questions.'

'What can I tell you? I say, Dr Fritzweiler, it's very decent of you to listen to me like this. I feel it's not quite fair on you to hand you all the moral responsibility for this decision. But I just don't feel capable of making it on my own.'

'Let's be clear Polly, the decision in the end can only be yours. I can give you some guidelines to help you think it through, but that's really all.'

'That's exactly what I want. Someone with experience to share the decision with. Not someone to dump it on. If I said that before then I spoke without thinking.'

'Well Polly, first do you think there is any way of advising

Andrew effectively without exposing yourself to the risk of, as you put it, being shagged?'

'Not really. Given his state of ignorance I just have to show him and then he won't be able to control himself. Probably I won't either if it comes to the point.'

'Do you generally enjoy having sex with men?'

'Very mixed. Most of what has happened to me has been with boys who didn't know much or with men who knew far too much. To such a point that since last academic year I've pretty much taken the veil. I feel much better about myself in consequence.'

'You said "pretty much".'

'There's one guy. A graduate student. I enjoy myself with him, but he has other fish to fry and I don't want to be a pain.'

Annie can't help thinking what a very self-aware young woman she has seated in front of her. She must give her the best advice she can. Or rather she must try to nudge her into making the best decision she can make for herself.

'But you don't think you would enjoy helping Andrew? I mean you don't anticipate getting any physical satisfaction from his penetrating you and so on.'

For a moment Polly is puzzled by Annie's formal use of such a term, but quickly she understands. Annie sees the hesitation.

Stick to the demotic from now on.

'Not really. But I would really like to help in making things come right for him with this woman he's so gone on.'

Now it's Annie's turn to be puzzled by nomenclature for a moment. But actually, it's clear enough.

'You don't think that if you allow him to shag you and then he goes and does it with this older woman that you might feel resentment, jealousy even. As if he's selfishly exploited something precious between you.'

Polly laughs.

'Sorry, but I really don't think so. Sex is such a common currency among kids of our age that it's hard to think of it a precious. Unless you're in love with someone I suppose.'

'But as you said yourself, Andrew is not a typical kid of your age. Would you be prepared for him to fall for you as a consequence of your helping him?'

Polly ponders this.

'It would be a new experience for me. I mean with someone serious like Andrew. But honestly, I don't think I would mind. I think of myself as pretty smart, intellectually. But though he's only in his first year, Andrew is light years ahead of me. He has such an original take on things. One would never be bored being with him.'

'And he is dishy?' Annie ventures.

Polly laughs. She does, Annie has to concede, have a certain charm as one gets to know her.

'Dishy, yes, I almost forgot that.'

'Polly as I told you at the start, I'm not going to tell you what to do. But are you now any closer to making up your own mind?'

'Oh yes, Dr Fritzweiler, thanks to you. Oh, one last thing. You don't think Andrew would freak out or something when it comes to the point?'

Annie considers her responsibility to be objective.

'I'm a philosopher, Polly, not a psychologist or a therapist. But as a lay person who has seen Andrew regularly over one term and the start of this one, and become quite friendly with him, I'd be very surprised if he went to pieces in your arms. Quite the contrary.'

'You are so sweet to say that, Dr Fritzweiler, Annie.'

The girl gets up and kisses Annie. Then she is at the door apologising for taking so much of Annie's time.

'Just before you go, Polly. What is the answer?'

'The answer?'

'Are you going to do it or not? With Andrew.'

'Of course, I am,' says Polly.

Annie can hear the girl's laughter echoing up the stone staircase as she goes to the door to close it after her. She hopes the girl is not mocking her but she does not think so. Or is Andrew mocking her? But the quality of his lust makes her feel this is not so either.

59

Darkness at Noon

Four of them, on the top floor of the County Police Headquarters, in the Chief Constable's office. The Chief grey with anxiety. The Crown Prosecutor white with anger. DI Tench seemingly bemused. DS Smogulecki obviously triumphant.

'You'd better go and bring her in,' the Chief Constable says. 'Take six uniformed officers with you. We can afford no mistakes with this one. Go on the pair of you. Do it now. No time to lose. I don't want to hear that the bird has flown.'

After her heart to heart with Polly, Annie has buried herself in finishing an article for Ethics Review, which is overdue. One does not lightly renege on one's commitments to what is a leading journal in her field, widely read by specialists on both sides of the Atlantic.

Annie has the gift of being able to seclude herself from the world, and more to the point from her own troubling thoughts, while she is working. Even if it is some toe-tinglingly boring administrative matter. Her Ethics Review article, 'Some Practical Applications of Moral Theory' is by contrast important to the success of her current research.

Even when she becomes aware of it, she is tempted to ignore the ringing of her phone. But it is persistent.

'Yes.'

'It's Higgins, Ma'am, at the Lodge.'

'Yes Mr. Higgins.'

'Some uniformed gentlemen are asking for you. Very urgent it seems. So urgent that once they got your staircase number, they rushed into College without waiting...'

'You mean the police? Coming here? Now?'

'Well not exactly now, Ma'am. An unpardonable mistake on my part but I sent them to the back quad. To the top of the tower. So, you've got a minute or two to....'

Annie's mind is suddenly clear. She shuts down her laptop. Grabs her wallet, keys and lipstick from her bag and sticks them into the pockets of her jeans along with her phone. She pulls on a thin jacket and her trainers, and she is gone from the room.

In the way of things, after the snow, today is mild, in that damp insidious Oxford way that makes one wish the cold was back. Head down, she hurries out of the main gate, raising a hand in thanks to Higgins who smiles back. Then she is running for her life.

Over the cobbles of Brasenose Lane, left and then right under the Bridge of Sighs into New College Lane, following the road sharp right, where a student falls off his bike trying to avoid her headlong flight. Annie is already sweating. Then out between Queens' and Teddy Hall, across the High as if there were no buses shipping people into the City from suburbs of which she is scarcely aware. What she is aware of, though, is a single pursuer. Smogulecki.

When the uniforms rushed off at the direction of the Porter to climb the tower in the back quad and DI Tench pondered on things in the middle of the main quad, Smogulecki in a black police top, black lycra wind pants and black trainers, hovered unnoticed in the lea of the Lodge. Even so, she almost missed Annie Fritzweiler as she hurried past and was only just quick enough to get herself through the main gate in time to see her turning into Brasenose Lane, running.

DI Tench standing where he was, apparently aimless, sees Annie Fritzweiler too, as she hurried across the main quad. But the Detective Inspector thinks he might just as well not have seen her. For he dislikes the current proceedings even more than the Crown Prosecutor does. It is just plain wrong. Whether she did it or not.

Just before Magdalen Bridge, Annie crosses back over the

High. She realises now that she cannot outrun the Polish woman who is bigger, stronger and at least ten years younger than she. And certainly fitter, with, she imagines, police training in unarmed combat.

Annie slows to glance over the balustrade at beginnings of Magdalen Bridge. The elegant structure has anchored itself to the land here for the last two hundred odd years. But the drop to the river bank beneath is too daunting. So, she doubles back a few yards before abruptly turning right into the narrow passage, always crowded with students, which runs past the Lodge of Magdalen College. She slides through the crowd but the Porter's practiced eye catches sight of her.

'Hey, you there.'

'Police,' shouts Annie, holding her credit card high in the air and not looking back. Clear of the crush she resumes running. But she has not shaken off Smogulecki, who is now too close to be deceived by any sharp turn offs or doubling back.

Annie knows she now has very little time. She turns abruptly right, down a sharp bank to the river where it comes to the bridge, just where the boat houses are. It is still January so there are no boatmen, in fact nobody at all, and only two punts in the water. Punts means punt poles. There is one leaning against the boathouse.

Smogulecki comes into view, her feet stuttering to a stop, looking around, for a moment disoriented. Annie knows that her only chance is to use her first mover advantage. And her anger.

From her experience in the GDR, Annie knows better than to swing the long pole at the detective. It would give a trained opponent too much time to react, she remembers. So, stepping quickly out of the shadow of the boathouse, holding the pole halfway down its eight-foot length, she runs at Smogulecki and jabs her sharply in the groin.

The detective staggers backwards towards the river and falls. Annie is on top of her, gripping the woman's groin through the thin lycra. Smogulecki is screaming in Polish now. With her right-hand Annie forces the woman's chin back so her fair hair, almost the same shade as Annie's, is trailing in the murky water of Cherwell, as the Thames is called here. She'll break the damn woman's neck if she has to.

'Why?'

Squeeze harder; push the woman's chin back further. The detective is slithering inch by inch down the muddy bank into the muddy water. The back of her head is in the river. Soon her nose will be under the surface.

'Why?'

This time in German. This time an answer.

'To get the Russian.'

It's enough for Annie. Keeping pressure on the policewoman's chin, she releases her grip on the woman's groin, to pull the police radio from her belt and to throw it into the middle of the river and to stuff Smogulecki's mobile phone into her own pocket.

Annie scrambles off the woman, who is starting to recover. No time for justice or fairness here. Annie takes the long punting poll with its small metal hook at the end and drives it between Smogulecki's thighs. An uncontrolled scream. The pain must be excruciating. But Annie has achieved her purpose. The policewoman, in order to escape the pain has scrambled backwards into the river.

This gives Annie what she needs. A couple of minutes' leeway. She scrambles up the bank and joins the crowd jostling through the passage by the Lodge. Then she is walking quickly along the High, away from Magdalen College back into Oxford. In a minute she turns into Longwall Street. There are few people here. So, Annie is running, eight hundred metre speed. All the way under the long curve of the long wall, crossing St. Cross Road and into Holywell Street.

By the time she reaches the Broad, her breath is coming in gasps and there are again crowds of people. Here she slows to a brisk walk, regaining her breath, in and out of the pedestrians and the occasional vehicle. Across the Broad into the Turl, then right into Market Street. She's running again now. Still no hue and cry. But now she has to be lucky.

Catching her breath, Annie trots up the bleak stone staircase of the obscure multi-storey car park by the covered market, empty beer bottles and piss as always on the stairway. She is only a few steps from the back of her College where her morning began. Third floor. She pushes cautiously at the door onto the deck. She has to be lucky.

Her car is still there. She scans the deck carefully. Then scans it again. No sign of a police guard. Then she spots him. A uniformed Constable. He's standing by the lift, chatting to a car park attendant. About some parking infraction. More likely football. It's Saturday after all. OK risk it.

Annie walks to her car. She inspects the wheels. No clamp. All the tires seem to have air in them. She tries the infra-red lock. For a moment her heart is in her mouth. The buggers have disabled it. Then she hears the comforting click. She's in the driving seat and has the engine running, her seat belt on and the car in motion before you can say 'Who's a clever girl then?'

Annie drives slowly toward the ramp. There is no avoiding the police Constable and the car park attendant. She looks in her mirror and with one hand smooths her hair. Her make-up must be a mess? No, not too bad. More as you see in the movies after a fight to the death than you would expect in real life. She smiles at the two guardians of the place as her car crawls past them. Neither gives her a glance.

One more hurdle. Have they disabled her exit card? She has no idea whether revving the engine and running full tilt at the barrier will crash through it or just leave a nasty mess of barrier, car and driver.

Slowly she approaches. Lowers her window. Inserts the card. The barrier doesn't move. Her hand is shaking. She tries again and the card falls to the ground beside the car. Her heart thudding in her chest, she pushes open the driver's door and leans down to retrieve the card. Just beyond her reach. She gets out, forcing herself to breathe more slowly, picks it up and stuffs it into the machine. This time, reluctantly, jerkily, the barrier rises. Annie is back in the car, the door slammed, revving the engine.

Fastest way out of the tentacles of the centre of Oxford? No question. Go north west and then turn off toward Wytham just after the by-pass. She wants, she thinks, to go east, but she wants more than anything to get out of Oxford before there are roadblocks.

Wytham woods. Haunt of lovers, though hardly at this time of year, and, for some reason she thinks, detectives. Annie pulls off the road and bumps the car along a logging track far enough so that the trees hide the car from the road. Detectives? Yes. Again, late night TV in the unified Germany. British detective series. That's it. The guy who is a bit like DI Tench. Wytham Woods truly the haunt of detectives.

Finally, Annie can make the call she's been dying to make since she started running for her life down Brasenose Lane. Only which call has she been dying to make the more?

To her lawyer, obviously. Martin Peters will calm her down and tell her what to do. Wrong. What had Smogulecki gasped out, her head nearly under water, her groin in Annie's angry grip?

'It's the Russian.' Something like that. No. 'To get the Russian.'

Of course. The Government, the Security Services, whoever takes these decisions in this constitutional democracy. For some reason they have decided they must be rid of Sergei. But they don't dare just to do it.

Sergei is connected. Media. He owns a bit of a London radio station. Football. He owns a bit of some famous club now fallen on hard times. Politics. He is most generous, by various obscure payment routes, to certain politicians come election time. So, the authorities need the cover of apparent legitimacy.

Aiding and abetting a kidnapping seems a reasonable basis for deporting someone. But for that to work there has actually to be a kidnapping and preferably a kidnapper.

They have previously decided they can't prove it, but at a pinch they have enough circumstantial stuff to arrest her and charge her, don't they? Or at least to get the Attorney General to give a legal opinion on behalf of the Government that they have enough evidence to arrest her and charge her. Then they might get away with it.

Sergei Dzhugashvili, imminent threat to the safety of the British State and almost proven abetter of Annie Fritzweiler, the almost proven kidnapper of her own student.

In this wasps' nest Annie does not need a lawyer to protect her. She needs the Russian. And the Russian needs her.

Sergei will protect her. Not because of his feeling for her, though that might be enough. But because his survival in Britain depends on keeping her out of the hands of the police. No visible suspect, no deportation.

She makes the call.

60

To Russia with Love

His squeeze of the moment, his creditors and the Kremlin. Only calls from these is an Oligarch likely to answer at once. But Sergei has told her as if he meant it, for him it is his creditors, the Kremlin and Annie Fritzweiler. His once and future squeeze?

It's still ringing. Of course, he wouldn't trust an answering service.

'Yes.' The unmistakable gruff voice.

'They came for me this morning. I've been running ever since. It is days only since they told me, told me they wouldn't charge me. Now this. No warning.'

Sergei knows exactly what she is saying.

'This can only be about me.'

'Yes. They need me in custody, to charge me, to get to at you. As an accessory.'

'Give me your co-ordinates.'

'I drove West out of Oxford, took the Wytham turn and then..'

'No stupid, your map reference co-ordinates off your smart phone. It's OK the guys have it. And if we have it the police have it. Annie, get out of there now. Dump your phone and leave the car.'

'And go where?'

'Just a second. The guys are working on it. Brilliant my people. OK Annie. No more communication after this. So, listen, carefully. From where you are, on your feet go back to the road, turn left and follow the road for a mile, maybe it's a mile and a half. And Annie, run as if your life it depends on it, because it does. There's a bus stop.'

'A bus?! Out here there is perhaps one bus a day.'

'Exactly and it will be at that stop in ten minutes from now precisely.'

'And the cops won't check a bus?'

'Annie you're getting off after six miles at, what is this, at Buggers Corner.'

Probably Badgers, thinks Annie, but Buggers was for sure what it was originally.

Then two miles cross country. A bit north of west. Ploughed field, pasture, we don't know. Then you are at the perimeter of an airfield, Windrush.'

'Sergei no. No plane can land there. The runway is too broken up.'

'Trust me, my love.'

Does she have an option? She drops the phone next to the car. Smogulecki's too. With her foot she sweeps some very dead leaves over the two mobile phones. There is nothing incriminating on her phone. On Smogulecki's, she is not so sure, but no time to check, so she leaves it anyway.

To make the time she has to run on the hard tarmac of the road. When on a couple of occasions, she hears a vehicle approaching she swerves off into the woods. But no police, so far. Exhausted she's at the bus stop in nine and a half minutes.

Twenty minutes later Annie is still at the bus stop. What the hell is Sergei playing at? She continues skulking at the edge of the woods so she won't be spotted by a passing police vehicle. She feels hungry and desperately thirsty. And she has to pee.

As she slides her jeans and knickers over her thighs, she hears the bus coming. Pulling her clothes back on she realises the driver is not going to stop, since he can see no one at the bus stop. She sprints after the bus, and it slows to a stop.

There are only three other people in the bus, all elderly country women.

'Bless me I nearly missed you, Ma'am.' The driver can see Annie is several cuts above his regular passengers even if a bit dishevelled. 'You was having a piss in the woods I'll be bound. So many do you know. Whilst they'm waiting like.'

Annie offers a five-pound note to Badgers Corner. The driver takes an age sorting out the change. Annie forces herself to wait quietly, though a police car could come at any time.

'You were very late,' she says when, finally she gets her money.

'Don't you go blaming me,' says the driver, at once truculent, putting the bus into gear. 'Police block coming out of the City wasn't there? Insisted on questioning those three old biddies back there. As if any of them could beat a woman police officer to within an inch of her life. It's one of they psychopaths I shouldn't wonder.'

Annie quickly agrees and sits down. Finally they are on their way. She stares out of the window trying to judge six miles. Several times she asks the driver.

'Don't you go worrying, my dear. I'll tell you in good time.

Though what in the world a nice woman like you could want in a place like that?'

'Friends,' she says airily. 'A house near there.'

'Bless my soul. I never known of a house at Badgers Corner all these years I've been driving along here. The planes taking off and so on, you know. All closed down now, mind you. Council couldn't afford to keep up the runway.'

What kind of garden path was Sergei leading her up, wonders Annie for the twentieth time?

'Tis just here Miss.'

The driver's voice rouses her from deep sleep. She is so grateful she doesn't even mind her demotion from 'Ma'am' to 'Miss'.

Scrambling off the bus, Annie wonders how she is to know without her smart phone where 'a bit North of West' is. Of course, it's where the sun is already starting to set.

She sets off across country. Just her luck its plough, making for very heavy going on the wet, clay soil, most of which sticks to her trainers. But finally, it is at an end and she walks through the perimeter fence, since the wire that once protected the airfield is long gone.

Then she sits on the ground under a clump of trees to wait. Well enough hidden, if there were anyone to look. In addition to a raging thirst, she is hungry and beginning to get cold. Still worst comes to worst she could seek shelter in the house which she reckons is directly the other side of the airfield from her.

She is roused from a dream, in which a very angry Polish woman is eviscerating her with a serrated butcher's knife, by the sound of a helicopter engine.

The pilot is clearly nervous of the runway surface and of the wet clinging soil he suspects is under the grass around the runway. So, he hovers. Three feet above the ground.

Cautiously she emerges from the trees. Then runs towards the helicopter. She doesn't want to miss her ride since, unlike the bus earlier, one can't really run after a helicopter once it decides to leave.

But she is too slow. The machine is lifting off. In a couple of minutes, it will be a speck on the setting sun.

There were several occasions during the day when Annie might reasonably have given way to despair. When the police arrived at the College. When it was clear that Smogulecki would overtake her. When Sergei told her to abandon her car, her phone and trust entirely in him. But each time she has borne up bravely. Now she flings herself down on the wet grass and cries.

So, she doesn't notice an athletic looking man approaching her out of the sunset until she is taken up in his bear hug embrace.

'You are interested in this I think.'

Sergei pulls something from the inside pocket of his jacket and hands it to her. It's a copy of the first edition of that day's London Standard...Does he own a part of that too? The front-page headline:

"Police Chase Don Thru Oxford."

There is a blurred picture, from a mobile phone for sure, of a woman, herself for sure, running across the High.

"Police are anxious to interview Oxford don, Dr Annie Fritzweiler." The only good thing is that the name of the College seems not to appear. But Sergei is speaking to her again.

'When you are running from police, it's best to keep your eyes open, Annie my love. Don't you see me jump from the helicopter? That shit face pilot doesn't risk a landing and "endanger his aircraft", as he says it.'

For a moment Annie is happy. In her mind she has surrendered the crushing responsibilities of the day, of her whole future, to Sergei. But then she pushes him away.

What is happening? She is a wanted person, sought among other things for inflicting grievous bodily harm on a police office. She needs to run, to hide. Has Sergei come to detain her and hand her over to the police, trading her in as an exchange for his own freedom?

'What the hell are you playing at, Sergei?'

'Oh that. The team and me, we stormed our brains for a while. Then it seems best that you and I hide out in the most obvious place. Where no one is thinking of looking.'

Annie's got it now.

'Windrush,' she says. 'The farmhouse?'

'Come on,' says Sergei. 'By now the team makes it a bit more comfortable than for Felix.' He laughs.

'And then what, Sergei?'

'Then I get my expensive English lawyers to earn their bread. And the politicians, maybe a couple of Ministers even, who are so grateful for my help when it's time for elections. And of course, your man, Martin. The runner.'

Sergei laughs at the memory of Martin Peters wallowing in his wake running by the Horse Guards barracks under snow.

'I talk with him just before I take the helicopter. A couple of days and things will be fine. You and me, my love, we just keep out of sight till then.'

Annie can think of nothing to say. So, she takes out her

lipstick. She can't actually see her reflection in the Russian's depthless dark eyes, but she does the best she can. Then Sergei takes her by the hand and leads her across the rough surface of the runway to the other side of the airfield and the back door of the abandoned farmhouse.

61

Back in the USSR

It's Friday. Less than a week since she ran for her life out of the College gates, Smogulecki at her heels

She is sitting exactly where she sat then. At her laptop. Trying to finish her long overdue article for Ethics Review before ten o'clock, when the day's stream of students will start to arrive for their tutorials. The last of these will be Andrew David Felix Cameron.

As promised, Sergei's people, whom Annie recognised as the protection and who perhaps also are the gang of four who kidnapped Felix, have made the place sufficiently comfortable.

She eats, drinks and showers. Then, in a bath robe supplied by the team, she climbs into Andrew's single bed.

She is instantly asleep and by the time she wakes, at eleven the next morning, Sergei is gone. To fight the good fight for Annie's freedom. Or so the two remaining members of the protection tell her. They speak only Russian. She understands them well enough, but they are unwilling to chat to her. Always on their guard.

Annie eats an enormous breakfast. Then sleeps until it is dark again. At six, the protection brings her a portable TV, tuned to a leading rolling news channel. She wonders vaguely what is happening in the world and quickly discovers that she is what is happening in the world.

There is an enormous row. The police are beleaguered.

Having notified Annie Fritzweiler formally that she is no longer under investigation in connection with the kidnapping of her student, Andrew Cameron, on what basis did they try to arrest her without warning? Without speaking to her solicitors? Was the police warrant for her arrest honestly sworn?

Or was this nothing at all to do with Annie Fritzweiler, but actually a way of getting at her friend and supposed accomplice, Sergei Dzhugashvili? A Russian Oligarch resident in London for some years. Financial stalwart of a charity for British Army personnel disabled in war, as well as saviour of various failing bits of the British media and of a famous football team.

'They make your boss sound as if he is a saint,' she says in Russian to the man who has just brought her supper. No answer but the ghost of a smile.

There is more. She is now an 'Affair'. The Commons is still in Christmas recess but several MPs appear on screen demanding a statement from the Prime Minister on police mishandling of the Fritzweiler Affair. In particular they want him to say what role the British security services have played?

The County Police are leaking like a sieve in a desperate attempt to ward off the onslaught of criticism. There are bits of film from mobile phones of her running and Smogulecki chasing. Hector and Achilles, thinks Annie, though in her case Hector turned the tables. Classical education in the GDR was relatively good. At least hers was.

But there is no mention of her ambush of the Detective Sergeant. No witnesses of course. Or of the injuries Smogulecki sustained. The Detective Sergeant gagged and spirited out of press range by her superiors.

Annie's cup runneth over. The TV press review suggests that every newspaper in the land is on her side.

And then the showstopper.

'We are hoping shortly after eight o'clock,' says the familiar news presenter, 'to bring you a live interview with Annie Fritzweiler from the secret location at which she is in hiding while the Fritzweiler Affair is resolved.'

Annie says in Russian to the protection, who has lingered

beside her to watch the news, 'But I've nothing to wear'. It is not the protest of women through the ages when surprised by a visit. It is the literal truth.

'It will be OK,' says the protection. Translated from the Russian, this presumably means, 'Sergei will arrange everything.' And so, he does.

A few minutes later, Martin Peters is in the room.

She stands up and she can't stop herself from hugging him.

'What a silly goose you are, Annie.'

Has he just finished reading a fairy story to his youngest?

'What you mean is, Martin, that you think I'm a damn fool. But if I hadn't run, I'd be in a police cell by now and none of this...She waves her hand at the TV screen. '...would be happening. Beyond a certain point Martin, human rights in this country are just like the GDR was.'

'Not entirely, Annie. For example, no interview with a rolling news channel in the GDR.'

A household name, household face rather, has just been ushered into the room. Martin introduces them, though each woman knows very well who the other is. Then comes the team. Two cameras and attached cameramen, a make-up artist and a hairdresser, and a producer. Though she can't see it, Annie knows there must be a van outside to upload the interview. Two thick black cables snaking through the door suggest she is right.

'So, you want me to appear in my bath robe?'

The face that has launched a thousand news bulletins laughs.

'That would certainly boost my viewing figures, Annie. But no, I've brought something for you. No tights I'm afraid. Orders from upstairs. What can I tell you? Women's rights still have some way to go in this country.'

Annie takes the dress in its cloth wrap into the bathroom. There is no long mirror but she can tell it fits better than her own clothes. But then none of her own clothes is as expensive as this.

There are shoes too. In six minutes, they do her hair. In another four her make-up. Ready to roll? Not quite. Annie complains that she has no knickers. The TV people look at each other aghast. Who is responsible for this total fuck up?

There is a media panic. People are shouting into mobile phones. No, they can't wait while someone goes into Oxford to Annie's flat or her College rooms. It's insecure anyway. We have trailed her for eight o'clock. Right after the headlines. Four minutes from now.

'OK,' says Annie wearily. She knows that this interview is important for her future. Possibly it will make the difference. It's prime viewing time. 'I've done worse.'

She crosses her legs and they are ready to go.

Even Annie has to concede afterwards that she hit exactly the right note. The household name, a woman, kisses her. The producer, a man, hugs her. The cameramen bend their thumbs in an upward direction. And the make-up artist and hairdresser squeal with excitement.

The household name apologises that they have to rush back. Annie looks at her uncertainly.

'Of course, you can keep the shoes and the dress, Annie….The fit? No, nothing to do with us. Some flunky of your Oligarch friend gave us the measurements.'

Sergei knows her body to the millimetre.

'I've been thinking about you, Annie,' the household name continues. 'As you were speaking in the interview. To be frank, a lot of women would wonder why you seem to be so attractive to a lot of men.'

'I'd like to know too,' says Annie. Because she really would.

'I think what it is that your face is quite severe, controlled, even when you allow yourself to smile. But your trim, good body works as a sort of challenge to men to make you lose that control. Anyway, my guys all have the hots for you, so I'd better take them away before something unseemly happens.'

She laughs. Annie laughs too, though conscious now that her

face remains severe and controlled.

The interview pulled no punches. But it is this kind of exchange on which Annie thrives.

'Do you in fact have any connection with Andrew Cameron's kidnapping? *No.*

So how come all the circumstantial evidence against you? *Innocent coincidence. The police should be able to distinguish coincidence from causation. What they can prove from what they cannot prove.*

Why did she run from police arrest yesterday morning? *Because I feared that matters had been taken out of the hands of the police and justice system and were now under the control of some unaccountable arm of the British Security Services.*

What evidence is there for that? *That the police have very recently notified me formally that I am no longer a suspect in connection with Andrew Cameron's kidnapping. If it was a kidnapping. Then there is the fact that I am a friend of and was once married to Sergei Dzhugashvili, the prominent Russian Oligarch living in London who may, though for no reason of which I am aware, be a target of the British Security Services.*

Tell us a bit about your upbringing in the former East Germany. *I grew in fear of the Government and its security services. I grew up longing for the kind of freedom of thought and speech that I believed I would find in a country like Britain.*

Were you a Stasi informer? *Yes, like many people at the time. I did it to survive.*

And afterwards? *In the unified Germany, I made a substantial academic career as a philosopher.*

What made you accept a Fellowship at an Oxford College? *The Oxford, the British, approach to philosophy is more congenial, more correct and more constructive, than the one in Germany. Shall I give you some examples?*

I'm not sure we have time for that, Annie. Instead, please tell us what you think will happen next in your case. *What I hope and believe should happen is that the police will recognise their mistake in trying to arrest me yesterday. I believe that the elected Government of this country has the same belief in the virtues of democracy and justice for each individual as I do. That in consequence it will restrain the Security Services and cause them to put a stop to their abuse of the rights of residents of this country.*

A message here for David Cameron. Not the novelist, who is in his writing room in the middle of working out the logistics of a sex and violence scene, in which Annie Fassbinder is just now lying naked and chained to an iron bedstead. But the Prime Minister, who by contrast is watching Annie Fitzweiler with attention and with his wife in their flat at 10 Downing Street.

Also watching with various levels of attention are four men with particular interest in Annie.

Just after eight on a Sunday evening is the busiest hour at The Bistro. But each time Luke Cameron returns to his broom cupboard of a kitchen he cannot resist looking up at the tiny screen peeping between the stacked cooking pots and longing with a physical ache for Annie's body.

Andrew Cameron's reaction is much the same as his brother's. But he has leisure to give his full attention to Annie's interview on screen of his laptop on which he is watching with Polly Philips.

Sergei Dzhugashvili also watches on his lap top as a chauffeur driven car takes him to meet a very senior member of the Cabinet Office. He feels proud of his protegée. He also forgives her for her less than ringing endorsement of his own innocence. After all, as she has told him, she is an analytic philosopher. She can only honestly assert what she truly knows.

Is she more to him than a protegée? The Russian romantic in him wants fervently to go back to their explosive relationship in the Tiergarten in the old time. But he knows that in practice he would at best pay her occasional attention. And Annie would never put up with that.

Martin Peters has the advantage of being in the room with Annie. He realises that as he watches her that he is falling for her. At the same time, he cannot escape the ever-present sense of being drowned in domesticity by his six children, urged on by his wife, as she competes ever more fiercely to be the one whose team first solves the problem of the Weak

Force.

When Annie wakes the next day, morning has broken like the first morning. Martin Peters is on the phone.

On the phone! This is supposed to be a secret location with a total electronic blackout. But Martin explains.

'Annie, good news. I think you can go home today.'

It's just as if a surgeon is telling you you've made good progress and....But then Martin does have rather a good bedside manner with clients. At least with her.

'The Cabinet Office has let me know, through channels, that you have nothing more to fear. The local Chief Constable has written to me saying you are no longer sought by them in any connection. He has apologised, also in writing, for chasing you through the streets of Oxford. The Government is due to make a public statement at noon. I have the text and it is entirely satisfactory to you, Annie. In fact, they would probably pay you compensation if you asked.'

'Martin, I can't keep thanking you. It's becoming embarrassing. But how can I get out of here? I have no phone and Sergei's people seem all to have gone.'

'I'll send a car for you. Hold on for half an hour.'

Annie directs the car to her flat. Someone, Martin perhaps, has had her fridge restocked and the flat cleaned. Annie takes off the expensive television dress and hangs it carefully. Then she gives herself the rest of the day off.

She writes emails to all her students, apologising for her unannounced absence. No need to explain that. It's in every headline. She tells them that the normal tutorial schedule will obtain as from tomorrow, Tuesday. She does not forget that his schedule runs to the end of teaching on Friday, when her last student will be Andrew Cameron.

Annie realises that for practical purposes the authorities cannot again attempt to arrest her. So, Andrew's power over her is gone. She does not need to sleep with him. This should make her happy. Instead, it troubles her throughout the week.

She gets a phone call from Priti who congratulates her effusively and asks if she may send Annie her bill.

'Annie you might be wondering whatever happened to Maria, DS Smogulecki?'

Annie wonders whether she gives a damn.

'The gossip round the local courts is that for some reason, despite having failed to catch you, she's been promoted. Into DI Tench's job. It seems he has been re-tenched.'

She laughs loudly at her awful joke.

'As the senior officer on the case, he caught all the flak for your escape I suppose. The word on the street is that you and Maria had a bit of a dust up when she finally caught up with you. Would you care to comment, Dr Fritzweiler? Well, fair enough. I'm impressed that you got the better of her, Annie. But you may like to know that Maria is OK. A bit sore in places that she doesn't want to mention, not to speak of her ego. But an overdue promotion goes a long way to.... Heavens I was due in Court five minutes ago. Don't forget my bill, and jolly good show Annie my love.'

When she gets into College on Tuesday, she slides an envelope containing five new fifty-pound notes under the hand of the Head Porter. She reckons Higgins is now as much her liegeman as Martin Peters. Her students all seem happy to see her. All are discrete enough to ask her nothing about the high drama of Saturday.

What she dreads though is the inevitable meeting with the Master. A hand written message tells her that Sir Alexander will be at home to her in the Lodgings if she cares to call at about seven the following day, Wednesday.

Annie is at once aware that the Master is radiating goodwill.

'Dr Fritzweiler. Do make yourself at home. Would a dry sherry suit? Your very good health. Good to have you back amongst us.'

'Master you are too kind.'

'I know we've had our differences recently, but I must tell you that I stand second to no man...or woman...in my admiration for your public defence of our liberties. I hope the proper authorities may in due course recognise your heroism. Birthday honours you know. I am certainly thinking of some way in which the College could suitably mark your contribution to our national life, Dr Fritzweiler, Annie. I hope I may still call you Annie.'

Annie waves an embarrassed hand.

'And do call me Duncan....Yes, yes, Alexander, I know. The fact is that for reasons lost in the mists of time my intimate friends call me Duncan.'

'Well, your good health, Duncan,' she says, sipping what she can tell is an excellent wine, though she detests sherry.

'And yours, Annie.'

He leans his bulk towards her to touch glasses.

'But the main reason I asked you to come over this evening is to tell you that Sir Siddhartha, Sir Sid, has also expressed his admiration for your stand for liberty. Sir Sid has in his time been a great battler for liberty of the individual, you know?'

'I really didn't Master.'

'I must tell you all about it on some future occasion. Sir Sid is most anxious to meet you.'

'And I him, Master, Duncan.'

'But you must be wanting to be off home. Suffice it to say that because of your recent actions and utterances, Sir Sid has decided to re-instate all the promised funding for the College which previously he was minded to withdraw. It is even in his mind he told me, though this is just between us for the moment Annie, to increase the amounts substantially.'

Oh well, thinks Annie, trying to finish her sherry and depart before she wakes up from her dream, the way to the establishment's heart is apparently viciously to attack a woman police officer in the honest discharge of her duties.

And so, Annie Fritzweiler sails through her week as if in a trance. She has the sense that everyone she sees is on her side. And then it is Friday.

62

Climax

Annie Fritzweiler knows that Andrew is in possession of information which could destroy her. Her mention to him of a restaurant as a good venue for a kidnapping could sink her should police enthusiasm to solve her case ever be revived. And who could be sure that this would not happen?

He may not be aware of the significance of this knowledge, but if he is not, David Cameron surely would be, were Andrew to mention it to him for some reason.

For now, she appears to be safe. Both the police and the Government have assured Annie that they would not seek to pursue her case further. It would be far too embarrassing for them to take action against her, even if they believed Andrew's further evidence. That is what her rational mind tells her. But she cannot disperse her fear that the police will again pursue her if they come to know all that Andrew knows. So, she still seems bound to honour her commitment to the boy. Anyway, she has promised him.

She telephones Martin Peters in his room. He tells her not to be a silly goose. There is no way the authorities could proceed against her, whatever new evidence Andrew might present.

She is convinced, but she is still undecided.

On Friday morning, she wakes early and goes for a run. It's bitterly cold but the rising sun is brilliant. The river almost sparkles and she runs fast but without effort. It's a day in a thousand.

After a cold shower, she goes over to the College Buttery to get something for breakfast. There she bumps into her new friend, Polly Philips.

'I'm so glad I met you,' the girl says. 'You look fantastic.'

'Just been for a run,' says Annie, embarrassed.

'Could I walk back with you to your staircase?'

They fall into step.

'I thought you might like to know the outcome of what I was asking you about the other day about Andrew.'

The shadow of a suspicion crosses Annie's mind, as it has before. Polly knows that Andrew's older woman is her.

'Oh yes.'

'Well Andrew turned out to be quite an apt student,' the girl giggles. 'Surprisingly advanced really. But when it came to the point, he wouldn't do it with me. To be honest, by that point I was quite keen. But Andy said it wouldn't be fair to her, you know.'

'Well Polly, thank you for telling me. That is interesting.'

'Yes, I thought you'd like to know. And Annie, I'm really glad you're back safe.'

They part at the foot of Annie's staircase. Of course, she knows. She's known all along, thinks Annie as she climbs up to her room two stairs at a time.

Her tutorial students have all written good essays, within their various compasses. It is as if they are all striving to do their best for her. Then at six the last of them has gone, leaving a cold empty space in Annie's mind.

Annie has deliberately left half an hour before Andrew is due. She wanders around her rooms. A good time to examine where she stands with the men recently in her life. An analytic philosopher ought to be able to do that in half an hour.

Sergei, her once and future lover? She would go to the ends of the earth with him. But she knows she would hate it when she got there. There is a vivid past but a blank future for her with Sergei. Perhaps he will visit her sometimes here or in her flat? That is all she can dream of. And it is only a dream.

David Cameron. A man she has come both to like and to despise. Well, if they run across each other and she is in the mood, she can no doubt put him in the mood too. But no. He will re-establish his reputation. His books will get worse, his earnings higher and Davina's possessiveness greater.

Luke Cameron. Even as she thinks of him, she wants to reach for her phone and call him. She knows he wants her as much as she him. But in a week, a month, a year, he will hire a very pretty waitress who can really be useful to him in building his bistro business. And they will have a life together. Not an affair which is all Luke and she could ever have. She is not sure she could bear that.

Finally, there is her Very Gentle Knight, Martin Peters. She owes him more than she has ever owed any human being. Yet physically he does not appeal to her. And in any case, he will be weighed down to the end of his life by all those children and a wife who needs him to attend to the children while she pursues some meaningless cosmic discovery.

With slight surprise she realises that she has not actually slept with any of these men. Well Sergei in the old time in Berlin of course. Only with that repulsive little weed, Andrew David Felix Cameron, will she do that. In approximately sixty minutes from now.

But as Martin has told her, the authorities would not dare try to arrest her a second time. She really is free, which means that Andrew no longer has a hold over her. She does not have to sleep with him, today or any other day.

But Annie believes that contracts freely entered into should be kept to whenever possible. She could safely deny Andrew but it wouldn't be right. It wouldn't be fair.

She and Andrew entered into an arrangement when Andrew seemed to have the key to a successful police prosecution against her. Through no doing of his, those circumstances have changed. No, it wouldn't be fair to deny him his bargain.

Such thinking is one of the burdens of being a moral philosopher.

There is a knock on the door. She should change. She calls out to him to come in and sit down. She will not be a minute.

In the closet, her eye catches sight of her TV interview dress in its bag. She has brought it in so she can have it cleaned. Why not? Give him a real thrill. But no, it is a dress to be seen in, not mauled by a first year undergraduate. So, she rejects it in favour of a serviceable short black skirt and white T-shirt, with...well he is only seventeen...black boots.

Invariably in a tutorial, her student sits across from her, both of them in easy chairs. The format of a civilised if rigorous conversation. But today for Andrew for some reason Annie sits at her desk, and turns her chair at ninety degrees from the desk, so he can see her clearly but has to look up at her.

The tutorial is a slog. He has written his essay, but it is well below the standard of what she knows he can achieve. He's probably been unable to work properly all week in anticipation of seeing her. His mind kept wandering to her body.

In the end she gives up and just lectures him on the topic. Russell's Theory of Definite Descriptions. Every few sentences she pauses to question him on what she has just said, forcing some kind of an answer from him.

Anyone else would have given it up, but Annie's German mind will not allow him to go without his full hour of education, even if she must force feed him.

She is almost as relieved as he is when the hour is passed.

'Would you like something to drink, Andrew?'

He sees that she is drinking tap water and asks for the same.

'Would you like to relieve yourself, Andrew? Why don't you use the washroom on the staircase while I use the one in here?'

But she doesn't want to relieve herself. She just wants it to be over. So, she is still sitting at her desk when he returns. Annie swivels her chair so as to face him.

'Now, Andrew, would you like to kiss me?'

'Andrew, your idea of sex between a man and a woman is quite wrong.'

Andrew is in despair. Where has he gone so wrong? Annie sees his look of anguish and laughs gently.

'No, my dear Andrew, physically it was quite all right.'

Well Beta, Beta Plus if one is making all sorts of allowances. But knowing how he can become almost suicidal if he is not always seen as Alpha Plus, she continues.

'I mean your idea that one feels the mind of the other more intensely in sex than otherwise.'

He breathes a sigh of relief.

'I do not feel your mind more intensely than otherwise. Quite the contrary. I feel my own body more intensely. But Andrew, it was perfectly OK. That is also very nice.'

For an unconsidered moment Andrew feels happy. But she is already standing over him. If she remains there for a minute or so, he will be ready to do it again, he feels sure.

'But now you must go, according to our arrangement. I will see you at the same time next week. The essay topic is on my web site.'

Can that really be all? The greatest experience of his life. Over in seconds. A minute or two anyway. For a few moments the arrogant, unattainable Dr Fritzweiler was at his mercy. But he couldn't sustain it.

And now she has coolly pulled down her skirt and is referring him to her web site for the topic of the following week's essay. To her, sex with him was a meaningless inconvenience. As in their tutorials she threw him a bone at the end.

'Well, it was very nice.'

That is what one says of a cup of tea and a cupcake not the greatest physical experience of which a human being is capable.

He grabs his shoes and clothes and rushes from the room. Only half way down her staircase does he realise. He stops hastily to pull on his trousers and then runs barefoot for his room. As he emerges from Annie's staircase, he passes Polly, her arms full of physics work books. He fails to acknowledge her greeting. The girl changes course to climb Annie's staircase and taps on Annie's door.

Annie, is looking immaculate, not a hair outs of place. She hesitates and then invites the girl in.

'Dr Fritzweiler, I'm sorry. I just couldn't resist. I just had to know.'

Annie invites her to put down her physics burden and sit down for a moment. Well, a horrible embarrassment shared is a horrible embarrassment halved. Isn't that what the English say.

'Did you by any chance see Andrew just now?'

'Yes. Frankly he looked as if he'd lost his mind. With delight or misery, I couldn't tell. He just blanked me.'

In other words what the hell have you done to him, Dr Fritzweiler?

'Polly, seriously, this is just between us. Not even Andrew. Not even your boyfriend, when you next have one.'

'Annie, I swear. But just tell me, how was he?'

'Better than might have been expected.'

Both women laugh together like conspirators.

'But Polly, why are you so interested? I mean, just between us, Polly, could you yourself be interested in Andrew?'

The girl flushes. Annie is suffused with hope.

'But I mean, you and Andrew?'

'To tell the truth, Andrew does not in the least attract me. And I am obviously much too old for him. This thing with him. It's really because he was so desperate. Against my better judgement I allowed myself to be drawn into it.'

She is very tempted to invite the girl back to her flat for a drink and a chat, but something in her German mind about the gulf between professors and students stops her. And after all Polly will be around for another couple of years.

Polly desperately wants to invite this woman for a drink. For Annie to be her friend for life. If only in thirty years' time she could turn out like Annie Fritzweiler. But she feels she may have pushed the boundaries as far as they will go for tonight. There is always tomorrow. Nearly a whole other year and more before she will graduate from Oxford.

'I must be going, Dr Fritzweiler. But thank you for trusting me.'

'Polly,' says Annie as she holds open the door for the girl, 'perhaps between us we can make things OK for Andrew.'

'Yes,' Polly replies, 'that would be great.'

63

Anti-climax

It is with relief rather than passion that he finally enters her. She encourages her body to respond though she is not much aroused by him. He deserves that much.

She does her best but, in the length of time he gives her, she cannot even pretend. She hopes he doesn't mind too much.

'Annie, you don't know what a relief it is to do that at last.'

She knows exactly what he means. For once to forget in a few minutes of sheer self-indulgence his responsibilities as a father and a husband. A provider and a help mate to his wife and her inquiries into the Weak Force in the Universe. Nothing weak about her domestic demands though.

Martin is expected to do his share at home. And he is expected to drag himself down to his Lincoln's Inn chambers in central London more often than is to his taste, to advise on and sometimes to appear in lucrative criminal cases of fraud, simply in order to pay the school fees. For all six of them. Endless.

Whereas all he wants to do is to bring as much clarity and structure to the Law as he can by writing his thoughtful academic books. To rescue the Law from what seems to him sometimes to be its descent into an inchoate, meaningless mass, as amending legislation is piled on inconsistent precedent.

That is why he first became enamoured of Annie Fritzweiler. Not for her short, fair, Baltic hair, which now he strokes. Not for her firm but yielding body which he now pulls close against him. Not for her strong thighs, up which he may soon feel an urge to run his tongue once again. But for the clarity which her mind has brought already to preparations for their joint Seminar on Law and Philosophy.

And for her, he is her champion, her faithful knight, her liegeman who has with extraordinary ingenuity and stamina saved her from falling into the toils of the legal traps her enemies have set for her.

She kisses him in sheer gratitude.

'Martin thank you. Sometimes it's just the way it is. And you are so exhausted what with your wife, your kids....'

Children she thinks, as she lies beside him. What little brutes they are. Whatever their affection for their parents it seldom comes anywhere close to the parental feeling lavished on them. They come to expect to be fed, clothed and, in the case of the professional classes, sent to extraordinarily expensive private schools for ten or more years of their lives, followed by not quite so expensive universities, followed these days by a large parental subsidy so they can afford somewhere to live in London.

London. Why is it always London, one of the most expensive cities on earth? Why not give Aberystwyth or Exeter or Oswestry a try?

And then at the finish, children may hover over the parental death bed making advanced dispositions of assets which they have done absolutely nothing to deserve, objectively assessing whether the ancient parent's quality of life merits another week or two in a fabulously expensive medical facility, the cost of which is daily diminishing the heritable asset base.

Annie breathes a sigh of relief. Lucky escape. Amazing as it now seems, it was only the fall of the Berlin Wall which had delivered her from the perils of parenthood. Otherwise, Sergei, who had disappeared back into the bosom of Mother Russia the night the Wall was breached, might have insisted on procreation. That after all was probably why he married her. That, and enabling her to travel to the West with him, where from time to time she was of service to him.

Martin is falling asleep beside her. She tries to sleep too, but her mind won't rest.

She's more than glad not to be bothered with an importunate partner night after night. She works very hard and needs to sleep well each night. Generally, she manages fairly successfully by herself and with the excitement she gets by teasing a few of her students in tutorials. But she is quite careful about that, as she knows she needs to be.

But now she has achieved this with Martin. She is sure he will never bother her too much, but as her true knight he would, she feels, be available on those occasions when she may be in need.

It is of course a drawback that he does not excite her much. Their minds are a much better fit than their bodies.

Now he is fast asleep.

She remembers that she has a dinner that evening with members of the University Philosophy Faculty. They are entertaining a visiting and very distinguished group of German philosophy professors. Though goodness only knows what they will find to talk about.

"Keine Brucke fur Mann zu Mann." No bridge from man to man.

As a philosopher she would not subscribe to this formulation of the Other Minds idea, as she explained to Andrew in that catastrophic tutorial. But if you substituted "English philosopher" and "German philosopher" for the first and second occurrence of "Mann" in the quotation, then the tag line was right on the money.

She smiles to herself. For once she is confident that she has got the English idiom right.

After Kant there is no German philosopher on the Oxford undergraduate syllabus, apart from Marx and he is included under Economics or Political Philosophy. The Anglo-American and the Continental traditions are so different as to constitute different subjects.

Annie showers and then starts to get ready for her evening out.

She wonders if she should wake Martin. Surely some family commitment should be claiming him by now. But that is his affair. She lets him sleep on.

By the time she is ready she is pleased with the effect. Her orange dress shows off to best advantage the swell of her breasts and shoulders, and her late spring tan. The outline of her thighs which is evident through the dress, she feels should impress the dourest of German professors.

The person who is impressed is of course Martin Peters. When he comes sleepily from the bedroom, he is wiping his glasses on his shirt end but is otherwise naked. She turns towards him, and stands at an angle to him, with her legs apart. She stands looking carefully at her new lover long enough for him to become fully aroused.

But he seems almost unconscious of that.

'Annie tell me.'

She wonders if she is going to be called on to lie to him about the degree of his physical attraction for her. But it is not that at all.

He has picked up the statuette of an elephant that is standing on a side table near the door. It had arrived, beautifully packed, a week or two before. No return address given. Annie had seen not harm in displaying it.

'Tell me, about the kidnapping. What really happened?'

Does he see a split second of alarm cross her expressionless face or does he see it because that is what he expects?

'Don't worry, Annie. Client privilege. I may, I must, never disclose what a client tells me in confidence.'

'Martin, bang shut the door when you leave. And call me soon.'

As she clatters down the stone staircase, she has hope that she might even turn a few heads in the High that evening.

END

About the Author

Patrick Docherty was raised and went to school in Cornwall, England. He is a graduate of Balliol College, Oxford University. He attended Columbia University in New York on a Fulbright, and is also a graduate of Harvard Business School, all providing peculiar familiarity with academic eccentricities.

Following a career as a government official and an investment banker in London, he continued in investment banking in Hong Kong. He has been a university lecturer in Singapore, where he now lives.

Patrick is also the author of **The Cornish Detective** series of crime novels.

Printed in Great Britain
by Amazon